wool shop, produced radio commercials, and ... voice-over agent representing a host of household names. *How to Lose a Husband and Gain a Life* is Bernadette's fifth novel. She is currently at work on her sixth, and a second stage musical with her husband, Matthew. They have one daughter, Niamh. Bernadette never eats carbs during the week.

For more information about Bernadette and her books, please visit www.bernadettestrachan.co.uk

Praise for Bernadette Strachan

'It's official: the drought of fresh new chick-lit is over . . . the sparkling language and hilarious scenes should keep you enthralled from the very first page'   *heat*

'No-nonsense sharp, dry wit with larger than life characters . . . a mosaic of sparkling fun'   *Woman*

'Fresh, funny and full of romance'   *Company*

'Delightful and refreshingly different'   *The Bookseller*

'Affectionately humorous at times, tongue-in-cheek and then poignantly astute . . . highly recommended' Lovereading.co.uk

Also by Bernadette Strachan

The Reluctant Landlady
Handbags and Halos
Diamonds and Daisies
Little White Lies

HOW TO LOSE A HUSBAND AND GAIN A LIFE

Bernadette Strachan

Sphere
An imprint of
Little, Brown Book Group,
100 Victoria Embankment,
London EC4Y 0DY

An Hachette UK Company
www.hachette.co.uk

www.littlebrown.co.uk

sphere

SPHERE

First published in Great Britain as a paperback original in 2009 by Sphere
Reprinted 2009 (twice)

Copyright © 2009 by StrawnyGawn Words and Music

The moral right of the author has been asserted.

A CIP catalogue record for this book
is available from the British Library.

ISBN 978-0-7515-4230-1

Typeset in Adobe Garamond by Palimpsest Book Production Limited,
Grangemouth, Stirlingshire
Printed and bound in Great Britain by Clays Ltd, St Ives plc

Papers used by Sphere are natural, renewable and recyclable
products sourced from well-managed forests and certified
in accordance with the rules of the Forest Stewardship Council.

This book is for Jen and Keith Strachan because they're great and I love them

Acknowledgements

Thank you, all you lovely people, for the following input:

James Little for the use of his phrase 'ergonomic shakedown'; Penny Killick for priceless early encouragement (and she may just recognise something she once said to me at the end of chapter twenty-five); Lily Gaughan, my mum, for being a cleaner with class and giving me the idea; Michael Anderson and Alison Last Anderson for making sure the legal stuff sounds sensible; Sam Strachan for translating the Latin motto; Elinor Lawless Basham for lending me her maiden name; Monika Moysová for Niamh-wrangling; Louis Vaughan for being my spy in the land of the boy; Annette Green for her agenty superpowers; Sara Kinsella, Suzie Dooré and Isobel Akenhurst for being there at the beginning of the book; the *über*-delightful Jo Dickinson at Little, Brown for being there at the end and hopefully a new beginning in all sorts of wonderful ways; and Matthew for being Matthew (something he's awfully good at).

PROLOGUE

Ruby Gallagher finally woke up at dawn on a rat-coloured January Monday. It was hard not to, with three CID officers built like sofa-beds hammering on her front door, but Ruby also awoke in the metaphorical sense. The complicated expression on her husband's face jolted her out of almost a decade of deep, deep matrimonial slumber.

'Manny . . . ?' Ruby tugged the duvet up to her chin as law-enforcing feet thundered up the new stair carpet.

'I can explain, babes,' rasped Manny, as insistent hands dragged him from the bed.

Ruby hated being called babes. Manny had never realised this in all the years they'd been together, and now, as he was manhandled into the ensuite with only a Homer Simpson hot water bottle to dent his nakedness, didn't seem the right time to tell him.

'Call my lawyer!' yelled the now fully dressed Manny as he was folded into the back seat of a Ford Mondeo. 'Call Simon!' The door slammed, but Ruby could hear his final, '*Now*, babes!'

I

It had been a mistake to let Manny name the house. Ruby knew he meant well, but the snooty neighbours sniggered up their bespoke sleeves at Château Rubes.

The art deco mansion's front door key, along with its fourteen remote controls and a panic button, had been handed to Ruby at her wedding, an event which triggered a tulle shortage in the South-East. Refurbished to Manny's brief of 'a palace fit for my princess', he believed it fulfilled his ulterior ambition to 'make Esher puke with envy'.

Since that day nine years ago Ruby had lived in a fog of luxury. The personal gym, the walk-in wardrobe and the account at Tiffany were head-turning for a nineteen-year-old fresh from the drab-hued family semi. Ruby's parents, Marjorie and Stan, were throwbacks to an austere postwar Britain that smelled of cabbage and was painted varying shades of 'bleurgh'. Sofas came with antimacassars, meals were eaten in silence, and Val Doonican was considered pretty near the knuckle. Panic-stricken by their only child's unaccountable red-haired beauty, they had regarded Ruby's looks as an unfortunate modern malady, such as homosexuality or Jonathan Ross. Their over-protectiveness discouraged friendships with girls her own age and ensured that Ruby entered sixth form with no girls' nights out under her belt, a complete ignorance of ITV, and less sexual awareness than a Victorian maiden aunt.

Marjorie found it impossible to call a spade a spade. Periods were 'monthlies', Ruby's panties contained her 'front bottom', and the word 'sex' was replaced by the more mundane (and confusing) 'relations'. One event in Ruby's life confounded even Marjorie's creative way with a simile, and she could only refer to it as 'the thing'. As in, 'Darling, we'd love to let you go to the cinema with the girls from school but since *the thing* . . .' Here a momentary closing of the eyes and a flutter of the hands would provide a full stop to the whole distasteful idea.

Ruby loved her parents, she really did. She understood them. To a point. When, not long after her marriage, they both died within three months of each other, she'd been plunged into a deep, blank sadness. Like the well-behaved girl she was, she'd gritted her teeth and waited for the grief to subside; questions an older, wiser Ruby might have asked had no hope of an answer now. Ruby didn't care to unravel how much bitterness there was in her mourning.

That sad year had seen her husband's generosity triple as Manny eyed her constantly, gauging her recovery. Ruby was accustomed to being watched, she'd had a lifetime of it, and she tried to be grateful. 'Marjorie and Stan were diamonds,' Manny would say, rolling a brandy glass in one of his huge paws. 'Salt of the earth.'

'They were,' Ruby would agree. She remembered how relieved her parents had been when her shop-worn Prince Charming had turned up. 'Now there's a *real man*.' Marjorie had stressed the term approvingly. 'He'll look after you.

Not a lot of men would take you on. You know what I mean, darling.'

Darling knew exactly what Marjorie meant. That phrase 'take you on' had rankled, but Ruby had been a dutiful daughter and repressed it: no GCSEs but a dab hand at repressing.

'At least they saw you living the dream before they . . .' Manny too had trouble with certain words. 'Before they *passed away*.' This sentimental side of him would have amazed his employees. The burly build; the rough-hewn accent; none of it pointed to a man who couldn't say 'died'.

The day before the CID entered stage right on the dream she was living, Ruby had got up early to put in a punishing hour on her treadmill. Rushing off to the local nail bar to have her talons burnished, she returned just in time to oversee the erection of a gazebo Manny had ordered that was a fraction higher than the neighbours' gazebo. Much of her afternoon was spent squinting at a Jamie Oliver cookbook in her dazzlingly glossy kitchen. She followed the fish pie recipe with the kind of baffled concentration a Neanderthal might bring to a sat nav. 'This time, maybe this time . . .' she whispered hopefully, sliding it into the only one of her four ovens she knew how to switch on. 'Maybe this time it will be edible.'

There was barely time to shower, dress, make peace with her shoulder-length russet tangles and pull her stomach in before she heard Manny's key in the door. Ruby froze, waiting for the front door to close.

There it was – a gentle clunk.

Ruby relaxed. She was a scholar of her husband's moods, and had many methods of judging them. The front door was a reliable barometer. A gentle clunk meant a relaxed Manny, one who would find a disastrous pie funny. A slam meant a

Manny who would push the pie away roughly. A slam and a grunt meant that the fish pie must be hidden with more urgency than Anne Frank.

Rushing down the stairs like a chic puppy, Ruby jumped into his arms. She loved doing that. It felt so sexy that Manny didn't even rock backwards when she launched all five foot nine of herself at him. He was built to last, her husband, and he smelled good too. 'Always smell posh,' was one of his maxims, and today he smelled posh but slightly sweaty, a combination that beckoned Ruby's pheromones out from their hidey-holes.

'All right, all right, let me get in the door.' Manny was doing his best to sound testy, but his wife knew that he was in good spirits and delighted to see her. Peeling her off, he twisted his head away, refusing to kiss her. 'Later, babes, later,' he admonished her, depositing her on the marble floor. 'I'm starving.'

It was a valiant try. Ruby felt for him as Manny rolled a forkful of her pie around his mouth, and came up with various noncommittal noises. Finally, though, he had to give up.

'Chinese?' asked Ruby, reaching for her mobile.

'Chinese,' confirmed Manny, frowning down at a prawn.

'I thought we'd watch a DVD,' said Ruby lightly. She knew better than to push: Manny was not a man to be pushed.

'Sure. No Ben Affleck shit, though.' Manny, jacket off, tie loosened, landed like a sack of Savile Row spuds on the white leather banquette. 'Nothing with that cross-eyed cow Sarah Jessica whatsit either. And nothing foreign language. Those subtitles do my head in.'

Settling down to a film where the body count reached

double figures before the credits, Ruby nestled in to her husband's hard contours. He held his arm wide to make her comfortable and she snuggled against him with a comfortable sigh. Ruby marvelled at the wild beast that her net had somehow snagged and civilised; pretty good going, she reckoned, for a girl who hadn't even realised she *had* a net.

Trying not to yawn at the predictably bloody swathe Wesley Snipes was cutting across the plasma screen, Ruby entertained thoughts of bed. Rather rude thoughts.

Beside her, Manny stirred, looking at his watch. 'Budge up, babes,' he whispered. 'Gotta few calls to make.'

The rude thoughts sighed, buttoned their coats and left. Ruby translated Manny's announcement as, 'I'll be in my den until 2 a.m.' 'Sure, darling,' she said, softly. 'Don't work too hard.'

A big bed is even bigger when you're alone in it. Ruby curled up beneath the downy duvet and closed her eyes. How long she'd been asleep when the bed suddenly lurched Ruby couldn't tell, but she half woke with a marshmallowy feeling of pleasure as she felt her husband scoot over and lay his warm arm across her.

'Babes,' he murmured, close to her sleepy ear.

'Mmm?' Those thoughts were back, tearing off their coats opportunistically, and Ruby half turned to burrow in to Manny's neck.

'You took your pill today, didn't you? Like a good girl?'

Her face invisible against his chest, Ruby nodded.

'We don't want any horrible little accidents, now do we?' Manny's lips started at her forehead, then slid down towards her mouth.

Blocking out his clumsy words, Ruby gave her husband the benefit of the doubt. He couldn't know how it made her feel, to be talked to like that. She surrendered and all was right with their small world.

Until the door was hammered down an hour later.

Like Sleeping Beauty, Ruby had dozed and snored and dribbled through her adult years. Listening to Simon made her long for the comfort of yesterday's drowsy innocence: 'Blah blah blah tax evasion blah blah blah illegal gambling blah blah blah money laundering.'

Her sheltered upbringing had groomed Ruby for just the kind of cushy existence her wealthy, older husband provided. Today was raw and real and demanding, not Ruby's style at all.

'Money laundering?' Sitting in Simon's orderly office in wrinkled jeans she'd ransomed from the washbag, Ruby examined a phrase she'd only ever encountered on TV shows such as *The Bill*. Vague notions of Manny washing and blow-drying fivers flitted across her mind as she said, 'Obviously Manny didn't do all those things, did he?'

It was less a question, more a statement, but Simon's bland, 'We will vigorously defend all charges,' didn't reassure her. 'Look, Ruby,' Simon leaned forward, as if spilling a secret. Pink cheeked and curly haired, he looked far too young for his dull suit and dull desk, as if he'd strayed from a school production of *Bugsy Malone*. 'Life is about to change. Manny's assets are being frozen.'

Another phrase from cops 'n' robbers TV. In response to Ruby's dumb look, Simon explained, uneasily, 'There'll be no money. No credit cards. Manny's nightclubs will have to be sold. The house might – will – have to go.' He looked far more upset than his shell-shocked client as he told her, 'The fairy tale is over.'

There was no need to tell Sleeping Beauty that. Ruby's

ears were ringing with the crash of castles in the air collapsing. The most pressing problem in her teeming mind wasn't money, cars, houses, or anything you could touch. It was her faith in Manny. 'Manny will sort this out.' Her voice wavered. 'He'll know what to do.' Her husband was strong. Resourceful. Dynamic. He was also ruthless, harsh and laughed until he wet himself at her belief in feng shui, but that didn't matter right now. 'It's all some stupid misunderstanding.' More pertinently, Manny was honest, the kind of man who made a song and dance about people being 'straight' with him.

'Manny is in a lot of trouble.' Simon was talking carefully, and with peculiar emphasis, as if trying to pass a message in code to an elderly foreigner. 'Ironically, you are now in a somewhat better financial position than your husband.'

'Me?' laughed Ruby. Manny had been careful never to burden her with a personal bank account. 'All I can get my hands on is the loose change down the back of the sofa.'

'Actually, you're the owner of a penthouse apartment in London.' Simon reached into a drawer and produced a bulky padded envelope. He was enunciating carefully in that meaningful way again, as if he suspected that the cheese plant was bugged. 'Manny signed it over to you some time ago. For tax purposes.'

Or tax evasion purposes? Ruby was stung by her own disloyalty as she took the envelope, her fingers encountering the hard contours of keys.

'It's *yours*,' said Simon pointedly. 'It's worth about a million and it's yours.'

'A million!' yelped Ruby, her voice up with the polystyrene ceiling tiles. Recovering slightly, she said, 'What's mine is Manny's.'

'Of course.' Simon nodded solemnly.

'We'll get through this together.'

'Of course you will,' said Simon. 'Of course.'

The day got more and more *Bill*-esque. Hoping that a taupe trouser suit was appropriate garb to bail out your husband, Ruby kept her head down as she signed forms at the police station reception desk, her flaming wavy hair shielding her freckled face. An ex-Brownie, a prospective organ donor and a card-carrying member of the RSPCA, she had never been on the wrong side of the law before. 'I've got a Waitrose account, goddammit!' she thought, scrawling her name on the last dotted line, too mortified to meet the eye of the bored constable dealing with her.

Creaking double doors delivered Manny to her. 'Not here,' he snapped, sweeping out of the building when she raised her face to his. He strode off across the tarmac with Ruby trailing him and didn't stop until he reached their four-by-four.

'Darling . . .' Ruby hobbled to a stop in her heels. Unlike his wife, Manny didn't look mortified. He looked furious. Beneath the impeccably cut pinstripes his body vibrated. Anger crackled from piercing blue eyes set deep in his broad, inscrutable, *über*-masculine face. Ruby looked up at him. She never tired of looking at him, of admiring the neat, sooty shape of his close-cropped dark hair. Maybe it was the fairy tale thing again: Manny was the Beast to Ruby's Beauty. Or maybe she was just kinky for blokes who looked like boxers. His earthy physique battled with the finesse of his tailoring: the tension created was potent. 'It's going to be all right.' She stole his line, the words she'd been waiting for him to say. Hoping to diffuse some of his fury, she reached up and wrapped her arms around him, laying her head on his chest. He was her rock.

Ruby's rock was silent all the way home in the passenger seat, staring down at his hands writhing in his lap. The stormy bad humour seemed to be receding, and Ruby silently prescribed a long bath for her husband, followed by a long talk. A very long talk.

As she slowed the car, waiting for the automatic gates of their rambling spread to inch open, Manny finally spoke, his voice like gravel on velvet. 'Not here.'

'Not here?' echoed Ruby, with a laugh. 'Then where, darling?'

'Tania's.'

'Eh?' Tania was manageress of Manhattan Nights, Manny's swishest (and, Ruby privately believed, tackiest) nightclub. 'Tania's?' She felt a stab of unease, possibly triggered by a sudden memory of Tania's push-up bra and its contents. 'What's at Tania's?'

'My kid,' sighed Manny.

Later, much later, when she was able to tell the tale without banging her head off the coffee table, Ruby would express amazement at her ability to coolly deliver her husband to his mistress like a minicab driver.

There was no goodbye from Manny, no attempt at an explanation, just a, 'This is killing me, babes.'

'Really?' asked Ruby, crunching the car into gear. ''Cos I'm loving it. *Babes.*'

Simmering in the hot tub like a boil in the bag ready meal, Ruby hoovered up another enormous glass of wine and laughed sardonically, the way she'd seen bad actors do. She was hot, and more bothered than she'd ever been.

This was her inaugural dip in the outdoor Jacuzzi. She'd argued against installing one, but it had appeared anyway. Tonight was an opportune moment to give it a whirl, before the police froze it. She'd flicked on all the other expensive gizmos that would be covered in icicles before long – the underfloor heating, the hi-fi wired into every room, the plasma screens, the swimming pool's underwater lasers. Every light in the house burned. Upstairs in Ruby's dressing room her remote-controlled wardrobe doors slid back and forth as if deranged, and the gates at the front of the property clanged open and shut with metallic grunts.

Château Rubes was probably visible from space. Ruby was surprised that the neighbours weren't complaining. But then, she wouldn't be able to hear them over the concert-level music and the high-pitched whinge of Manny's Alfa Romeo car alarm attempting to alert its AWOL owner to the fact that his missus had caved in the windscreen with his rowing machine.

A lifelong good girl (sleepwalkers tend to be well behaved), Ruby was surprised by the satisfaction her rampage brought. The alcohol, she guessed, helped. A novice at drinking, she was taking to it like a duck to wine. Bashing open the lock on Manny's temperature-controlled wine cellar with a heavy bronze statuette proclaiming him 'Esher's Brightest Businessman 2001', Ruby had contemplated inviting her friends over to join in the carnage. The only snag was her utter lack of friends: princesses are traditionally rather lonely figures in their ivory towers.

'Mug,' Ruby had chastised herself while manipulating the super dooper vacuum thingy Manny insisted on to open his precious wine. 'He *bought* you, you mug,' she enlarged on her own foolishness as she tossed the super dooper vacuum thingy in a high arc into the swimming pool. 'And your price was this pile of tat!' She'd wobbled across the lawn, taking in the sprawling white house. Every detail was the best that money could buy, and every detail was, as Ruby roared, 'NAFF!'

Up to her chin in bubbling water, Ruby tortured herself with random thoughts of what Manny might be doing right now, with Tania and their child. The mention of his 'kid' had been the turning point. Now she could believe anything of Manny. The tacky crimes all seemed plausible, now that his – she gulped at the tabloid phrase – *love child* had come to light.

Manny had 'baggage'. Not his matching Prada holdalls, but an ex-wife and two teenage children. 'Been there, done that,' was Manny's shorthand whenever talk had turned to babies. 'You're my family now, babes,' Manny had told her, again and again.

Presumably he was telling Tania just that in their love nest over the Pang Wang all-you-can-eat buffet. Ruby slumped in the hot tub, torturing herself with images of Manny cooing over a tiny version of himself, a foot-long bruiser in a pinstriped nappy. 'Been there, done that,' she slurred bitterly. 'But what about me, Manny?' Ruby started to cry. 'I haven't been there. I haven't done that. I haven't done anything!' Prone to melodrama, Ruby reckoned she deserved a histrionic wail or two.

Replaying her last moments with her husband, Ruby was perversely glad that she'd been sarcastic with Manny, what he would call 'mouthy'. Why the hell hadn't she been mouthy more often? she wondered, wrinkling her slender nose. Something about Manny made people tread carefully. That repressed air inhibited folk, as if he might tear off his suit and start howling like a werewolf. Ruby had tiptoed around him through their entire marriage.

'Twat!' she shouted. 'Baldy twat,' she added, amazed by her own daring. Manny's bullet head, with what was left of his hair cut snugly to the contours of his skull, was a tender subject. 'Erm . . .' Ruby scrabbled around for swear words.

She wasn't good at this being angry stuff. 'Cow,' she shouted, blushing at her lack of finesse with a curse. 'BASTARD!' That was more like it. Ruby squeezed her eyes shut and shrieked, bouncing in the water with the sheer effort of it, 'BALDY TWATTY BASTARD PIG MAN!'

'Err, hi.'

'OhmyGod!' Ruby opened her eyes and slid off the Jacuzzi's tiny underwater bench. Spluttering to the surface again, her wine glass floating away, she focused with difficulty on the small figure on her patio. 'Maria. Hi.' She pushed tendrils of damp hair away with a clumsy hand, attempting to look composed in front of one of Manny's bar staff, raising her voice to be heard over Elvis giving it loads from the speakers.

'Do you know your house has gone mad?' asked Maria, childishly small in her combats and sweatshirt. She was dark and Mediterranean looking, with a neat olive face that always seemed to get a joke Ruby didn't know had been cracked yet.

'Oh that.' Ruby nodded in the direction of the floodlit house of horrors. 'It'll be frozen any minute.'

'I see.' Maria righted one of the aluminium garden chairs that Ruby had carefully knocked over, and sat down. 'I wanted to make sure you were OK.'

'Did Manny send you?' Wine and hot water evidently made Ruby suspicious.

'Hardly.' Maria sneered at the mention of her boss's name. 'I'm homeless thanks to him. Two of his heavies chucked me out of the flat I shared with the other bar staff over the Vegas Rooms.' Maria leaned forward, hands on her knees. 'Just thought I'd pop by and see how you are. This must be a shock for you.'

'You sound as if it isn't a shock for you' isn't easy to say when you've been knocking back vintage claret for hours, but Maria must have had some sort of bartender's degree in drunk-speak, because she understood.

'Not really. He's a bad 'un.' She sat up suddenly, perhaps aware she'd gone too far. 'Sorry. I mean, he's your husband and everything.'

'No, no, don't apolo-, apol-, say shorry.' Ruby exonerated her visitor with a regal wave of her rescued glass. 'He is the baddest 'un I've ever met. Shomehow I never noticed.' Ruby did another of those mirthless laughs. Through the fug of Jacuzzi steam and priceless wine, she squinted at Maria. 'Where will you live? What will you do?'

'Don't worry about me. I'm always all right,' said Maria, briskly. 'I'd better, you know, get away. I just wanted to make sure you were coping.'

'Thanksh.' At the girl's kindness, Ruby felt tears threaten but then, with the abrupt changes of mood common to drunks, toddlers and serial killers, she grinned. 'Let me see you to the door.'

Creating a tsunami that lapped over the patio, Ruby stood up. Maria goggled up at her, amazed. 'I assumed you had a bikini on . . .' she gasped.

'Nope.' Ruby swayed as she stepped out of the tub in killer heels. 'I've got all my deshigner gear on. All presents from my loving husband.' A chic sumo wrestler, Ruby could barely walk in the layers of Gucci, Chanel, Roland Mouret and Stella McCartney. Manny had good taste in clothes and the sodden leggings under the trousers under the skirts under the dresses were all exquisite, none more so than the top layer, Ruby's strapless satin wedding dress embroidered with Swarovski crystals. Waddling back through the house after waving off a perturbed Maria, Ruby caught sight of herself in one of the mirrored walls of the James Bond-style living room. Mascara down to her chin, her hair a knotted beehive and her newly size 28 body swathed in a dripping wedding dress, she murmured, 'Shame Manny's not here. He loves me in white.'

2

It was turning out to be a festival of firsts. Ruby's first dip in the Jacuzzi was swiftly followed by Ruby's first night on the utility room floor, her first hangover, and her first grilling by the CID.

Perhaps, Ruby later conceded, *grilling* was too dramatic a term for the litany of dull questions punctuated by chipped mugs of milky tea. With Simon beagle-like at her side, Ruby answered that no, she knew nothing about Manny's secret bank accounts, nor his aliases, his sham businesses that folded owing thousands, his moneylending venture that charged one hundred and twenty per cent interest.

In scarily wooden language, the officer finally declared himself 'satisfied that the spouse was ignorant of Mr Gallagher's wrongdoing'. Outside in the nippy car park, Simon enthused that this was the best possible outcome, but Ruby translated the police-speak as 'this is a thickie of such impressive calibre that she would accept an invitation to dinner round Hannibal Lecter's'.

'Unless you're charged, they can't compel you to testify,'

explained Simon. As they parted company on a handshake, he promised, 'I'll protect you from as much of the process as I can. There's no reason why the police should interview you again.'

Shuddering, Ruby thanked him. The steamroller of the law was chugging inexorably over her old life, rendering it flat as a cartoon pancake. The prospect of a court case – an actual court case with a judge and barristers and everything – was both chilling and preposterous.

Another first was coming up: Ruby's first journey by public transport since she'd met Manny.

This, she told herself, was exciting. It was real life after her near-decade in the Land of Nod. Tucking her suitcases under her seat, she threw back her shoulders and grimaced: any sudden movement annoyed the little men with gongs who had taken up residence in her head.

Real life was noisy and brash and left chewing gum on her pink suede vanity case. The bus driver shouted at her for holding up the bus as she struggled off with her luggage, and a schoolboy offered to help in return for a blowjob.

Ruby declined.

On the train crawling towards town, Ruby felt naked without the armour of her wealth: flash jewellery, flash car, flash husband. The pain of Manny's defection smarted like a fresh tattoo. (Or so she supposed – Ruby had never had a tattoo: too sensible. Or perhaps too scared.) Manny knew how it would scald Ruby. And yet he'd done it.

There was nothing to save, nothing to salvage, from the wreckage of her marriage. It had finally sunk under the waves with the words, 'My kid'. Sleeping Beauty had taken a good look at her fairy tale and realised that it was bloody Grimm.

The penthouse was no longer 'theirs'.

It was Ruby's.

*

Fulham was as exotic a destination as Mesopotamia. Growing up in the tidy suburbs, Ruby had only ever nibbled at the edges of London proper. Too nervous to hail a taxi now that she was officially poor, Ruby dragged her cases along Fulham Road. How, she wondered, could council estates rub shoulders with expensive antiques emporiums? She passed a shabby, depressed wreck of a house attached to a mirror image property refurbished to within an inch of its life, sporting a loft extension, discreet double glazing, and potted bay trees either side of the gleaming front door. Could there really be a million-pound penthouse round here?

As a devotee of *Location, Location, Location*, Ruby should have known that the London property market is a wayward beast. Laughing in the face of common sense, it mesmerises house hunters into gladly paying hundreds of thousands of pounds for a two-up two-down with a coffin-sized yard that their gran will describe as 'poky'. Million-pound penthouses pop up everywhere in London, often with a wonderful view of sunset over the young offenders' hostel.

The *A–Z* informed Ruby that she was ten minutes away from her new home on Parsons Green. Veering away from the main road, the streets grew quieter, although they couldn't entirely escape the low-level hum of the traffic. Prettier houses, their cosy basement kitchens overshadowed by steps leading to their front doors, were appealing but much too close together for a suburban lass. Making her footsore way down a Clancy Street, Ruby felt hemmed in by the terraced houses and the cars parked nose to bum.

Clancy Street. The name rang a distant bell in Ruby's consciousness. Drowned out by those diligent little men and their gongs, it chimed on, gentle yet insistent, until Ruby stopped dead, dropping her vanity case into an oily puddle.

Clancy Street. A typewritten form appeared in livid red

in her mind. Her remorseless memory went further: *fourteen* Clancy Street, it recited.

Ruby looked slowly up at the nearest door. Eighteen. So number fourteen was two houses back. She didn't turn. She snatched up her bags and marched on.

When a few roads had been safely put between Ruby and that address, she turned a corner and confronted one of London's abrupt mood changes. Suddenly, all was smug and moneyed, as she crossed a glossy grass triangle skirted by tall redbrick houses, which wore their porches and balconies and turrets as nonchalantly as Eurotrash display their bling.

This was Parsons Green, and soon Ruby would be looking down on it from the eighth floor of the building in the opposite corner. A gleaming glass tower, it could have looked incongruous in such a stately setting, but Hannah House's strict modern beauty meant it would be welcome anywhere. Its precise lines made Ruby feel tossed in her keep-the-cold-out woolly strata, and her vanity case dripped a grotty trail across its white marble lobby.

After a minute or two of staring, chimp-like, at the buttons in the lift Ruby realised that the penthouse had its own elevator across the lobby. One of the keys in Simon's envelope fitted and soon Ruby was headed skywards, whizzing towards her post-dated independence.

The lift doors whispered open. Ruby blinked and tried to close them again, convinced she was on the wrong floor. In a private lift, there *is* no wrong floor, so Ruby had to accept that this was home.

A vast room stretched in front of her, two of its walls glass, and its floors and the other two walls a shimmering virginal white.

So far, so tasteful. But somebody had gone berserk with

a credit card at Bordellos R Us and crammed the space with pink chaise-longues, rococo gilt tables, heavily framed mirrors, furry rugs, life-size china panthers baring their teeth, candelabra, chandeliers . . . Ruby was reeling.

'It's hideous!' she squealed, hands on her head. Peeking into a bedroom, she shuddered. A baroque four-poster, bigger than Manny's ego, dominated the dark-walled room, its slithery black sheets reflected in the giant mirror suspended from its canopy.

Ruby looked up to confront her horrified reflection among the winking cherubs milling about up there. Unless she had plans to open a whorehouse, this place needed sweeping changes. Thoughts of what might have gone on in the penthouse (Simon had mentioned 'entertaining business contacts') were postponed indefinitely as Ruby swooped on a laptop computer sitting on an onyx table. Punching the air when she discovered it was connected to the internet, she Googled house clearances.

Two hours after Ruby had first set foot in Hannah House, the huge main room was empty. Ruby had sensibly hung on to the bed linen, towels, and the kitchen ephemera, and the house clearance chap had refused to take the monster four-poster. 'Now what?' thought Ruby, sitting on the glossy white floor, her legs stuck out in front of her.

The beauty of the empty rooms was obvious, but all that elegant white space felt like tundra. Ruby was alone with only three bedrooms, a shower room, a wet room, a bathroom clad in limestone, a kitchen that looked as if it came from the future and two terraces for company. The sky, so close outside the eighth-floor wall to ceiling windows, was clogged with smoky clouds, and Ruby yearned for an open fire and a squashy chair.

Jumping up, she headed for the lift. It was exhilarating to

know that everything in her universe had to happen by her own hand. Ruby was accustomed to life being handed to her on a plate (usually a Versace Homewares one). 'Yes, exhilarating,' she told herself. It sounded better than 'terrifying'.

Handing over her debit card in the scruffy second-hand shop was nerve tingling, but the transaction went through smoothly: evidently the police hadn't closed all Manny's bank accounts just yet. 'Can you deliver today?' Ruby didn't give much thought to her looks as a rule, but she knew that it was her even features, her tilted greenish eyes and the dramatic rise and fall of her V-neck that clinched an, 'Oh go on then,' from the roll-up-smoking, dirty-nailed proprietor.

By dusk, the snooty white space at the top of Hannah House was a leper colony of strangers' furniture. A plain wooden bed, dressed in white, was installed in the second bedroom, as Ruby was unable to face the four-poster and its dubious history. In the main room a long, squashy, rather tatty crimson sofa lounged against one pristine wall, facing a low coffee table tiled with garish seventies flowers. Along the back wall, a sideboard, veneered in acid bright colours, squatted self-importantly. An office swivel chair, re-upholstered by some enterprising imbecile in fuchsia towelling, admired the view from the plate glass wall, flirting with a tapestry footstool resting on the glossy flooring after a lifetime supporting elderly feet.

The effect was horrendous, a mish-mash of clashing fabrics and deservedly forgotten styles. And Ruby *loved* it, for its eccentricity, its soft edges and the defiant snook it cocked at labels and lifestyle.

Switching on her new orange standard lamp, Ruby smiled at the cosy, anti-minimalist glow it spread over the room. All that second-hand furniture had been grubby when it arrived, but now every surface sang. Ruby had polished the tables, hoovered the sofa, and beaten the bejaysus out of the rugs. If there was one skill Ruby could boast of (and there probably was only one), it was cleaning. Château Rubes had never been touched by a daily's hand, its chatelaine did all the scrubbing. Cleaning cleared her head and made her feel useful, but nothing in Ruby's cleaning history had challenged her like this collection of cast-offs, with their years of accumulated fingerprints and footprints and teacup rings. Her purchases were now fragrant, their lurid colours and various textures refreshed.

Ruby flopped down on the rejuvenated sofa, her limbs aching. She was wearier than she'd ever been after a workout. An orchid in Manny's hothouse, Ruby had never worked for a living, but she fantasised that this was how 'normal' women felt at the end of the day.

She closed her eyes.

Mistake.

Stationary at last, after a frantic day, Ruby was prey to dark thoughts that had been circling for hours. She was on her own. She opened her eyes. She was on her own in Laurence Llewelyn-Bowen's subconscious with no husband, no income, no bleeding idea of what to do next. Ruby had never had a plan. Things just happened. Other people made them happen. Hot with shame, she reviewed her sleepwalking career, and blushed at how first her parents and then Manny had organised everything in her life. She was as helpless as a newborn baby, and this self-knowledge, which had always lurked just outside the campfire of her consciousness, pounced.

Her mobile trilled. Ruby jolted upright. 'Manny,' she breathed, and then paused, her hand halfway to her bag. Shocked at her reaction to the innocuous ringtone, Ruby swallowed: she had thought 'Thank God', she had thought 'At last', she had thought 'Rescue me'. She hadn't thought, as any sensible adult should, 'Oh, that'll be the conniving, lying, unfaithful, tyrannical, baldy crim I've been enslaved to for years.'

Ruby snatched up her phone and tore off a Post-It note obscuring the display. She sagged: the ident wasn't Manny's. It was her gym, no doubt reminding her about renewing the membership she could no longer afford.

Hugging a cushion to her tummy, Ruby stuffed the mobile back into her bag. The yellow sticky note fluttered to the floor, and Ruby swung forwards to retrieve it, almost losing her balance on the edge of the violently red sofa. Idly, she smoothed it out. 'JUST IN CASE!' she read, then a line of digits.

Without thinking – it was an overrated hobby, in Ruby's view – she tapped out the mobile number.

'Hello?' The voice on the other end was wary.

'It's Ruby.' Wading in without preamble, she asked, 'Have you found anywhere to live, Maria?' and within two minutes her new lodger was on her way over.

3

'Change the locks,' suggested Simon, casually, when he called early the next morning.

'Isn't that a little dramatic?'

'Just change the locks.' Simon didn't elaborate. 'The case they're building against Manny is a good one.'

'Oh God.' Ruby squirmed.

'A lot of people have talked. He's going to need money for his defence, and that penthouse would come in handy. He's going to have a few scores to settle.'

'Manny would never hurt anybody.'

It could have been a scoff, it could have been a cough, it could have been a Tic Tac losing its way. As Simon recovered from whatever it was, Ruby went further. 'He'd certainly never lay a finger on me.'

'He has to behave himself or he'll be taken into custody, but Ruby, you know too much. So . . .'

Never before had Ruby been accused of 'knowing too much'. She could conjure up only the vaguest details about Manny's business affairs. Should she, Ruby wondered, thank him for keeping her in the dark? All Manny's strategies to protect his wife turned out to be double-edged, also serving to make her feel dumb and helpless.

The litany of Manny's crimes had been on her mind since that morning in Simon's office. They weren't just arcane words, they were real deeds, which had damaged real people. And she was implicated.

'I know. Change the locks.'

'I'm covered in bruises,' moaned Maria, hunched over the marble breakfast bar as they shared a breakfast of eight Polo mints and a very old muesli bar. There had been no time to shop, so the women were reduced to handbag foraging. 'Why anybody considers satin sheets sexy is beyond me. I kept slithering off.'

'I heard.' Ruby tried not to smile. 'Bump . . . bump . . . bumpbump –'

'*Bump*.' Maria wryly completed the sequence. 'If I pull, any and all naughtiness will have to take place on the floor. I don't fancy rolling up to casualty in suspenders, concocting an excuse for my dislocated rude bits.'

'So you don't have a boyfriend?' Ruby wondered if she was being pushy. Out of practice at making friends, there was lots she was keen to know about the raven-haired little stranger suddenly sharing her home and her past its sell-by date cereal bar.

'Nah.' Maria seemed unconcerned. 'Bit of a dry spell. There'll be another one along in a minute.' She picked a grain of something wholesome but old from between her strong, white teeth. 'Men are like buses.'

Having recently been reversed over by one, Ruby silently agreed.

'What's with the violin I found under the four-poster?'

26

In response to Ruby's gormless look, Maria produced a shabby looking instrument from beneath her chair. 'There's kinky,' she said, scowling at it, 'and then there's kinky. God knows what this little fella got up to.'

'Oh, I recognise that,' smiled Ruby, taking it from her, and cradling it fondly. 'Manny picked it up for a few quid at a car boot.' She looked at it, and past it. 'Just to make me laugh, I think.'

'Hmm.' Maria sounded sceptical, as she rose to put her glass in the dishwasher.

'Will you be in or out tonight?' asked Ruby, as Maria gathered the myriad kit that somehow fitted into the pockets and flaps of the omnipresent combat trousers: mobile, keys, purse, paperback, mini action figure of David Hasselhoff. 'Not that it's any of my business,' Ruby backtracked. '*Beware the nosy landlady*. Just ignore me.'

Hoff in hand, Maria looked amused. 'I'll be in. And if the job interview goes well, the winebox is on me.'

More wine, thought Ruby, horrified, as Maria clattered noisily out of the space age kitchen. She didn't remember single life being quite so boozy, but perhaps that was because she'd lived with parents who got giddy on wine gums.

In what Ruby was already thinking of as the olden days, Wednesdays had meant two hours of expensive humiliation at the hands of her personal trainer. Along with reiki sessions, facials and walking around the house with her tummy pulled in, he had been abandoned. Full of energy that had nowhere to go, Ruby polished and dusted the already immaculate apartment, grateful to Maria for slopping water on the work surfaces and leaving half a bootprint by the front door.

Such elementary cleaning (how Ruby longed for a challenging red wine spillage, or even – O bliss! – some dried-in blood on a man-made fibre) couldn't be spun out for long and she flopped on to the sofa.

Sitting down meant thinking. Thinking meant imagining Manny either cooing over his extramarital mini-me, or turning up at Hannah House sporting Gucci knuckledusters. Ruby sprang up. She would be her own personal trainer.

Glad that she'd allocated precious suitcase space to her gym gear, Ruby hit Parsons Green running. It turned out to be trickier than her usual session on the treadmill. She had to swerve for pedestrians and poodles and the like. Darting past hedges and bins and gates, Ruby congratulated herself on keeping fit *and* getting to know her new area. She noted her nearest newsagent, wine bar, mini-mart, tramp.

It tickled Ruby to see the homeless man park his rag-laden supermarket trolley in the doorway of a super-smart shirt-maker's, and she wished she had her purse with her: she had never passed a homeless person without pressing some change into their hand. Galloping over a zebra crossing it occurred to her that the tramp very possibly had more disposable income than she did.

After an hour's running, Ruby paused to try not to die. Bent double, her breath came in rasping heaves. Holding on to some railings with the iron grip of a hamster, Ruby glanced up at the house she'd chosen to expire in front of. Sweating, dizzy, she saw the number fourteen on a sky blue door at the top of some chipped steps. Ruby panicked as the blue door swung open and she realised that she was back on Clancy Street.

Trying to stagger away, Ruby only succeeded in catching the attention of the woman striding down the steps.

'Are you OK?' The woman paused, and bent down to take a good look at Ruby. She was a muddle of wintry accessories, a walking pashmina exhibition, laden with bulging bags. Under an untidy, curling fringe, her face was kind and wore the expression of a woman who was really, really hoping that the hacking wreck in perfectly matching sportswear clinging to her wall would live long enough to move on.

'I'm fine,' gasped Ruby, attempting nonchalance while trying to stop her lungs jumping out through her mouth. 'Just a bit, you know, out of breath.' She flapped her hands and smiled hopelessly and the woman looked even more alarmed.

'If you're sure . . .' The stranger backed away, picking up speed, finally turning on her laced-up boots with an unusual look that combined irritation and sympathy.

'So that's her.' Ruby sank to her knees. 'That's Mrs Olivia Friend.'

The retro coffee table was pimping bad wine, Doritos and sundry dips: Maria had got the job.

'This is nice.' Ruby wondered if she should deduct the price of the snacks from Maria's rent. Maybe half the price, as they were sharing. Having a lodger threw up all sorts of dilemmas. 'Tell me about the job.' She sat stiffly on the towelling office chair. Perhaps Maria was just being polite, having a quick drink with her lonely landlady before meeting up with her real friends.

'It's another bar job.' Maria poured wine into two glorious crystal goblets she'd unearthed in the kitchen. Nestling among the sofa cushions like somebody who was hunkering down for the evening, she said, 'Should be a giggle. It's just up the road. The Velvet Glove.'

'I passed there today!' squealed Ruby, as if this was stop press news. Emboldened by Maria's relaxed demeanour, she tucked her legs under her on the swivel chair, only to regret it as the seat spun wildly round. 'Hang on! Hang on!' she laughed, scooching herself round to face Maria again. 'Right. I'm back. You mean the little bar between the dry cleaner and the chemist?' Ruby had been amused by the blood red façade with dramatic gilt lettering, so decadent between its sober neighbours.

'It's a gay place.'

Evidently the startled glance that Ruby threw at Maria and hastily converted into an oh-so-casual look around the whole room was noted, because Maria went on, 'And no, I'm not. Although . . .' she said dreamily, 'there was that time in Margate. But I think that was a one-off.'

Filing away 'Margate' as a subject to return to when she knew Maria better, Ruby raised her glass in a toast. 'Here's to you! Your new flat and your new job.'

'And my new mate.' Maria said it easily, and perhaps she didn't notice the blush that started around the collar of Ruby's dressing gown and threatened to start a forest fire in her hairline. 'What about your plans?' Maria harassed the sour cream dip with a Dorito. 'You getting a job or what?' She didn't seem to share Ruby's qualms about boundaries. 'I suppose you'll be rolling in it after the divorce.' She halted, laden Dorito halfway to her lips. 'You *are* going to divorce him, aren't you?'

The question took Ruby by surprise. Her thinking hadn't got that far. It hadn't got anywhere. 'Erm . . .' she said.

'In the meantime it would make sense to sell this place.' Maria cast a sideways glance at Ruby.

'Oh no, definitely not,' said Ruby resolutely.

'Why not?' Despite her puzzlement, Maria looked gratified by Ruby's answer.

'I've got too much on my mind. And besides, I don't have a clue how to go about it.'

'It's easy!' scoffed Maria.

Ruby had been frightened by an estate agent at an impressionable age and now harboured an irrational fear of hair gelled into a point, but that wasn't the real reason. She'd had enough upheaval, and the stacks of cash tied up in the apartment didn't tempt her. Wealth had been a sleeping pill for Ruby: she was wide awake now and her agenda was simple. She wanted freedom. 'I'll look for a job.'

'Perhaps,' Maria went on, 'this flat is your last link with Manny.' She spoke slowly, as if working out a maths problem. 'That's it. You don't want to sever your last connection to him.' She nodded, pleased with herself. 'Just like the violin. It has sentimental meaning for you.'

'Oh for God's flipping sake!' expostulated the amateur swearer. 'As if! I mean!' Confirming any suspicions by the ardour of her response, Ruby crossed and uncrossed her legs so fast her fluffy slippers were a pink blur. One foot caught a glass on the coffee table, and red wine splattered across the rug.

'Shit!' shrieked Maria, leaping up. 'Balls!' She was a much more accomplished curser than her new friend.

'No problem.' Ruby shot into the kitchen, glee all over her face.

'It'll stain,' groaned Maria.

'No it won't.' Flourishing one damp cloth and one dry cloth like a vaudeville magician, Ruby returned and sank to her knees. 'You just make it even wetter like this . . .' She pressed the wet cloth over the scattered islets of Beaujolais. 'Then blot with the dry one.' Deep in concentration, Ruby didn't catch Maria's bored look. 'And ta daah!' Ruby held up the dry cloth which had absorbed a surprising amount of wine. 'And then you—'

Butting in on the stain removal masterclass, Maria asked, 'What kind of job will you look for?'

That stopped the masterclass dead. Sitting back on her heels, Ruby's feline face fell. 'God knows. I'm useless.' She waved away Maria's polite attempts to pooh-pooh. 'No, really, I am. I was a pampered child, an over-protected teenager, a kept woman.' It was time to confess all. 'I don't know how to pay a bill, or stick to a budget, or buy a car, or complain in a shop. I can't type, I never really got the hang of alpha-betical order, and my one GCSE is in Looking Pretty. And,' she added miserably, 'I'm so thick I didn't even realise my husband, the missing Kray triplet, was bonking the help.'

'Nobody says bonking any more.'

'Rogering, then. Schtupping. Whatever. You see my problem?' appealed Ruby, getting back to business with her arsenal of cloths.

'You must be good at something. Everybody's good at something.' Maria didn't seem fazed by the rollcall of short-comings.

'This!' Ruby mocked herself. 'Cleaning.' She held up the cloth like an Oscar. 'I'm the world's best cleaner. I can get rid of any stain. I can bring order to chaos. I scrub. I hoover. I polish. I even steam clean if the wind's in the right direc-tion.' Ruby sighed. 'But so what?'

'So what?' Maria was on the edge of the sofa. 'If you can clean you can make a living. Be a cleaner. As long as there's money coming in, you'll survive, and I'll talk you through the boring bits, the bills, the council tax and stuff.' Ruby's look of amazed horror evidently wasn't lost on her. 'Of course, it won't keep you in designer clothes, like you're used to.'

'Me? A cleaner?' Tussling with layers of prejudice, Ruby recalled how the highlight of her mother's week had been patronising her 'Mrs B'. Cleaners were invisible drones, doing the mucky stuff nobody else wanted to. 'I don't know . . .'

'You'd be your own boss. You'd decide who you worked

for, what hours you did.' Pacing the floor, Maria pushed her idea. 'You'd be independent.'

That last word shone, and quite dazzled Ruby. 'I would, wouldn't I?' The notion took a firm grip of Ruby's excitable imagination: she was practically working out who'd play her in the biopic. 'And I'd have a nice little uniform. And a logo. And a motto.'

'Hang on,' laughed Maria, who had far more experience of the harsh realities of work than Ruby did. 'First things first. What will you charge? How will you find your customers?'

'*Clients*,' corrected Ruby. 'I'll have cards made and I'll target homes I like the look of. I'll be picky,' she warned. 'I'll charge the going rate plus . . . two pounds. And I'll be worth it.'

'You definitely will.' Maria ran an exploratory toe over the rug. 'It's like new.'

Like new – Ruby liked that phrase. It was how she was starting to feel.

I am the world's best cleaner
Let me transform your life
Ruby 07871 3340924

In less than a week the cards were done, earning a smile and an, 'I like your confidence,' from Maria, who had lent Ruby the money to print them, and to top up her mobile. Or 'work phone' as Ruby had taken to calling it. Between them, they compiled a list of houses to target.

'Posh houses.' Maria was adamant.

'*Interesting* houses.' Ruby was equally so. She slipped a card into her sports bra. It would be delivered tonight on her daily run.

*

33

Clancy Street was dark, the feeble dark that London thinks is night time, despite the street lamps. Having trotted up, and then down, the steps of number fourteen (noting that the knocker needed a good going over), Ruby jogged the rest of her usual route.

The tramp was rifling through his packed supermarket trolley outside the launderette. Ruby always threw him a 'good evening' but that was all she could give him.

A few steps beyond him, Ruby halted, then jogged backwards until she was level with him again. 'Excuse me,' she said politely.

'Yes, my love,' answered the tramp with equal good manners. He was a proper, old-fashioned gentleman of the road, from his battered trilby, via his ancient raincoat belted with string, to the brogues that peeled back like sardine tins to display blackened toes.

'Do you . . .' Halfway through the sentence Ruby realised how ridiculous it would sound. 'Play the violin?' she ended, apologetically.

'Of course,' came the immediate reply. The tramp's eyes widened in his filthy face, as if everybody knew that.

'I'll be back in two ticks.'

With the window open, Ruby could just hear the strains of 'Yesterday' from the pavement eight floors below her. The music had kept her company after Maria had set off for her shift at the Velvet Glove.

That had been three hours ago, and even a devoted Beatles fan would wilt after hearing 'Yesterday' played thirty times in succession on a faltering, scratchy violin.

Ruby, trying not to regret her good deed, pulled the window shut just as her mobile rang. It was a local number.

She bit her lip, stared at the phone for a long moment, then picked it up.

A male voice on the other end asked, 'Can you really transform lives?'

Ruby had her first clients.

4

'What should I call you?' Olivia Friend's face seemed designed to express concern. Her brows knitted, her hazel eyes narrowed, her lips thinned. 'All that Mrs G stuff is so patronising. Makes my blood boil.'

'Ruby'll be fine.' Ruby was crouching on the (very grubby) floor of Olivia's basement kitchen, nervously decanting the tools of her new trade from a toolbox. She'd bought dusters, rubber gloves, sprays and potions: her clients needn't supply anything except the dirt.

'Ruby.' Trying the name out for size, Olivia seemed reluctant to leave Ruby to it.

'Any other instructions?' asked Ruby gently, pulling on her Marigolds with a satisfying snap.

'No, just, you know . . . *clean* the bloody place, I suppose,' said Olivia vaguely, waving a hand over the muddled room. She was a strong and sturdy looking woman, her sandal-clad feet rooting her firmly to the earth. 'I don't think we need a cleaner, but Hugo seems to feel we do.'

Any casual onlooker would agree. Ruby had struggled to

control her gasps at the state of this pretty terraced house. Every room was blanketed in dust, the crumbs of long-dead sandwiches were trodden into every carpet, and the windows had last been cleaned when God was in short trousers. The priorities of the well-spoken couple, every bit as scruffy as their home in their baggy layers, were obviously elsewhere. Both something in further education (Ruby, typically, hadn't been listening when the pertinent facts were given out); evidence of their reading addiction lay piled up on the landing, in the hall, in the sitting room, in the bedrooms. There were books in the loo, and in the kitchen, bringing colour and the promise of other lives into the shabbily genteel house.

'I can't help feeling it's wrong.' Olivia was standing over Ruby as she bent down to pick up her bucket. 'I mean, as one woman to another, isn't it demeaning?' she asked, urgently. 'Cleaning up after us, as if you're a . . .'

'Servant?' offered Ruby, cheerfully. 'No. It's not demeaning. It's a job. And I'm happy to do it. Honestly, I am!' Ruby had to laugh at the anxiety on Olivia's face. It was a handsome face, naked of makeup, with clever eyes that sought to understand. 'Please don't worry.' She wondered what Olivia would say if she knew that Ruby had given the Friends a special low price. And why.

'Bloody Hugo,' huffed Olivia, making for the door. 'Next time he calls himself a feminist I'll remind him of you.' She glanced back at Ruby, and pulled a face at the mop in her hand. 'I feel like paying you *not* to clean.'

'Now that *would* be demeaning,' Ruby gently pointed out.

Olivia's discomfort was embarrassing. Ruby was glad when the squeaky kitchen door shut behind her new employer. Gender politics had passed Ruby's corner of Esher by: there was no room for a feminist in Château Rubes. Ruby had no qualms about her new career, didn't feel compromised or belittled. She felt excited: the soft yellow dusters in their cellophane packets were hand grenades. To use a word Olivia might approve of, Ruby felt empowered as she filled her shiny new bucket with scalding water.

'It looks like somebody else's kitchen!' marvelled Hugo, staring awestruck about him.

'It does, doesn't it?' murmured Olivia, with what sounded like nostalgia for her cobwebs.

The only dirty thing in the sparkling new room was Ruby. Two hours of archaeological housewifery, unearthing the artefacts buried under the grime, had left her feeling grubby. 'I'll have a quick cup of tea before I attack—' She hurriedly modified her language. '*Tackle* the rest of the house,' she said, dropping into a rocking chair that now smelled of beeswax.

'I'll make it for you.' Olivia was over to the kettle like a greyhound, obviously relieved to contribute.

'Rightiho.' Hugo gestured upstairs. 'I'll get back to my, you know, study and let you get on with it, kind of thing.' He bumbled out backwards.

Ruby had taken a shine to Hugo, who was a born bumbler and as comfortable as his worn corduroy trousers. She suspected him of having hidden depths, and felt certain that he was a lovely dad. Ruby reached out and straightened a framed family snap she'd just polished. Hugo, Olivia and a gap-toothed boy grinned out at her, leaning on each other in a higgledy piggledy, just-about-to-collapse-in-giggles way. 'Where's your son today?' she asked, suppressing a yawn.

'Joe?' Olivia turned sharply. The question seemed to surprise her. 'Out,' she said curtly.

'Oh. Right.' The change in atmosphere was tangible. *I see*, thought Ruby. *As a cleaner I'm entitled to exaggerated respect and the benefit of your middle-class guilt, but not the right to ask a personal question.* Olivia was contradicting her own code. 'He's a beautiful boy,' ventured Ruby. She looked into Joe's innocent eyes, soft and happy in the black and white print.

'We like him,' said Olivia.

'Ruby, sweetheart, we beauties must stick together,' said the stocky man in the scarlet evening gown.

'Er, yes.' Ruby cowered on her chrome bar stool, and sucked on her blue cocktail. She attempted to smile with her eyes over the rim of her glass. The thump of the music made conversation difficult.

''Scuse me a sec.' The chap hoicked his sequined hem up to his groin and rearranged, with much huffing and puffing, whatever it was he kept down there. 'That's better. This girdle plays havoc with me crown jewels.'

'I can imagine,' said Ruby, who, unfortunately, could.

The bijou interior of the Velvet Glove pulsed with raucous high spirits. The inevitable glitterball dazzled, the music deafened, and Ruby's new friend was demure in comparison to the diva wiggling about on the minute stage. In response to Maria's nagging ('Come on! *Double entendres* and free booze, what more could you want?') Ruby had finally given in and visited her at work. Another night on the red sofa with only the TV and the distant scrapings of a maudlin violin for company hadn't been tempting earlier, but now Ruby harked back to them as a lost nirvana.

Ruby had never really 'gone out'. She didn't know how. The teenage rite of shuffling round handbags at pulling palaces had passed her by in favour of marriage to the uptight Manny. Tonight was a baptism of fire. The room was painted the colour of a midnight sky, with twinkling fairy lights standing in for stars. Maria's bar was curved and silver, fashioned from the finest MDF: the venue's pretensions outstripped its budget. The Glove (as Maria's shorthand termed it) was drenched in pheromones, a pulling palace of the finest calibre. Except that all the pullers, and pullees, were male.

Ruby was trying hard to be modern. To not notice. To not mind. To be absolutely, totally, utterly nonchalant about a bloke in a suit snogging a skinny guy in cycling shorts at her elbow.

'Knock it off, you two.' The chap in the dress gave the passionate pair a shove. 'There's a lady present.' Leaning in conspiratorially to Ruby, he whispered hoarsely, 'Sorry about that, love. It's like a safari in here some nights.'

Ruby laughed awkwardly, plotting her escape. The booming music, the off-key caterwauling from the stage, the high octane chatter was too much for her. Frowning as another free cocktail was plonked in front of her, Ruby hissed, 'Maria, what if your boss finds out?'

'He already has.' The paunchy man in the dress laughed, a scratchy throttle that just remembered to segue into a girlish tinkle halfway through. 'I'm Teddy, darling. I own the joint. A beauty like you drinks on the house. You bring a touch of class to this dump.'

From the other side of the bar, the flick of a tea towel sent Teddy's wig over his eyes. 'Might I remind you of two things?' said a small neat man with a cropped head and ascetic demeanour. 'One, you are not the sole owner of this *dump*, mate. My name, Kendall Brontë, is over the door as well. And two – you're on.'

'I'm ALWAYS on, darling!' roared Teddy, pushing his way to the stage. 'Wonderful performance, just wonderful,' he complimented the knobbly-kneed amazon who'd been miming badly to Cher. 'Now fuck off.'

Teddy clambered with splayed, fishnet-clad legs on to the

tiny stage, manhandled the microphone from the departing artiste, and swung into his act in front of purple lurex curtains which were a fraction too short. Singing, swearing, telling ancient jokes and insulting the clientele, he was clearly having the time of his life.

And so was the audience. Even as they groaned at the knackered gags and winced at his musings on the sexual attractiveness of the front row, the whole room was focused on this stout, middle-aged man in unconvincing drag. Behind her, Ruby heard Kendall sigh, 'Silly old tart' fondly.

Slowly, Ruby relaxed. Possibly she would never relax sufficiently to hear the punchline of Teddy's joke about the vicar and the corn on the cob without feeling faint, but she felt less out of place than she'd expected to. The mood in the crowded room was friendly and celebratory, and there was no risk of being chatted up.

Ruby got chatted up a lot. It made her wriggle, like an insect on a botanist's pin. She couldn't understand why men were drawn to her, why they felt compelled to mouth trite versions of, 'Come here often?' as she ordered a frappuccino, or waited in the post office queue, or even, one memorable afternoon, as she stood outside a hairdresser's during a fire alarm with her hair in curlers. Ruby's beauty was an accident, a genetic roll of the dice: she didn't prize it, and it puzzled her that men seemed to. Every bit as innocent as her parents had hoped, Ruby took her looks for granted. She would have preferred a man to compliment her on her kindness, her ability to stand on her head, or her way with a hoover: telling her she was beautiful was old news and only served to make her slightly uncomfortable. It was one of the reasons that Ruby had found it easy to comply with Manny's request to stay away from his clubs. 'Too tacky a setting for my diamond,' he'd told her. She knew the truth now: she might have got in the way of impregnating the help.

A prod in her back made her swivel round.

'You all right?' Maria checked.

'I'm good.' Ruby corrected herself. 'I'm great.' To feel so at home in a bursting bar was unexpected, and Ruby raised her free drink as her mobile buzzed in her jeans pocket. 'Ooh. Maybe it's another client.' She dug out her phone to check the message.

U being a good girl babes?

It was as if Manny's meaty hand was on her shoulder. By his standards she wasn't being a good girl at all. She was propping up a bar, half tipsy and loving it, surrounded by men. Ruby swallowed. Could she reinvent herself so speedily? One minute a devoted wife, the next a barfly. It didn't say much for her loyalty. Ruby stared at the message, wondering where Manny was, who he was with.

A small hand reached over and grabbed the phone.

'Hey!' Ruby complained, as Maria deleted the message.

'He's trying to get into your head,' spat Maria, handing back the phone.

'He's my husband,' Ruby reminded her, annoyance prickling her tone. 'He's already in my head.'

'You're moving on, girl.' Maria was resolute, as she was about everything. She was as resolute about which cereal she preferred (Coco Pops) as she was about which political party she voted for (Monster Raving Loony). 'Aren't you?' she asked, scrutinising Ruby like a particularly scary PE teacher.

'Yes.' Ruby took another sip of her cocktail. Texting Manny, as she wanted to do, probably didn't fit in with moving on. But joining in with the chorus of 'I Am What I Am' with her hands in the air did.

5

'*Detergeo ergo sum.*' Ruby patted the embroidered motto on the breast pocket of her unimpeachably white cotton overall.

'Is that foreign?' Maria was propped on one elbow in her four-poster, a sleep mask pushing her hair up into a tousled nest.

'Latin.' Ruby pirouetted to show off her uniform, newly released from its cellophane.

'Only you could look sexy in a bloody overall.' Maria slumped back into her pillows: last night's shift had ended in a shot-drinking contest with a man known only as Dockyard Doris.

'I'm not trying to look sexy.' Mildly affronted, Ruby stopped mid-twirl. 'I look efficient. Capable. Professional.'

'And sexy,' mumbled Maria from under the covers. 'Sorry, but you do.'

Ruby's trusty right-hand man, Henry, had no opinion on her sex appeal: all he wanted to do was suck up dust, and lots of it. Ruby scooped up her new hoover and headed for the lift. Another day, another client, she thought smugly. That made four in total. Today she was heading across the green, to a grand redbrick house that seemed to have strayed into London from the countryside.

Mrs Vine turned out to be an elegant lady of tiny dimensions who made barely a dent in her massive home now that her husband had died. Room after room opened off the wide hallways, all studded with antiques and sofas and armchairs laden with cushions. There were rugs to beat, parquet floors to polish, and oil paintings to dust. But, thought Ruby, somebody else had got there first.

The whole house was sparkling. Ruby couldn't fault it. Locating Mrs Vine in a kitchen large enough to stable an elephant, Ruby was about to suggest that there was no cleaning for her to do, when Mrs Vine pre-empted her with a hearty, 'Tea? Cake?'

Ruby shut her mouth and nodded. Since her marriage broke up, or dissolved, or imploded, or whatever it had done on that damp Monday, she'd been in thrall to food. She'd taken to eating between meals so diligently that breakfast carried on until the last Twix of the day, eaten in bed by the light of her clock radio.

The cake was home made, and very good. In between appreciative mouthfuls, Ruby endeavoured to ask Mrs Vine why she'd taken on a cleaner she patently had no need for, but there was no chink in the genteel wall of sound the woman created.

'Cake orlright?' began Mrs Vine in the sort of refined accent that has quelled peasant rebellions and intimidated bus conductors for generations. 'Good. My eldest nephew adores my cake. Of course, his wife can't bake. She can ride to hounds but a jammy sponge is quite beyond her. I told him. Darling, I said, that gel will never make you happy.

44

Breasts are not everything. He went ahead and married her of course. Never listens.'

The Vines were a large family and Ruby could have sat an exam in their peccadilloes by the time she'd chased the last crumbs with a licked forefinger. It was evident that the junior Vines rarely visited their widowed relative. Mrs Vine had answered Ruby's unasked question: there was, Ruby learned, more than one way to earn her ten pounds an hour. 'Same time next week, Mrs Vine!' she called out buoyantly as she went out through the heavy front door.

It was a short walk home across the green to Hannah House, the damp grass squeaky under her trainers. Ruby allowed herself a curtailed wallow in the satisfaction her unexpected new career was bringing. With some hand-holding from Maria, she'd managed to change all the apartment's household bills from Château Rubes Enterprises to her own name. It had been pretty straightforward, confounding Ruby's fear of such humdrum practicalities.

Money was coming in, bona fide cash that she could touch and feel and arrange in pleasing little towers. So much better than the baffling columns of figures that Manny had frowned at and cursed over. Maria was unamused by the cereal box that lay smugly under Ruby's bed, crammed with tenners, and warned her landlady that a savings account was the next step in her independence. Still wary of waking up frozen by the CID, Ruby was content to sleep above her modest fortune for now.

Switching her mobile back on, Ruby wondered if she'd had a reply to the card she'd dropped through the Honourable Millicent Flatbush's front door. Or, to be precise, the door of the house, where, according to its blue plaque, the Honourable Millicent Flatbush had once lived. Ruby had never heard of the lady, but the gloriously outdated name made her smile, and the house was possibly Ruby's favourite of the homes she'd targeted, a pretty flat-fronted cottage painted lavender blue whose wonky, doll's house charm made Ruby itch to get through the front door.

A text had come in. Ruby stiffened. The spectre of Manny loomed, even though it was a while since his message. According to Simon, Manny never mentioned her at their almost daily meetings: a detail which managed to both sting and reassure her. It was, she knew, preferable that the new, Guy Ritchie version of her husband keep away, but she felt sore that he could keep away so easily. Her marriage was now an open wound. There was no way to approach it without smarting.

The text was a banal one from Maria. It was quite a feat to be bitterly disappointed and deeply relieved at the same time, but Ruby pulled it off.

'You the cleaner?' asked a squeaky voice from behind Ruby, battling with Henry's greedy roar.

Ruby switched the hoover off. She had finally been allowed into Hugo Friend's dark and cloistered study and was evicting dust that had lain undisturbed since Jim Davidson was funny. 'Yes, I am.' She turned around. 'And you're Joe.'

'Yup.' Joe was as lovely as his photo, with all the peachy promise of a scoop of cold ice cream. He was pale with round grey eyes and the worst pudding bowl haircut that Ruby had seen outside of a Dickens serialisation. 'The house smells different since you've been coming.'

'Thanks, Joe.' That was the kind of compliment Ruby liked. 'I haven't done your room yet. It's always locked.'

'I have a lot of personal stuff in there,' said Joe gravely.

'That's what I reckoned.' Ruby had scant experience of ten-year-old boys but she doubted that they were all as self-possessed as this one. In his Fair Isle jumper and tweedy trousers she could be dealing with a bite-size Dr Jonathan Miller.

'*Detergeo ergo sum*'. Joe pointed unexpectedly at Ruby's left breast. 'I clean therefore I am.'

Christ, he could speak Latin. He could probably direct an opera if somebody gave him a box to stand on. 'You old clever clogs,' marvelled Ruby.

'Dad teaches me bits and pieces of Latin,' shrugged Joe. 'I can say bumhole if you like,' he offered, veering away from the Jonathan Miller template somewhat.

'Go on then,' Ruby dared him, folding her arms.

A clatter of Birkenstocks on the stair interrupted Joe before he could educate Ruby. 'Stop pestering Ruby, sweetheart,' scolded Olivia, placing a proprietorial hand on her son's shoulder. 'Sorry about him,' she muttered, leaning over Joe to slam the door shut.

Ruby, alone again with Henry, tucked her chin into her chest and smiled. 'Bumhole,' she whispered happily to herself, before flicking a switch and destroying the ancestral homes of countless Clancy Road spiders.

A regular now at the Velvet Glove, Ruby was as relaxed in its hyped-up atmosphere as a monk at prayer in a cathedral. Sipping a complicated drink which supported three separate swizzle sticks on what she now regarded as 'her' stool, Ruby was enjoying the relative peace of Happy Hour.

Behind the bar, Maria was applying gloss to Teddy's pucker. 'More!' he bayed. 'More!'

Elbowing them both out of the way, Kendall frowned disapprovingly as he heaved a crate of bottled beer under the bar. 'Don't mind me,' he carped. 'I'll just work meself to death while the staff play Girls' World.'

'How do I look?' smouldered Teddy.

'Like a past-it faggot who's fallen face down in the jam. Next question.' Kendall pushed his partner out of the way to do something mysterious with the slimline tonic pump.

Ruby was past reacting to this kind of banter. It was normal for Teddy and Kendall, as harmless as any other couple discussing the garden. She relished the bickering of this Terry and June *manqué*, knowing it to be camouflage. She saw love in the way Kendall watched Teddy's act no matter how busy the bar was; in the way they found each other's eye in the crowd. She saw it, and rather envied it.

'Tell him, Rubes,' drawled Teddy, in his broken glass rumble. 'A lady likes to be treated with respect.'

Without looking up from the pump, Kendall sniped, 'You're the only lady I know who can wee wee her own name in the snow. Her Majesty Queen Elizabeth II, for example, would find that quite beyond her.'

With a shriek Teddy covered Ruby's ears. 'Pas devant les enfants!' he hissed at Kendall.

'She's no child.' Now Kendall did look up, and he threw a brief penetrating glance Ruby's way before shaking out a tea towel with a snap.

'She is,' cooed Teddy, wrinkling his large and flabby nose at Ruby. 'Don't mind him. He's just bitter that I got the looks, the talent and the charisma while he got the ability to dry glasses really really well.'

But Ruby did mind Kendall. It wasn't the first such look she'd had. Despite his small stature, Kendall had presence. Perhaps it was the carefully tended moustache. Ruby sat up straighter when he was around. His shrewd reserve brought out her only child need to be teacher's pet. Taut and tidy in his unchanging armour of white T and jeans, Kendall had the austerity of a colonel, even in the salty environs of the Velvet Glove.

In contrast, Teddy was a marshmallow confection of dresses and boas and heels, all held together by Jack Daniel's and insecurity. 'I could have had my pick of men, you know,' he was telling Ruby, not for the first time. Emerging from behind the bar to take the stool next to hers, he elaborated. 'A very well known actor, whose name I shall never reveal under pain of death, once begged to kiss my feet.'

'Kinky for Odor-Eaters, was he?' Kendall scrutinised a glass then polished it again.

'I have the feet of a geisha!' shrieked Teddy, jumping down from the stool on his size eleven T-bars. 'And look at my knees!' He lifted his marabou hem to expose legs encased, like disco sausages, in glittering tights. 'They are the legs of a twelve-year-old girl.'

'Unfortunately attached to the arse of a fifty-year-old poofter. Get on stage,' ordered Kendall evenly. 'We're filling up.'

As Teddy swept off in a huffy cloud of feathers and expletives, Ruby chanced a conversation with Kendall. 'Cold out,' she ventured.

'Wouldn't know.' Kendall was short.

'Oh.' The atmosphere was glacial. 'Too busy to get out, I suppose.'

'Not all of us can prop up bars sinking free booze.'

Ouch. Hoping to diffuse the bitchiness, Ruby said without rancour, 'Perhaps you need some more staff. It might take the pressure off you.'

Maria butted in, ostentatiously topping up Ruby's drink. 'What you really need is some help upstairs. No, no,' she said hurriedly, as Kendall raised a protective hand to his shiny head, 'I mean, in the flat.'

'If Teddy would lift a finger . . .' said Kendall darkly.

'I could help.' Ruby recognised Maria's cue. 'I'm a cleaner.

I can give you a few hours a week.' Kendall didn't respond. 'Special rates. Seven pounds an hour.'

'Eight,' snapped Maria.

'Seven,' repeated Ruby. 'To say thanks for all those free drinks.'

'Hmm.' Kendall appraised her, those squirrel-bright eyes calculating. 'OK,' he said at last. Then he smiled.

Ruby jumped. He looked like a different person.

'It's not that there's anything wrong with Kendall's teeth,' explained Ruby as she linked arms with Maria on their way home much later that night. 'It's just that I'd never seen them before.'

'It's not personal,' mused Maria, leaning on her taller companion. 'He was like that with me at first. Cagey. As if I'd done something.'

'Exactly!' Ruby was slightly over-emphatic as a result of the conveyor belt of drinks Maria had laid on. 'Just wait till I get my hands on his flat. I'll clean like I've never cleaned before and then he'll *have* to like me.'

'So you reckon a mop and bucket are the way to a man's heart?' queried Maria as the mirrored lift sped towards the penthouse.

'It's *a* way to *anybody's* heart.' Ruby knew the power of her mop and bucket. She knew she was doing good with them, spreading love along with the Flash. 'Joe told me I made his house smell nice today.'

'Which one's Joe? The kid?' Maria headed straight for the sofa and stretched out like a medieval martyr on a tomb, albeit one in combats and a Sex Pistols T-shirt. 'Aren't there any eligible men on your customer, sorry, client list?'

'Nah.' Ruby shouted through from the kitchen where she had embarked on an ambitious tea and toasted sandwich combo. 'The word "eligible" is not in my vocabulary. I've been neutered. My marriage was . . .' She faltered, struck by her easy use of the past tense.

'Was what?' prompted the martyr in the other room.

'Was plenty for one lifetime.'

When Ruby set down a tray of excellent things, including a rogue Bakewell she'd surprised at the back of a cupboard, Maria sat up. 'Has he texted again?'

'No.' Ruby shook her head. 'That was a one-off.'

'Never,' scoffed Maria. 'He'll leave it ju-u-st long enough so you start to relax and then BANG!' She thumped the coffee table and the battered little cake jumped. 'Another creepy message. He'll keep that thread nice and taut.' She paused. 'Do you miss him? Be honest.'

Ruby was rarely anything else. 'Yes.'

'Nooooh!'

'I spent every day with him for nine years.' Ruby refused to be embarrassed by her emotions. 'I'd miss the Antichrist after all that time.'

'He was unfaithful, for God's sake.'

'I don't really need reminding, thanks.' A thought, solid and stony, took sudden shape. 'Did you know?'

Mid-chew, Maria pulled a face and nodded. 'Not about the baby,' she clarified, her voice thick with ham toastie. 'But we all knew he and Tania were—'

'Enjoying each other's company.' Ruby saved Maria from finding a polite way of describing something very impolite indeed. 'I suppose that's why you used to be standoffish with me,' she theorised.

'Was I?' said Maria. 'Maybe.'

'You were. Kind of shifty.' Ruby smiled. 'That's sweet. You didn't even know me but it made you feel awkward.'

'I honestly don't remember feeling awkward.'

Ruby gave up trying to squeeze a warm moment out of the past and asked instead, 'Were there others?'

Maria shrugged. 'Dunno. Yes. It was the coke. It gets some men like that.'

'The coke?' Ruby was puzzled for a moment, wondering why a fizzy drink should affect her husband's libido. Then she said, stunned, 'Manny took cocaine?'

'Oh God,' groaned Maria. 'There's so much you don't know.'

'He wouldn't even take an aspirin for a headache!'

Maria took a bite of her sandwich. 'Look, this is horrible.'

'Too much Branston?' Ruby looked contrite.

'What? No. Not the sandwich, you idiot.' Maria's cheeks darkened. 'Talking about Manny to you.' She shuddered. 'I don't want to casually tell you stuff that might hurt.'

'That's the only sort of stuff left.' Ruby pulled her hair back into an approximation of a bun and coaxed an elastic band around it.

'How do you do that?' Maria sounded almost annoyed. 'Bollocks your hair up any old how, yet look like an Edwardian beauty?'

'Hold it, missus. You're not in Margate now, you know.'

Maria guffawed and a piece of ham hit Ruby's lap. 'Seriously, you've no idea how beautiful you are. If I had your looks I'd be shagging Brad Pitt, with George Clooney on standby for bank holidays.' Ignoring Ruby's unhappy, 'Give over!' she said wonderingly, 'How the hell did somebody like Manny Gallagher ever get his mitts on you?'

'He bought me from my parents.' Ruby almost laughed at the abrupt change in Maria's expression. 'Not literally. Not quite.' Slithering to the rug, she hugged her knees. 'They were very old-fashioned, my mum and dad. Churchy. Respectable. They loved me but they worried about me. They could be very stiff. I was a bit . . .' She groped about for a word, settling for one that didn't really fit the bill. 'Wild, I suppose.'

'You? Wild?' Maria looked unconvinced.

'By their standards,' smiled Ruby, without further explanation. No need to share everything with Maria just yet. Or perhaps ever. 'Let's just say they were very keen to see me settled down. They had a lurid imagination about all the terrible fates that could befall me, and it made them overprotective. I can see that now but at the time I went along with it.' That bloody sleepwalking again. 'Even looking for a job, like my mates were doing, was discouraged. They suggested I help out with the family business until something came up.' Ruby threw her hands in the air. 'I ask you, Maria, what was going to *come up* for a spoilt teenaged knownothing who wasn't even looking?'

'What was the family business? My lot are in coffee bars.'

'My lot were in air conditioning components.' There was a brief pause for the sake of politeness, before they both snorted with laughter. 'And it's not as exciting as it sounds. I helped out in the office, putting callers through to the wrong extension, spilling coffee on the first aid box, that kind of thing. Then one day Dad asked me to take a spare part around to his new customer at the Vegas Rooms.'

'Enter Mr Emanuel Gallagher, stage right.'

'I'd never been inside a nightclub before.'

'Get off.' Maria looked as shocked as if Ruby had admitted a fondness for flashing. 'You were, what, nineteen? You must have been to a club by then.'

'No, really. I was a wimple short of a nun.'

'What did you make of Manny?' Maria seemed genuinely intrigued.

Ruby closed her eyes and recalled her first sight of her

husband. He'd had his back to her, that broad beefy back, encased in a black suit. At her timid cough he'd turned and his canny eyes had met hers. A firework was lit in her tummy. 'I thought he was OK,' she lied.

'Didn't you think he was *old*?' Maria repeated a face she made if caught downwind of their violinist vagrant.

Lashes down, Ruby recalled her impression of Manny. She'd thought him different, she'd thought him exciting. Male. Impressive. Dark. And sexy. 'No, I didn't think him old,' she said sadly.

'Bet he came on to you.'

'Yeah,' sighed Ruby. 'Offered me a free pass for all his clubs. I turned it down. There was no way my parents would let me go.'

'But they couldn't stop you,' protested Maria. 'I was bored with clubs by that age.'

'I don't mean they'd physically stop me.' It was difficult to explain to somebody who hadn't grown up in that claustrophobic semi which always smelled of greens and disappointment. 'It was the worried looks, the wringing of the hands.' She remembered her mother's ornate plans for getting home on the odd occasion she escaped for a pizza with a school friend: 'Daddy will be outside in the Honda at ten. If he's late, wait. Don't get the bus or –' a visible maternal shudder, 'a minicab. They're all rapists, Ruby.' 'So I scampered back to the white heat of air conditioning components and forgot about him.' Another lie. You don't forget being struck by lightning.

'Let me guess. Flowers.'

'God. Is it that predictable?'

'Lilies?'

'Peonies.'

'He'd moved on to lilies by the time . . .' Maria tailed off.

'I'd have preferred lilies,' said Ruby brightly, saving her friend's feelings. 'But anyway, huge bunches started arriving. The office looked like a funeral home. The cards all said more or less the same thing: what a fool he was to think a lady like me would want a free pass, could I forgive him, he couldn't stop thinking about me.'

'Was he already divorced?'

'Of course.' That detail was vital. Ruby had had nothing to do with the break-up of Manny and the original Mrs Gallagher. Or the She Beast, as he called her. 'Eventually he asked us all out to dinner.'

'You and your mum and dad?' Maria was as incredulous as if hearing of life on other planets. 'That has to be the weirdest first date ever.'

'We went to a very chic place he had a share in. All the waiters fawned over us. My mum and dad were naïve, simple people: I could see how impressed they were. I heard them thinking "This man could take care of our little girl".'

'Little did they know.'

'Over liqueurs, Manny produced a list of his contacts who were interested in doing business with our company. Pound signs came up behind Dad's bifocals. And then Manny formally asked if he could take me out one night.'

'Prince Charming crossed with Tony Soprano,' murmured Maria.

'Six months later we had the biggest wedding Esher has ever seen.'

'Hang on! It couldn't have happened just like that.' Maria snapped her fingers. 'How did he pull the wool over your eyes? Make you fall in love with him?'

'He was nice to me.' Ruby looked down at her tea rather than discover how that went down with the bolshy Maria. 'I could tell he was excited when he saw me, that I meant something to him. I felt lucky that somebody so dynamic and powerful made time for me.'

'He was the lucky one!' interjected Maria.

'We were both lucky,' insisted Ruby. She had to say it, so she took a deep breath. 'We fell in love.' She couldn't deny Manny that little truth.

'And you exchanged one prison for another, more luxurious one,' suggested Maria.

'That's the way it turned out. But there was a time . . .' Ruby would keep some of the memories to herself. How she'd felt the urgency of real sexual desire for the first time, how she'd race down the stairs when she heard his key in the door. She certainly wasn't going to tell Maria how he'd cried after their first row. 'Manny's not a complete monster, you know,' she protested gently. 'He's complicated. And, what's that fashionable new term? He's *conflicted*. I know now that he's one of the bad guys. But there were moments when you'd understand how I came to fall in love with him. Passionately in love,' she added, sadly.

Far from being sceptical, Maria looked mournful. 'Yeah,' she answered softly, and the subject was closed.

'You're the Honourable Millicent Flatbush!' squealed Ruby delightedly.

The man on the other end of the phone protested, 'I'm not actually her, I just live in her house.'

'Sorry. That's what I meant.' Ruby stopped pretending to polish Mrs Vine's already gleaming bidet. 'So, do you want me?'

'Blimey, you're direct.' The man was laughing. He had a playful voice that easily erupted into a deep chuckle. 'Shouldn't I ask some questions? Like how much?'

'I charge ten pounds an hour. How about Fridays? Ten a.m.? A couple of hours?'

'Great. Do me this Friday.' There was a pause before the man coughed and said, 'Would you mind if I rephrased that? Ten o'clock Fridays is fine. I'll leave the key under the bay tree and twenty quid under Elvis.'

Elvis? 'Er, OK.' Ruby was going to get a peek inside the little blue house. 'Bye.'

'And my name's Tom, by the way,' blurted out her new client just before Ruby hit the off button.

thinking of u babes

Ruby turned the TV up louder, wishing Maria was back from work. Four innocuous words, they crawled all over her tired body like red ants. She peered out at the midnight view of strangers' roofs.

Somewhere out there, Manny was thinking of her. She shivered. It was foolish, Ruby knew, to feel perversely re-assured. It wasn't foolish to feel threatened.

The thread was taut again.

6

The key waited, as promised, under one of the potted bay trees outside the blue house. 'Hi, the Honourable Millicent, I'm home!' shouted Ruby, winking up at the plaque as she wiggled the key in the unco-operative lock.

A four-by-four with darkened windows slowed to the kerb behind her. Ruby tensed, her senses hyper alert. A runty child hopped out of the car and ran up to the house next door.

Relaxing, Ruby cursed her twin burdens of imagination and timidity. Manny was not Mephisto: he would not materialise behind her out of the blue. Her fear was granting him powers he couldn't possess, but it was difficult to prophesy what he *was* capable of, now that he had been revealed as a completely different man to the one she'd shared a Posturepedic with all those years. What if he was having her followed? What if he had a – what was it – a *contract* out on her?

The lock suddenly capitulated. Ruby shook herself. By seeing him in every shadow, Ruby was doing Manny's dirty work for him. Enough. It stopped here, she promised herself, lugging her equipment over the threshold.

The Honourable Millicent's house smelled good. Not musty, like the Friends' had. Not of superior coffee, like Mrs Vine's. It smelled fresh. The sunny hallway led into a sitting room that offered a glimpse of grey-green garden through long french windows at the other end. The room was all whites and blues and yellows, as if summer had been captured and kept alive in it, despite the gloom outside. Ruby liked it: inviting and welcoming, it was still messy enough for her to make a difference.

The cheerfully unmodernised kitchen needed her, she decided, rolling up her overall sleeves and rooting through her toolbox for rubber gloves. Tom seemed to be a tea drinker and a toast maker, but he was no mug washer or crumb clearer.

A ruled page torn from a notepad was sellotaped to a blue and yellow chequered teapot. In messy handwriting, it read:

Hello Ruby, or World's Best Cleaner,

~~Hope you found the key okay. Well, you must have, mustn't you or you wouldn't be reading thi~~

~~Glad you found the key okay. Sorry about the state of the place. But then you are a cleaner, so . . .~~

Please make yourself a cup of tea. Or coffee. Or something cold. There's wine in the fridge. And cake. Altho' the cake is old. I have left the money under the small statue of Elvis on the mantelpiece.

I have run out of bin bags. This is shameful, and I don't have a proper excuse, except to say that I have been

working very hard and bin bags have not been on my mind. Could you improvise?
  Thank you
  Tom

It was chattier than the note Olivia had left the day before: 'Pls clean fridge if hv time'. It was chattier than it needed to be. Ruby wondered how one would improvise a bin bag. Luckily, she had a crinkly roll of the things in her arsenal.

A smile seeped over Ruby's features as she ran the hot water tap and watched bubbles bloom in the sink. A small, content sigh escaped her. Washing-up and fantasies of a murderous Manny couldn't coexist: she was going to enjoy her couple of hours at the Honourable Millicent and Tom's house.

The textured weave of the seagrass stair carpet challenged Henry, and the grout between the white bathroom tiles had tales to tell that Ruby would rather not hear. She leaned back on her haunches and surveyed the bathroom proudly, like a stage mother whose offspring has just got an encore. This Tom character was basically a clean type, but Ruby had raised his house to another level of hygiene. She wondered, as she rubbed a tap, if he lived alone. There was no evidence of a woman in that most crucial place, the bathroom cabinet. There were no tampons, no makeup, no cotton wool balls, just some shaving foam and a packet of plasters. The tube of antiseptic cream, all rolled up and almost empty, Ruby didn't dwell on: some clues were best ignored.

Ruby pushed open the door to the bedroom at the front of the house, overlooking the narrow street. Evidently the master room, it was dark thanks to the closed curtains. Feeling like an intruder, Ruby padded across the seagrass and tugged at the drapes. No, she concluded, there definitely wasn't a Mrs Tom. A trail of (male) clothes conga-ed from the door to the bed, and no woman would tolerate a teetering pile of *FHM*s that served as a bedside table. It was the work of a moment to straighten the bed, a curvy old French piece, and toss the dirty clothes into a wicker laundry basket. The room seemed to shake itself, and stand up straighter.

The way the struggling sun caught the far wall and lit the newly tidy bed made Ruby sag a little: she'd never had a room like this, simple, welcoming. Her childhood bedroom had mirrored the rest of the house in its drabness, and her Château Rubes boudoir was Vegas-brash. A pleasant little room in a pleasant little house. Ruby shrugged at her modest ambition, and marvelled that it had never been achieved.

The two hours flew by. By the time Ruby was finished, Tom could have taken out a guest's appendix on the coffee table if he so desired. Picking up the note to toss in the (fully bagged up) kitchen bin, Ruby instead flipped it over and scribbled,

> I'll hang on to the key, if that's all right with you. Next time I'll hose down the patio. Do you want me to polish your gnome? (I've never asked anybody that before.)
> You have a lovely house.

Tutting at the biro as if it was all its fault, Ruby stuck the note to the teapot. 'You have a lovely house?' she read, appalled. Was it, she wondered, the type of thing cleaners said to clients? Why would Tom be interested in her opinion of his house?

'Come on, Henry.' Ruby was just about to pull the front door shut when a glimmer of white in the front garden caught her eye. She reached over and twisted off a branch of jasmine and raced upstairs.

A little blue vase stood on the chest of drawers in the master bedroom, and Ruby plopped the flower into it. 'There,' she said, pleased with herself. 'Perfect.'

Joe was stamping down the top steps of number fourteen as Ruby placed a foot on the bottom one. 'You off out?' she asked, animatedly. She wasn't used to children, and became overbearing and slightly toothy around them, like Basil Brush in a skirt.

'Sitar lessons,' said Joe, with the air of a man condemned to hang.

'Christ, you poor bugger,' said Ruby with empathy. She sensed, rather than saw, Olivia at the front door and decided not to look up and see what effect this response might have had on her.

With a sneaky sideways slant of his tilted eyes, Joe accepted the sympathy. Ruby watched him trudge down the street, that haircut an insult to his puppyish beauty.

'There's mould in the breadbin,' said Olivia, by way of hello.

Stairs were Ruby's nemesis: the Moriarty to her Holmes. Fourteen Clancy Street had a lot of stairs, and on these stairs were books, magazines, odd shoes, unopened post and the occasional mug, all of which had to be tidied away before Ruby could struggle up and down with Henry, hoovering up the rubble the three Friends left in their wake.

Red faced, Ruby made it to the top landing. Once again, Joe's room was resolutely locked. Shame, she thought. She was keen to get in there, rejuvenate it, and, if she was honest, look for clues. This passion for snooping had been conspicuously absent from her high-minded discussions with Maria about why she wanted to be a cleaner, but domestic detective work was turning out to be one of the most satisfying aspects of her new career. She was careful never to intrude – she wouldn't, for example, open a diary or read a letter. It was the clues in plain sight that fascinated her.

Right now, she was struck by the MUM KEEP OUT felt-tipped sign on Joe's door. Hugo was welcome: Olivia was not. 'Interesting,' mused Ruby, twirling an imaginary moustache. She laid a hand on the door, as if it was breathing, and stood for a moment before polishing the handle vigorously.

Joe was out of place in this adult house. The book ruled, leaving no room for roller skates. Ruby dusted plenty of Aboriginal art, but she hadn't stumbled across a single piece of Lego. It reminded her of her childhood home, not because her parents were big on Aborigines, but because her Barbies had been relentlessly tidied out of sight by her mother. Ruby recalled their brittle, pleading hands stretching out to her as they were shoved into cupboards. She'd learned her cleaning skills from watching her mum, but she'd rejected the Stalinist application of them. Ruby would have liked to see some proof that Joe lived at fourteen Clancy Street.

From the basement, came a tentative shout. 'Fancy a cup of tea with me, Ruby?'

The biscuits Olivia had set out were posh. Thin, flaky and scented with almonds, they weren't what Ruby would call a bickie, but she didn't like to hurt their feelings by letting them know that. Her new eating habits were having no discernible effect on her waist (a fact which irritated Maria no end) but they had a huge effect on Ruby's sense of wellbeing. Freed at last from the tyranny of Manny's expectations – he considered a size twelve female to be one Hot Dog away from Jabba the Hutt – she was scampering barefoot through the output of Messrs McVitie, Kipling and Jacob, but a diversion into Bahlsen couldn't hurt.

'What a week. We're short-staffed and I'm feeling the pressure,' sighed Olivia, taking her glasses off and rubbing her anxious, makeup-free eyes. Pouring a splashy cup of tea with one hand, she swept the other through her brush-wary mass of hair. The flecks of grey weren't masked; they were, apparently, welcome. 'How's it going with you, Ruby?' The question was earnestly put, as if Olivia was deeply interested in the response.

Not sure what 'it' was, Ruby plumped for it being the process of cleaning the house. 'Fine,' she smiled. 'Getting there.' She squirmed. Talking to Olivia made her feel lacking, as if the older woman was squinting past Ruby's pretty exterior and revealing the paucity of clever thoughts, and opinions about Cubism, within.

'Is this what you . . .' Olivia twiddled one of her omnipresent tasselled scarves: she made a point of dressing like a peasant fleeing the Cossacks. 'I mean, do you see yourself always being a cleaner?'

It was an unexpected question, obliging Ruby to realise that she didn't have a plan. She looked no further than her next session in a stranger's house. The past had tripped her up so spectacularly that she mistrusted the future in case it held another such show-stopping, knicker-flashing pratfall. 'I don't know,' she said, slowly, before laughing. 'It's not as if I'd be splitting the atom if I wasn't cleaning.' She had no idea what an atom was, just a vague suspicion that it was very very wee, and therefore tricky to split.

'Don't run yourself down,' said Olivia gravely, revealing where Joe got his demeanour from. 'You can do anything you set your mind to. I spend a lot of time with young women from overseas in my department, and I'm appalled at the glass ceiling they set for themselves, just like you're doing. We women have to nurture our inner warrior queens, don't we?'

Olivia appealed to Ruby, who nodded daftly: she was trying to recall what Olivia's department might be. She excavated a vague memory about adult education. She'd overheard ('eavesdropped' is such an ugly word) conversations between Olivia and Hugo about various calamities involving students' housing benefit, visas or love lives. More than once Ruby had heard Hugo advising, 'Darling, don't get involved,' and had smiled at his wife's equine snort.

'I admire you.'

'You do?' Ruby thought this was absurd, coming from somebody with enough letters after her name to qualify as the *Countdown* conundrum. 'That's nice,' she said lamely, looking into her tea and kidnapping another biscuit.

'Absolutely,' said Olivia, nodding vigorously. She was ignoring the biscuits, seeming more interested in, and nourished by, her idea. 'With limited options you're making the most of your labour skills. Never think that you're unimportant, that you're just a tiny cog in a vast machine. That would be quite wrong.'

'Right.' Ruby didn't think that cleaning was unimportant. On the contrary, she considered it vital. Without the likes of Ruby and her Cillit Bang, the country would be left to moulder by the intellectuals, the lazybones, and the blokes.

'Women like you have toiled for centuries without recognition, or proper recompense.'

Hmm. *Women like you.* Ruby was starting to feel itchy. She wondered just what Olivia was basing her notions on.

'It makes me livid,' Olivia carried on, sounding, well, livid. 'A vast female army of under-educated, under-appreciated women have cleaned up society's mess without ever having a voice. I mean, why should cleaners be looked down upon? It's sexist and snobbish.'

'Mmm,' murmured Ruby in agreement, a traitor to her real feelings. She had never looked down on cleaners, and she didn't feel any stigma now that she was one of their number. 'Look, I'd better get off,' she said, standing up to curtail what was becoming an awkward conversation. She knew that Olivia meant well, but she wanted to get out of there before her client sent her skidding even further down the rungs of the 'society' she seemed so irate about.

'Oh. Fine. God. Was I ranting?' Olivia looked sheepish and years fell away from her. Her fine-boned face softened as she twisted her lips into a wiggly line of contrition. 'Sorry.' She seemed to have come back to the present, abashed by her *alter ego*'s diatribe.

'No, not at all. It was interesting,' lied Ruby, snaffling a last biscuit for luck. She stood for a moment before saying, 'So, if you could . . .'

'Could what?' asked Olivia distractedly, already shaking out a broadsheet newspaper.

'Pay me!' Ruby said it with an artificial laugh. Olivia's comments had turned their simple transaction into something with the weight of history upon it.

'Sorry, sorry, sorry!' flustered Olivia, searching for her purse in the hammock of a bag she brought everywhere. Handing over a crisp twenty pound note, she asked, 'Are you off to another job? Or is it hometime?'

'I'm off home,' said Ruby, fishing the change out of her jeans pocket.

'And where is home?' asked Olivia, looking at Ruby as if she'd never seen her before. 'See what I mean? Isn't that odd? You come to our house every week and yet I don't even know where you live.'

'Just around the corner.' Ruby paused. 'Hannah House, on the green,' she continued lightly, knowing she'd just tossed a grenade into Olivia's preconceptions. 'The penthouse,' she clarified.

'The penthouse,' echoed Olivia limply.

On her way home, Ruby waved up at Mrs Vine, who was standing like a very well dressed ghost at her drawing room window.

7

'Why am I here?' asked Ruby. She wasn't dabbling in philosophy, merely asking Simon why he'd asked her to come in and see him.

'Just to catch up.' Simon smelled very strongly of cologne, as if his office was in the middle of a lemon grove. 'It's been a while and, after all, I am your solicitor as well as Manny's. How are you coping?'

'Fine.' Ruby said it without thinking and it was true. Ish. 'You know, there's the odd moment when I sit with my head in my hands and go *my husband's a monster and he lied to me for nine years and I have nothing*, but on the whole I'm all right.' She grinned at Simon, who was looking aghast. 'Don't worry about me, Simon!' she pleaded. 'I'm standing on my own two feet at last. About time, if you ask me.'

'I'm having a hard time convincing Manny that the penthouse really is yours.' Simon reached down and fiddled with a lever on his chair, raising himself up. He still looked like a schoolboy, albeit a slightly higher up schoolboy. 'He's been getting very agitated, repeating that he hopes you haven't changed anything there.' Simon held out his hands, palms up. 'I reminded him that you have no income any more, so you're hardly in a position to redecorate.' He smiled sadly, as if regretting having to be so frank.

'Hmm,' said Ruby.

'If you don't mind me asking,' began Simon, looking trepidatious, 'what *are* you doing for money?'

'I'm managing to pay the bills,' said Ruby, endeavouring not to look proud: after all, most human adults paid their bills. It had just taken her longer than most to get around to it.

'Really? How?'

'I work for myself,' she said, trying to quash her smile. It was still a novelty to be *a* something. 'I'm a cleaner,' she said, knowing she sounded smug and unable to do anything about it.

'Oh God, Ruby, I'm so sorry.' Simon seemed to have misheard. He was reacting as if her parrot had died.

'No, I'm—' she began.

'You brave girl.' Simon was looking soggily at her.

Ruby didn't like the self she saw reflected in his sympathetic gaze. 'I'm cleaning houses, Simon, not rushing into burning buildings to rescue orphans.' She stopped short, wondering where such sarcasm had come from. 'Sorry. Sorry, Simon. You didn't deserve that. Sorry.'

Looking confused, Simon frowned at her. 'But you can't clean houses, Ruby, you're a—'

She cut him off, trying not to sound so harsh this time. 'Cleaner, Simon. I'm a cleaner.' She could have gone further: she was a happy cleaner, an independent cleaner, a busy cleaner who didn't sit around all day waiting for her husband to come home trailing his mistress's perfume. But she didn't, she changed the subject instead. 'How's the case going?'

Simon exhaled. 'Slowly. Something new comes up every day. It's very complicated.'

With no desire for details, Ruby asked, 'Will I have to, whatsit, *testify*?'

'I'm doing my best to keep you out of it. There's no reason to drag you into court.'

'Tell me, Simon, is he going to jail?' Ruby had no idea what answer she wanted.

'We will vigorously defend all charges.'

The familiar line was as good a 'yes' as any that Ruby had ever heard. 'I see.' Suddenly she thought of the baby. 'What a mess,' she whispered.

'I've got some good news, though.'

Ruby brightened. 'What's that?'

'I can return your jewellery to you. As gifts, they don't come under the police's remit.' Simon grinned.

'But I left it behind.' Ruby made it clearer. 'I don't want it.'

'It's worth thousands.' Simon looked mildly shocked.

'It was guilty conscience stuff, bought with other people's money. It belongs to Manny's victims, not me. It's dirty.' Ruby wrinkled her nose. It was hard to explain without sounding pious, but there was no place for those sparkly reminders of Manny's dishonesty in her new life. She was clean now. 'Honestly, I don't want it. Manny can have it. Might help him pay for his defence.' Ruby crossed and uncrossed her legs, keen to be away. 'Is that it, Simon, only I've got a client in an hour.'

'There was something else.' Simon stopped short and began twiddling a pencil with his firm's name on it very fast indeed. 'I was wondering if . . .' he began, very slowly, as if dictating a letter, before racing on, 'you'dliketocomeouttodinner-withme?'

70

Unravelling his blurt, Ruby opened her eyes wide. 'Dinner dinner?' she queried.

'Ye-ah,' said Simon uncertainly. 'Hang on, no. Um, what do you mean, Ruby?'

'Well, is it just, you know, menus and food and waiters, or is it –' Ruby swallowed. 'A date?'

In a new deep voice Simon said, 'A date.'

Ruby was flabbergasted. 'You're my solicitor,' she reminded him.

'I'm not a priest. It's morally acceptable,' grumbled Simon.

Now the cologne made sense. 'I'm a married woman,' she reminded him, attempting regal disapproval, achieving slight peeve.

'Well, separated.' Simon seemed to be trying to win his beloved's heart on a technicality. 'And you're going to divorce him.' He leaned forward a fraction. 'Aren't you?'

'Why does everybody keep asking me that?' snapped Ruby, deftly promoting Simon and Maria to 'everybody'. 'I'm sorry, Simon, I'm not on the market. I couldn't go out on a date if my life depended on it.' She bundled her arms into the sleeves of her jacket, snatched up her bag and ricocheted off a filing cabinet, *à la* the Chuckle Brothers, on her way out.

Teddy let Ruby in, and gallantly carried her shopping bags up to the flat over the Velvet Glove. Off duty, Teddy dressed in 'civvies'. Apart from the waxed eyebrows, his ordinary garb, although flamboyant, gave no clue to his night job, except for when he lounged about the flat, indulging his love for negligees. Today a vibrantly scarlet polyester kimono gaped over his hairy chest, which, along with his towelling turban, gave him an exotic air only slightly compromised by the tartan slippers. 'Welcome to the love nest!' he declared with a wry pout as they reached the top of the stairs.

Cramped and dark, the love nest was small, with lots of knick-knacks, and lots of photos of Teddy showing his legs.

'Nice,' fibbed Ruby.

'It's a hellhole, darling, but it's *our* hellhole,' rasped Teddy. 'I'm going to snatch some beauty sleep. Just prod me with a squeegee when you want to do the bedroom. Don't knock yourself out,' he advised, plodding towards the next, shorter flight of stairs. 'Just threaten the kitchen with a J-Cloth and spray some polish in the air.'

Teddy was an undemanding client, but Ruby was a diligent professional. To the casual eye the flat looked as if a jumble sale monster had vomited in through the window, but to Ruby it was the perfect opportunity to flex her cleaning muscles.

There were ornaments to dust, shelves to wipe, mirrors to polish, cushions to primp and a rug to beat insensible. Flying at her task, Ruby spent a contented afternoon taking the flat by the scruff of the neck and shaking it.

The small functional kitchen was separated from the living area by a fifties-style room divider made up of interconnecting MDF cubes, all showcasing cutesy ornaments. Pottery cats shared a cube with rabbits on a swing. Plastic flowers, furred with dust, sprouted from funfair vases, which in their turn sat on plastic doilies. So many *things*, and all of them neglected. Ruby wondered when the Messrs Glove last had a clearout.

A thought struck her. By Ruby's standards, it was an exciting thought. Perhaps, though, it would entail stepping over the boundaries of the client/cleaner contract. Kendall had the look of a man who liked staff to know their place.

It was a risk Ruby was willing to take. This ramshackle flat was crying out for an ergonomic shakedown.

With an evangelical burst of energy, Ruby thinned out the

ornaments. Every third artefact, be it a weeping clown or a shepherdess with her nose missing, went into a cardboard box. Every third cushion was whipped off the sofas, every third studio portrait of Teddy in soft focus came off the walls.

The bathroom shed the crinoline lady protecting the spare toilet roll from questing fingers; the kitchen gave up the greasy jars of elderly pasta; the landing lost another portrait of Teddy (as Marilyn Monroe, presumably after a lifetime of carbs).

Her nose streaked with dirt, Ruby surveyed her handiwork. It looked like a home now, no longer the sort of gaff that features on regional TV news bulletins about the discovery of long-dead pensioners. She hoped that the home owners would agree.

One of them was coming up the stairs. Ruby recognised Kendall's light jog.

'Oh. My. God.' Kendall stood stock still at the top of the stairs, his keys limp in his hand. 'What have you done, Ms Mop?'

'I'm sorry.' Old habits die hard, and Ruby clicked back into her default setting of frightened guilt.

'Oh, don't apologise. It looks like a proper flat,' marvelled Kendall, moving slowly through the sitting room. 'Where actual people with lives live.' He came to a stop in the kitchen, and leaned against the pristine worktop, his arms folded.

'It only needed a little TLC,' said Ruby.

'Don't we all,' sighed Kendall, before reverting to terrier-esque sharpness. 'You're more than just a pretty face, I'll give you that. How did you get on with the bedrooms?'

'Oh, I haven't—' began Ruby.

'That old sow still in her sty?' tutted Kendall. 'I'll get Teddy out of your way. His naps are like comas, but it only

73

takes the promise of a bacon sandwich and a look at Posh's cellulite in *OK!* to get him down those stairs.'

The 'boudoir', as Teddy termed it, was his interpretation of the bedroom of a Hollywood starlet, albeit one on a limited budget who decorated in the dark. Where a screen goddess might employ oyster satin, Teddy had used bubblegum pink polyester. Ruched and frilled, yards of the stuff covered the bed, the windows and a dressing table that supported a mirror framed with lightbulbs and more makeup than a Boots sale.

'Right!' Confident now, Ruby made short work of the boudoir. The dreary ruffled curtains were the first to go, leaving just the plain roller blind to preserve the guys' modesty and their neighbours' peace of mind. An eerie mannequin draped with Teddy's costume jewellery was next to surrender to Ruby's zealous new broom. Whisking a gypsy scarf from the top of a lamp and using tongs to remove an ancient sheepskin that lay like roadkill by the bed, Ruby was finished.

The whole flat glowed with the wholesome air of one who knows all its crevices can withstand scrutiny. Sufficient bargain basement glitz remained to invoke the spirit of Teddy, but now it looked like somewhere Kendall could exist too.

Satisfied, Ruby gathered up the lolling shopping bags. They contained the makings of lasagne, Maria's favourite: Ruby's cooking skills were improving now that she wasn't under so much pressure to perform. She bit her lip, then turned back. Tonight the tiny kitchen's fluorescent tube wouldn't glare down on a takeaway. She pulled out an onion and a bag of mince. Maria could make do with Welsh rarebit.

Pink and scented and dressing-gowned after an epic bath, Ruby rejoined Maria by the huge penthouse windows. 'I'm soooo tired,' she declared happily. 'Tired from good honest graft.'

'Huh,' snorted Maria, who had been getting up close and personal with a winebox. 'It's still tired. Personally I'd rather be knackered from having manicures and shopping too much.'

'Been there, done that, as my saint of a husband would say. I prefer this feeling. I've earned my sleep.'

'It's like living with Goldi-bloody-locks. Well,' Maria looked across at Ruby. '*Reddi*-locks, I suppose.' She stretched like a cat. A feral one. 'How come nights off go so quickly but shifts go so damn slow?'

'I thought you liked your job.' Ruby peered down at her toes, all happy and clean, poking out of her towelling mules.

'I do. But it's still a job. I'd rather eat Twiglets all day.'

'You'd soon get bored.' Ruby spoke from experience.

'Not a chance. I could watch *Cash in the Attic* back to back for a month without any side-effects. I'm not like you,' Maria pointed out. 'I don't have a conscience.'

'You do,' protested Ruby. 'You confessed to nicking my cream polo neck and getting chutney on it.'

'The word is *borrowing*,' elucidated Maria, holding up a stern forefinger to make her point. 'And you would never *borrow* anything of mine. I only confessed because nobody else ever comes in the flat so it was an open and shut case, m'lud.'

'Don't believe you.' Ruby was indulgent towards her lodger. The small, dark tomboy had built a bridge to normal life for Ruby: she would never forget that.

'I'd never hurt you.' Maria's neck was against her chest as she sprawled the length of the sofa. 'You know that, don't you?'

That sounded like the wine talking. 'Of course.' Disguising her slight embarrassment, Ruby growled, 'That's Manny's job.'

'He's never sent you another text!' Maria sat up, her eyes flashing. The cat was stretching her claws. 'Don't tell me he's been hassling you again.'

'No, nothing like that.' Ruby leaned over to refresh Maria's glass of nail varnish remover. 'I meant, in general.'

'You know what he's trying to do, don't you?' Ignoring Ruby's weary nod, Maria rattled on. 'Manny wants you to feel unsettled. Unsure. So you'll be a good girl and do what you're told and give him this penthouse.'

'You're forgetting something,' said Ruby, with a kind of timid stubbornness. 'He's not making any threats. In fact, he's being quite . . . sentimental.' She added a rueful, 'by his standards'.

'That's to keep you dangling. Don't you see?' Maria banged her forehead with her palm. 'Whatever you do you mustn't call him. He'll know he's broken you. Promise me you won't crack and call him.'

Another nod from Ruby evidently sufficed as a promise, because Maria had more to say. 'A little kiss. Then a little slap. Just to keep you on your toes. Classic macho bullshit.'

'You seem to know a lot about it,' murmured Ruby, wishing she could locate Maria's off switch.

At that Maria twitched. 'Yeah, I do,' she muttered angrily. 'Wish I didn't, but I do.'

After a short pause, Ruby dared to say, 'Do you want to talk about it?'

'Shit, no,' barked Maria, clipping the end of Ruby's question. Abruptly she stood up. 'I'm off to bed.'

The slammed bedroom door provided an emphatic full stop to their conversation. Ruby felt admonished, and wondered if her offer to talk about it had sounded nosy. She hadn't meant it that way, but Ruby was a beginner at this friendship stuff.

Delving into the pocket of her dressing gown, she pulled out her mobile. *Good thing Maria didn't see this*, she thought, scrolling through her saved texts to find today's message.

I MISS YOU

No 'babes'. Not even an abbreviation for 'you'. It didn't read like macho bullshit to Ruby.

8

Spring was nudging its way around the city. The tramp had shrugged off his winter plumage of filthy black raincoat tied with string in favour of a filthy cream raincoat tied with string. The organic greengrocer was offering first crop artichokes that cost more than gold ones might. And up in her tower, the erstwhile princess was striking catwalk poses in front of the mirror, all the better to admire the new, light-weight wool jacket she'd just dragged ravenously out of a carrier bag.

It was grey, and waisted, and cheap. Even so, Ruby had had to save up for it. During her years as Manny's dress-up dolly Ruby had worn new clothes every other day. Few of them had given her the thrill she felt slipping on this garment.

Stroking her cheek along the meagre collar of fake fur, Ruby purred with satisfaction. She took immense pride in the knowledge that every button was paid for out of her earnings.

Reality had bitten. The new Ruby knew how expensive it was to live even the simplest of lives. She continued to post her cards through likely-looking letterboxes as she sprinted from one job to another. 'The more the merrier,' she thought banally, ever conscious of the gaping maws of the electricity company, BT, Sainsbury's and, on the rare occasions she felt the need of an aristocratic root vegetable, the organic grocer's.

New clients slotted into her schedule where they could. She wasn't too fond of the Sniffer, a supercilious woman who ran a gloved finger along the picture rail before handing over Ruby's fee with the good grace of a wolf sharing its kill. The Divorcee followed her new cleaner around with a glass of Chardonnay and listed her ex's faults at tedious length, before borrowing back half the money she paid out. On Tuesday evenings Ruby spent precious *EastEnders* time primping an apartment two floors below her own. The Bachelor lived in a kind of millionaire version of Comet, with electronic doodahs lining his suede-covered walls. He was extremely proud of his plasma screens, his iPods, his Bang & Olufsen this, and his Bose that.

Immune to the lure of hard things with plugs on, Ruby listened patiently to the Bachelor's boasts about his equipment. His striped shirt and generous behind suggested he worked in the city, but the Bachelor always made sure to be home from work when his cleaner arrived. Following her around with a whisky in his hand, he presumably believed that Ruby was unaware of the close scrutiny he gave her bottom when she leaned over to wipe his bath, or his scholarly examination of her legs when she stood on steps to tickle his cornices.

His cleaner was perfectly aware and valiantly resisted the urge to squirt Toilet Duck in his bouffant. Ruby gritted her teeth and reminded herself that she charged the Bachelor a special rate above the usual one, and contented herself with de-alphabetising the porn DVD collection he thought he'd hidden.

Drama Queen was another new face. Chain-smoking, slender and so trendy that the hat she wore in the morning was old-fashioned by lunchtime, Drama Queen lived in a tiny flat off the Fulham Road. As groomed as a *Vogue* cover girl, she emerged from a pit that made the London Dungeon look shipshape. Marmite toast lay tangled in her bedclothes, her plain sofa was patterned with an intricate design of ancient spillages, and more one-cell brainless life forms could be found on her toilet seat than at a *Big Brother* reunion. Drama Queen never had time for housework because she was too busy crying.

'Oh dear,' Ruby would say as she uncovered her client under a cashmere throw liberally dotted with marmalade and menstrual blood. 'What's he done now?'

'The bastard!' Drama Queen would howl, lighting a cigarette and shuffling after Ruby wrapped in her grotty security blanket. 'He said he'd be half an hour. Half a fucking hour. And when does he get back? Midnight! Got his shoe stuck in a drain. Does he think I'm stupid?'

The stories piled up around Ruby's feet as she scrubbed and scoured and buffed. Yes, thought Ruby, he did think Drama Queen was stupid. Unless the bastard boyfriend was sensationally unlucky and really did keep getting locked in the loos of lap dancing clubs when he'd only popped in to ask the time, or truly had caught chlamydia off a glove puppet he found in the street.

'Eat that,' Ruby would finally advise, placing a sandwich in front of Drama Queen. The sobs would subside, to be replaced by sniffly munching, giving Ruby a chance to tackle the greasy cavern of the oven, or the netherworld of fluff in the land under the bed, without interruption. The girl's inability to cope touched her, and Ruby hoped that one day the accident-prone boyfriend would be replaced with a more reliable model. One thing was certain: Drama Queen would never opt for being alone.

Shame. Ruby was a convert to the benefits of celibacy. Nobody to answer to. Nobody to tiptoe around. Nobody to shatter your modest dreams by turning out to be an unfaithful, sperm-spraying money launderer. That last benefit was, admittedly, pretty specific to her own situation but on the whole Ruby considered being single to be a very good thing.

*

Dear World's Best Cleaner (WBC),
These days I love getting home on
Fridays . . .
Tom

Even when there was nothing to say, no request to 'have a go' at the oven or shine his knocker, Tom always left a note. He was much more reliable than the tedious European penpals Ruby had corresponded with back at primary school ('Today is Tuesday. I go in school today. I come in home and say hi Wolfy to my little dog'). Those relationships had petered out after just two or three envelopes covered in doodles. This correspondence was unique among Ruby's clients, and she looked forward to it.

Ruby did her bit by leaving a newsy note of her own, always taped to the kettle, as tradition dictated. Today she wrote

Tom,
I like Fridays too! Have hung out the washing
I found in the machine.
Ruby

81

She would have liked to add a PS, *What on earth do you do for a living?*, but restrained herself. She was just the cleaner, she didn't have the right to probe. Her attempts to discover Tom's job from the clues in his house had come to nothing. There was no uniform, no specialist equipment, no certificate on the wall. Ruby felt sure he did something brainy, and terribly grown up. Not knowing was driving her mad.

There was a new fixture in his kitchen. A cork noticeboard had gone up, providing a home for dry-cleaning receipts, theatre tickets, blurry photos and a voucher for a free burger.

'So you're not a vegetarian, Tom,' mused Ruby, taking in the photographs as she parted the clingy remains of a fried egg from a pan. A photo booth strip was fruitful for the detective/chronic nosy parker. 'Can't keep a straight face, can you?' she murmured. In the top frame the clean-jawed face was passport serious, but in frame two the blue eyes began to crease. In the third picture the wide mouth was shunting dimples towards his ears. By the last shot his head had dropped forward and Tom's black curls were blurred with his laughter.

The good humour was catching. Ruby giggled as she studied the other pictures. There was a fuzzy Polaroid of Tom on a stripy sofa holding a cat very carefully away from his body as if it might explode. 'And you don't like cats,' Ruby said approvingly. The obligatory drunken snap was tucked into the bottom of the frame: a gurning Tom, bleary eyed and holding up a pint glass as a male friend stuck his tongue in his ear. 'Uurgh.' Ruby guessed that Tom's hair was a reliable indication of his spirits – the cheerier the expression, the wilder the hair.

Ruby skimmed over the photo taken at some children's party: a clown loomed large in it and Ruby did not do clowns. One last photo was partly hidden by a Post-It shouting 'CALL AMANDA!!!' Ruby put the frying pan down on the draining board and picked up a tannin-tattooed mug as she moved the Post-It gently to one side. Tom, his strong features in profile, was grinning at somebody or something out of shot on a beach that could only be English, with a sea that grey and a sky that milky.

'That's a big old nose you've got there, Tommy boy,' smiled Ruby. She stopped her mug in mid-swish through the bubbles in the washing up bowl. 'Oh.' Her eyes ambled down the T-shaped strip of dark hair on his chest, took a tour of the pecs and lingered over the pleasingly taut but not too self-consciously ripped six-pack. Who'd have thought giggly old Tom was hiding such quality under his shirt?

Certainly not Ruby.

With a cough, Ruby turned her attention back to the mug. Tom's chest was neither here nor there. It was none of her business. All her clients had chests, after all. The mug was clean, but she continued to harass it with a scouring pad.

And who, she thought haughtily, was bloody bleeding Amanda?

It was a quiet night at the Glove. The guest artiste had been invalided home after tumbling off the stage during his first chorus of 'Like a Virgin', and Teddy was sulking upstairs after Kendall's remark that his new leopardskin catsuit made him look like Barbara Windsor's nan.

Either side of the bar, Maria and Ruby were filling in some of the dots about each other. 'Five?' gasped Ruby, on learning how many older brothers Maria had.

'Yup. Now you know why I'm so cynical about blokes. I grew up watching them wind their girlfriends up and run rings around them. Before marrying them and getting them pregnant every five minutes.' Maria pointlessly rearranged the liqueur bottles. 'I'm an aunt eight times over.'

Maria wasn't Ruby's idea of an aunt. Her aunties had double chins and committed hara-kiri if their wide-fit shoes didn't match their handbags. 'Your family get-togethers must be fun,' she said, enviously.

'You're kidding.' Leaning her elbows on the bar, Maria snorted. 'My mum and dad's tiny sitting room packed with people who look vaguely like me? The ones who aren't old enough to talk throw toys and wet themselves, while the older ones ask *When are you going to settle down? When are you going to stop messing about?* Italians, see. It's all about family.'

'You don't feel that way?'

'Don't get me wrong, I like them. No,' Maria corrected herself. 'I love them. But in small doses. I don't fit in, because I've never gone for that whole package. The husband, the house, the kids. So my family don't know what to make of me.'

'Have you ever tried explaining the way you feel?' Ruby asked.

'They wouldn't listen. It's not that sort of set-up.' Maria spoke without rancour. 'Besides, how do I tell people who worship the traditional family that I don't believe in marriage? That I think it's based on lies?'

'Yeah.' Ruby braced herself. She knew what was coming next.

'I mean, look at your marriage!'

Ruby didn't really want to look at her marriage, thanks very much, and she was tiring of the way Maria held it up as proof of love's shortcomings. Ruby was mute on the whole subject of love, right through from hand-holding to bringing up triplets together: a door had slammed somewhere deep inside her when Manny defected to Tania and his child. She had nothing to say, nothing to offer, but she did nurse a faint flicker of hope that one day, when this tricky chapter of her life was closed, she might be able to join the debate again.

In the meantime, however, Ruby had no wish to trash love. It was a good thing, something to aspire to: she resented Maria's attempts to make her the poster girl for crap relationships. A change of subject was called for. 'What are you doing with your night off tomorrow?'

'Big plans,' grinned Maria, slinging together a G and T for a regular at the other end of the bar. 'B-i-i-g.' She carried the gin to its recipient, saying over her shoulder, 'You. The telly. Possibly an oven-ready lasagne. I am Italian, after all.'

That sounded like a good plan to Ruby. She'd revised her initial opinion of Maria. Her lodger was no party girl, she was essentially a solitary person with a Ruby-shaped gap in her life.

Flattered by this, and grateful that she'd stumbled upon somebody else who seemed to contain a gritty kernel of loneliness similar to her own, Ruby raised her glass. 'Here's to us. And convenience foods.'

9

The door was unlocked. Ruby was inside Joe's domain. So he trusted her. That was good.

Looking around, it was hard to fathom why she'd been kept out for so long. Or why, according to the sign tacked to the door, his mother was still banned. Maybe this room had its secrets, but at first glance it was a plain square space, painted the kind of harsh blue only a boy could love.

Ruby began to instil her own brand of calming order. Not too much. She didn't want to tidy herself out of another invitation. She tucked the books strewn across the floor like stepping stones back into the rickety bookcase, tutting at the titles – *Maths Is Fun!*, *Tell Me About the Industrial Revolution*. No annuals, no joke compendiums.

Making the bed, she noted the stripy flannel bedclothes. Presumably the *Doctor Who* duvet covers she saw in her local Woolworth's were too lowbrow, too consumerist, too something or other for the Friends' parenting philosophy.

In no time the room had been Ruby-ed. 'Oi, you,' said Ruby accusingly to an Aran sweater which had escaped her

Mary Poppins eye. 'Get back where you belong.' She opened the bottom drawer of a wooden chest and tucked it in. Or tried to. Even though the drawer was quite deep, she had to squash the jumper right down to close it. She tugged the Aran out and peered at the bottom of the drawer: her nerve endings did a Mexican wave. She was staring at a false bottom, and very probably the reason Joe was so paranoid about adults poking about in his lair.

A tussle ensued, between Good Ruby and Bad Ruby. Good Ruby knew her place, knew she must respect clients' privacy, knew she had to slam that drawer and walk away. Bad Ruby's wheedling voice whispered, 'What if you accidentally, by accident, somehow, just kind of pressed on the drawer and it . . .'

Snorting with impatience, Disgustingly Nosy Ruby elbowed them both out of the way and jerked the false drawer up, quaking all the while at the prospect of what she might find there. It might change her opinion of soppy, big-eyed Joe for good.

'Oh my God . . .' There was a stash of magazines, plus an outfit that made Ruby's eyes widen. Perhaps she just wasn't worldly-wise enough.

Fingering the glittery cummerbund and the elasticated bow tie, Ruby turned the pages of the uppermost issue of *Ballroom Dancing Times*. The images were shocking indeed. Hurriedly, she jammed the false bottom back into place and fled.

*

it aint over till its over babes

It would never be over while Manny had a functioning forefinger. Leaning on her mop in Teddy and Kendall's kitchen,

Ruby growled at the unpunctuated message. As usual it freeze-framed her into a statue of herself.

Ambiguous, it promised or threatened a dozen different outcomes to Ruby's wonky fairy tale. Standing transfixed with her hair bundled up into a spotty scarf and a steaming bucket of pine-scented water at her feet, Ruby didn't know what she wanted Manny's message to mean: she had no idea what would constitute her Happy Ever After. Right now, she'd settle for a Numb Ever After.

Kendall's crisp diction cut through the fug of cleaning products and self-doubt. 'O LOVE OF MY LIFE!' he was hollering as he took the stairs two at a time. 'I need one of your special foot massages before I – *oh*.' He came to an abrupt full stop when he spotted Ruby through the room divider. His ears went a vivid pink. 'Sorry. I didn't realise we had company.'

'She's not company.' Teddy tottered into the room in a silky dressing gown, his heavily made up face contrasting dramatically with his wigless short hair. 'She's part of the furniture.' He folded Kendall into a bear hug worthy of the name. 'Come here, handsome. Has that nasty old outside world been at you again?'

Acquiescing to Teddy's messy affections far more meekly than Ruby would have imagined, Kendall mumbled something about 'those oafs' and 'the worst alcopops delivery it's been my misfortune to deal with'. Peering out from Teddy's embrace he caught Ruby's eye. 'You'll know us if you see us again, won't you?' he asked.

It had none of his old waspishness. Kendall's attitude to Ruby had turned a corner. She regarded him as human natural yoghurt: a little too tart for her tastes but essential in a balanced diet. (And good with fruits.)

'Wassamatter, Rubes?' Nothing escaped Teddy's gaze, despite the tarantula-like false eyelashes. 'Something's up.

C'mere. C'mere,' he flapped urgently, as if she were a recalcitrant farmyard animal. 'Group hug.'

'You and your group hugs,' muttered Kendall. 'We're not the cast of *Friends*, you know.'

'Quickly!' chided Teddy, as Ruby hung back.

The woebegone look already replaced by a downturned smile, Ruby dumped her mop and joined them.

Smearing lipstick on her left cheek, Teddy wrapped his brawny arms around her, blotting out the light and almost choking her with mingled scents of Anaïs Anaïs and shaving foam. 'Kendall, get on with it!' he hissed.

Gingerly at first, then tighter, Kendall's wiry arms snaked around the other two. To Ruby's surprise she got a kiss from him too, a smart, clean one precisely aimed at her right cheek. 'It'll be all right,' he whispered.

It was as if all the cuddles Ruby had never had in her childhood and marriage were being administered at once. There was a ring of veracity to Kendall's banal assurance: Ruby chose to believe him.

That grey jacket looked *good*. Ruby's reflection in shop windows pleased her no end, and a hint of swagger crept into her stride. She even pursed her lips.

'GORRRRRJUS!' A man in a white van critiqued her and Ruby reined in the swagger and undid her pout. A dot of pink blooming on each cheek, she almost ignored the cheerful, 'Afternoon!' from the alley beside the Glove.

'I *said*: afternoon.'

'Oh. Sorry. Hello.' Ruby stopped for 'her' tramp. 'How are things?' she asked awkwardly. The man was, after all, a tramp: how could things be? He was unlikely to have got a raise, or taken up French at degree level.

'Fantastic,' he answered. 'I have a new dog.' The tramp

pointed to a lean black mongrel sitting somewhat self-consciously in the supermarket trolley.

'Aww,' said Ruby dutifully. She motioned to the violin poking out from under the new arrival's none too clean bottom. 'Learned any new songs?' she asked hopefully.

'No need,' said the tramp comfortably.

'S'pose not. Must rush. I'm meeting someone.'

That someone was Joe and he pulled a gurn of surprise at seeing Ruby at his school gate.

The lame, 'I was just passing and . . .' didn't seem to convince him, so Ruby dispensed with any pretence as they walked. 'There's something I'd like to talk to you about.'

Joe's eyebrows disappeared up into his dreadful fringe, eloquently signalling, *You* want to talk to me? Fists rammed into parka pockets, he was trundling speedily along, keeping just in front of Ruby.

Flailing, wondering why she'd started this, Ruby staggered on. 'I did your room yesterday.' Pregnant pause. 'I gave it a really good clean.' Pregnant pause. 'Especially the drawers.'

Joe would have made an excellent poker player. He wasn't biting. Ruby resorted to nipping in front of him, blocking his way and saying, 'I know about the ballroom dancing.'

'Sssh!' Joe reacted violently, putting his finger to his lips and darting paranoid looks about him. 'That's a secret. You shouldn't have.'

Ruby had to agree. 'I know. And I'm really sorry.' Ruby fell into step beside him. 'Why do you hide the magazines and the clothes? Why the secrecy? There's nothing wrong with ballroom dancing.' That wasn't entirely true. There was a lot wrong with it, from the high Lycra content of the trousers to the wisdom of ruffly sleeves on men, but there was nothing *morally* wrong with it.

'I know there's nothing wrong with it.' Joe's mouth was a hen's bum of discomfort.

'Your mum and dad might be pleased you've got a hobby.' Even one involving sequins and Brylcreem.

This earned a grunt of juvenile disbelief from Joe.

'You're obviously very keen on it. Those magazines aren't cheap.' Especially on a pocket money income. 'Maybe if you share it with your—'

'Why are you so interested?'

'Because . . .' Ruby faltered. Why, she wondered, *was* she so interested? Best to be honest. Up to a point. 'Because I like you, Joe.' She hesitated before adding, 'I want you to be happy.'

The disbelief on Joe's face was comical. He shifted his rucksack to his other shoulder. 'I can't tell my mum and dad,' he said finally, and as grudgingly as if each word cost him money. 'They'd go apeshit.' He looked sideways at Ruby.

She looked sideways right back. 'You can say apeshit if you like,' she told him. 'I've heard worse. But you could have just said they'd go mad.'

'OK, *OK*,' huffed Joe, as if Ruby was mercilessly interrogating him. 'They'd go mad.'

After a second's deliberation, Ruby eschewed the *maybe they wouldn't* approach. This wasn't a sitcom, it was real life, and Ruby knew Olivia well enough to know that her employer would indeed go several shades of apeshit if Joe admitted to such plebeian leanings. 'Yeah, you're right,' she sighed, surprising her little hostage.

'Do you like ballroom dancing?' asked Joe, with that trademark gravity, so odd in a face too cute for the Mickey Mouse Club.

'Erm . . .' The honest approach ('Christ! NO!') was ditched in favour of a more diplomatic, 'It looks very difficult.'

Suddenly Joe threw down his rucksack. 'In the paso doble,'

he spluttered, all gravity dissolved, 'you have to be a bull-fighter.' He struck a dramatic pose, arms haughtily above his head, his parka riding up to cover his face. 'See?' he coughed, through the fake fur. 'It's not that hard.'

It wouldn't do to laugh. And it *really* wouldn't do to cuddle him. Instead, Ruby retrieved his rucksack and told him, 'I think you've got a flair for it.'

'Nah.' Joe shook his head, but couldn't shake off the sneakily pleased look on his face. 'I'll never find out, will I?' he grumbled, as they started to walk again. 'I can't see Mum taking me to classes. Even though they're only eight pounds an hour, at St Matthew's church hall, every Thursday at four until six.' He rubbed his nose, suddenly and viciously, like a squirrel might.

Joe had obviously done his research. Ruby could almost smell the need wafting from him. 'Stop a minute.' She yanked Joe back by his hood. They were almost at the corner of Clancy Street and she didn't want Olivia or Hugo to spot them together. 'Let me think for a sec.' She felt like an adulteress, lurking on corners, fearful of being seen with a certain somebody. 'How about if I took you to a—' she began.

Joe was way ahead of her. 'YESSSSS!' he roared, punching the air.

10

The text interrupted Ruby's unabashed adoration of Sarah Beeny in a repeat of *Property Ladder* that she'd already seen eight times. Tearing herself away from the on-screen talk of third bedrooms and load-bearing walls, Ruby looked sideways at her phone.

Unless his personality had changed somewhat, the text wasn't from Manny.

BRING SLIPPERS, FEET KILLING ME

Earlier, an unamused Kendall had described Maria's style as 'bulldyke meets SAS' and requested that she glam up for that evening's talent night. Cursing and tutting, Maria had dug out a pair of hardly worn 'hot date shoes'. Sparkly and strappy, they had perfectly rounded off Maria's outfit of little black dress and too much makeup, but had the unfortunate side-effect of making her walk like a chicken. Ruby had prophesied that they wouldn't last the night and now she was proved right.

'Slippers.' Ruby banged down novelty bunny footwear on the bar.

'Free booze.' Maria banged down a glass. With a heartfelt 'Oooh', she pushed her toes into the bunnys' offal. 'That's better.'

'Hardly what you'd call glam, though.' Ruby sipped her drink gingerly. Maria liked to create new cocktails and the results were variable.

'That's a Thong Twister.' Maria looked eager to hear Ruby's verdict on it. 'What do you think?'

'I think . . .' Ruby thought it would be useful for getting barnacles off boats, but was saved from finding a polite way of saying so by Kendall, who pushed through the crowd brandishing a plunger.

'Good evening, Ms Mop.' Kendall slung the plunger behind the bar. 'Pray don't expect small talk from a man who's spent the last half hour with his head down a bog. People are animals,' he shuddered, declining to elaborate. Kendall flicked a thumb in the direction of Maria, who had scuttled over to the other side of the horseshoe bar to pull a pint. 'The minute I appear, the little vixen tries to look busy.' He gasped. 'And sodding slippers! I'll have her,' he promised darkly.

'The talent night's going well,' Ruby noted, as up on the stage a small man in a bow tie persuaded a pregnant-looking poodle through a modest hoop of flame.

'Just call me Simon Cowell,' muttered Kendall, leaning over the bar to pull out a mini fire extinguisher. 'Just in case.' He patted the red cylinder. 'Teddy is especially flammable tonight.'

That was true. Teddy, at the side of the stage, was twirling about in a nylon crinoline that brought to mind Shirley Temple. Albeit with an Adam's Apple. And a habit of saying 'fuck' a lot. 'Pink suits him.' Ruby's aesthetic sense had shifted. She could now see the beauty in a paunchy middle-aged bloke wearing lipstick. Admittedly, it was a bonkers, off-kilter beauty, but it qualified as beauty all the same when the paunchy middle-aged bloke was Teddy.

A roar of approval went up from the tipsy crowd as the poodle lay heavily down, exhibiting an entirely sensible reluctance to brave the hoop. Teddy stepped in, made a number of weak dog-related gags and broke into song to distract attention from the contestant's red-faced exit.

Hands in the air, the audience joined in good-naturedly with Teddy's off-key and rather rude version of, 'How Much Is That Doggy in the Window?'

Turning to Kendall, Ruby said, over the noise, 'God, he's good, isn't he? He's got them in the palm of his hand.' She enjoyed basking in the warmth that the two men showed each other: it was an emotional sunbed in Ruby's slightly arid new life.

But Kendall didn't reply. He was looking straight at his partner but seemed not to see him. Wherever he was, Kendall was miles away.

Ruby sipped her Twisted Thong, and gagged delicately. No doubt he'd be back soon.

What is it now? thought Ruby, trudging home in the dark as her mobile beeped at her. She was looking forward to a long bath in her absurdly fancypants bathroom and had resisted all Maria's entreaties to linger at the Velvet Glove until last orders. She flipped open the phone, anticipating text-based emotional blackmail from her lodger.

For the second time that evening she was wrong.

I CAN SEE U BABES

A fleeting desire to vomit up her Twisted Thong shook Ruby. She snapped the phone shut. Feet stapled to the spot, she glanced about neurotically. Common sense dictated that Manny couldn't actually see her, but hysteria was of the opposite opinion. Hysteria could see him in that bush, behind that bin, wound around that lamppost like a viper. Hysteria won hands down (as it tends to do) and Ruby took off, racing home at speed with a tear-splashed face and a heart banging so hard against her ribs that she half expected it to wake the neighbours.

Safe indoors, Ruby laid her phone on the tiles of her coffee table and prowled around it. She didn't even take off her beloved new jacket, so intent was she on thinking this one through. Accustomed to handing problems to the nearest grown-up, it took a while for Ruby to unscramble her thoughts.

Proper good old-fashioned, knee-knocking fear surrounded the whole idea of Manny, like the tendrils around Sleeping Beauty's castle. In lieu of a knight on a white horse, Ruby would have to hack at the creeper herself.

Pacing around her opulent-stroke-kitsch sitting room, Ruby gave herself a good talking to. There was no way that Manny, with all his pressing problems, not to mention his lack of superpowers, could be watching her. That 'I CAN SEE U' was an attempt to unsettle her. For whatever psycho reasons, Manny wanted to keep her comfortably under his thumb.

So far, so Maria. Now Ruby added her own spin. It was a far more compassionate take. Still pacing, Ruby ironed out the wrinkles of her reasoning. What if, she thought, this bullyboy posturing was a cry for help? Cries for Help, after all, came in all guises: some men cried for help by gambling away life savings, film stars tended to do it by snorting their own weight in cocaine, her parents' next door neighbour had cried for help by learning Esperanto. Ruby couldn't forget the ambiguous tenderness of Manny's earlier messages. Maybe, she theorised with increasing confidence, this menacing text was designed to provoke her into replying.

Ruby packed in the pacing and lunged for her phone. Ignoring the imaginary Greek chorus of Marias, all singing *'No no no, for Christ's sake no!'* Ruby called the familiar number.

It rang. As each tense moment tumbled past, Ruby was at war with herself, longing to press 'cancel', and longing to hear his customary curt, 'Manny here.'

Then, suddenly, she heard it. 'Manny here.' He paused, leaving a gap which a breathless Ruby didn't feel able to fill. 'Rubes?' he said, quietly.

That tender tone did it. 'Oh Manny,' snuffled Ruby.

'Darling,' he whispered. It was as if a man-eating grizzly had morphed into Winnie the Pooh. 'You called. Thank you, babes.'

Ignoring that 'babes', Ruby allowed herself a second's amazement at being thanked by Manny before she said, 'If you can see me, what am I doing?' in quite a playful way for somebody who was shaking.

'You're looking fucking gorgeous, as usual.'

Manny was keeping his voice low and Ruby couldn't quell the suspicion that Tania was in earshot. 'Are you alone?'

'And lonely.'

Another deeply un-Manny word. 'Don't say that.' Ruby could imagine those broad shoulders sagging. 'This is all a horrible mess, isn't it?'

'I never thought it would come to this. Not with you.'

The spectre of Tania, in her Wonderbra and précised skirts, reared up, but Ruby suppressed her in the interests of the status quo: a habit from the old days. 'Do you miss me?' she murmured, ashamed to let even the walls know the true depth of her dependency.

'*Miss* you?' Manny made the word sound insufficient. 'You're all I think about.'

With a jolt, Ruby realised that she couldn't answer in kind. A couple of weeks ago she'd have said, quite truthfully, that Manny was constantly on her mind, but now her conscious-ness was cluttered with Joe's ballroom dancing, how to get the Ribena stains out of Tom's pouffe and the everyday practicalities of paying the bills. 'I've changed, you know,' she told him warily. 'I've done a lot of growing up.'

'That's my fault,' said Manny quickly, as if growing up was regrettable. 'I should never have left you on your own. Why did I go to Tania that day? I regret it every minute of every hour. If I hadn't been so rash we'd be together now.'

Hmm. Even a seasoned wearer of rose-tinted specs would have to query that. There was, after all, a baby in the mix. 'But you did go to her.' Some of Maria's chutzpah had rubbed off on Ruby. She held the phone away from her ear for the explosion.

It didn't come. 'Yeah, but you know why? The real reason? Because she's like me. Bad. I was so ashamed. I couldn't bear to see myself through your eyes. You're so good, so pure. I had to run away from you. Tania knew I was a bad boy and she accepted it, 'cos she's been around the block a few times too. But you . . . you're perfect, babes.'

Squirming at the moronic Alice In Wonderland figure he described, Ruby endeavoured to square Manny's words with her memory of the day her life had gone pear shaped. She didn't recall his shame. Fury, yes, and lots of it. Maybe, she chided herself efficiently, she'd misread the signs. 'Manny, the baby . . .' she began, not knowing where the sentence was taking her.

Her husband's voice changed. 'Yeah. Well. Yeah.' He sounded cornered, got at, as if Ruby was poking him with a compass. 'That was Tania's doing. He wasn't exactly planned.'

Even the sheltered Ruby knew how babies came about: she doubted that Tania had made one with her chemistry set. 'What's his name?'

'Why do you want to talk about him?' Manny was sounding more and more uneasy, like a man reclining on broken glass.

Rather enjoying the lassitude of their new circumstances, Ruby pushed her husband in a way that had been impossible during their marriage. 'Come on. Tell me his name.'

'Alfie.'

'That's lovely.' Ruby hesitated, then ploughed on. Perhaps it was time to allude to the hinterland of hurt that Alfie's conception had caused. 'Ironic, really. That was one of the names I'd have liked if you and I had ever— '

'You know I love you, don't you?'

Ruby mewed. Both at hearing that word from Manny's lips, and at his brusque tone. He could just as easily have said, 'You know I hate you, don't you?' 'Do I know that?' she breathed.

'Christ, babes, I let you live in my penthouse, don't I?'

It had been a while since Ruby had experienced the sensation of her spirit dribbling down the plughole. 'You don't let me live here, Manny.' She spoke shakily but with clarity. 'I own this place.'

'Oh you bought it. I didn't realise.' Manny's smooth sarcasm became something darker. 'Did you graft for it? Did you work your knackers off for it? You didn't even know the place existed until that toerag Simon handed you the keys. Lady La-di-fucking-da.' Manny's voice was as hostile as the stubby finger Ruby felt sure he was stabbing in the air.

'There's a lot I didn't know.'

Complete silence met this uncharacteristically 'mouthy' retort. Eventually Manny said, in a more low key way, 'This is getting us nowhere. I shouldn't . . .' He seemed to collect himself. 'It's a tough time for me, babes. A lot of people who did very nicely out of me are getting all pally with the police. I'm under a lot of stress.' He sighed, half laughing. 'I never believed in stress before. Now I have it for breakfast, lunch and dinner.'

'Simon's told me how serious things are.'

'If he'd only pull his public school educated finger out,' flashed Manny, 'things might improve. I'm paying him hundreds of pounds an hour to tell me what I know, that I'm in schtuck. Look,' he said, an appeal in his voice, 'it's hopeless talking on the phone. Why don't I come over?'

'What?' Ruby looked around, spooked, as if Manny might suddenly emerge from behind the crimson sofa.

'I can be there in forty minutes.'

'But—'

'Babes, I want to see you. I want to see my beautiful girl.'

A straitjacket was snaking its tapes and buckles around Ruby. 'It's not a good idea, Manny.' She had no desire to be his beautiful, silent, *obedient* girl again.

'Go on.' Manny could be silky when he wanted to be. 'I miss the way you smell, Ruby. I miss the feel of you. I'm dying here. Without my girl it makes no sense.' When a pause produced no response, he carried on. 'Just an hour. I'll behave, I promise. It would be like having a gourmet meal after living on takeaways.' He paused again. 'Please?' This, thought Ruby, may well have been the first time Manny's lips had framed the word. 'I just want to see you. And the apartment. Make sure you haven't made too many changes to the place, got rid of my stuff.' Despite an obvious attempt to keep his delivery light, there was an undercurrent to his, 'You haven't, have you, babe?'

Ashamed of herself, Ruby lied. 'No, no, not really.' She was, she knew, different and stronger these days, but she still wasn't up to facing Manny's wrath.

'Good. Good girl.'

'I'm getting a divorce.' Perhaps that 'good girl' did it.

'Don't be silly.'

Silly. Manny dug his hole deeper. 'I'm divorcing you.' The idea had only just solidified, and saying it out loud felt good. 'We're divorcing,' she said, by way of variety.

'Now shut your mouth, Ruby. You're a Gallagher and you're staying that way.'

Ruby could sense that Manny was battling to keep a lid on it. 'I mean it.'

'Throw your toys out of the pram if you like, babes. I know you're pissed off. In some ways I don't blame you. But this'll all blow over and we'll sort something out.'

'Babies, as a rule, don't blow over.' Ruby was starting to enjoy her spectacular new mouthiness. Power over another person was intoxicating: she was beginning to understand Manny's abuse of it for all those years. 'I don't want anything from you, Manny. I just want you to leave me alone.'

'And what about what I want?' Manny's patience sounded thinner than his hair.

'You've had it all your own way for years.' Never had a worm turned so dramatically. 'It's my go.'

'You'll be back. You're mine.'

'I'm nobody's. I manage without you. Me and Maria are doing just fine.'

'Maria?' Manny sounded surprised. He wasn't a man who liked surprises. 'What's she been saying?'

'Nothing about you, don't worry.' For the first time in her

life, Ruby was bored by her husband. 'It's not all about you, Manny. Maria's my mate, that's all.'

'Yeah. Well. I'd watch her. She's not such a mate.'

'What do you—' began Ruby, before stepping back from the precipice that Manny had so deftly carved out. 'I'm allowed to have friends these days, Manny.' She glanced at her watch. 'It's late. I'm going. I've got to be up for work.'

'Work?' Manny made a horrible noise that just about qualified as a laugh. 'You? What do you do, quality control at the Dozy Bint factory?'

'If you really want to know, I'm a cleaner.'

The creepy laughter stopped. 'You are fucking having me fucking on.' Manny, who could happily sanction all sorts of criminal activity, drew the line at bleaching U-bends. 'My wife does not go out and skivvy. I'm telling you, Ruby, you pack that in right now!'

'Goodnight, Manny.'

And Ruby finally took her jacket off.

11

It was wrong. So very wrong. And Ruby hadn't enjoyed herself so much since her headmistress's tights had fallen down during assembly.

There was no name for her crime, but crime it surely was. Perhaps it needed a whole new category: Taking a Child to Ballroom Dancing Lessons without Consent. Not as dastardly as Manny's impressive list of misdemeanours, but racy stuff for a woman who came out in hives if she spilled jam on her library book.

The brightly lit church hall was scuffed and shabby, bearing the scars of the classes and meetings and toddler groups that used and abused it. Ruby sat on an uncomfortable plastic chair with the other adults on one side of the peeling boards as Joe and a dozen of his peers wheeled awkwardly about on the far side of the room.

Sneaking Toffos from her handbag, Ruby suppressed squeals of delight. It was all so unbearably cute. She'd assumed she was immune to the delights of ballroom, but she was watching Joe with the rapt delight of an OAP watching Alan Titchmarsh.

'Heads *up*!' bellowed the imperious Miss Delmar, whose colourful surname was at odds with her elasticated trousers and bobbly cardigan. Her nasal voice booming, she wielded absolute authority over her class. She was a kiddie Hitler. 'Shoulders, Isobel!' she scolded. 'Suzie, dear! *Your feet, dear!*'

Partnered with the scowling Suzie of the wayward feet, Joe was tense and straight backed. His face was even graver than usual. Ruby's heart went out to him. He was trying *so* hard. For a complete beginner, he was doing rather well, even if he was a little jerky and occasionally pulled Suzie when he should have pushed her. Suzie looked the kind of girl who liked to lead.

A woman in the chair next to Ruby, knitting a messy garment that could be a hat with sleeves, leaned over to whisper, 'Your son's doing very well for a first timer.'

'Oh, he's not my son,' smiled Ruby. 'He's my friend,' she said, looking over at the stumbling Joe. The smile wouldn't dissolve. She was proud of Joe, however unreasonable that was. To hell with E numbers, that boy was getting a Cornetto after class.

The tube carriage on the way back to Parsons Green station was empty enough for Joe to practise his steps.

'Point. Ball. Change,' he chanted, galumphing the width of the train.

'So you liked it?' Ruby enjoyed her rhetorical question.

'*Liked* it?' Joe dropped into the sticky velour seat beside Ruby. 'It's incredible. I've never had so much fun.'

'You were good.' It wasn't exactly a lie: Ruby couldn't distinguish good from bad in this instance. Her heart told her Joe was good and she chose to take its biased opinion at face value.

'Really? Am I, though?' asked Joe, very seriously. 'Mum says everyone has a talent, but we haven't found mine yet.' He frowned, chewing his lip. 'It's certainly not trigonometry.'

At Joe's age, Ruby wouldn't have been able to *spell* trigonometry: hell, she wasn't sure she could spell it now. 'We can't all be good at maths,' she said soothingly.

'Or chemistry. Or history. Or geography. Or—'

'I get the picture.' Ruby touched the sleeve of Joe's blazer. 'Maybe you're creative.'

'I'm rubbish at the oboe, too.'

Try as she might, Ruby couldn't picture an oboe. Was it, she wondered, a small farm animal? 'What if your talent is in your feet?' she suggested.

'I promise I'm going to work really hard,' vowed Joe, looking and sounding like the juvenile lead in a low budget TV movie, subtitled Overcoming The Odds. 'I'll practise like mad. And next week I'll bring my sparkly cummerbund.'

It was shocking to hear a young lad use the word cummerbund so freely. 'Next time you have a birthday party you can stun everybody with your unexpected dancing skills. But,' mused Ruby, 'you'd have to invite your partner Suzie . . .' Suzie wasn't her idea of an ideal party guest. Although only four foot three she had the air of a menopausal spinster.

'We don't do birthday parties,' said Joe.

'What, never?'

'Nah. Too much noise and stuff, I suppose. Mum doesn't really like having loads of people in the house. She gets one of her heads.'

'But . . .' Ruby was torn. To meddle or not to meddle?

'I'd love to have a birthday party, though.'

Meddling was now compulsory. 'Does your mum know you feel that way?'

'Ye-ah!' Joe swung the word upwards for maximum

emphasis. 'I'm always saying it. She gives me the Look. You know –' Joe mimed an Olivia-esque peer over the top of imaginary glasses.

Ruby jumped. 'Jeez. You look just like her.'

'Everyone says that.'

'Maybe this year she'll let you have a party.' A reckless, probably doomed plan was taking shape under Ruby's bobble hat.

'Nope. Mum doesn't change her mind.' Joe didn't speak judgementally. He talked about his mother as if she was a force of nature, like a storm or a sunny day: she was what she was. 'It'd be cool to have the guys from my class over. We could have burgers. And ice cream. And maybe beer.'

Ruby snorted. 'Yeah right. Perhaps Olivia will book a stripper too.'

Pink as a prawn, Joe said stiffly, 'I wouldn't want an old stripper. But some sort of entertainer would be brill. A magician. I love magic.'

'How about a clown?'

'I *hate* clowns,' spat Joe, vehemently, as the train lurched out of a station.

Delighted, Ruby high-fived him. 'Me too!' she squealed. 'They're so spooky!'

'They paint their smiles on. That's just weird.'

'And those big feet.'

'And the stupid clothes.'

'And they're not funny.'

'And they think it's clever to fall over.' Joe sneered. 'Anyone can fall over.'

'Underneath they're all serial child killers.'

That seemed to be the definitive word on clowns. Exhausted by their rant, Joe and Ruby grinned conspiratorially at each other. 'Does your mum like clowns?'

'Why are you so interested in my mum?'

The question sideswiped Ruby. She'd thought she was being subtle. 'Am I?' she asked, eyes wide. 'I'm not. Just, you know, chit-chatting.'

Joe looked at Ruby without comment for what felt like a month, but was more like twenty seconds. 'Do you have a boyfriend?' he asked finally.

'I've got a husband.' Ruby enjoyed seeing surprise on that guarded little face. 'We don't get on very well, so I live with a friend now.' It was tricky simplifying chewy adult stuff for childish digestions.

'Are you getting a divorce?'

'Blimey Joe, you don't shy away from a blunt question, do you?' Ruby floundered, but said 'Yes'. She couldn't lie to his grey eyes.

'Everybody gets divorced,' pronounced Joe. 'Our stop.' He jumped up and Ruby tailed him out on to the platform.

Parting company just before the corner of Clancy Street, Ruby asked, 'Where did you tell your parents you were going?'

'Extra sitar.' Joe couldn't hold back his snigger. 'As if.'

Ruby sniggered too. 'You little liar.' She cuffed him lightly on the side of his woeful haircut.

In response Joe leapt up and tugged off Ruby's knitted hat. 'Not cold enough for this any more,' he said.

That was true. The March evening sky was streaked with the pink remains of a mild day. 'The year's racing past,' murmured Ruby. She felt as if she was on the top of a hill, preparing to hurtle down on a home-made go-kart held together with twine. The right thing to do was encourage Joe to tell his mother about the ballroom lessons and end this deceit. 'Same time next week?'

'Deffo.'

*

A cup of tea would help. What Ruby's mother had always referred to as 'a nice cup of tea', presumably in order to differentiate it from a nasty cup of tea garnished with clumps of hair.

The venue for this problem-busting beverage was Tom's kitchen. Clean and bright, it repaid her hard work by making her feel at home. It was just the kind of cosy, functional kitchen she'd like to create one day when, if, she ever chose her own home.

As night follows day, as Ant follows Dec, cake follows tea. A sizeable slab of iced Madeira lolled provocatively on a striped plate in front of her. Being a girl who needed permission to do anything remotely naughty, Ruby flattened out Tom's latest note as she unbuttoned her overall.

W.B.C.,
    Since you came into my life my house is so clean that I allow my mother access to all my nooks and crannies. She is a devious individual, given to running a finger along curtain rails and picture frames: imagine an older Anthea Turner with bad legs. I am now her favourite son. (I haven't owned up about you.) Feel free to eat her homemade cake in the fridge. I can't face any more of it. Although I <u>insist</u> that you don't wash the plate up afterwards.
    Do you suppose we'll ever meet?
    T.

There it was, in black and white: Ruby would do him a favour by eating the sponge. She lunged at it in a way only possible when alone, like a lioness on a wildebeest. It helped with her problem. A bit.

Ruby was accustomed to guilt. She'd lived with it all her life, and now looked out for its wan little gob at every junction. She felt guilty about being attractive, about living in a mortgage-free apartment, about her rude good health, about laughing at the spotty, sobbing folk on the *Jeremy Kyle Show*. If she gave it a minute, guilt about eating such a massive wodge of cake would kick in.

All those pangs could be shooed away, blamed variously on her upbringing, her genes, Jeremy Kyle. The guilt she shouldered about Joe's dancing class was different: it was – she gulped down a hit of medicinal tea – *deserved*.

Perhaps it was the Madeira cake. Perhaps it was the calming effect of the clock ticking on the kitchen wall. Ruby began to feel better. *Hey*, she asked herself chummily, *what vices do I have, after all?* She led a low key, blameless life. She was nice to people. She did her best. She gave violins to tramps. So where was the harm in facilitating a ten-year-old's cha cha cha once a week?

None, she decided. Or very little. Olivia's face reared up in her mind.

To distract herself from this compelling witness for the prosecution, Ruby re-read the note. As it had done both times previously, it made her grin. She glanced over at the snaps of Tom on his noticeboard, now dominated by a long, curling list of dates. Hoping they'd provide a clue to his job, Ruby was disappointed. A word-processed list of addresses and dates, they were annotated in Tom's handwriting. 'B.A.', he'd written by one date. 'Bachelor of Arts?' wondered Ruby, intimidated already.

Whatever Tom did for a living, he was a natural flirt. Even a sheltered (or, to quote Maria, 'sexually autistic') woman like

Ruby could tell that. His notes were just too different to her other clients'. The last one from the Bachelor had been a succinct, 'Sorry about the bog'. The question was *why* Tom flirted with a faceless person who, for all he knew, looked like Billy Bunter having a fat day, when all he had to go on was her prowess with a mop and her way with a note.

Ruby opened the kitchen drawer where the mismatched odds and ends lived, a sad place where the scissors had to pretend to get along with the sandwich bag ties. Grabbing a pen, she turned Tom's note over to write on the other side. Attention from men usually brought out Ruby's inner Mother Superior, but this was different. She admired Tom for his open-mindedness in flirting with a faceless cleaner.

> Lovely sponge. I arranged your FHM archive in date order, and I fixed the sticky cupboard door in the bathroom.

She paused. She wanted to flirt. She had an impulse to write something coquettish. Something minxish.

> I can't shift the damp stain in the downstairs loo, but I'll keep trying.

That would have to do.

The shouting drowned out even Henry's basso profundo. Ruby clicked the hoover off with her trainer and cocked her head towards the stairs. It couldn't be a *real* row, surely? Teddy and Kendall specialised in operatic set pieces where nobody got hurt.

'I've never been so insulted in my life!' Teddy was howling.

'With your dress sense, I find that hard to believe.' The

sound of a slammed door suggested that Kendall was putting some space between himself and his partner.

'Don't you run away from me, you little snot.' Teddy's deep voice sounded choked. Ruby's suspicions were correct, this was a bona fide row. Hurriedly, she bundled up the hoover's cord, ready to flee and give her clients some privacy.

A loud hammering was followed by the creak of a door opening upstairs. 'For God's sake, can't a man have some PEACE!' yelled Kendall.

Kendall *never* yelled. Ruby crammed her dusters into her holdall.

'Don't think I don't know what you're thinking!' blustered Teddy, whose size eleven marabou mules could be heard thundering along the landing above.

'What you don't know is a biiiig subject.' Kendall was storming down the stairs. 'Have you even looked at me recently, Ted. Really looked?' Kendall appeared in the doorway of the sitting room, cutting off Ruby's escape route. 'Ah,' he said, chastened, when he spotted her crouched, cringing, over her cleaning fluids.

'Look at *you*? What would I want to look at you for?' gabbled Teddy as he flounced in behind Kendall. 'There's only room for one star in this establishment, honeybun, and it ain't *you*.' He too stopped dead when he saw Ruby, before flying to her side like a wounded swan. A lumpy wounded swan who'd eaten all the pies. 'We're upsetting the child,' he said gently, laying his hands protectively on her shoulders.

'Don't worry about me, I'm fine.' Ruby rearranged her features into a less stricken expression. 'I'll just creep out and leave you to it.'

Nobody was creeping anywhere. Those gentle hands of Teddy's were like vices. 'We have no secrets,' he said loftily, nose in the air. 'Everybody knows I live with an inhuman monster who will work me and work me until I stagger and die, like the beast of burden that I am.'

'I merely suggested,' said Kendall calmly, 'that my better half might like to help me with the weekly accounts for a change, instead of taking *yet another* nap.' He breathed out noisily, fluttering his moustache, in his effort not to rise to Teddy's bait.

'I'm an artiste,' wailed Teddy, appealing to Ruby. 'He knows I need my beauty sleep.'

Kendall rolled his eyes. 'If you had all the beauty sleep you needed you'd be in a coma.' He stepped out of the room. 'If anybody needs me, I'll be the one running the place.'

Piggy in the middle, Ruby was mute. Luckily, Teddy always filled any conversational gaps. 'I've wasted the best years of my life on that mincing dwarf.' He put his head on one side. 'And the worst, come to think of it.'

'Is everything OK? You both sounded deadly serious.'

'Oh, you know us.' Teddy gave Ruby a playful push that sent her careering into the room divider. 'We're a three act circus.' He righted her and planted a kiss on her forehead. 'Don't worry, sweetie. If anything happens, I'll get custody of you.'

12

There it was again, that tang of cologne. Ruby winced as she took a seat. She wished Simon would revert to smelling of whatever it was he used to smell of. Ink, maybe. Or law.

'*Another* visit,' he noted, loading the two words with sultry meaning. 'You're spoiling me, Ruby.'

Ruby goggled at him. Simon was attempting a leer and it didn't sit well with the loo paper on his shaving cut. Deciding it was best to ignore his attempts to manoeuvre her down Love Lane, she stuck to business. 'I'm here to discuss a very delicate matter,' she began, carefully.

'Delicate!' Simon pulled a face Kenneth Williams would have envied. 'Ooh, matron!'

For God's sake. '*Simon . . .*' Ruby implored him. Why, she marvelled, did men mutate into such dummies when their willies were awake? 'I really need your help.'

'Sorry.' Simon coughed and folded his hands in front of him, newsreader-like. 'Go on.'

Taking a deep breath, Ruby set a momentous ball rolling. 'I've decided to divorce Manny.'

'That's terrific!' Simon bounced out of his seat as if he'd won an Oscar. The look on her face sent him plummeting back down to say, soberly, 'If that's what you really want, I'll hand you over to one of my colleagues. You can trust her. We'll do all we can to make it as painless as possible.'

'Thank you.' Ruby fell silent. Tears, uninvited and unexpected, were gatecrashing the meeting. It was such a mundane way to end a marriage, sitting here in an office with a pot plant, a *Top Gear* calendar and an amorous solicitor.

'Oh. Here.' Simon leaned across his desk to offer her a monogrammed hanky. 'Ruby, don't cry.'

'I'm not,' lied Ruby. 'Well,' she smiled, 'obviously I *am*. But I don't really want to. It just feels so . . .' She tailed off as Simon launched into a dull litany of divorce facts and figures. A roll of drums, some poignant strings, anything to mark the moment would have done. She sighed and stood up, cutting Simon off mid-flow. 'Do you fancy a drink?' she asked, peremptorily.

'What? Yes.' Simon gathered up his briefcase as if the building were on fire. 'Yes. Oh yes. Yes.'

'I need to celebrate,' said Ruby. With a wonky smile, she said, 'Champagne!' and blew her nose.

Mrs Vine was surprised to see Ruby's face at her door. 'It's ten o'clock at night, dear,' she said, wonderingly, pulling her high-necked dressing gown closed. Behind her, the house was lit up as if ready for a ball, even though its only occupant was one elderly lady in slippers.

'I know.' Ruby, with her exaggerated sense of responsibility, hoped that her breath wasn't too champagny. 'I forgot to give you this when I was in earlier.' She held out a small box of teabags. 'They're fennel. Your favourite. I noticed you'd run out.'

Looking suspicious, Mrs Vine slowly reached out to take the box. 'My dear,' she said, 'you shouldn't have.'

'I know you love your fennel tea,' smiled Ruby, ramming her hands back in the pockets of her special jacket.

The suspicious look faded from the old lady's papery face, and she answered Ruby's smile with one of her own. 'You're very kind.'

'No problem.' Ruby backed out of the reach of the porch light. 'Goodnight.' No need to tell Mrs Vine that the fennel-teabag mercy dash wasn't entirely altruistic. Her hour drinking champagne with Simon needed to be walked off. Or, more precisely, the sight of one of Manny's 'guys' at the other end of the swish bar had to be walked off.

The 'guys' had never had a proper job title. Once Ruby had asked what the guys actually did, and had received a terse 'Stuff' from Manny in reply. When pressed, he went further: 'Guy stuff.' With hindsight, Ruby could see that guy stuff didn't include flower arranging or yoga. The guys were built like King Kong, and shared his sunny disposition.

The guy at the champagne bar was Frankie, and he'd stared at Ruby and Simon as if they were fascinating, occasionally raising a glass of water to his lips. It couldn't be coincidence. The guys were pub men: it would short-circuit their macho wiring to stray into an establishment which offered paper coasters.

'Manny sent him.' Ruby stated the bleeding obvious to herself. For all she knew, Frankie could be on her tail right now, as she crossed the darkness of the green. She sped up, valiantly trying to stay calm. In a way, she should be grateful to Manny: he'd certainly proved that she was doing the right thing divorcing him.

Think about something else, Ruby counselled herself, as she tapped her security number into the Hannah House entry phone. Ruby recalled the look of pleasure on Mrs Vine's face. Fennel teabags had never meant so much. That house was far too big and grand for her client. The guest rooms were kept pristine (by Ruby) for guests who never came to tousle the sheets or untidy the ensuites.

Quick to spot loneliness in the lives of others, Ruby wasn't sure how to handle her own. Pressing plasters over strangers' grazes provided only vicarious relief.

The lift doors opened on to the penthouse, neatly framing Maria. 'Table tennis!' she oinked, jumping on the spot and waving two new bats. 'NOW!'

Tearing off her jacket and grabbing a bat, *Thank God*, thought Ruby, *for Maria*.

The feather duster halted. Ruby was distracted by the row of biographies she was dusting. Olivia and Hugo had far-ranging tastes: on this evidence they were interested in Pol Pot, Einstein and Charlie Chaplin. The bookshelves stretched the length of the knocked-through reception room and all that learning took a lot of dusting.

Sinking on to a Moroccan leather pouffe that had travelled further than Ruby ever had, she opened a biography of Gandhi at the photographs. Maybe she would have got into the habit of reading if she'd grown up in a house like this. Ruby had always assumed that her goldfish-style attention span was to blame for the fact that she read nothing more intellectual than *heat*'s 'Spotted' page, but perhaps her parents' 'library' hadn't helped. Barbara Cartland's way with an exclamation mark had left Ruby cold, as had the procession of virginal heroines getting their ringlets in a twist over the nearest duke. The spy thrillers favoured by her dad, with their covers of blood-caked swastikas, had never tempted her away from her magazines either.

The familiar click of the front door propelled Ruby off her pouffe. She set to with her duster again, bending to straighten the pile of DVDs that sat beside the house's one, small television set. She allowed herself a secretive smirk at the copy of *Harry Potter and the Goblet of Fire* she'd inserted into the pile during her last visit. The cellophane was gone. Ruby hoped that Joe had enjoyed it: the man in the shop assured her that every self-respecting ten-year-old in the land owned a copy. It was impossible to imagine Joe curling up in front of his parents' collection of worthy dramas and documentaries.

Now that the initial overhaul of Clancy Street had been achieved, Ruby's visits entailed keeping on top of the incredible amounts of mess that three people can generate. Tucking sweaters back into drawers, straightening duvets, emptying wash baskets, wiping down the kitchen units, rubbing the section of wall where food aimed at the bin actually landed, Ruby was far happier than a human might be expected to be. Restoring order, bringing comfort and ease, she was a fairy with a toilet brush instead of a wand.

Clattering down the bare wooden stairs to the basement kitchen, Ruby's arms were full of heavy navy blue material. 'These curtains from Joe's room need a wash,' she told Olivia, who was at the pine table with a newspaper.

'Oh. Right.' Olivia was distracted by a long newspaper article with no pictures, just the sort of closely typed page that made Ruby press on in search of the cartoons. The headline was about asylum seekers; if Ruby had declared, 'I'm putting Hugo through the Heavily Soiled cycle,' Olivia wouldn't have looked up.

This vagueness suited Ruby very well. The curtains were doomed. They were never going back. They blocked out the light and gave the room a cold, unwelcoming air. The striped blind exposed by the curtains' removal was much more suitable.

'Hold on!' Olivia came back to the present as Ruby started up the stairs again. 'Sit yourself down for a moment. Have a rest.' It was time for the tea ritual. Olivia's constant admonitions to 'take it easy' and 'take the weight off your feet' came directly from her guilt gland, and were therefore more about her peace of mind than Ruby's comfort. But Ruby wasn't the sort of girl to analyse anything too closely, and if letting Olivia make her a cup of tea made Olivia happy, then Ruby was glad to accept the (too weak, too perfumed) tea that Olivia made.

'And a biscuit,' fussed Olivia, pushing her half-moon glasses up her nose with a jerky, impatient move that was typical of her. 'I'm sure there's a nice Bath Oliver in here somewhere.' She threw open the pantry door and gave a surprised, 'Oh!'

Knowing what was coming, Ruby arranged her features carefully so as not to look guilty as hell. She'd been getting some practice at this lately.

'Where did these . . .' Olivia held up a Tupperware box full of Mars and Twixes and Milky Ways. 'I don't remember . . .' She frowned at them as if they were baffling archaeological finds hinting at other ways of life.

'I saw them last week.' This wasn't a lie, it was an omission: Ruby had seen them when she'd put them there. 'I did wonder.' *That* was a lie.

'Oh well.' Olivia's curiosity didn't last. She was so thoroughly undomesticated that she was unsurprised when her own cupboards rebelled and started filling themselves. 'I don't really approve of Joe eating too much chocolate but . . .'

Disapproving of chocolate was as alien to Ruby as watching *Newsnight* by choice: admittedly, too much of the stuff could render him morbidly obese, but, she shamefacedly reminded herself, the boy could dance it off.

'Would you like a – what are these jobbies, I never touch them – *Bounty*, or something?' Olivia held out the box, shrugging at the contents.

Not waiting to be asked twice, Ruby chose a bite-size Mars. Her eating habits were still out of control. This morning her jeans had been tight around the waist.

The question came out on a cough, as if Olivia was trying to disguise it. 'Are you married, Ruby?'

'Er, yeah.' It was a shorthand answer, but the unexpurgated version would have tried Olivia's patience and meant leaving the back of the fridge until next week.

'So . . .' Olivia pondered, as if working out a sum. 'You weren't always a Gallagher?'

'No, that's my husband's name.' Ruby was wrongfooted by the question.

'Right,' said Olivia contemplatively.

'Erm, why?' asked Ruby.

'Oh, no reason.' Olivia licked her lips and framed a word, but nothing came out. Instead she asked eventually, 'And you're how old?'

This was turning into an interview. 'I'm twenty-eight,' said Ruby, with a wondering air. 'Is that,' she asked, feeling it to be a silly question, 'all right?' These queries had to be leading somewhere.

Olivia was sucking her lips contemplatively and took a moment to answer, shaking her head as if to toss away an unsettling thought. 'Are you busy next Thursday?'

'Nope.' Ruby's social calendar was as blank as her CV. Was she about to be asked to dinner? Perhaps Olivia was setting her up with one of her glittering intellectual circle. Ruby would have to buy a new dress. And a new brain.

'Could you babysit?'

Demoted in a split second from sparkling guest to Joe-wrangler, Ruby felt it was just as well: an evening on the sofa alongside Joe, ingesting too much chocolate and introducing him to the delights of E4 was well within her capabilities; small talk about the rights of women in the workplace probably wasn't. 'Sure. I'd love to.'

'You're a godsend.' Olivia didn't smile, she just let her shoulders sag under her mohair handknit. 'Hugo and I have been invited to supper.' Olivia rattled through some exposition. 'It's at Hugo's old chambers. Once upon a time, before he got into FE, he was called to the Bar. Lots of old faces from Middle Temple will be there.'

'Hmm, nice.' Ruby couldn't have been more baffled if Olivia had explained in Elvish. 'What time will you need me?'

'Ooh, about—' Olivia was cut short by the slam of the front door above their heads and the scuffling of schoolboy feet on the varnished boards of the hall. 'Seven,' she finished, raising her voice to be heard over the noise of several elephants, or one Joe, racing down to the basement. 'You must have smelled the Twox,' she said indulgently to her son, getting up to fetch his milk out of the fridge.

Behind Olivia's back Joe executed a clumsy but serviceable glide with back dip, earning him a furious shake of the head from Ruby. Furious, but delighted.

Another night, another cocktail. Ruby contemplated her pink drink.

'What the hell is in that glass?' asked Kendall, backing away from it as he laid out peanuts.

'Oblivion, probably,' laughed Ruby.

'Give it here then.' Kendall grabbed the glass and knocked it back in one. His eyes crossed and he slammed the side of his head with his hand. 'I may never play the piano again,' he croaked, before disappearing towards the door marked Private with an armful of ledgers.

Ruby stared at her empty glass. Kendall was a teetotaller, both from inclination and common sense. As he was fond of saying, there had to be one sober man in the place.

'You're thirsty tonight!' marvelled Maria, appearing from the far side of the bar to scoop up Ruby's glass. 'I'll do you another one.'

Managing to smile (she was sure she'd seen smoke coming out of the pink drink), Ruby accepted another toxic offering. 'I saw Yehudi on my way here,' she said, Yehudi being their name for the violin-playing tramp. 'I gave him a quid.'

'Was he playing—'

'*Yesterday*,' the two girls chorused.

''Fraid so,' said Ruby.

'I've been thinking,' said Maria, assuming a suitably thoughtful expression. 'That Frankie fella wasn't watching you, you know. You've got that all wrong.'

'Oh come on,' spluttered Ruby. 'I told you what the "guys" are like. They come out in hives if they meet somebody who can do joined-up writing. There's *no way* Frankie would ever venture into anywhere as poncey as a champagne bar in the West End unless he was tailing me.'

'Let me finish.' Maria held up a small, imperious forefinger. 'He was watching somebody, but not you. He was watching . . .' she took a moment, evidently enjoying the caveman-like frown on her friend's face, 'Simon.'

'But why would Manny want Simon watched?'

'Now *that* I don't know.' Maria was unapologetic for the sudden collapse of her theory.

'Maybe Manny suspects Simon of co-operating with the police or something.' Ruby tutted. She was back in *Bill* territory. She couldn't follow this kind of stuff on the television, so there was no way she could puzzle it out in real life. 'Who knows? He was always a bit paranoid.' She remembered, with very little nostalgia, the drama when Manny had accused the dry cleaner of wearing his suits 'to dance about in out the back'.

The wander down Memory Lane (a rather crowded dirt track in Ruby's case) was interrupted by the Private door banging back on its hinges and the emergence of Teddy in full regalia. His feather head-dress nodding in the air conditioning, he bellowed over his shoulder, '*And you can stuff your VAT calculator where the sun don't shine, Kendall fucking Vorderman!*' Realising he had attracted stares from everybody in the bar, Teddy coughed and giggled girlishly, his massive shoulders hunched up round his ears. 'A lovers' tiff,' he cooed, before stomping past Ruby like a navvy in glittery platforms. '*Another* one.'

13

The bed looked so inviting. She'd made it herself, so Ruby knew how taut the sheet was, how downy the duvet, how bosomy the pillow. She longed to creep into it, to sleep for just an hour, without any dark dreams of Manny.

The only problem was, it wasn't her bed. It was Tom's bed, and by now she should be sprucing up his ensuite. Instead, Ruby's bottom found its way, as if mesmerised, down on to the white duvet. It welcomed her with a clean soft sigh and, without thinking, Ruby folded herself into a contented S and was asleep in moments, her red hair like a banner across the pillow.

Ruby didn't dream. She didn't wrap herself in her bedclothes like a shroud. She didn't wake up every hour convinced that Manny was bending over her, deciding whether to opt for the traditional garrotte or the more challenging freehand strangulation. In Tom's airy bedroom, with its crisp blues and whites, Ruby found the peace that had eluded her since she'd spotted Frankie, the guy across a crowded room. She turned over, mewing happily to herself.

Just an hour. That's all she wanted. An hour of peace watched over by the spirit of the Honourable Millicent.

The outlines of the windows glowed cold in the gloom. Ruby sat bolt upright, an unfamiliar check blanket sliding off her torso. 'Ynngh,' she said, dribble icy on her chin. 'Flruh.'

As her surroundings sharpened into focus, Ruby squinted at her watch, its little fluorescent numbers telling her the horrible truth, that it was half past eight at night. 'No, no, noooooo!' she squealed, leaping off the bed and hitting the light switch.

Then she saw the note, propped up against the bedside lamp. Cringing, Ruby approached it bent double with self-loathing. A note meant that Tom had been in. He'd seen her, snoring and dribbling on his bed. His cleaner. On his bed. She presumed the note would give her notice, or warn her of legal action.

> Dear WBC,
>   I feel like one of the three bears. Although I bet they didn't shout 'holy fuck' when they saw Goldilocks. You've obviously had a hard week. Sleep it off and let yourself out when you're done. I've got to get to work (it's usually during the day but tonight is a one-off) so I won't be lurking about downstairs.
>   You look very peaceful.
>   Tom

Ruby was far from peaceful now as she ran about the bedroom like a toddler on hot sand. Yipping with embarrassment she realised that Tom must have laid the blanket over her, and tiptoed out. She had made the poor man feel like an intruder in his own home.

Things got worse when she went downstairs and saw her usual fee sitting tidily on the mantelpiece. Tom had paid her to sleep. Ruby emitted one more grunt of regret and let herself out.

'Joe's worn out, poor kid.' Olivia ruffled her son's silky, ruffleable hair. 'Extra sitar,' she mouthed to Ruby, over his head.

'Ahhh,' answered Ruby conspiratorially, certain that her visa to Heaven was being shredded in some celestial admin office.

'No I'm not, I'm fine,' said Joe, in his customary flat way. 'You doing my dinner or what, Ruby?'

'Joe!' admonished Olivia, who had turned away and was checking herself out in the mirror, peering past the flyers and money-off coupons she'd slipped into the gap between the glass and the frame. What she saw evidently didn't please her. Tutting, she pulled at the velvet gathered skirt and the fluffy jumper she'd excavated for her supper date. 'Don't be so rude. As it happens, yes, Ruby has agreed to give you your dinner.' Sighing, Olivia dashed some peach lipstick on to her lips as if she didn't believe it would do any good but was contractually obliged to do so. 'I've left some marinated tofu in the fridge, and there's a lovely quinoa risotto to go with it.'

Quinoa was, as far as Ruby knew, a war-torn province in Africa. She nodded, and held her bag a little closer to her chest. She wished she could reach out and line Olivia's bright eyes with a khaki pencil, and dust some blush along her high, neglected cheekbones. Tonight Olivia's inner lights were on, and in her flowing muted outfit she reminded Ruby of those warrior queens she banged on about. 'Like your hair,' she said.

'Really?' Olivia sounded incredulous. She raised a hand to the writhing curls tamed tonight by a barrage of clips, staring at them in the mirror as if they'd just appeared. 'I never know what to do with my damned hair. If it wasn't for Hugo I'd have a crew cut.'

Thank goodness for Hugo, thought Ruby. She gave a little smile at the thought of such an oblivious man being sentimental about his wife's hair.

After some last minute toing and froing (Hugo was, apparently, in the wrong crumpled corduroys and was ordered upstairs to change into different crumpled corduroys), Mr and Mrs Friend were waved off the premises.

'Hungry?' asked Ruby.

'Nah. We had that quinoa risotto last night.' A gruesome memory seemed to flit across Joe's face. 'Just some cornflakes, thanks.'

'Or . . .' With a dramatic flourish, Ruby tugged a warm paper bag out of her holdall. In scintillating red lettering the bag spelled out its provenance.

'I've never had Kentucky Fried Chicken before!' squeaked Joe.

'Thought not.' Ruby raced him down to the kitchen.

'Next time, you can cook us something,' murmured Ruby, lying back with a sated, naughty, greasy, post-takeaway feeling.

'I'm not allowed. Mum says it's quicker if she does it herself.' Joe was slumped along the knackered chesterfield, gnawed chicken bones on the bare boards alongside him.

'That's silly, you should . . .' Ruby stopped herself. It was one thing to bring a little childish sparkle into Joe's life, but quite another to ride roughshod over all Olivia's rules. 'OK, no cooking then,' she said. 'Where's the remote?'

'What remote?'

That was how Ruby discovered that Joe wasn't allowed to watch television. This was, she knew, an attempt to protect him from the bilge that flowed through the nation's sitting rooms every night, turning the UK into a nation of binge-drinking, chain-smoking, Simon Cowell-worshipping zombies. She appreciated the Friends' motives, and she respected them. But she reckoned a little soupçon of *I'm a Celebrity . . . Get Me Out Of Here!* couldn't hurt.

'Simon! I've been trying to get hold of you.' Ruby hoicked her bag up on to her shoulder as she pressed her mobile to her ear. The Friends hadn't got back until midnight and now Ruby was dashing across Parsons Green, eager to get in out of the cold. Joe had fallen asleep with his head on her lap and it had been a wrench to wake him and help him up to bed, but she'd managed to destroy all evidence of their E-number, Z-list bonanza.

'I haven't been at work.' Simon sounded muffled, like Ruby's impression of Marlon Brando in *The Godfather*. She didn't do impressions all that often, and she found that nobody clamoured for them in the intervals. 'Is this too late to call? I've been kind of out of it all day.'

'No, it's not too late at all,' Ruby reassured him. 'What's the matter? Is it this flu that everybody's getting?' Instinctively Ruby held the phone a little further from her ear.

'No. I'm fine. I'm calling to make sure you've heard. About Manny.'

The phone was clamped back on to Ruby's ear. 'What about Manny?' she asked in a low, urgent voice.

'He's back in custody.'

It took a moment to compute, and then relief surged through Ruby. 'How come?' she whispered, marvelling that it had happened without her knowledge. She'd been so close to Manny once; now she had to hear about his life second-hand. Surely some kind of wifely telepathy should have alerted her?

'He broke the conditions of his bail.'

'Idiot,' said Ruby, with feeling. It was a word she wouldn't dare use if Manny wasn't behind some nice thick iron bars. 'Simon, I don't know if it's relevant any more, but I was trying to get hold of you to tell you that Manny's having you watched.'

There was a laugh, the kind described in books as 'hollow', from the other end of the phone. 'I figured that.'

'Oh. Really? Why would he do it?'

'He told me he wanted to make sure he was getting his money's worth. And he suspected me of colluding with the police.'

'How ridiculous.' Ruby caught up with the sense of what Simon was saying. 'Hang on, *Manny* told you this?'

'Yes.' Simon sighed. It was a deep, long sound with a reservoir of feeling in it. 'As he was beating the stuffing out of me.'

'NO!' Ruby stopped dead, in the milky light of a street lamp. 'I'm so sorry!'

'Ruby, it's not your fault,' said Simon, sounding stern. 'It's down to Manny and he's paying the price.'

'Is it bad?' winced Ruby.

'Pretty bad. He jumped me in the car park. Gave me a good pounding. He can be vicious.'

'I'm finding that out,' murmured Ruby.

'Cuts. Bruises. A cracked rib. A missing tooth.'

A missing tooth . . . Ruby shuddered at the horror of it. 'That's terrible,' she murmured. 'But Simon, what made him risk jail?' Even if Manny had his doubts about Simon, it would have made far more sense to send one of the guys.

'He made it clear I was getting the personal touch,' said Simon bitterly. 'It was about you.'

'*Me?*' Ruby squawked.

'When Manny heard we were in a bar he assumed it was a date.' Simon laughed again and the lack of a front tooth could plainly be heard in his wry whistle. 'Admittedly, it wasn't for the want of trying on my part. He didn't believe me when I said there was nothing between us.' Simon sounded tired now. 'He's still nuts about you, Ruby.'

Nuts being the operative word. 'Not about me personally,' she said sadly. There was nothing personal about Manny's jealousy: he would have reacted the same way if he'd heard that Simon had fondled his Porsche. 'I'm really, really sorry, Simon.'

'It's not your fault.'

In some Byzantine way, Ruby felt, it must be.

14

'You'll never guess what he's done now!' Drama Queen was waiting to pounce as Ruby put her key in the girl's front door.

'No, I probably won't.' The gritted teeth and the thin lips were lost on Drama Queen, who followed Ruby's stomping progress down the hall to the kitchen.

Over the angry hiss of the hot tap, Drama Queen settled herself down to begin her tale. 'I got home, all upset anyway because of work, you know what's going on there, and he hadn't rung all day and I said to myself, *If he hasn't left a message on the home phone then I'll really kill him this time,* and do you know what?'

Ruby spun round. 'There was no message. You didn't kill him. He went on to do something even worse. You still didn't kill him. Now, do you mind if I get on with the bathroom floor, please?'

Drama Queen went completely still. She wobbled slightly, like a skittle, as Ruby barged past her.

Taking it all out on the bathroom floor, Ruby wondered

if this was how people became horrible. Did everybody start out quite nice really but get beaten down by life and suddenly start stomping and barging and snapping? Since talking to Simon the night before, Ruby was entirely capable of GBH. The injustice seared: Simon was minus a front tooth courtesy of a suburban psycho's paranoia about 'his' woman.

'His' woman was boiling with a rancid mixture of responsibility and revulsion. Ruby, who had never raised her hand to anybody, who experienced post-traumatic stress disorder if she swatted a bluebottle, was now an accomplice to violence, by dint of downing a glass or two of overpriced bubbly in the company of a diminutive solicitor.

Ironically, that made her feel like wringing somebody's neck. 'This is *not* the person I want to be,' growled Ruby, slapping down a wet sponge. It took some more growling and a lot more slapping but Ruby calmed down a little, and began to feel uneasy about the silence. Usually Drama Queen was on in the background, like the radio.

Peeling off her rubber gloves, Ruby went to find her client. Plonking herself on the bed beside Drama Queen, she held out a small peace offering in the shape of a Rolo. 'So. What's he done now?' she asked gently.

'Well,' began Drama Queen, her old self immediately. 'Remember I told you I have a morbid fear of lychees?'

'We've been invited to a girly afternoon,' said Maria, meeting Ruby at the lift door of their apartment. 'Manicures, pedicures, face packs and gossip.'

Lacking girlfriends, Ruby had never experienced anything so exotic as a girly afternoon. 'Sounds good,' she smiled. Her morning with Drama Queen had tired her out. 'But who invited us?'

'Teddy.' Maria tried to keep a straight face but it was

beyond her. 'Obviously, he's not exactly a girl, but he's far girlier than either of us. Should be a laugh.'

Candles flickered and tinkly music played in the master bedroom over the Glove. Teddy was in character already, a towelling turban on his head and a monogrammed silk dressing gown draped over his boxer's build. Beauty products were laid out on towels, and some grim looking manicure tools glinted in the afternoon sun.

'Robes on, ladies!' he ordered benignly, chucking two towelling dressing gowns their way. 'We have a *lot* of beautifying to get through.'

Luminous green face pack on, Ruby reclined on a tattered chaise-longue as Maria attended to her toenails and Teddy fussed over her hands.

'These could be miners' mitts!' he spat, horrified, through the pink pack on his own face. 'Your cuticles are a disgrace, missy. If the nail police were to swoop you'd be in beauty jail for a long, long time.'

Talk of police swoops and jail weren't going to help Ruby relax. 'How did you and Kendall meet?' she asked. It was something she'd often wondered about, imagining Teddy in a polka dot sundress dropping his hanky at a church hop.

'In a bank,' said Teddy, enjoying the surprise on the girls' faces. 'Yes, in my other life I was a cashier in a suit and tie, the very picture of normality.' He paused, emery board in mid-air as he looked into the middle distance of the past. 'Of course, nobody knew about the suspenders under my pinstripes.'

Hooting, Maria splashed Ruby's little toe with cherry red polish. 'I can't see you in a bank, somehow, Teddy.'

'It was over twenty years ago. I was another person.' Teddy set to work on Ruby's nails again, filing like a demon. 'I'd been in the closet so long I had a travel card to Narnia. I was a grenade: if I pulled the string, if I told anybody, I imagined my whole life would blow up around me. I wasn't very brave,' he said, darkly.

'Where does Kendall come into the story?' asked Ruby eagerly, extending her other hand.

'Doesn't she do little things like that elegant-like?' commented Teddy approvingly, taking the proffered fingers. 'Kendall? He was a customer. And a more obvious queer I've yet to encounter.' Teddy took a moment to enjoy the shocked gasps, and to counter Maria's 'You can't say that!' with an, 'I can say what I like, I'm one of them. This was the eighties, girls, and Kendall was a clone. Do you remember them? Big handlebar moustache, leather cap with a chain across it, and tight tight tight leather trews. Oh, you can laugh,' he scolded as Ruby and Maria hooted. 'He looked *gorgeous*. Clean jaw. Piercing eyes. And, yes, his trousers squeaked but nobody's perfect.'

'Did you fancy him?' Maria cut to the chase with her usual speed.

'I was in denial. Still doing my best to find lady newsreaders sexually desirable.'

'Didn't your family guess?' Ruby was amazed that anybody could have believed the burly man in the face pack to be heterosexual.

'My mother thought I hadn't found the right girl yet.'

Ruby butted in. 'When in fact you *were* the right girl.'

'Oi, cheeky.' Teddy tapped Maria on her nose with the emery board. 'Dad wasn't a very hands-on father. I don't think he could have picked me out in a line-up, never mind divine my secret sexual orientation.'

'The story!' said Ruby impatiently. 'The bank. Kendall in leather. You in a suit. Carry on.'

'Right. I started to notice that this gay gentleman was always in my queue. Very polite he was, very direct. Just like he is now. And he started to come in for little things he could have done over the phone, like checking his balance, or ordering a new chequebook.'

'He fancied you!' sang Maria.

'What's not to fancy?' pouted Teddy. 'Like I say, I was too dumb to read the signs. I knew something was going on, I just didn't know what.'

'And meanwhile you were still trying to imagine Moira Stewart in her underthings,' prompted Maria.

'Yes, guttermouth,' admitted Teddy. 'But I would never be so gross about the lovely Ms Stewart. I was more of a Sue Lawley man.'

'Story! Story!' demanded Ruby.

Unscrewing a bottle of pale nail polish, Teddy carried on. 'One afternoon, while I was stamping his chit – and for once that's not a *double entendre* – Kendall asked me, very formally, to join him for a beer after work.'

'Oooh!' said both girls together.

'You're a fabulous audience,' said Teddy approvingly. 'So I goes *Yes* and he goes *Good, see you at the Speckled Cow* and I goes –' Teddy drew in his breath sharply. 'The Speckled Cow was a gay pub, you see. And I thought, he knows. This little sod knows my blackest deepest darkest –'

'Bleeding obvious . . .' muttered Maria.

'– secret!' finished Teddy. 'I got there, in me suit, all buttoned up and nervous as hell. He was already there. We talked. Not about anything, really. I made him laugh. I remember that. I remember how it felt to make this serious chap laugh. And then he leaned over and said, all meaningful like, "Do you like it here?"' Teddy stopped painting Ruby's nails and put his chin in his hand. 'And I looks around, at all these men, some of them dressed like visitors from another planet, some of them dressed like me. I see them all laughing and talking and *relaxing* and I goes, "Yes, Kendall, I love it here."' He cocked his head to one side. 'And the rest is history.'

'Aww,' said Ruby, far more delighted with the story than she was with her polish-splattered feet and half-finished hands. 'How lovely.' She was avid for detail about people. There was a terrible lack of information about how her own parents got together. When pressed, her mother had only offered un-connected phrases like 'church youth club', 'minibus' and 'dreadful eczema'. Perhaps more detail about her parents' early days would have given her more insight into relationships, and stopped her screwing up so spectacularly.

And perhaps it wouldn't.

'It was. It was lovely,' agreed Teddy, standing up to stretch in his robe. 'It still is. But lately . . .' He turned suddenly to Maria, asking her greedily, 'Have you noticed anything funny lately? About Kendall?'

There was a moment of silence, before Maria said, 'Well, yeah, as you ask. He's very moody.'

'I knew it!' Teddy was triumphant and defeated all in the same breath. 'He's not happy. I knew it. You've noticed too. What about you?' He spun round to Ruby on the chaise-longue.

Taking Maria's lead, Ruby tried to be honest too. 'He does seem to be under a lot of strain.'

'We argue all the time.' Teddy let out a fruity groan. 'Not like we used to, not silly rows. These are proper arguments. He never tells me I look good in a stage outfit.' He flashed a look at Maria. 'And don't say that's because I don't look good in a stage outfit, missy.'

'Wouldn't dare,' smiled Maria.

They all heard the feet on the stairs, and entered into a

sudden unspoken pact to act normal. When Kendall stuck his neat head around the door he saw a scene that could have come straight from a harem.

'Ah. The girly afternoon,' he said, in a bored voice. 'I could smell the Dettol at the front door.'

'It's not easy looking this good,' twittered Teddy, back in character.

'And it's not good looking that easy,' answered Kendall. He looked at his watch, half his body inserted into the room. 'You haven't forgotten the boiler man's coming at four?'

'How could I?' cooed Teddy.

'We've just been hearing,' said Ruby hurriedly as Kendall started to retreat, 'how you two met.'

'More than twenty years ago,' said Maria, beaming approval.

'To be precise,' said Kendall, 'twenty-one years, nine months, two weeks and four days ago.' He closed the door behind him and nobody spoke until they heard the front door slam.

'What he said was nice . . .' started Ruby encouragingly.

'It was the way he said it,' sighed Teddy.

'He said it,' said Maria wading in fearlessly, 'as if he didn't like it.'

'It's just a phase.' Ruby undermined the certainty of her tone with an 'Isn't it?' to Maria, as they strolled back to Hannah House.

Picking errant flakes of face pack from the sides of her nose, Maria said, 'How the hell would I know? If you want me to tell you everything will be all right, I can't. Life isn't like that.'

Ruby *did* want to be told everything – or at least the important bits – would be all right. She'd cobbled together the framework of a life since that day the CID popped in, and now an unseen hand was wobbling it. 'Teddy and Kendall love each other. That's what binds people together in the end.'

'Don't you find,' began Maria, in a tone that warned something cold blooded was coming up, 'that usually one person does more of the loving than the other?'

'Can't you see the glass half full for five minutes?' begged Ruby.

'If it is, it's half full of sick.'

'Lovely. Glad I asked.'

'Sorry. I'm a bit of an Eeyore.' Maria grabbed Ruby's arm and swung off it, like a handbag. 'I should be cheering you up. The divorce. Simon. All that pooey stuff.'

'Where's your pooey stuff?' asked Ruby, wishing she'd taken the time to phrase her question better.

'I beg your pudding?'

'You know what I mean. In one way I know lots about you but in another way . . .'

'I am an international woman of mystery.'

'You can offload on me, you know.' Ruby looked earnestly down at her dinky chum. 'I am . . .' she hesitated over the cheesy words: 'here for you.' She pulled an appalled face, mirrored by the one Maria pulled.

'Oh Gawd, don't,' spluttered Maria. 'It always tickles my gag reflex when people start spouting stuff like that.'

'Sorry. You know what I mean.'

'Luckily, I do.' Maria squeezed the arm that was tucked through her own. 'You're the one who needs therapy. Feeling guilty about what that . . .' she faltered. Ruby had asked her to stop describing Manny with swear words and she seemed to be struggling. 'About what that *naughty fellow* has done. You've got to cut out the pointless guilt. Promise?'

'Promise,' said Ruby weakly.

*

137

Ruby searched for the note straight away. Best to get it over and done with. Today might be her last day at the Honourable Millicent's.

WBC,
　There's been a tomato/cheese orgy in my grill, and I can't get rid of the evidence. Could you have a go with your superhuman cleaning skills? Ta.
　Oh, and do try to stay awake . . .
　Tom

The little house received the Beethoven of cleans, the Taj Mahal, the *Mona Lisa*, the *Sex and the City* boxed set of goings over. Every inch of Tom's domain was wiped and rinsed and pampered.

Finally satisfied, Ruby allowed herself a peek at the noticeboard. The snap of his pecs had been removed (boo!) but a scribbled memo about his work had been added (hurrah!). It begged more questions than it answered, however: 'COLLECT NEW WORK SHOES! DON'T FORGET!!'

A career that demanded both a BA and special shoes? Ruby was confounded.

'I need more clients,' moaned Ruby, screwing the paper she'd been scribbling on into a ball and aiming it at the back of Maria's head as her lodger enjoyed *Countdown*.

'Sums not adding up?'

'Nope. Maybe I need to sell this place after all.'

Maria shifted around so that she could see Ruby, whose head was now resting on the nice cool dining table. 'Really?' she asked warily, as two men in tank tops who had never had a girlfriend unscrambled an anagram on the screen. 'You'll give me decent notice, won't you?'

'Notice?' The word alarmed Ruby. 'You're bloody coming with me.' It wasn't a joke. Ruby had had enough change in her life to last until the menopause.

'Oh, I am, am I?' Maria arched an eyebrow. But, Ruby noted, it was a delighted and gratified eyebrow. 'Have you heard from that house you left a card at yesterday morning?'

'The one with the rocking horse in the window. No.' Ruby's phone buzzed and she jerked her head up. 'Ooh, Maria, you're a witch. I don't recognise the number. Bet it's them.' Ruby picked up her mobile and said 'Hello' in a voice that Maria referred to as 'Ruby's phone voice': nice, approachable and just a smidgeon less common than she really was.

Swivelling back to the duel of the Mummy's boys on *Countdown*, Maria didn't see Ruby's face lose all its colour.

'All right, babes?' said Manny's deep, familiar, yet half forgotten voice.

'Oh my God.'

'Not quite. Just your husband. I suppose you heard about my spot of bother.'

'I heard you bashed up Simon,' whispered Ruby urgently, darting looks at Maria. She instantly regretted that 'bashed up': it sounded like a 1950s housewife.

'He was asking for it. Frankie told me how cosy you were. All over each other.'

'What?'

'I never had you down as a slut, babes. The minute my back's turned. Thanks a lot.'

'I'm not—' Ruby closed her mouth with a snap of her teeth. This time Manny wouldn't lure her into defending something she hadn't done. 'Where are you calling from?' She bit her lip. 'Are you out?'

'Nope. It's all very civilised inside these days. I'm allowed to make some calls. But sooner or later I *will* be out, babes. You know me well enough to guess that it'll be sooner. Then I intend to clean house. My house. The one you're squatting in.'

'This is my home,' quavered Ruby. 'And it's perfectly clean.'

'You know exactly what I'm referring to, Miss Innocent.'

'I don't, and I don't want to. I've changed the security codes.'

'Oh no,' deadpanned Manny coolly. 'That'll definitely keep a law-abiding individual like me out. Forget I spoke.'

'I was with Simon that evening because I'd set a divorce in motion, Manny.'

'Don't like that word,' laughed Manny. It sounded like a genuine laugh, and Ruby took time off from being shit scared to admire his detachment. 'Ain't gonna happen. But you do whatever turns you on, babes, and like I say, I'll pay you a little conjugal visit and we'll sort out all these misunderstandings.'

'You've stopped pretending to love me,' noted Ruby dismally. She felt lost, no longer able to strategise, and she was tired of editing what she said to her own husband.

'I never pretended nothing,' said Manny, each word a bullet. 'I've always been straight with you. You're mine. I love you like I did the day I met you. If only you'd get that into your thick skull everything would be all right.'

'Give my love to Tania,' said Ruby, switching her phone off.

Maria, who presumably could ignore a bullfight behind her if *Countdown* was on, turned her head to ask, 'Was that the rocking horse people?'

'No,' said Ruby, wiping her eyes. 'It was somebody else. Someone from my past.'

'Right,' said Maria, half listening.

'I hope,' whispered Ruby.

15

The house was empty. There was no answer to Ruby's yodelled 'Hellooo!' She found Mrs Vine out in the garden, doing something with secateurs and the kind of trug that Ruby had only seen in old films. 'Weather like this makes me wish I had a garden,' smiled Ruby, taking out a tray with a pitcher of lemonade and two glasses on it.

'Oh. You *are* thoughtful.' Mrs Vine held out a gnarled hand for a drink. 'Don't you have a garden, dear? What a shame. In one of those high rises, are you?' she tutted.

High rise it certainly was, but Hannah House was far from the slum in the sky that Mrs Vine was evidently visualising. Ruby thought it best to indulge her client: a cleaner who lived in an apartment that was worth more than her house would only confuse the traditionally minded old lady. ''Fraid so. Thought I'd give the utility room a seeing to today,' she said, with far more enthusiasm than might be expected. 'And if I have time I'll get down the good crockery and freshen it up.'

'Very good, very good.' Mrs Vine sipped her lemonade.

'We used to go to the South of France every May, you know. Avoid the crowds.'

'Are you going away this year?'

'Oh dear no.' Mrs Vine looked as if Ruby had suggested a little light bestiality. 'I can't leave this place. What if somebody comes? I like to spoil my family when they visit.'

The blameless sky suddenly frowned at this, and clouds appeared from nowhere. 'We'd better get in,' said Ruby. 'Looks like rain.' She gathered up the tray and the trug and the secateurs and preceded Mrs Vine across the lawn.

Nobody would come. Ruby knew that now. Nobody ever came. Presumably there were phone calls – *hopefully* there were – but there were no visitors to this comfortable house. Ruby fetched the stepladder to reach the chilly high shelves where the best, unused dinner service lived.

With a series of the sort of whoops and yowls that might be expected from a squirrel trapped in a dishwasher, Ruby was whirled across the chipped quarry tiles of number fourteen's basement kitchen.

Grimly determined, Joe concentrated on his footwork, forcing out 'one two three, one two three,' between gritted teeth as he manhandled his babysitter in wobbly circles.

'Aargh. Ouch. Eeek,' recited Ruby as Joe bounced her off the washing machine, barged her into the table and finally deposited her in the recycling bin as the wheels came off his attempt at a waltz.

'I'll never get it,' he whined, thumping his leg in frustration. 'I'm not going back.'

'You're improving every week.' Ruby longed to rub the bruise blossoming in the small of her back but managed not to. 'You've got talent, Joe. Honest.'

Changing his attitude abruptly, Joe grinned. 'Do you think I could go in for competitions?'

'Definitely.' *In about thirty years' time*, Ruby added silently, giving in and rubbing her back surreptitiously. Joe had rhythm, but he also seemed to have extra feet, most of them left. Ruby intuitively felt that encouragement at this early stage was vital. After all, Miss Delmar had praised his 'precision' last week, earning Joe an envious glance from the competitive Suzie. 'Suzie's nice, isn't she?' Ruby felt that Suzie was about as nice as shingles, but she had a suspicion she wanted to explore.

Throwing himself full length on the sagging sofa like a stuntman, Joe offered only a studied 'Mmm' in reply.

'Do you like her?' asked Ruby casually, feigning deep interest in her cuticles.

'S'pose. She's quite . . .' Joe pouted. 'Prettyish,' he finally conceded.

She shoots, she scores. Ruby was right. Quietly triumphant, she hid her smile from Joe.

Joe had moved on. 'I'm *starving*,' he moaned. He looked at his watch. 'We'd better order now if we're going to finish the takeaway and get rid of the evidence before Mum and Dad come home.'

Such a glib admission of their criminality took Ruby aback. A pang of conscience made her ask, 'Why don't we just heat up the quiche and have that?'

'Yeah,' laughed Joe, reaching for the Chinese menu he'd tucked behind a poster of Martin Luther King. 'Right.'

Later, as Joe slept in his tidy room, with the moon glowing through his blind and his dance shoes wrapped in a scarf under his bed, Ruby sat in the kitchen, her feet tucked beneath her on the sofa.

The old, oversized clock above the cooker ticked and

tocked the silence away. Ruby was tired enough to appreci-ate the softness of the cushions that didn't match, and awake enough to enjoy the calm of the rambling, empty house. She loved this house, she thought. And she loved the little man upstairs.

She loved Joe, this house, and she loved the Friends. The fact that none of them loved her back wasn't important. Ruby was proving Maria's theory: hers was a lopsided love affair but none the worse for that.

It was an hour that the Friends thought of as scandalously late (Hugo had insisted on giving her an extra tenner when they'd tapped up the stairs to the front door) but which was still half an hour from closing time at the Glove.

Reluctant to be alone, and reluctant to examine why, Ruby pushed through the packed bodies, most of whom were dancing as if they'd been electrified, and quite recently.

Up on the bar, high kicking in heels that Ruby would have found it difficult to stand still in, Teddy seemed back to his old self. His outfit had a flamenco theme extending, as Ruby could plainly see, to ruffled knickers.

'You're not getting a cocktail tonight.' Kendall's voice sounded in Ruby's ear, cutting through the sweaty fug of the music.

'Oh. OK.' Ruby managed a laugh, surprised by his blunt rudeness.

'Not with that face,' said Kendall, producing a mug. 'Alcohol won't help. But hot chocolate might.'

'You're a very wise man.' Ruby was impressed that someone who seemed to ignore her most of the time could read her so efficiently. 'How are things?' She gestured towards Teddy, who had produced castanets.

'So-so.' Kendall shrugged, and leaned on the bar so that

their faces were closer and Ruby didn't have to strain to hear. 'Sorry you've had to witness our scenes. Teddy is . . .' Kendall rolled the words around his mouth before letting them go. 'Teddy is a very *needy* man,' he said, carefully. 'Just like the little girl in the nursery rhyme, when he's good, he's very very good, but when he's bad he's horrid. But there's nobody with a bigger heart.' He glanced up at his gyrating lover. 'Or arse, come to that.' Ignoring the playful slap that Ruby dared to deliver to his wrist, Kendall said, 'He's also a bottomless pit when it comes to attention. And reassurance. It would be nice if we could get on an even keel and just coast for a while. It's always a drama. With lots of costume changes.' Perhaps Kendall noticed the effect his words had on Ruby, because he straightened up and said briskly, 'But I knew what I was getting myself into two decades ago when I signed on the dotted line.'

It wasn't enough for Ruby. She needed effusiveness. She needed certainty. Kendall's resigned acceptance was paltry. The man had love and security (albeit with a bloke in flamenco knickers): why didn't he appreciate it?

If ever I find it, Ruby promised herself, I will appreciate it. And I will hang on tight.

16

The statutory cup of tea prepared by Olivia and drunk by Ruby was becoming more bearable. It felt less stagy with each week, and Ruby was surprised by how much she had in common with her client. 'Yeah, me too,' she nodded, delighted, when Olivia confessed to a 'thing' about umbrellas. 'I love them, but I always lose them.'

'I thought I was the only person who lost umbrellas!' Olivia gawped at Ruby. 'Once Hugo bought me a gorgeous one, black, shaped like a birdcage, with a bamboo handle, and I left it on the bus the very first time I took it out.'

'I managed to leave one on the big wheel in Littlehampton,' said Ruby proudly. 'I buy the cheapo ones they sell in chemists' these days.'

'Me too,' agreed Olivia sadly. 'Or I just get wet.'

The two women giggled together, and Ruby felt the gulf between them shrink.

But then Olivia opened it up again by sniggering about Hugo bringing home 'one of those rubbish magazines' by mistake. '*OK*! I think it was. Dreadful tosh. Who wants to read all about celebrities' pathetic love lives?'

'Who indeed?' mused Ruby, a woman who jumped up and down on the spot waiting for the newsagent to open on Thursdays.

A rhythmic tapping on the stairs announced Joe. A quick glare from Ruby and he clunked in, not at all ballroom-dancer-like. 'All right?' he mumbled.

'A *hello* is too much to ask?' grumbled Olivia, pushing her glasses into the maelstrom of her hair. 'How was school?'

'All right.'

Raising her eyes conspiratorially at Ruby, Olivia prodded her son on the arm. 'I asked you a question. May I have a proper answer? How was choir?'

'Choir was cr-awful.'

With a sharp look for the word he'd almost said, Olivia tutted. 'Just because it's not the yowling you get on *Top of the Pops* doesn't mean it's awful, Joe.'

'*Top of the Pops* isn't on any more.' Joe pinched an apple from a bowl on the dresser.

'Did you hang around with Lucian at playtime?'

'Yeah.'

'Good.' Olivia said in an aside to Ruby. 'Lucian's father is very active on the Race Relations Board, and Lucian himself is something of a prodigy with woodwind.'

'Lovely,' said Ruby approvingly, conjuring up a boy whom Manny would deem 'a right twonk'.

'Joe and Lucian are very close,' said Olivia, ignoring a warning '*Mu-um!*' from her son. 'I keep telling him, men can be friends.' She coughed slightly and said, rather woodenly, as if rehearsing lines, 'They can be more than friends.' Olivia turned to Joe and told him earnestly, 'You know it's OK if you're gay, poppet.'

Joe groaned and threw himself on the sofa as if he'd been shot by a sniper behind the recycling bin. 'Shut uuuuuup!' he begged.

'Isn't it, Ruby?' Olivia turned to her cleaner for moral support. 'Isn't it absolutely fine, and actually rather nice, if Joe is homosexual?'

'Of course.' Ruby nodded enthusiastically, able to state quite sincerely that some of her best friends were gay. *But Joe isn't,* she added vehemently to herself. Didn't Olivia know her own son? His heart belonged to Suzie, scowling, carping, female Suzie. She looked over at Joe, and they shared a secret smile.

*

Dear WBC,
    I notice you 'did' the loft last week. That must have taken longer than usual, so please accept an extra tenner from Elvis today.
    Do you have a temper to match that red hair?
    Tom

'Cheeky sod,' thought Ruby, delightedly, with a backdated blush for the time Tom had seen her fast asleep. The irony was that she'd happily clean Tom's house for free.

That thought sideswiped her. 'Why would I?' she wondered. Ruby needed the money (*OK!*s don't grow on trees) and she'd never even met Tom. And she would certainly never meet the Honourable Millicent Flatbush. Was it because he had superlative pecs? Because he flirted with her via the medium of Post-It notes? *Was she really that easily captivated?*

The answer, apparently, was a resounding 'yes'.

*

'I have important news.' Miss Delmar looked at each of her pupils in turn, fixing them with a glare that dared them to move, sneeze, breathe audibly or otherwise insult her. She patted her immovable perm before announcing, 'We have been invited to take part in the borough variety show at the town hall on the twelfth of September!'

Joe gasped and even Suzie gulped. The dancers all looked excitedly over at their adults on the hard chairs across the hall. Ruby caught Joe's eye and sent him a breathy 'Wow!'

'We must work. Like dogs!' roared Miss Delmar, stamping her foot.

Ruby jumped. Miss Delmar frightened the tripe out of her, but Joe seemed to thrive under her dictatorial guidance. She watched her charge stand to attention and then hold his head just so, and his torso just so, and extend his arms elegantly around the waiting Suzie. Joe had discovered poise. Under her breath, Ruby counted with him. '*One* two three, *one* two three.'

Some people achieve inner calm by meditating; Ruby's mother had achieved it by sucking Fisherman's Friends; Maria achieved it by watching David Beckham take free kicks and saying 'God, I so would' under her breath; Ruby achieved it by cleaning.

It had been a quiet weekend, enlivened only by a special Sunday lunch of fish, chips and all the little extras the chipper could muster (Ruby regretted the pickled egg but had grown to love the battered pineapple). Ruby was glad it was Monday and she could get back to work.

First on her agenda, as ever, was the flat over the Glove. The loud snores wafting like alien music down the stairs told her that Teddy was still enjoying his beauty sleep, and the state of the sitting room told her another story.

Empty bottles littered the carpet like downed skittles. Whisky, wine, sangria, curaçao – the partygoers had certainly been game. Gathering them up as quietly as she could, Ruby marvelled that the men had had time to entertain. They worked, as Kendall tirelessly repeated, every hour that God sent.

'Could you turn the noise down to "loud"?' begged Teddy, with the sticky diction of the furry-tongued, from the doorway.

'Quite a do. How many people did you have round?'

'This carnage is mine and mine alone,' said Teddy, with hung-over pride. 'Yes, I mixed the whisky with the wine, the wine with the curaçao and the martini with the grappa. Let me tell you, after the fifteenth glass they all taste *wonderful*!' He threw an expansive arm, and then winced with regret and held his head. 'My brain feels like Ozzy Osbourne's in there, trying to sing his way out.'

Ruby crossed to the kitchen and cobbled together a carb-heavy breakfast. As Teddy picked at it from a tray, she probed a little. 'What were you celebrating?'

'Darling,' Teddy waved a morsel of fried egg sandwich. 'Nobody drinks on their tod to *celebrate*. I was consoling myself.' He dabbed his eyes with the froufrou collar of his robe. 'Kendall was missing, you see. Could have been dead. Could have been split in half on a level crossing somewhere. He wasn't answering his phone. Not to me, anyway.' Teddy took a large and spiteful bite of the sandwich. 'The sod had the cheek to come home healthy, when I'd planned me funeral outfit. Black takes years off me.'

'Where had he been?' This was very unusual behaviour. Ruby could – and occasionally did – set her watch by Kendall.

'Thinking.' Teddy scoffed. He was a seasoned scoffer and did it well. 'Walking and thinking, apparently.'

'That sounds . . .' Ruby couldn't put a word to how it sounded, apart from *unlikely*.

'Like a sack of shit?' Teddy was more prosaic. 'That's what

I said. Snogging, maybe. Shagging, certainly. But walking and thinking? I'm sorry, but nobody walks all night.'

Wiping the mirror over the fireplace, Ruby studied Teddy's face in it as he said, 'I told him, you're out on your ear, mate, if you don't pull your socks up.'

The voice was bold: the woebegone face in the mirror anything but.

The day ran away with Ruby. Mrs Vine held her up by chatting on her step, oblivious to Ruby's need to tube it into town and meet her divorce lawyer. Ruby had loyally loitered, unwilling to spoil Mrs Vine's pleasure in announcing the upcoming visit from her niece. She made it sound like a state visit from a monarch: rugs would be beaten, best china fetched, gooses cooked. Ruby had almost missed her train.

It was peculiar passing Simon's office. She'd looked in on him, gasped at his bruises and apologised for the umpty-fifth time. One of Ruby's wishes had been granted: the lecherous light in Simon's eye had died, replaced by a wariness that was much harder to take. Her jokey, 'Maybe we can risk a drink again some time?' had been met with muted panic.

The meeting with her divorce lawyer had been difficult too. Not because of Sheila, a lively woman who didn't know that gigantic bosoms and pussycat bows are incompatible. Sheila did an admirable job of explaining the intricacies of matrimonial law, but still Ruby fidgeted as if her chair was upholstered with quills.

Discussing divorce was all wrong: Ruby was programmed to be married for ever and ever, like the fairy tale princesses she'd emulated. Now that she'd cranked legal cogs into life, Ruby just wanted it all to be over.

'It's not that simple,' Sheila had told her, a motherly look on her face.

'But I don't want anything from him,' Ruby had reiterated. 'Not a bean. I just want to be free.'

'Mr Gallagher has declined to send an acknowledgement of service. That means,' Sheila must have caught Ruby's dumb look, 'that your husband hasn't sent us a response to the document we sent him, setting out your reasons for divorce. If he'd respond, we could proceed, but now we need to put some pressure on him.'

'I just want to get away from him,' Ruby repeated, forlornly. 'How long can he tie me up in knots for?'

Sheila had sidestepped the question but her middle-aged fortitude was reassuring. 'You'll get your freedom.'

The word *eventually* had hung in the air.

Now it was twilight. The first day of June was dwindling as she dashed across the green, determined not to be late for the Bachelor. Ruby had left her jacket behind for the first time since she'd bought it, and all around her London was unfurling for what promised to be a hot summer.

Yet still Ruby's buttocks were clenched, as was her mind. She tried to focus on her work: *that* was always 'there' for her.

Haranguing herself for not bringing her tools and uniform out with her, Ruby crossed the quiet lobby of Hannah House, her boots tip-tapping on the marble floor. A figure in her peripheral vision rose slowly from a chair. Ruby didn't panic because the figure was so small: it definitely wasn't guy-shaped. She glanced at it as she called her lift. She stared. Ruby would have preferred a guy. A platoon of guys would have been preferable to the sight of Tania crossing the lobby with a baby in her arms.

17

The first word belonged to Maria, passing the lift doors as they opened, a bundle of dirty washing in her arms. 'Eh? No way! You're having a laugh, Tania. Fuck off, and do it now and do it quickly, yeah?' she jabbered, unleashing an avalanche of knickers and bras and combat trousers on to the floor.

Stepping over the grubby pile, Ruby preceded her guest into the sitting room. 'She's got something to say, apparently,' she muttered, winded by this unexpected turn of events. Hoping that Tania couldn't see her discomfort, Ruby tried to pull herself together double quick, to fit an hour or two's hyperventilating into the time it took her to reach the sofa. 'Take a seat,' she said, as politely as one could when one wanted to hurl one's visitor out of one's picture window.

Tania sat on the edge of the sofa, laying her sleeping son carefully among the cushions. The white blanket wrapped around him fell open, and Ruby managed to pixellate the baby's face. She planned to get through this whole painful interview without fixing his features in her mind.

'You look as if you've seen a ghost,' said Tania, in her flinty accent.

Before Ruby could reply, Maria was at her side and answering for her. 'You've got a nerve, Tania. What could you possibly have to say that Ruby wants to hear?'

Impaling Maria with a glare, Tania said with complete self-possession, 'I could say a lot, an awful lot, that Ruby might be very interested in. Couldn't I, Maria, me old mucker?' She flicked her attention to Ruby. 'Does she have to stay? It's like having a Rottweiler in the room.'

Considering for a moment, Ruby turned to Maria. 'Can you give us a minute?' she asked, a pleading look in her eye. Ruby didn't like Tania's bossy manner but she'd decided to hear her out. She reached for Maria's hand and gave it a squeeze. 'Please,' she said.

With a throaty harrumph, Maria backed towards her discarded washing. 'I'll be in the kitchen if you want me.'

'With your little Italian ear pressed to the door, no doubt.' Tania raised her voice as Maria left the room. She bent down to scrabble in her bag, producing a toddler cup and a chopped apple.

Ruby took the opportunity to look Tania over. She'd never really taken much notice of her before, believing her to be 'just' the manageress of Manhattan Nights. Small and muscular, Tania's smooth brown limbs reminded her of Maria. Tania had the same springy strength, but their faces were very different. Maria's Mediterranean eyes had soul: Tania's face was pinched. Glamorous, modern, the hard-edged Tania somehow lacked any vestige of beauty.

Or, Ruby wondered, could that be jealousy talking?

Now it was Tania talking. 'I've come to ask you a favour.'

'Fine. Whatever. Do you want to borrow my hairdryer?' Ruby wrapped her arms around herself. She gave herself permission to be 'mouthy' with Tania, but her anger made her feel poisoned.

'Very funny. Hilarious.' Tania had a steady gaze, like a cobra. 'The favour is this: don't divorce Manny. Not yet.'

That took a moment to compute. Manny's mistress was asking her not to divorce him. 'You should be delighted. He's all yours when the decree nisi comes through.' Ruby hoped she'd pronounced the legal term correctly.

'You're breaking him,' said Tania, in a voice so clipped it could cut diamonds. 'He's got a lot on his plate at the moment.'

'Prison food, mostly,' murmured Ruby, quietly pleased with her quick thinking until she saw Tania's unmoved face. 'Sorry. Cheap jibe.'

'He still loves you.' Tania said it as easily as if she was telling Ruby the time. Only a jiggle of the sippy cup hinted at what might be going on inside. 'Do you want to break his heart?'

The easy, mouthy answer was a loud 'yes', but Ruby knew she would be lying. 'I'm going ahead with it. You've had a wasted journey.' She stood up. 'Sorry to throw you out, but I'm late for a job.'

'What, cleaning?' For the first time Tania smiled, and a sour little parody it was. 'I thought Manny was taking the mick when he told me. Lady Muck the cleaner. Who'd have thought it?'

'Me. I'd have thought it.' Ruby was liking Tania less and less, and she hadn't been that fond of her to begin with. 'I love cleaning. It's honest,' she said, with meaning. 'It's useful.'

'Listen to you.' Tania shook her head wonderingly. Her body language wasn't that of a woman preparing to go. It was more that of a woman preparing to dig her heels in.

'*Useful.* Where did this conscience come from all of a sudden? You weren't so particular when you were spending Manny's money, were you, love?'

'I'm not your love,' said Ruby coolly. It was tempting to describe how uneasy she'd felt during her marriage, to tell Tania that now, at long last, she felt as if she was presenting her real face to the world, but Ruby stopped herself. Some instinct warned her not to reveal too much to this woman. 'And my conscience is none of your business. Go back and tell Manny that I'm going ahead with the divorce, but he's not to worry. I don't want a penny.'

'Nah,' drawled Tania, settling back into the sofa. 'You don't want a thing. Except this million-pound property.' She skewered Ruby with another of her looks. 'You're doing all right out of his ill-gotten gains, aren't you?'

There were many irritating things about Tania, but the most annoying one was the fact that she was right. Ownership of the apartment, even though it was all perfectly legal and above board, was a niggly thorn in Ruby's side, one that kept her awake at night. 'I didn't ask him to sign it over to me,' she said, lifting her chin. Parroting Maria's rationale, she went on, 'It was a gift. He did it of his own free will.'

'Whatever.' Tania's use of the banal word was eloquent. She turned to the baby, who had begun to make soft snuffling noises. 'What is it, Alfie? You all right, cupcake?' The endearment sounded clunky in Tania's streetwise voice, but the love was obvious.

'How old is he?' asked Ruby before her self-censoring equipment could kick in. She still hadn't focused on his face.

'Just one,' said Tania, with a glimmer of pride. She turned to face Ruby with bravado. 'Manny dotes on him. You should see them together.'

Genuinely interested as well as genuinely hurt, Ruby frowned. 'Why do you want to say stuff like that to me? I've never done anything to you.'

'You're in the way, Ruby, as sodding usual.'

Something had gone awry here. The mistress was ticking off the wife. 'I'm just living my life.'

'You were in the way when you lived with Manny, treating him like dirt, making him look elsewhere, and now you're in the way again, insisting on a divorce just when it will look bad for him in court.'

'Whoah!' Ruby held up one pale hand, to halt the runaway train of Tania's bile. 'Treat Manny like dirt? I was a bloody geisha. I ran his baths. I made his favourite meals. I massaged his flipping verrucas, for flip's sake.' Months of living with Maria hadn't improved Ruby's cursing prowess.

'And nagged him to buy you more stuff. And refused to sleep with him. I know all about it, love.'

'I'm no more your love than I was a minute ago,' said Ruby, through lips as thin as Tania's thighs. 'And if you really want to believe that Manny and I didn't sleep together while you were having your scuzzy little "love" affair, that's up to you.' Ruby felt like a Renaissance saint tied to a tree while the local heathens enjoyed target practice. The air was thick with the sound of whizzing arrows and that last one had struck her right in the heart: Ruby's memories of the way she and Manny made love was one of the few untarnished relics of their marriage. That aspect of their relationship had never waned, never faltered, had scared her each time with its perfection and intensity. The look in Manny's eyes when they held each other had been one of the main reasons she had taken so long to accept the truth about him.

'You know what I *really* want.' Tania was making an effort

not to sound tired. 'You know what Manny needs. He said you're hiding it. His insurance policy.'

'All the papers were left in Château Rubes.' Ruby was weary and, on a shallower level, bored. 'Tell him to talk to Simo—' She pulled herself up short. 'To whoever is looking after him.'

'This is between you and him.' Tania leaned forward, and her top gaped to display those twin assets that had so charmed Manny back in the neon dark of Manhattan Nights. 'He said you'd know what he meant. *His insurance policy*,' she repeated meaningfully.

Folding her arms in what she hoped was a schoolmarmy fashion, Ruby said, clearly and carefully, 'I have no idea what you're on about. Manny never involved me in the money side of things. You know what he's like. The man is full of secrets.'

'He said,' repeated Tania, grimly, 'that you'd know what he meant. And Manny doesn't make mistakes.'

Ruby looked Tania up and down slowly. 'Oh, I think he does.'

'Are you going to give him the insurance?' Tania was getting worked up, and beside her Alfie stirred and grizzled. 'Am I wasting my time?' snapped Tania. 'Are you going ahead with the divorce?'

'That's none of your business.' Ruby's forehead was starting to throb. 'Christ, Tania, he's doing a number on you just like he did on me. He's got you doing his dirty work, coming here to talk me out of divorcing him even though, deep down, you *can't wait* for me to do it.' The flicker of Tania's stare confirmed Ruby's suspicions. 'You want me out of the picture. You want him to yourself. But you sit there, degrading yourself because he's told you to. What does that tell you about him? How could a man claim to love you, and then make you grovel to his wife?'

'Who mentioned love?' Tania was all action now, zipping her bag and scooping up her son. 'It's only the likes of you princesses who think the world runs on love. *This*,' she brandished Alfie like a trophy as she stood up, 'keeps Manny with me. And that's where I've got one over on you, Ruby Gallagher. And I always will.'

Speedily deciding against the retort *You really are horrid, aren't you* as being possibly too childish and definitely too mild, Ruby flinched as she took in Alfie's yawning face for the first time. 'Ohhh, he looks like Manny!' she said, in a voice too soft for the occasion. The little boy was beautiful, with a petulant pink mouth and eyes of the most serene blue.

'And he's mine. Not yours, you barren cow.' Tania evidently wasn't there to make friends. She strode across the room, every step a noisy insult to the slick floor. 'Couldn't give Manny what he really wanted, could you?'

More lies. Ruby didn't feel motivated to enlighten Tania: chuck her down the lift shaft, yes. Enlighten her, no. Just as Ruby's head drooped, Maria emerged from the kitchen.

'Don't let us hold you up,' she smiled at Tania. 'Do call again. Next time I'll bake a cake.'

'Go fuck yourself,' said Tania over her son's head of blond curls.

'No, no, the pleasure was all ours.' Maria pressed the button to call the lift.

As the doors closed over her, Tania spat, 'He wants that insurance, Ruby.'

With a sudden flurry of movement and a scream louder than anything she'd ever produced before, Ruby snatched up a vase of gerberas and hurled them at the lift. The vase shattered, and mutilated petals rained down on the floor. The scream kept going, underscored by the drumming of Ruby's heels.

Approaching her with caution, Maria said gently, 'Do you know what you need?'

'WHAT?' Ruby stopped screaming but kept up the volume. 'You need to go and do some cleaning.'

18

Now that it was June, the green was coming into its own. Jacketless, tightless, Ruby and Maria sprawled on a patch of stubbly grass, gazing up at a cloudless sky.

'Where is the year going?' asked Maria.

'I remember hearing adults say that and thinking they were mad,' said Ruby. 'Time goes much slower when you're a child.'

'Remember how long the summer holidays seemed?' Maria rolled on to her side and took an awkward bite out of her lolly.

'And now the weeks just fly by.'

'We must be getting old.'

'I don't mind getting older,' philosophised Ruby, 'as long as I get wiser.'

'Are you still thinking about Tania?' Maria held one arm over her eyes against the glare of the sun as she checked out her friend's expression.

'No.' Ruby reconsidered. 'Yes. She made me feel vulnerable, appearing out of the blue like that.'

'Like the Wicked Witch in *The Wizard of Oz*.'

'Only not quite so good looking.'

They enjoyed a companionable snigger before Maria spoke. 'You never really told me what she said.'

'She said a lot of rubbish,' said Ruby vehemently.

'About . . . ?' probed Maria, leaning up on one elbow to scrutinise Ruby more closely.

'The divorce. My inability to have a baby.'

'But that was Manny's decision!'

'Like I said, rubbish.'

'She didn't say anything about . . .' Maria shrugged. 'Anything?'

'Errm . . .' Ruby looked at Maria until they both laughed. 'You'd make a great interrogator,' giggled Ruby. 'Very specific.'

'Shuddup you.' Maria seemed to be mollified and sank back down on to the grass. 'Tania was a hopeless manageress,' she bitched dreamily, her eyes closed. 'Nobody liked her. She was so stroppy, and she never lifted a finger.'

This should have been soothing, but Ruby was uninterested. 'Really?' she said.

'I never got on with her.'

'You surprise me,' said Ruby levelly. 'And you such an easygoing little thing.'

'She was always watching me.'

'Pity somebody didn't watch *her* when she spent hours in the stockroom with my husband.'

'Oh, they didn't do it in the stockroom. They did it—' Maria pulled a face as if she'd just sniffed Satan's faeces. 'Sorry. Sorry. That's too much information.'

'*Far* too much information,' frowned Ruby. They lay side by side in silence, listening to the traffic. 'OK, where did they do it?' Ruby asked eventually.

'In the loos.'

'Nice.'

'Want a lift?' The red and black SmartCar almost mounted the pavement, forcing Ruby to leap back against a garden wall. Olivia leaned out of the passenger window, looking over-sized for such a vehicle. She was hunched over the dashboard, her hair wheeling like Medusa's snakes. 'Get in then!' she ordered while Ruby was trying to frame a polite 'No'.

'I'm only going a couple of streets,' said Ruby, meekly taking a seat beside her client.

'I'll get you there quicker.' Olivia checked her mirrors and then took off at speed. She drove the flimsy car as if it was a Lamborghini, her elegant hand expert on the gearstick. 'Right or left?' she asked.

Giving directions feebly, Ruby made small talk. 'Where are you off to?'

'Bloody shopping,' grumbled Olivia. 'I had to face facts this morning when one of my blouses just fell apart. It's time for my annual shopping trip.' She sailed across a roundabout, somehow bending other, larger, cars to her will. 'I wish we could all wear uniforms. Like your overall. With mottoes on. Get rid of all this competitiveness. Free up our time to do useful things.'

'S'pose,' said Ruby, who was mourned in every designer outlet in Esher. 'Ah. Here we are.'

'Excellent. Out you get. Good.'

And Olivia was gone.

'Hi Milly!' Ruby's merry shout, now a habit, echoed down Tom's empty hall. '*Hi Rubes,*' Ruby answered herself in an approximation of a posh accent. '*How are you, my deah?*' 'Oh, you know,' Ruby told the Honourable Millicent, 'the usual. My swine of an ex won't respond to my petition thingy so my divorce is going to take longer than one of Teddy's special baths, but never mind.' The Honourable Millicent was a good listener, and Ruby felt better for sharing.

Carrying Henry through to the kitchen, Ruby waddled about looking for Tom's note. Dropping her hoover chum with a disappointed 'Oh', she had to concede defeat. There was no note today. That was a first. 'Not that it matters,' she reminded herself.

It didn't matter, not at all, so the lack of a note couldn't have accounted for the grumpiness that distorted Ruby's pretty face as she stomped up the stairs to start on the master bedroom. Grasping the door handle firmly, she strode in, setting off a chain reaction of rapid movements inside the room.

Frozen in the doorway, Ruby watched as two figures reared up from the bed, then jumped down on the opposite side, tugging the snow white duvet with them.

A female voice shrieked, 'WHO IS SHE?!' from within the newly made bedding tent, and a dark male head burrowed out to meet Ruby's shocked gaze.

'Oh dear,' understated Ruby, as she met her client for the first time.

'This is very, very embarrassing. And awful. And I'm truly sorry.' Tom's face was trying valiantly to master the unruly smile that kept breaking out under his nose. Standing up, and winding the duvet around his lower torso, he advanced on Ruby, holding out his hand. 'You're Ruby, aren't you?'

'Yes.' Ruby nodded, chained to the spot.

From the carpet, hidden by the bed, that female voice was squealing again. '*Dar*ling! Leave me some decency.' An invisible hand grabbed at the duvet and Tom was abruptly naked.

'Oh dear,' repeated Ruby, with rather more conviction this time.

'This is not good,' said Tom, cupping both hands around his crown jewels.

'I'll . . . I mean . . .' Ruby turned and fled, her flat sandals thumping a rapid cha cha cha on the stairs.

'Wait!' roared Tom. To catch up with her so speedily he must have taken the bedroom in two strides. 'Ruby! Don't just walk out!'

'I'll come back, make up the time,' muttered Ruby, fussing with her toolbox, trying to pick up Henry at the same time. Averting her eyes like a Victorian maid, she hardly dared look at Tom, being the sort of girl who likes a formal introduction before genitalia are unveiled.

'I'm safe to look at.'

Tom's voice held a laugh, a faintly insolent one, and Ruby wasn't comforted by it. So far, Tom wasn't living up to her daydream. She'd created a painting by numbers gentleman and now she was confronted by – it was time to use one of her mother's words – a cad. She did, however, raise her eyes.

'See? Perfectly decent!' beamed Tom, holding up his hands. A cardigan tied backwards around his midriff, its sleeves cuddling his waist, protected his really rude bits from scrutiny. His bottom, which Ruby considered fairly rude in the great scheme of things, was poking prettily out at the back.

In the moment it took Ruby to renew her scandalised look, she took in the fact that Tom had a very nice bum. And face. Having made a study of the noticeboard, she'd know that wide mouth anywhere, and those blue eyes. She'd anticipated seeing them for real some day, but not like this. With a cardy round his equipment and a woman under his bed. 'I'll let you get back to your, erm, girlfriend,' she said, in the new low mutter that was the only voice available to her.

'Or . . .' Tom bit his lip. His teeth were very white and

his bottom lip was very red. 'You could join us.' He gave her a long, frank look up and down.

Tom's appraisal stripped Ruby down to her skin. She recalled that he had watched her as she slept, and a warm fuzzy memory suddenly transformed into a sleazy one, complete with porn soundtrack. 'I'm here to clean!' she reminded him, her mutter giving way to a shout. Hauling up the vacuum cleaner's nozzle, she employed it to poke Tom in the chest, forcing him backwards towards the stairs. 'Go on, shoo!' she ordered him as he staggered back under Henry's onslaught.

Turning to find the bottom stair, Tom stumbled and fell backwards, sprawling up the staircase. 'I can explain. I don't want you to go like this,' he gabbled, as Ruby wrestled with the door.

'There's nothing to explain,' said Ruby, bundling herself and her paraphernalia over the step. 'I just wish you'd called and cancelled. Could have saved a lot of embarrassment all round.' She paused. 'Sorry. About poking you.'

'Oh, I deserved it,' said Tom. 'Never apologise for a poke.'

Blushing, Ruby managed an, 'Oh for God's sake,' before legging it down the path.

'Promise you'll come back!' shouted Tom, leaning out of the front door. 'I'm just too dirty without you!'

'I think he sounds nice,' laughed Maria ironically, as she mixed Ruby a reviving glass of something orange and blue at the Velvet Glove.

'He's crude,' spat Ruby. 'And rude.'

'And lewd?' rhymed Maria. 'Oh, come on, Rubes. You're acting like he molested you.'

'He would have if he'd had the chance. Urgh.' Ruby shuddered, then jumped as two hands grabbed her shoulders.

'Good evening, my little bougainvillaea,' rasped Teddy. 'Why the forlorn look?'

Before Ruby could answer, Maria leapt in. 'She's just had her eyes opened about the filthy mind of your average man.'

'Oh purlease!' squawked Teddy, pulling up a bar stool. It took him a moment to nip up on to it, thanks to the yards of chiffon in the skirt of his 'Nobody Loves a Fairy When She's Forty' outfit. 'I could write you a book. Shandy, Maria, love, and lots of it.' He turned to the miserable Ruby. 'You're not used to the rough and tumble of the real world, are you, darl?'

Resentfully, Ruby said, 'I'm not doing such a bad job of living in the real world, am I?'

'You're doing a grand job.' Teddy chucked her cheek, rather hard, to emphasise his point. 'But you're a princess, sweetheart, and men ain't princes. They've got dirty hands and dirty minds.'

'Not all of them, surely,' protested Ruby. She'd been sure that Tom was a Sir Galahad, despite the fact that she'd got Manny so impressively wrong. 'There must be one or two gentlemen out there.'

'You're the only woman of your age who even uses the word.' Teddy beckoned to Maria. 'You don't want a gent, do you?'

'Wouldn't know what to do with one,' admitted Maria.

'Kendall's a gentleman,' Ruby asserted, glad to have found a defence.

Scowling as if he'd just bit into a thistle, Teddy's voice rolled even deeper. 'Pardon my panto, but oh no he isn't. If he was a gent, he'd be here, watching me do me turn, instead of being God knows where, with his phone switched off.' A tinny fanfare of synth drums rolled out of the speakers, and a hundred pairs of hands burst into applause. 'That's me.

My public want me.' Teddy hopped inelegantly off the stool, landing with his legs splayed. 'At least somebody does,' he sighed, downing his shandy and heading for the stage, a wide smile pasted on his face.

'Men,' said Maria.

'Men,' said Ruby.

19

Profoundly out of step with most other Londoners, Ruby was glad the weekend was over. That precious full stop at the tail of the working week meant nothing to her these days. In the past, Manny had insisted on their Saturday nights out, necessitating a day of buffing and painting and glossing on Ruby's part.

A mutinous fog would descend round about the time Ruby slipped on her newest dress and clipped her newest jewel to some part of her, because the truth was that she preferred a night in, with a DVD and the undivided attention of her husband. Saturday nights had meant the best tables at the best restaurants with fawning waiters and complimentary liqueurs. Ruby, who squirmed under scrutiny, had sat up straight and finished off her food like a good girl, all the while wishing she was at home with her feet snuggled in Manny's lap on their mile-long white sofa.

Saturday nights these days meant the television equivalent of ready meals, or propping up the bar at the Velvet Glove: Ruby's social life was in dire need of a spring clean and she had been nurturing a small, hairless and runty hope that Tom might be the man with the broom. How could she have been so wrong? His personality was completely different to the one she'd stitched together for him. All those clues around his house had been misleading. Perhaps, thought Ruby, as she mopped and scalded Teddy and Kendall's flat on Monday morning, she wasn't such a good detective after all. For all she knew, Mrs Vine could be a thousand pound a night hooker.

Wednesday brought another session at the Friends'. Olivia, usually a sedentary presence, was prowling the house in her sludgy jersey layers, a mug of something hot misting up her glasses. Pacing, preoccupied, she managed to be under Ruby's feet in every room.

Locked away upstairs, the rhythmic creak of the floorboards hinting at what was going on up there, Joe was safe from the troubling vibes his mother was leaking all over the house.

Straightening picture frames on the landing, Ruby had to ask Olivia to move out of the way.

'Oh. Sorry.' Olivia moved a fraction to her left.

Ruby gave up. The frames could wait. 'I'm dying of thirst here,' she said, meaningfully.

'What? Why?' asked Olivia querulously.

'Tea? You usually make me a cup round about now.' Ruby tapped her watch. 'Might take your mind off whatever it is.'

'Is it that obvious?' Olivia rolled her eyes. 'Sorry. Work problems. Students. It's a tough town, London, if you don't have the language or the street smarts. Tea. Yes. Definitely.' She stood, irresolute, on the worn landing carpet.

'Downstairs, then?' prompted Ruby gently. 'The kitchen?'

'Of course.' Olivia, galvanised, set off down the stairs to the basement. 'Come on!' she shouted, grumpily.

The tea was weak, devoid of sugar, just the way Ruby didn't like it. She didn't complain, just sipped it and watched as Olivia opened the post.

'Hmm.' Olivia studied a pamphlet. 'Should I go to this?'

Startled to be asked her advice, Ruby took the flyer. 'A fund raising evening for a women's refuge,' she read. 'Sounds like a good cause.'

'Good cause?' queried Olivia. 'It's a little more than that, surely.'

Feeling castigated, Ruby returned to sipping.

'Some of these women have horrific tales to tell. Not all men are like Hugo.'

That, thought Ruby, was true enough. She'd been married to the anti-Hugo for years.

'Have you ever suffered at the hands of a man?' asked Olivia, taking her glasses off and leaning over the table.

'Yes,' said Ruby simply.

'Physically?' Olivia sat down, with the absorbed look on her face that came over her when reading what Ruby thought of as one of her 'brainy' books.

'No. Mentally. Emotionally.' Ruby wasn't sure how best to describe Manny's masterly mindfuck.

'Only women bleed,' sighed Olivia.

Joe stepped into the kitchen. Despite his quirks, he was a standard enough ten-year-old to enter a room as if there were a dozen of him, some of them in clogs.

'Goodness, darling,' chided Olivia. 'How do you manage to make so much noise?'

'It's in his job description,' laughed Ruby.

Joe laughed, but Olivia didn't. Perhaps, reasoned Ruby, she hadn't heard her.

'I can't go.' Olivia crumpled up the pamphlet. 'It's too complicated, going out at night. There's Joe's dinner, and I'd have to arrange babysitting.' Olivia sounded defeated, unlike her usual confident self.

'Ruby can babysit!' Joe plonked his elbows on the table and his arched eyebrows disappeared under his fringe. 'You go out, Mum. Me and Ruby always have a great time.' Joe took his mother's ominous silence as indecision. 'Go on. You can go out every night if you want. Ruby'll look after me.' He was grinning, showing off every wonky tooth in his head.

'Yes, I'm sure she will,' agreed Olivia, in a tone that worried Ruby but skated over Joe's head.

'Yeah. I have a right laugh with Ruby.'

'You can laugh yourself back up to your room, young man!' Olivia's voice quavered. When Joe just stared and grinned, she snapped, 'GO!' and her son disappeared like smoke.

A tense silence hung over the two women. Ruby grasped her mug very hard. The diplomatic way to handle this new atmosphere would be silence, but Ruby couldn't bear it. 'Kids!' she tutted, with exaggerated bonhomie.

'Listen,' said Olivia, with an obvious effort to sound neutral. 'Just leave the rest for today.'

'But I haven't even made a start on the kitchen,' protested Ruby. The sauce-flecked tiles around the sink were taunting her: she'd enjoy showing them who was boss.

'I *can* clean my own kitchen!'

Ruby took the hint.

The divorce had all the impetus of a square wheel. Manny was not co-operating, and Sheila, Ruby's solicitor, was obliged to force the petition through. It was time consuming and expensive and distressing, one of those situations that, however one approaches it, has no good angle. As Maria said, a little like every man she'd ever slept with. 'Some men – and Manny's one of them – are the human equivalent of a tequila slammer. Wonderful while it's happening, but the next morning bits of you hurt, your best dress is torn and your shoes are flecked with vomit.' She laughed at Ruby's baffled expression. 'Honest. Manny is a slammer.' She thought for a moment. 'Whereas you are more of a champagne cocktail. Tall. Classy. Effer-whatsit.'

'I feel like the dregs in the bottom of the Baileys bottle at the back of the drinks cabinet,' said Ruby. 'Forgotten. Out of date.'

'Nah. Champagne,' insisted Maria.

'End of the Baileys bottle,' repeated Ruby.

This argument went on for some time.

That Ruby was a coward had been proved time and time again. She would never complain in a shop, even if an assistant tried to stab her; all through her marriage she had told Manny that she considered bald men to be more sexy when she actually considered them to be more bald; she would rather lick her way to the centre of the earth than be the first to dance at a party. That Friday, however, Ruby learned just how much of a coward she really was.

In her new incarnation as the World's Best Cleaner, Ruby prided herself on her professionalism. A professional cleaner might not sound impressive when compared to, say, a professional President of the United States, but Ruby took her commitment to her clients seriously. Therefore it took some serious, big league cowardice to resign from Tom by text.

As of toady I can no longer clean your house for you. Ruby.

Tutting up a storm, she sent another.

    I meant 'today', obviously.

Feeling shabby, she placed the phone on a high shelf and
quelled her shame with a Wagon Wheel. In a few moments
the phone called out to her.

    OK. But why?

Snorting, and splattering her T-shirt with Wagon Wheel
shards, Ruby tapped out:

    I think you know why!

Surprised when the phone beeped again, she picked it up to
read:

    Fair enough.

20

The spare room in Teddy and Kendall's flat was a wasteland of cardboard boxes, garments drying on a herd of clothes horses, and a suspiciously pristine exercise bike. Every Monday Ruby gave it a basic tweak, but today she noticed that the single bed was rumpled. There was an empty glass and a paperback on the bedside table. As the book was a literary biography and didn't involve the words 'Jackie' or 'Collins' on the cover, Ruby surmised that it wasn't Teddy's. Kendall had been banished to the Siberian salt mines of the spare room.

Sighing inwardly at this escalation of the cold war, Ruby swapped the desk light by the bed for an amber-shaded lamp, and exchanged the squeaky nylon sheets for plain linen. She bullied the boxes into some kind of order, and evicted the damp clothes. 'There, that's better,' she puffed, as she manhandled the exercise bike alongside the wardrobe.

'Quite the palace,' said Kendall from the doorway.

'If you have to sleep here, it might as well be comfy,' said Ruby, patting the plumped-up pillows with a tender hand.

'I think certain people would prefer me to sleep on a bed of nails.' Kendall hung his white cotton jacket carefully on a hanger. 'Teddy is giving me the silent treatment.'

It was rude of Ruby to look so surprised but she couldn't help it. 'Teddy has a silent treatment?' she asked, amazed.

'YES I BLOODY DO HAVE A SILENT TREATMENT!' roared a voice from the main bedroom.

Kendall displayed his patented long-suffering expression and shouted, 'I thought you weren't talking to me?'

'Ruby, darling,' came Teddy's gritty yell. 'Kindly tell that old man with the comedy moustache that I'm not talking to *him*, I am talking to *you*.'

'OK,' shouted Ruby. She turned to Kendall. 'He's not—'

'Oh for the love of God you don't actually have to tell me,' snapped Kendall.

'No. Sorry,' said Ruby, feeling foolish. 'Are you all right?' she asked, in a low voice that Teddy's radar couldn't pick up.

'I'm fine,' said Kendall automatically. 'I've weathered worse. You weren't around when he found his first varicose vein,' he grimaced. 'If I can survive that, I can survive anything.'

'Can't you just, you know, sort this out?' asked Ruby, a touch more pathetically than she'd meant to.

'It's complicated.' Kendall hesitated, his face weary. 'Madam isn't exactly approachable just now.'

'Madam loves you,' said Ruby.

'Not as much as Madam loves himself.'

'MADAM FUCKING HEARD THAT!'

Another Thursday, another ballroom class. The hall had been airless, and Miss Delmar more irritable than usual, hurling a Fox's Glacier Mint at Suzie during a tense left cross turn. Ruby blamed the heat for that, and for Joe's surliness on the way home. A minute or so after she left him at his corner, she heard a voice call her name.

'*Ruby!*'

Turning, hands in the pockets of her stripy dress, Ruby saw Hugo bounding up behind her. She grew even hotter than the weather merited, and attempted a noncommittal face. Her breathing quickened as Hugo drew nearer, and she nervously anticipated the questions about just what she was doing with his son.

'Gosh. Oh. Crikey.' Hugo's vocabulary was as period as his cords, which hadn't been relinquished despite the sunshine. He was panting with the exertion of catching up with Ruby. 'Not much of a runner. Not much of a mover at all.' Hugo bent down to put his hands on his knees and took some deep breaths. 'More of a sitting down with a book chap.'

'Take your time,' said Ruby uneasily, gauging his mood. It was hard with Hugo, whose face was qualified only to smile sheepishly. If announcing nuclear war, he'd do so with a sheepish smile. So, with a sheepish smile, he got his breath back and said, 'I'm glad I spotted you. I think I owe you an apology.'

This was so far removed from what she'd been expecting that Ruby's expression had to execute a sharp about-turn. 'Whatever for, Hugo?'

'Well, not me, but Olivia. She feels terrible about it. Snapping at you the last time you were at our place. Practically threw you out, she told me.'

'It wasn't that bad,' said Ruby, keen to curtail a drawn-out apology from the father of the child she kidnapped weekly. 'Honest.'

'We owe you a lot,' said Hugo, with feeling. 'The house is . . . different since you came along. I mean,' he smiled, 'obviously it's cleaner, but there's something else. I don't want to talk about Olivia when she's not here, but my wife . . .' Hugo faltered. 'My wife isn't very confident some-times.' Perhaps he noted the surprise Ruby endeavoured to cover up. 'Oh, I know she seems certain of herself, and if you're talking about her work or her politics, then she's fearless. But sometimes she just wavers and then, well,' Hugo shrugged his shoulders. Ruby could tell he wouldn't elaborate out of loyalty to his wife. 'Suffice to say, Olivia really didn't mean to chase you out of the house. Will you be back next week? No hard feelings?'

'None. As if.' Ruby risked a gentle punch on Hugo's shoulder and he laughed too loudly and jumped a foot in the air.

21

There was a Tom-shaped hole in Ruby's Friday. She'd taken on a new client – a Polish family with a cat that shed so much hair their toddler looked like a yak – but it had felt treacherous to allot them Tom's two hours between ten and twelve. So, instead of pottering about, titivating Tom's crevices, Ruby was out on her terrace, trying to get comfortable in one of the ultra-modern steel loungers she'd inherited along with the apartment. Glad of the privacy the penthouse afforded, Ruby was test driving a new bikini. Egged on by Maria, she'd purchased three triangles of green polka dot material that, if joined together, would barely make a hen's hanky. It was a departure for Ruby, and she felt half daring, half daft as she squirmed on the mesh fabric of the lounger.

'Visitor for you.' Maria suddenly slid the glass door to one side, leading a tall man out on to the paving.

It was like a dream. Whether good or bad Ruby wasn't sure, but Tom was standing on her terrace. 'Yerks,' she said, or similar.

'Hi.' Tom's dark head was bowed, like a schoolboy entering

the headmaster's study. 'Are you busy?' He lost faith in the question halfway through, and started to smile. 'Obviously you're not.'

There was nothing for Ruby to grab and cover her body with. She wondered if her blush was bleeding all over her legs, her arms, her breasts, all of which were offered to Tom as forthrightly as a chicken in a butcher's window. 'I'm busy sunbathing,' she said, in a clipped voice.

Maria, who had happily folded her arms, obviously wasn't going anywhere. 'So, you're the famous Tom,' she began, deepening her friend's beetroot tint.

'Am I famous?' asked Tom, scratching his black curls. 'What for?'

A warning glare from Ruby must have worked, because Maria only said, 'For living in the Honourable Millicent Whatsit's house.'

'Oh. Yes. Me and Ms Flatbush, we're like that.' Tom entwined two of his fingers. He returned his attention to Ruby, who was stock still on the sunlounger. He looked resolutely and definitely at her face, as if the rest of her body was forbidden territory. 'Thought I'd drop by. See if we could talk about things. Sort something out.'

'Hmm.' Ruby, who would have swapped all her worldly goods for a towel, was tempted to mutter that she didn't recognise him with his clothes on. He looked heavier in his battered jeans and washed-out T, and his hair was more unruly than she remembered. 'I don't think so,' she said. Tom had disappointed her, which she could take; but he'd gone on to suggest a threesome, which she couldn't. A thought occurred to her. 'You don't know where I live,' she said accusingly.

Producing a puckered envelope from his back pocket, Tom said, with a hint of triumph, 'You wrote one of your notes on an electricity bill.'

'Ooh, Columbo,' teased Maria. She lifted her chin and said, with narrowed eyes, 'You kept her notes, then?'

'Oh, well, I,' Tom flailed. 'Yes,' he said eventually.

Ruby stood up. 'Look,' she said, in a distracted, rather unfriendly way, 'I can't talk while I'm wearing less than I do in the bath. S'cuse me.' She approached Tom and he leapt out of the way as if she was on fire. Stamping to her room, Ruby grabbed her white towelling dressing gown and rejoined the others out in the sun. 'Right. What do you mean, sort things out?' She was aware that she was being brusque, and she wasn't a brusque girl, but she wanted this man out of her flat. He smelled nice, she noticed, irrationally disliking him more for his pleasantly masculine odour. 'It's no big deal. I don't have time to do your house any more.'

'Obviously.' Tom looked around the terrace, taking in the glass of lemonade and the half-read bonkbuster. 'It puzzled me, your sudden departure. I wondered if there was anything I could do.'

'Drop the pretence, Rubes.' Maria elbowed in before Ruby could answer. 'Tell him the real reason. It won't be a surprise.' Maria waggled a finger at Tom. 'You should think twice before you ask a girl to join you and another lady for some hi-jinks, mate. You propositioned the last good girl in London.'

'Propositioned?' Tom squeaked. When he spoke again, he'd cranked his voice down to its usual bass tone. 'You must have misread one of my notes,' he said, shaking his head. 'But I can't think how.' He frowned at Maria. 'Are you being serious?'

He was a good actor. Ruby might have admired him if she hadn't wanted to toss him over the chrome railings. 'You can't have forgotten. Don't treat me like an idiot.'

'Forgotten what?' Tom kept up his spirited pretence.

'Me walking in on you and your girlfriend? You following me down the stairs with nothing on? You asking me to . . .' Ruby tapered off. 'To, you know.'

'Shag you both,' sang Maria cheerily.

'Are you mad?' Tom seemed quite angry. 'Is she?' he appealed to Maria. 'Is there something wrong with her? Because none of this ever happened.'

Ruby bristled. 'Excuse me, don't ask my friend if I'm mad. I can tell you. I'm not.'

'That,' said Tom, holding up a pompous forefinger, 'is exactly what a mad person would say.'

Suppressing a growl, Ruby said in a low voice, 'One minute I'm sunbathing, the next I'm defending my mental health. If there's nothing else?' The post-Manny Ruby could be stroppy when irked.

'Nothing else? You accuse me of going around propositioning born again virgins in the altogether and that's it, I'm dismissed?' Tom did a good line in stroppy too. 'You're—' He pulled up short, his mouth half open to form a word that was now redundant. 'Oh my God,' he said slowly, raising a hand to his head. He had lovely long fingers, Ruby noticed. Horrid long fingers, she corrected herself. He was groaning, much like Ruby groaned the morning after accepting too much hospitality at the Velvet Glove. 'I don't believe this. *Carl*,' he said, distorting the short name with venom.

'Carl?' said Ruby and Maria in perfect unison.

'My brother.'

Ruby unpursed her lips a notch. She looked closer at Tom. She knew what was coming. He didn't look heavier in his jeans, he *was* heavier. He wasn't the man Henry had fended off. Her blush was back.

'My shithead brother. My sod of a brother. My I-will-kill-him brother,' Tom was elucidating. 'He used to live with me.

I threw him out because of the constant shagathons. He's a kind of Russell Brand with a proper job. He keeps finding excuses not to give the key back and now I know why.'

Dubiously, Maria asked, 'You mean it was him that Ruby met? Why can't he have sex in his own house?'

'His wife wouldn't like it,' said Tom, darkly. 'I'm guessing,' he added, with a shrug of his shoulders.

Maria laughed, but Ruby didn't. She felt like a heel. 'I'm sorry, I should have realised.'

'We look alike,' said Tom kindly. 'Everybody says so. And you'd never met me, so it was an obvious thing to assume.'

His efforts to absolve her were welcome, but didn't do much for Ruby's embarrassment. 'I should have known. I mean, from the photos on the noticeboard . . .' She tapered off. Now Tom knew that she studied his noticeboard.

'Honestly, it was a simple misunderstanding. Could have happened to anyone.' He shuddered suddenly and violently. 'Urrgh. I haven't changed the bed!'

That got a laugh out of both Maria and Ruby. 'Sounds like you need me back,' smiled Ruby.

'Oh, I so do.' There seemed to be a little more emotion in Tom's intonation than was strictly necessary when welcoming back a prodigal domestic worker.

Ruby looked sharply at him, noting that Maria did exactly the same. She took him in properly for the first time since he'd appeared like a panto genie on her terrace. Tom was tall, and broadish. He looked as if he had an acquaintance with the gym, without getting all silly about it. The clothes were scruffy and nondescript, evidently chosen for comfort rather than style. His hair was – she couldn't suppress the adjective – fab. Thick, black, curly, it flopped and waved all over the place, even cheekily dangling over his knowing blue eyes. Dark lashed, they were intelligent eyes, eyes that seemed to get the point. 'I'd better put some clothes on, and get round there, then.'

'Yeah,' said Tom, tapping his watch. 'You're late.'

Ruby had been away from the terrace for no longer than three minutes. It was impressive how much Maria could achieve in such a limited window. Stepping back out into the sunshine, she heard her friend say bullishly, 'Well if you don't ask her, I will. And believe me, you don't want that.' Maria jumped as Ruby materialised in her work overall and a pair of cutoff jeans. 'Oh. What are you doing, creeping up on people like that?'

'I was just walking normally,' protested Ruby, looking from Maria's tanned little face to Tom's pale visage. 'What's going on?'

'Tom has something to ask you.' Maria nodded encouragingly, and ever so slightly menacingly, at Tom. 'Don't you?'

'Er, yeah.' Tom wasn't half as certain as Maria. 'I do.'

Ruby assumed a receptive expression, despite the prickling in her palms.

'Go on!' nagged Maria.

'Shut up,' hissed Tom, whose hands were writhing around each other. Addressing Ruby, he said, 'Um', and then 'Ah', and finally 'Erm'.

Evidently losing patience, Maria rounded on Ruby. 'He wants to ask you out. For dinner.' She glanced at Tom to double-check. 'Dinner, right?' On a groan and a nod from him, she reiterated. 'Dinner. What do you say?'

'I'm married,' was what she said, setting off a chain reaction of 'Oh God' from Tom and a flurry of waved hands and 'No no no!'s from Maria.

Determined to broker this deal, Maria moved towards Tom. 'She's getting divorced. It's over. Really over. You have no idea how over it is.' Ignoring the glare that this précis of

Ruby's situation elicited from her friend, she repeated the question to Ruby. 'Dinner. Yes or no? Or do you want to phone a bloody friend?'

'I'm sorry about her, Tom,' said Ruby in a small voice, more mortified than she'd ever been, even taking into account the time she'd overbalanced and fallen into the frozen gateau section in Waitrose.

'I'm not.' Tom puffed out his cheeks, and held her gaze with his astute blue eyes. 'I would never have got around to asking you without her.' He put his hands behind his back, like a naughty boy. 'So, to quote your friend – yes or no?'

'Yes,' said Ruby, and she was rather afraid that she simpered.

The next morning it was a close run thing as to who was annoying the other more, Maria or Ruby.

Maria was getting on Ruby's nerves by uttering variations on, 'So, on a scale of one to ten how much would you say you fancy Lover Boy?' every few minutes as they passed each other in their spacious reception room.

Ruby was irritating Maria by insisting, 'It's not a proper date. Just dinner. Not a real date, as such.'

Finally Maria shrieked, throwing down the Aunt Bessie's Yorkshire pudding which was the only thing she could source in the kitchen for her breakfast, 'Will you *please* stop saying it's not a proper date? It's two people in a restaurant all dressed up and leaking pheromones! *Of course it's a date!*'

'Keep your voice down,' said Ruby with maddening calm. 'And stop calling him Lover Boy. He has a name.'

'Yes. I know. Tom.' Maria bit into her insufficiently defrosted yorkie. 'Lover Boy Tom.'

'Any more of this behaviour and I won't let you come to the funfair with me and Teddy.'

'You're not that cruel,' said Maria confidently.

Ruby wasn't. So at noon the trio set off for the park, with their differing ambitions for the afternoon. Teddy wanted to fill his face with candyfloss and forget all about Kendall's behaviour for a few hours; Ruby wanted a go on the chairo-planes; Maria spoke of pinning down the boys who spun the waltzers.

Their route took them down Clancy Street. Joe was hanging about outside number fourteen. Any other boy might be on a skateboard, but Joe held an English/French dictionary. He said polite hellos when introduced to Maria and Teddy. 'I've never been to a funfair,' he said, pushing a fringe that was in dire need of cutting out of his smoky eyes.

'Never?' Teddy was as appalled as if he'd just learned that Joe's parents only fed him when there was an R in the month.

'Boys and funfairs go together,' protested Maria.

Ruby said nothing. She was accustomed to these gaps in Joe's experience. He'd been to the ballet. He'd seen Michelangelo's *David*. But he'd never thrown up on a Big Wheel. 'We'll save you some candyfloss,' she promised, fixing his collar.

'Can't I come?' Joe was all eagerness, leaning forward in his desire to escape with them.

Casting an anxious glance up at the front door, Ruby shook her head. 'Your mum wouldn't like it, Joe.'

With a theatrical cough, Teddy hissed behind his hand, 'Does Mum have to know?'

'Yes,' said Ruby, not quite drowning out Joe's 'No'.

'I'll say I'm going round Quon's. She likes Quon. His grandad's a prisoner of conscience in China.'

'That's a fib,' said Ruby, repressively.

'More of a lie,' said Maria happily. 'Go on then. We'll meet you round the corner.'

As Joe nipped up the steps, dropping his English/French

186

dictionary on the way, Ruby frowned at Maria. 'Are you going to be butting in all my life?'

'Possibly.' Maria linked arms with Ruby and Teddy, leading them away from number fourteen. 'Don't go all virtuous on me, Rubes. You take him dancing every week without his mum knowing.'

'And that's bad enough without enticing him to the funfair.'

'Ooh,' Teddy shivered joyfully. 'Is that what we're doing? It's years since I enticed.'

For a novice, Joe got the hang of things pretty quick. The eighteen pence he had on him didn't go far, so Ruby paid for him to go on everything once and quite a lot of it twice. 'This is wicked,' he grinned, showing off those pointed canines that touched Ruby's heart for some reason.

'Waltzer next,' she said, leading him to where Maria had already snaffled a carriage.

Puffing and wheezing, Teddy joined them. 'I'm too old for all this,' he griped, slapping away Ruby's hand as she tried to fasten the safety bar over his tummy.

Ignoring him, Ruby clicked the bar into position, smiling into Joe's eyes as she did so. She liked looking after him.

'Look at this piece of machinery,' Maria was grunting in a low voice as one of the waltzer team swaggered towards them in torn jeans and a cocky expression.

'Shush.' Ruby elbowed her, motioning at Joe with a slight tilt of her head.

'Joe,' Maria leaned over Ruby. 'You don't mind if I chat this up, do you?'

'Nope.'

'Thanks.' Maria licked her lips and turned back to the attendant, who had reached their car. 'Four,' she said, with a pout.

'D'you like it fast?' One would never guess that he used this line a hundred times a day: the waltzer guy put his all into it.

Ruby tutted, but Maria lived up to the challenge. 'Oh, I can go as fast as you like,' she purred. As the object of her affection sashayed back to the cashier, she dug Ruby in the arm. 'Don't look at me like that. This is how I do it, OK? You do it by being ethereally beautiful and untouchable, I do it by being obvious. I know what I'm up to.'

Teddy had pulled his glasses out of his shirt pocket. Vanity meant that he rarely used them and consequently thought the whole world was like modern art. 'Hmm,' he said, with the air of a connoisseur, squinting at Maria's target. 'Rough. Mean. Dirty fingernails.' He folded his glasses again. 'Looks the type who'd snog your face off.'

'Here's hoping,' grinned Maria.

'There is a child present,' said Ruby through gritted teeth.

'Oh, he loves it,' claimed Teddy, poking Joe in the ribs. 'Dontcha?'

'I do!' agreed Joe, all smiles. 'I love it. This is the best day out I've had for ages.'

Knowing that the most recent competition was an exhibition about the flora and fauna of Ecuador didn't taint the pleasure Joe's remark gave Ruby. She was savouring it as the ride creaked into life and their carriage started to glide.

'I feel sick,' complained Teddy.

'We haven't got going yet,' warned Maria, craning her neck to keep an eye on her fairground beau.

'Hold on to the bar, Joe,' whispered Ruby.

'All right,' said Joe, tetchily, making her smile.

And then Maria's dirty-fingernailed chap got his hands on them. The fairground became a blur as their little carriage spun. The sensation that her head might come off marred it slightly for Ruby but she whooped and screamed with the others. The guy was good at this: with the merest touch of his little finger he was spinning his four victims like a smoothie in a food processor. Teddy's hoarse appeals to God went unheard as they picked up speed.

'*Faster! Faster!*' yelled Maria provocatively.

'*Fuck off!*' yelled Teddy desperately.

'*Language!*' yelled Ruby, wishing she could remove her hands from the safety bar to cover Joe's ears but lacking the courage.

Wobbly legged, Teddy and Ruby helped each other off when their ride eventually ended. Bent at the knees and staggering like orang-utans, they made a sharp contrast to Maria and Joe who bounded down on to the grass, giggling and pushing each other.

'Can I have a burger?' asked Joe.

'Of course,' said Teddy. 'And candyfloss. And a Coke. As soon as your Uncle Teddy's recovered.' He sank on to the steps of the waltzer. 'Which might be some time.'

'Teddy, sit there until you get your breath back,' said Ruby. 'I'll get them. A burger each, yeah? All the trimmings?' Ruby shook herself to ensure all her bits were still in the right order. 'Maria, what do you want?' Ruby did a Scooby Doo double take: Maria had disappeared. 'Aha.' Ruby spotted her at the other side of the ride, laughing up into the smut-stained face of the waltzer guy. '*That's* what you want.'

22

It was good to be alone. Saturday night offered a few empty hours with nothing to do and nobody to do it with. Maria was at the Velvet Glove, working a truncated shift before nipping over to the park to meet Birdie.

'Birdie?' Ruby had queried. It didn't sound like a proper name to her.

'Birdie,' Maria had confirmed, standing before her full length mirror, comparing the bosom-boosting properties of a variety of vest tops.

Alone in her eyrie at the top of Hannah House, Ruby combed her wet hair and gazed out at the darkening roofs. Birdie's dangerous looks had done nothing for her: she hoped Maria would be careful.

But being careful wasn't in Maria's nature. She hadn't been careful when Tom visited: without Maria's interference, Ruby's path ahead would be straight, smooth, safe. A little dull, perhaps, if you discounted the psycho ex, but that was what Ruby was accustomed to. Now, thanks to Maria, Ruby had a dinner date to disrupt the vanilla blandness of her new life.

For most women, a date with a tall, dark-haired bloke with sexy eyes might come under the category 'good things'. Depending on one's point of view, it might be promoted to 'bloody good things'. For Ruby, it was a problem.

For a start, Ruby was married. Separated maybe, but until the decree nisi was signed (and if Manny had his way that wouldn't happen until some time after Ruby's teeth fell out) she was legally married. And that meant something to her.

Further, she was out of practice. If she'd ever been *in* practice. What, Ruby fretted, as she turned away from the window and rushed to the kitchen to reassure herself in the arms of a Jammie Dodger, would Tom expect from her at the end of the dreaded date? Some hand-holding? A chaste kiss on the lips? What if he demanded a full-on snog? Or sex? Proper, knickers-off, breath-mingling sex?

Sex meant Manny. She knew how he liked it. Stockings were good. Talking dirty was bad. She knew where to kiss him, how hard to pinch. What if fashions in sex had moved on? She imagined Tom naked and laughing at her: 'You're not seriously going to try and put that *there* are you?'

That image of a naked Tom necessitated a Chunky KitKat. Ruby shivered, partly because her damp hair was tickling her shoulders, partly because she had the oddest sensation that those floor to ceiling windows were offering her up to scrutiny. She glanced down at the street, half expecting Manny to be down there, slouched against a street lamp in a hat, like an old-fashioned baddie.

There was no Manny down there. Manny's location was as predictable as a location can be. He was in jail. Whenever Ruby imagined him there, she conjured up a vision of a stark brick cell, with one of those doors that have a little grille in them. Perhaps prisons, like sex, had changed over the years. She wondered if he had his own television. And would he be allowed to have a shower first thing? Manny was impossible until he'd showered.

For a man who loved his luxuries, prison would be hard. A door eased open somewhere in Ruby's mind, but she slammed it hurriedly. She couldn't risk feeling sorry for Manny. He'd made his own bed (presumably a hard one with a thin mattress) and he had to lie on it. Why waste sympathy on a man who'd pounded Simon like a piece of steak? Perhaps, she thought, Manny could befriend a little mouse in prison, and find his better self that way.

While Manny bonded with his rodent, his wife would be on a date. It seemed inconceivable that Manny wouldn't find out about her adultery: Manny knew everything. Could he, in between heart-to-hearts with his mouse confidant, arrange to have Tom beaten up from his cell?

A long, Manny-shaped shadow loomed over the apartment.

Birdie was not shy. Leaning against the fridge freezer in inadequate underpants, he chirruped a cheerful 'Morning, treacle!' to Ruby when she wandered into the kitchen, sleep-befuddled, on Sunday morning.

'Morning,' murmured Ruby, suddenly self-conscious in her dressing gown. She put a hand to her matted bed hair. 'Can I get you anything?'

'Got it.' Birdie raised a bowl of cereal in salute. 'I believe in getting things for yourself. Don't ask, don't get.'

Unaccustomed to absorbing personal philosophies so early, Ruby managed a wan smile. She didn't much like Birdie, and she hadn't much liked the noises he and Maria had made for most of the previous night. Either they were training zoo animals in the second bedroom, or their date had ended in the kind of raucous and enthusiastic sex *Nuts* readers fantasise about.

Muscular and tousled, the squat morning-after Birdie still wasn't Ruby's type. His eyes were stripy amber, like a cat's, and like a cat Birdie seemed to sense her antipathy and thrive on it, edging closer and keeping up his rapid fire chatter. 'Nice place you got here. Must have cost a bit. You a model? You could be. You've got the looks. I've got contacts in the modelling world. I know people. You'd be surprised. I've got a lot of contacts. I can get you anything.' He clicked his fingers. 'Like that.'

Except soap, by the look of him. Ruby made noncommittal noises as she lowered a bagel into the toaster, keeping some space between her and Birdie. 'Did you have a nice evening?' she asked politely.

'Ten out of ten,' leered Birdie. 'Your mate's a red hot chilli pepper.'

'I meant . . .' Ruby tapered off. She'd meant their date, but it occurred to her that there had been very little time between the closing of the funfair and the couple's arrival at Hannah House to fit in traditional date-style activities like eating or drinking or dancing. 'Are you working today?' she asked hopefully.

'After some free rides, are ya?' chuckled Birdie. 'Nah. Day off.' He stretched and his toned midriff undulated like a rubber xylophone. 'Might get back to bed.' He waggled a finger at Ruby, who cowered from it. 'Now, now, you naughty girl. I know what you're thinking. I need some kip. Didn't get much last night.' He dumped the bowl in the sink, and passed Maria on her way in as he made his way back to the black silk sheets. 'She's got a dirty mind, your mate.'

Looking at Ruby quizzically, Maria said, 'Really?' Stealing the bagel as it popped up, she teased, 'You after my bloke?'

'So not. So very not.' Ruby waited until the bedroom door slammed shut. 'Maria!' she hissed. 'He's awful!'

'I know,' nodded Maria happily, slathering butter on her bagel and casting about for the jam. 'He's a lowlife.' She paused, then said dreamily, 'But oh my goodness, what a—'

'Don't!' warned Ruby. 'I kind of know what you're going to say and I don't want to hear it before I've even brushed my teeth. He's good in bed. I get it. In fact,' she said testily, 'I could hardly miss it. I heard the soundtrack.'

'Sorry,' said Maria, contrite. 'We got a bit carried away. It's been a while.'

'We are now so far into the realm of too much information I fear we'll never get out,' sighed Ruby, nicking back half of her bagel. 'Do you always go the whole way on the first night?'

'If I feel like it.' There was a whiff of defensiveness to Maria's reply. 'If I want to. Why?' She knitted her brows together. 'Do you think I'm a slag now?'

'No!' spluttered Ruby. Then, more tentatively, 'No.' She struggled to deliver her thoughts in a palatable way. 'It's just not what I'd do, that's all. I thought maybe you'd get to know him first.'

'Get to know Birdie?' giggled Maria. 'What for? What you see is what you get, I suspect. We're never going to have deep conversations about the nature of the universe. He's too busy staring at my chest.'

'Then why do you want to, you know, make love?'

'Nonono.' Maria waved a buttery knife like a conductor's baton. 'That was not making love, Rubes. What you heard was the scratching of an itch. It was animal. It wasn't love.'

'It was certainly animal,' agreed Ruby. 'At one point I worried that a troop of baboons had wandered up in the lift. But if there's no feeling there, why do it?'

Tenderly Maria pushed Ruby's hair back from her forehead

and studied her as if she'd never seen her before. 'You really are a romantic, aren't you?' she said fondly. 'We're poles apart, you and me. I've never made love, as you call it. I've only ever had sex.'

'Maria . . .' That admission seemed poignant to Ruby.

Not so, apparently, to Maria. 'And I've enjoyed every sweaty minute,' she laughed. 'Maybe one day I'll find somebody to get real with. But I'm not holding my breath.' She shrugged, an exaggerated 'so what?' that didn't quite convince. 'Men haven't been all that nice to me, Ruby. I don't attract the likes of Tom. I'm more . . .' she stammered for a millisecond, 'Birdie's type.'

'Manny wasn't nice to me in the long run.' That was an understatement, similar to the one Ruby employed when she told Teddy his outfits looked 'interesting'.

'You'll be all right. You've got it, whatever it is. I've got . . .' Maria held her hands out, palms up, in search of inspiration. 'I've got almost it. I'll always get the bargain basement guys.'

Disturbed by this revelation of low self-esteem, Ruby objected. 'We don't know what Tom is like. He could be a right cow.' She noted Maria's wince. 'Pig, then. Sorry. I am trying with the swearing, you know.'

'I know,' said Maria kindly. 'Tom is nice. I can smell it on him. Just like I can smell the last girl's perfume on Birdie. What does he do for a living?'

'Dunno. Can't work it out. I know he has a BA.'

'Bachelor of Arts?' Maria looked impressed. 'See? Nice.'

'That's hardly a guarantee.'

'It's a start, though. Maybe he does research into . . .' Maria stumbled. 'Something. Or he might be a teacher.'

'Yeah.' Ruby hadn't thought of that. She liked the idea of Tom as something staid and respectable: it would be such a relief after Manny's fly-by-night business affairs. She reined herself in. Her thought process was galloping into very dangerous terrain. 'Hadn't you better get back to your Mr Birdie?'

'Yes. He's a dirty job but somebody's got to do him.'

23

Another Saturday. Another smorgasbord of reality shows, talent shows, chat shows and a popular movie with all the swear words snipped out. Full length on the sofa with a bucket of popcorn on her chest, Ruby realised it was almost 3 a.m.

She sat up abruptly, showering the rug with popcorn. Maria was always in by now. From somewhere deep in the cushions, her mobile hiccuped, and Ruby scrabbled for it. She had inherited her mother's dread of the late night call, always expecting it to be the police.

It was Maria. 'Could you get round to the Glove?' she asked, in a whisper. 'I know it's late.'

'Of course I can.' Ruby was already reaching for her keys. 'But what's going on?'

'You know that new fan the guys had installed?' said Maria. 'Well, the shit's just hit it.'

The pavements were grey and quiet beneath Ruby's feet as she sped along the familiar route to the bar. As she was passing the doorway of the delicatessen, a snore startled her. Yehudi slept, head on knees, by his laden trolley, arms cradled around his violin and his dog.

'Sleep tight,' breathed Ruby, smiling at his bowed, unkempt head. He was fantastically filthy, an affront to Ruby's love of the hygienic, but she had a soft spot for her tramp.

The Velvet Glove seemed dark, but when Ruby peered through the glass of the door she saw the glow of the spotlight over the stage. She made out Maria, bending over what appeared to be a large blancmange.

At Ruby's knock, Maria bounded across the deserted bar to let her in. 'Look at him,' she sighed, motioning at the stage with a nod of her head as she noisily relocked the door. 'He's in pieces.'

The blancmange was Teddy, sitting on the edge of the stage, legs a foot apart, feather boa quivering with each sob.

'It's Kendall,' said Maria, before Ruby could ask. 'He had a little confession to make.' She swiped a bottle of Jack Daniel's from the bar as they passed it. 'He's interested in someone else.'

'*Nooo!*' Ruby couldn't hold the exclamation in. Teddy and Kendall were her quasi-parents: their relationship had to be in good shape for her to make sense of the world. She sank down to sit beside Teddy and draped a long arm around his buckled shoulders. '*Interested?*' She examined the word and didn't much like it. 'What does Kendall mean by that?'

'He means,' Teddy's voice was even hoarser than usual, 'that I'm old news. Not wanted on voyage. Fit for the knacker's yard. Ready for re-fucking-cycling.'

'Kendall didn't put it quite like that,' interrupted Maria gently. Her face grey after an hour of Teddy duty, she poured some Jack Daniel's into the pint glass Teddy was waving.

From the other side of the darkened bar came a voice.

'No, I didn't. I was sensitive and respectful and honest.' Kendall emerged into the spotlight's scrutiny. 'And this is what I got for my trouble.'

Ruby inhaled sharply. She'd never seen a man with a glitter-ball dangling round his neck before.

With a growl, Teddy shouted, 'It was all I had to hand. Believe me, he got off lightly.' He slurped a loud mouthful from his glass. 'Take it off, Kendall, you're only looking for attention.'

'You tried to throttle me with it!' Kendall sounded offended. 'I'm keeping it where I can see it.'

'Pity I didn't try that strategy with you,' sneered Teddy.

'I give up.' Kendall wandered back to the darkness.

'Go on! Play the martyr like you always do!' spat Teddy.

Ruby gave Teddy a covert once-over. At some point his wig had scarpered, leaving his fluffy head vulnerable and small. The flamboyant eye makeup was smudged down his cheeks, there were tear stains on his bodice, and his big, lumpy feet were shoeless. 'Oh, Teddy,' she murmured.

'What would I do without you girls?' he asked sorrow-fully. 'Never depend on love, ladies. It lets you down every time.'

'You don't really think that,' scolded Ruby. She needed to resurrect something from this shambles. 'He's only *interested* in someone.' Privately she was wondering why Kendall had to open his big mouth. 'He's still with you, that's the import-ant thing.' She contemplated a rousing speech about winning back your man, but Teddy was in no state to do any such thing. 'It's not like he's moving out.'

'He'd better not try,' boomed Teddy. 'He's mine. He's a little shit, but he's my little shit. I don't let go that easy.'

Exchanging a worried glance with Maria over Teddy's head, Ruby decided to investigate further. With a 'Back in a mo', she stood up and tiptoed across the floor to where Kendall had melted, like a ghost in a Victorian tale. Groping about in the darkness, Ruby found the fire exit. Clanking through it, she came upon Kendall out in the alley, sitting on an upturned barrel, turning the glitterball over in his hands.

'Death by glitterball,' he said without looking up. 'What a way to go.'

'Teddy's trying for death by Jack Daniel's.'

'Or self-pity.'

With lips slightly pursed, Ruby said, 'Can you blame him?' She took a seat on an adjacent barrel. It was surprisingly comfy.

'Poor Teddy.' Kendall raised his eyes, sharp and alert even in the midnight gloom. 'Poor, poor Teddy.'

'Don't use that tone of voice,' begged Ruby. Once again, life was not following her script. 'You love him. Or you did last time I looked.'

'I'll always love him,' said Kendall, simply and with a touch of weariness, as if discussing an incontinent cat. 'That doesn't guarantee a happy ever after, princess.'

Folding her arms, Ruby said, with a hint of huff, 'Nobody over the age of eight expects one of them.' Deftly she forgot the rose-tinted glasses she'd thrown away only when the CID came knocking. 'Talk to me,' she said bravely, uncertain whether Kendall would play ball. 'Who are you interested in?'

'Nobody you know,' said Kendall.

'And how interested are you?'

'If you're asking am I interested in a trousers off, let's get jiggy with it kind of way, then not very.' Kendall paused, then surprised Ruby by taking her hand. 'But if you're asking if I'm interested in a my God, somebody actually wants to listen to me kind of way, then I'm very very very interested.' He looked intently at her, as if trying to see past the tired eyes and untidy fringe. 'I haven't been happy for a while, Ruby, and now somebody is showing me glimpses of a wonderful, comfortable, *quiet* world.' He dropped her hand. 'It's hard to look away.'

'But you haven't . . .'

'No. I haven't,' said Kendall firmly. 'I don't do affairs. Never have. And I've had offers, you know,' he said archly. 'But I haven't been unfaithful to the old slapper yet.'

'So why mention this . . . somebody?' Ruby already hated this whoever-it-was with their glimpses and their listening. 'Unless you're thinking of going?' She had meant to keep the fear out of her voice.

'If you want the truth, I'm torn.' Kendall tutted at the melo-dramatic gasp from his interrogator. 'Keep your hair on, Rubes. I won't do anything rash. It's hard to imagine a life without Teddy. He's my other half. Believe it or not, I still look at him and see the skinny lad in the bank. He was a beauty, you know. Amongst all those suited, buttoned-up straights, Teddy was like a rose growing on an allotment. And I plucked him.' He half laughed. 'Good thing Teddy's not out here, or we'd be fending off some pretty grim *double entendres*.'

'Are you going to take things further with this mystery man?'

'There's so much you don't know,' said Kendall, madden-ingly. 'It's not straightforward.'

'Teddy's in agony, Kendall. Is this the beginning of the end?' Ruby asked, desperate for a *no*.

'Who knows?'

'Not good enough,' said Ruby as sternly as she could. 'As answers to vital questions go, Kendall, that is not nearly good enough.'

'Is *I hope not* any better?'

'Not really.'

Kendall stood up slowly, as if his joints ached. 'Here. Give this glitterball to Dusty Springfield in there and tell him if he wants to finish the job I'll be upstairs.'

The glitterball didn't glitter out there in the gloom. It just reflected dozens of tiny crestfallen Rubys.

The house was quiet, like a museum, as Ruby padded about with her dusters. Mrs Vine was upstairs, lying on her sumptuously dressed bed, prey to a headache.

When everything was in order, Ruby pushed open the door to her client's room. Opening the heavy curtains just a chink, she rested a china cup of tea on the bedside table. 'Thought you might like a hot drink,' she whispered.

Sitting up, Mrs Vine looked perfectly pressed and neat, with none of the disarray that Ruby exhibited if she took a nap: after forty winks in front of *Judge Judy* she woke up looking shipwrecked, but Mrs Vine could have gone straight to a job interview.

'You *are* thoughtful,' she smiled, unbending just a little. 'What a blessing you must be to your parents.'

That smarted, so Ruby changed the subject. 'Are you looking forward to your niece and her family arriving? It's tomorrow, isn't it? I aired the two bigger spare rooms and put your best bedclothes on.'

Mrs Vine looked down and said thinly, 'There's some problem with her husband's work. They won't be coming.' She took a sip of tea and said, 'She's terribly disappointed, poor gel.'

I bet she is, thought Ruby murderously. She'd seen the cake Mrs Vine had baked sitting on a stand down in the kitchen.

She'd seen the little handwritten jottings of places the children might enjoy, on her desk. 'Oh well.'

'Oh well indeed,' echoed Mrs Vine.

'Has Birdie rung?' Ruby, fresh from two hours of hosing down the Bachelor's pad, bustled into her own kitchen and dumped her toolbox noisily on the floor.

'How could he?' Maria was ladling coleslaw out of a tub into her waiting mouth. 'He doesn't have my number.'

'Oh. So you don't want to see him again?' Ruby hoped the naked relief wasn't too apparent.

'The fair's moved on.'

The Friends' house was quiet. Joe was in his room, Hugo was out bumbling in the wider community, and Olivia was in her study, a small room apparently made entirely of books. With a respectfully discreet knock, Ruby disturbed her with a whispered, 'Do you want me to do in here, or shall I leave it till next week?'

'Oh. Ruby.' Olivia put down her glasses, with a weary rub at the bridge of her nose. 'Leave it for today.' She looked her full in the face. 'I'm glad you looked in on me. I need to apologise.'

'Nah you don't,' said Ruby airily, hoping to curtail any doomy dissecting. 'All forgotten.'

'Not by me,' said Olivia, holding her gaze. She studied Ruby's expectant face for an instant longer than was comfortable. 'I know,' she began slowly, 'how much we owe you, Ruby.'

'Oh, come on,' laughed Ruby, still hoping to lighten the tone. 'I only clean the house. Anybody with a mop can do that!' Her gaze was more skittish than her employer's, and danced all over the room.

'I know how much we owe you,' repeated Olivia carefully.

There was hidden weight to her words and Ruby wriggled like a butterfly on a pin. 'How do you mean?' she asked.

After a moment of charged silence, Olivia's demeanour softened. 'I do see all the little touches, you know. The extras. I'm not completely preoccupied with my work.'

'Oh, them,' scoffed Ruby, uncertain how this might pan out. 'They're nothing.'

'They make Joe happy. There's been a change in him. In us.' Olivia rubbed a metal paperweight shaped like a monkey with its hands over its eyes. 'Joe even trots off to his sitar lessons like a lamb.'

'That's nice.' Ruby maintained her neutral expression, willing herself not to confess with a shout of *Don't be nice to me! We do illegal ballroom behind your back!*

'I'm trying to say, and you'll have to forgive me because I'm not very good at expressing myself at moments like this, I'm sorry for letting off steam at you.'

Ruby waved away the apology but Olivia ploughed on.

'To be honest,' she said, 'I'm not very confident.' She pushed her rebellious fringe back from her forehead and said, 'Oh, I can stand up in front of two thousand people and explain exactly why my college needs more funds and exactly how I plan to spend the money. No problem. But, here at home, with my boy . . .' Olivia looked past Ruby. 'As a mother,' she said quietly, 'I'm not sure of myself at all.'

'Joe loves you!' Ruby exclaimed, believing this simple fact to be a cure-all.

'Yes, I think he does,' said Olivia, in her analytical way. 'And I certainly love him. More than he can ever know,' she added crisply, as if wary of letting too much emotion creep in. 'But, Ruby, it's my weak spot. It's the one important segment of my life where I've never earned a qualification.

I don't have a diploma in being a mum. And it shows. I think too hard about how I should be with him. Then you come along, and you're such a natural.'

'I'm not a mum,' said Ruby carefully.

Ignoring her, Olivia said, 'Maybe now you can understand why I flew off the handle. I'm . . . oh God, this is a terrible word, and very hard to admit, but I'm jealous, Ruby.'

'Don't be jealous of me,' said Ruby with feeling, wishing that she had the nerve to reach out and touch Olivia. 'I'm just some daft bird who cleans your house. You're Joe's mum. You're the warrior queen.'

Ignoring her again, Olivia rose abruptly from her chair. 'I'm glad we cleared that up. I'd better . . .' She stuttered, and finally said sheepishly, 'Well, I'd better sit down again, and get on with my work.' Olivia laughed, and she looked like a little girl.

Red eyes peeped out from under a blanket that Yehudi's dog would have rejected as too unhygienic. 'Is that you?' asked Drama Queen weakly, as if about to breathe her last.

'What happened?' asked Ruby, helping her client up to a sitting position. They were surrounded by empty mugs, screwed-up tissues, bottles lolling on their sides and one sandwich with the imprint of a shoe on it.

'He chucked me.' Those sore eyes closed, like a silent movie heroine on her deathbed.

'I'm so sorry,' said Ruby, with as much sincerity as she could muster, which wasn't much: the boyfriend was bad news. The only way was up for Drama Queen. 'You poor thing. Oh well,' she sighed, philosophically, standing up to make a start on the debris of heartache.

'I begged and begged and begged. I got down on my knees. I told him I'd kill myself,' said Drama Queen, working herself up by retelling it. 'But he said I didn't have the nerve. So I threw myself out of the window. But I—'

'Live on the ground floor,' Ruby butted in. 'Well, let's not dwell on all that. I'll make you some soup.'

'Oh would you?' Drama Queen brightened. 'And some toast? And perhaps a bit of cheese. I think there's a pickled onion in the cupboard. You might have to go to the shop for bread.'

24

Preparing for a date – especially your first date since early in
the millennium – shouldn't be a spectator sport. Quite how
Teddy and Maria had wangled their way into her bedroom,
Ruby wasn't sure, but they had taken up residence on her
bed with a bottle of wine and a bowl of Doritos. They were
there, they claimed, to offer encouragement and support. As
Ruby finished drying her hair, Teddy was showing his support
by lying on his back and kicking his heels in the air, cack-
ling with laughter.

'You'd better scoot,' said Ruby through gritted, flossed,
whitened, Listerined teeth. 'I need to get dressed.'

'Oh, but this is the best bit,' bleated Teddy, righting himself
and brushing crumbs from his shirt. 'Change in the ensuite
if you're shy. Although as a professional homosexual of some
years' standing I can promise not to ogle your assets.'

Ruby's assets were, she felt, none of Teddy's business whatever his sexuality, so she cloistered herself in her super-chic
bathroom. Glad of the flattering light, she surveyed herself
in her grey jersey dress. The boat neck suited her broad

shoulders and the demure length felt comfortable. Emerging, she asked confidently, 'Will I do?'

Silence from the bed. Then Teddy spoke. 'I hope Tom is aware that he's wining and dining his old nan.'

'Far too frumpy,' grumbled Maria, leaning across Ruby's pillows to slop more wine into Teddy's glass. 'Back you go.'

Luckily Ruby had a standby outfit. The cunningly cut black trousers were sophisticated, a relic of her old incarnation as Queen of Esher's designer boutiques. The black ruffled silk blouse set them off perfectly, she thought. 'Take two!' she laughed, stepping back out into her room.

Maria was too busy tutting to critique, but Teddy asked, 'Are you stopping off at a state funeral on the way?'

'It has to be this or the grey dress,' said Ruby mulishly.

Sliding off the bed, but managing to hold his wine glass steady, Teddy padded over to the wardrobe. 'Let's have a look,' he said to himself, pawing the clothes hanging in there. 'Nah. Nah. Nah.'

'That gold dress I helped you buy,' said Maria suddenly.

Helped as in *bullied remorselessly*. 'Too short,' said Ruby, shortly.

'No such thing, doll.' Teddy had found the garment, hanging limp like a glamorous bandage on the last hanger. 'This is more like it.'

Back in the bathroom, Ruby didn't quite recognise the redhead in the mirror. Her legs, long and white and supple, seemed longer than she remembered, and her appley bosom more rounded. 'I can't wear this,' she whispered, unnerved by the sexually knowing vibes given off by the apparition.

The bathroom door flew open and her twin tormentors' giggles died as they drank her in.

'You'll knock him out,' said Maria admiringly.

'Where have you been hiding those pins?' demanded Teddy.

'I can't wear this.' Ruby wrapped her arms around herself, as if to obliterate the babe in the mirror. 'It's too much.'

'It would be a crime not to wear that dress,' said Maria, her chin sticking out in a way that Ruby recognised. And dreaded. 'It's perfect with your colouring. It suits your shape. Tom won't believe his eyes.' She said, more softly, 'It's OK to be sexy. Manny's not here to tell you off.'

'It's settled,' said Teddy firmly, taking a hold of Ruby's arm. 'She's wearing it. And now she's going to have a wee snifter before she goes out.'

Sitting down without treating the others to a grandstand view of her gusset was a challenge. Teddy was pacing back and forth, asking questions about Tom like a concerned father. 'What does he do for a living?' He was irked that Ruby didn't know, but the BA went down well. 'Good head on his shoulders, then. Is he polite? Clean fingernails? Not a potty mouth, I hope?' he enquired, with magnificent hypocrisy. 'As long as he appreciates you, he's all right by me.'

'I've seen the way he looks at her.' Maria winked at Ruby. 'He appreciates her, Ted.'

'Good. Only the best for our little Ruby. She doesn't even know what a jewel she is.' Teddy's button eyes went foggy, and he patted Ruby's hair absentmindedly as if she was a Labrador. 'Anybody who hurts her will have to deal with me.'

'Thanks.' Ruby tried to repair the damage Teddy had wreaked on her artfully natural hair.

Gulping, Teddy turned to the panoramic window and lifted his head in a stance obviously calculated to depict great emotion. 'Just because my love life lies on the floor, trampled underfoot by insensitive paws, it doesn't mean I can't be happy for you.' He turned away from the window. 'We're talking again, but Kendall's still in the spare room.' Teddy struck another dramatic pose. 'He doesn't deserve my lily-white body until he can state categorically that he's not *interested* in anybody but *moi*.'

'Where is he tonight? Back at the bar?' asked Ruby, glad to deflect attention from her date. She didn't welcome all the fuss. It was just dinner: a plate of food and a glass of wine. She wasn't looking for a knight on a white charger to take her away from all this: she'd just arrived at all this.

'He's out.' Teddy sneered. 'Part of our new attempt to be *civilised*.' He spat the word, as if it tasted bad. 'Reckons he needs some freedom, some time off from me now and then.'

'Don't look so hurt, Teddy.' Ruby felt for him. 'Sometimes people in relationships need to give each other some space now and then.'

'If you plan to use the phrase "if you love someone set them free" I may have to vomit on your shoes,' warned Teddy. 'I know, I know, I read all that self-help bollocks too, but I don't have to like it.' He took a deep breath and lifted his head. 'But I have promised no more rows. No more scenes. We're going to get through this.'

'That's the spirit.'

Maria checked her watch. 'We have to get back to the Glove, Ted. That new barman is on his own.'

'Duty beckons. I'm a slave to that place,' claimed Teddy melodramatically. 'I should be having a nice quiet nervous breakdown somewhere but instead I'll be on that stage, giving an undeserving public my Miss Tammy Wynette.'

Maria pulled Ruby around by her shoulders, then looked her over like a hard-to-please stage mother. Licking the end of her finger she cleaned a mark from Ruby's cheek, ignoring the 'Yew!' her victim emitted. She tweaked her hair, moved the strap of her dress, handed her a gold clutch. 'You'll do,' she said.

From within the clutch, Ruby's mobile twittered. As the

trio walked towards the lift she fished it out. 'Maybe it's Tom saying he can't make it,' she said, with a small flicker of hope that she could tear off this OTT dress, and the butterflies in her stomach could call it a day. It was Sheila. 'Sheila! You're working late. I'm guessing Manny got the new papers. How did he take it?' Ruby had been expecting this call. 'Not well, I dare say.'

'Now don't panic,' began Sheila, in a tone designed to make any sane human do just that.

'What?' Ruby clutched the phone.

'Manny is out.'

'They let him out?' squealed Ruby, incredulous. 'He's dangerous!'

'He let himself out.' Sheila's voice was tight. 'He was being driven back from yet another court hearing when he overpowered the warders. Held a knife to one of their throats. Busted out of the back of a van on Euston Road and hasn't been seen since.'

'When was that?'

'An hour ago.'

Enough time to get to Parsons Green. Ruby turned away from the windows. He could be outside. He could be in the lift. She almost laughed at Sheila's next line.

'Don't worry.'

'He'll come for me, Sheila. This is all about the divorce.'

'The police reckon he'd be crazy to turn up at your place. It's too obvious. And your husband is not an obvious man.'

'Thanks for letting me know.' Ruby had to end the conversation. She wanted to vomit, to purge herself of all the Manny years.

'Take care.'

Maria and Teddy had put two and two together. 'You're

not going anywhere,' said Teddy stoutly. 'I'm sleeping here tonight.'

His reaction broke through Ruby's nausea. 'Teddy, I'm going to carry on as normal.' Moments ago, Ruby had been hoping to hear that Tom couldn't make it, now she was fired up and ready to date, date, date for all she was worth. 'If Manny wants me he'll find me. Hiding indoors won't stop him.' She allowed herself an inward smile at the thought of portly old Teddy protecting her from her gangster husband. 'He wants me to be scared.'

'And,' said Maria, catching her drift and liking it immensely, 'you don't do what Manny wants any more.'

'Correct.'

But Ruby jumped when the lift doors opened, all the same.

Snug in a taxi (on Teddy's insistence), Ruby's initial panic soon faded. To be replaced by secondary panic. She bit her lip, chewing off her carefully applied gloss, as the cab took her into W1, gazing out unseeingly at normal people leading normal lives.

Thank goodness, she thought, that Maria and Teddy had been with her when she'd got the news. Her world was so shrunken that there was nobody else to call with this development.

How ironic that Ruby's immediate instinct had been to call Manny. She was still, somewhere in the loamy depths of her psyche, looking to him for protection. Looking to Manny to protect her from himself was so very nuts that Ruby was rather impressed by her own mental dexterity.

The taxi purred on the spot at traffic lights. Ruby peered out. Already in Soho, she was only a street away from Tom. Her stomach lurched. She reminisced about her earlier nerves with fondness: the butterflies had found hobnail boots.

Ruby fanned her face and took deep breaths. Two people stepped off the kerb, speeding up as the traffic lights flashed amber. The taxi revved, almost clipping the couple's heels. The man put his arm protectively around his companion's shoulder, and half turned as he hurried them both to safety. Ruby swivelled on her seat, her hair flying in her eyes. 'Kendall!' she squeaked.

The restaurant was small. Romantic. Ruby, who had been dealt a couple of impressive sideswipes by fate on her way there, didn't feel terribly romantic. She was shaken by the sight of Kendall and his lover, and fearful of Manny, before she even approached her mixed bag of emotions about Tom.

Peachily lit by the flattering candlelight, Ruby checked herself out in a mirror across the restaurant. She put a hand to her hair, tossing it a little, in case it looked too 'done'. Her makeup was perfect, the gold dress twinkled discreetly and she smelled delicious; but the inside didn't quite match up to the wrapping. It was simple for Ruby to look good, far more elusive to feel that way. She looked at the dainty watch on her wrist and before she noted the time, realised that it was one of Manny's last gifts to her. It seared her wrist, and she tugged it off, secreting it in her clutch bag.

The waiter brought her a calming glass of wine, and Ruby tried not to watch the door. The minutes ticked by, and dread crawled over her. She had another glass of wine, but stopped sipping halfway down, realising that her thoughts had begun to melt and meld and slip away from her.

A couple of scenarios occurred to her, neither of them good. Tom had forgotten – bad. Tom had been jumped by her escapee husband – really very bad indeed.

Ruby tried to focus on the more banal reasons a man might be late for a date – leaves on the line, working late.

To her frantic brain they didn't seem half as likely as her lurid imaginings. He'd either forgotten all about her or was lying in the gutter with his features rearranged, like a Picasso.

Ruby looked at the menu. She studied the other diners, all of them arranged in cosy groups of two or more. She was the only soloist in the place. She fiddled with her cutlery. She tapped a tune on the tablecloth. She coughed. She rearranged the bra strap chafing her shoulder. And she tried not to imagine Manny out there in the London evening like a modern day Jack the Ripper. And she tried not to remember just how happy Kendall looked with his *amour*.

Even without checking her watch, Ruby knew that Tom was very late. He'd forgotten. Her head bowed, she tried to swallow this fact. It was a blessing in disguise, she told herself, utilising one of her mother's favoured sayings: it hadn't helped during Ruby's teens and it didn't help now. Suddenly Tom's eyes were bluer, his hair more touchable and his plain way of speaking more comforting. Oh well, she thought, draining her glass, she'd got along without him up to now. Him and his eyes and his hair and his plain speaking.

A kerfuffle at the door made her look up. She looked back at her glass – that wine must be potent. The kerfuffle continued, and reluctantly she dragged her eyes back to the scene by the gilt reception desk.

Ginger wig wobbling, a clown in full, terrifying regalia was arguing with the manager. His padded tummy knocked a pile of menus from a shelf as he pointed agitatedly across the room. The manager followed the line of the finger in its oversized white glove, and found Ruby's startled face.

Ruby sat up straight, a blush burning her carefully made-up face as all the staff and all the guests switched their gaze between her and the clown, like enthralled tennis fans. Clowns ranked high in her personal list of scary things (just behind touching the taps in a public loo and Vanessa Feltz) and this one was pointing straight at her, *walking towards her*: it was like a nightmare.

Shrinking back in her seat as the tall figure made his way through the warren of tables in his long patchwork coat, Ruby watched the feeble efforts of the manager to hold him back. The clown's massive yellow shoes kept catching on chairs and turning over ladies' handbags, but he was undeterred.

Snaking her arms tightly about herself, Ruby pressed back in her chair as the clown stopped to loom over her. 'Sorry I'm late,' he said, and a small horn sticking out of his coat pocket honked, making Ruby jump. 'I couldn't get away from work.'

Unexpectedly, the voice wasn't helium high-pitched. It was plain. It was Tom's. 'That's all right,' she heard herself saying. 'You're here now.'

25

The walk down the busy Soho street was the longest of Ruby's life. His huge feet slapping along the pavement beside her, Tom was nonchalant about the stir his outfit was causing, but Ruby found it hard to be so blasé. She stole a look at him as they turned a corner, taking in the bright orange tufts of hair beneath his undersized bowler, his painted smile and his red ball of a nose. *This man*, she thought, *is my date*.

Her fear of being overdressed had faded: it's hard to be overdressed beside somebody wearing a suit that is tartan, floral, and five sizes too large. 'Could you stop that thing, you know, honking?' she asked testily: the horn tooted sadly with every step Tom took.

'Oh. Sorry.' Tom took the horn out of his pocket and fiddled with it. 'It's faulty.' He grinned, his teeth very white against the shiny red greasepaint. 'It's a mistake to try and save money on horns.'

'Just what I always say,' murmured Ruby, the giggles and exclamations of the people they passed striking her like hurled stones.

'Sit here. Have a coffee.' Tom gestured to a metal chair outside one of the coffee bars that stud Soho. 'I'll disappear into the Gents and come back a changed man.'

'Like Superman in the phone box.'

'Only I promise not to be wearing tights.'

Tights, thought Ruby, as she watched him bump and bounce his way through the coffee bar clientele, *would be an improvement.*

So. Tom was a clown. Ruby would rather he was a child-catcher, or made tampons, or sold his bottom on Piccadilly. Clowns managed to scare and bore her all at once, and she'd just been thrown out of a restaurant with one. As first dates go, it couldn't get much worse. Unless, of course, Manny turned up and fed them to each other.

Fifteen minutes passed before Tom reappeared, long enough for Ruby to gulp down two espressos. This time his progress through the bar didn't attract any attention: he was just an ordinary, if rather nice looking, bloke.

'Right.' Tom sat down heavily in the chair opposite Ruby, dumping a bag that strained at the seams. 'May we start again?'

'I'd like to,' said Ruby, wholeheartedly.

'Good. You look gorgeous.' Tom looked doubtful. 'Is that good enough? Should I say stunning? Because you are.'

'Gorgeous will do.' Ruby examined the bottom of her cup.

'Is that too much? Should I pace the compliments?'

Tom was teasing her, but he wasn't to know how uneasy Ruby was about her looks. 'You look nice,' she said shyly, because he did. His messy hair dangled in his eyes, and his white shirt was crisp under his black linen jacket.

Smiling broadly, in a way that creased his entire face, Tom said, 'Better than I did when I arrived. Sorry about that. You looked horrified. I assumed you knew.'

'How would I know?' asked Ruby, unwrapping a sugar cube to give her nervous fingers something to do.

'The photos on my board. And surely you saw my work clothes lying around?'

'The photos . . .' Ruby said slowly, realising long after the fact that the well-swaddled guy with the squirty flowers was Tom. 'I've never come across your work clothes.' She paused. 'I'd remember,' she said, emphatically. 'I saw a note about a BA. I assumed you were some kind of brainbox academic.'

'BA?' Tom looked into the navy night sky, screwing up his face in puzzlement. Something dawned, and he seemed to be struggling not to laugh. 'I use the abbreviation BA,' he said, his mouth twitching dangerously, 'for balloon animals. Sometimes clients request them.'

'Balloon . . .' began Ruby, but she couldn't finish the phrase. She was too busy wincing at the thought of those squeaky little misshapen poodles that threaten to burst any moment.

Tom slapped his thighs, stood up, threw a fiver down on the table and held out his hand. 'Hungry?' he asked.

Her slender hand heading for his in slow motion, Ruby nodded. 'Starving,' she admitted, as her fingers disappeared in his clasp.

'Good. Classy or not so classy?'

'Chinese, please!' giggled Ruby, whose mood had improved sharply thanks to the ditching of the comedy clothes and the warmth of Tom's hand.

In contrast to the bustling streets outside, the Chinese restaurant was calm and quiet. Pink shaded lanterns shed a blush over the room and on to the blue-black topknot of the impossibly pretty girl who brought them the banquet of food they'd recklessly ordered.

'I take it,' said Tom, watching with amusement in his eyes

as Ruby fell on a spare rib, 'that you're not one of those girls who can't eat in front of men?'

'Gnnbhle grof,' said Ruby, masticating enthusiastically. She swallowed and repeated herself. 'Absolutely not.'

'Good.' Tom's good humour was imperturbable. He seemed delighted with everything: the table, the food, the strange cloudy wine that came in a carafe and called to mind goat urine. 'I had a girlfriend once who only pushed her food around, and acted all flabbergasted if I suggested afters.'

'Afters is the best bit,' said Ruby knowledgeably. 'Unless they bring you chocolate mints with your coffee. That is, I think, *officially* the best bit.' She liked herself with Tom; she was free and easy, talking with the voice that she recognised from inside her head rather than the stilted one that sometimes escaped. 'Have a rib. They're orgasmic.' She blushed, then blushed because she was blushing.

'That's quite a claim,' said Tom, amused. He had a little pout at odds with such a generous mouth. 'So. That mate of yours. Maria? She's quite something.'

'She's very protective,' said Ruby. 'And very very nosy.'

'Without her we wouldn't be sitting here. I like her. Although she has claws, I bet.'

Bridling slightly, Ruby said, 'She's my best friend,' warmed by the truth of it. She'd never said it before.

'I used to think my brother was my best mate,' said Tom, chasing a prawn ball with his chopsticks.

'Don't let what happened come between you.' Ruby didn't want to be responsible for a rift. 'I overreacted.'

'No, you didn't. Some girls would have stuck the hoover where the sun don't shine,' pouted Tom. 'He just laughed when I tackled him about it. Sod.'

'You do look alike.' Ruby wanted to add that Tom was more handsome, but the moment passed.

'That's where the similarity ends. I couldn't cheat on anybody the way Carl does on my poor sister-in-law.'

A gold star went up on the scoreboard Ruby was keeping. Loyalty was a plus. But, she reasoned, regretfully taking the star down again, nobody would admit they were the cheating kind. It wasn't something people boasted about on their lonely hearts profiles: *I love long walks, log fires and sleeping with your friends behind your back.* 'Look,' she said carefully, dabbling her digits in the finger bowl. 'We have to talk about the C word.'

Looking blank for a moment, Tom nodded comprehendingly. 'I'm not really a clown,' he began.

'Then you have to radically rethink your dress sense.'

'I mean,' smiled Tom, 'I'm really an actor. I'm a clown on the side. It's just that, for the last five years, I've been a clown who's an actor on the side. There's loads of clown work out there, but precious little acting.' He folded his arms on the table and leaned closer. 'I was down to the last three for a regular part in *EastEnders*.' He accepted Ruby's admiring whistle. 'There's the odd bit of fringe. I did an ad last year. But it's not enough to keep body and soul together, hence the clowning. Or children's theatre, if you catch me in pretentious mode.' He shrugged. 'It's hard to be pretentious when you're wearing a Day-Glo wig and several tiny people are climbing all over you.'

'Do you enjoy it?' Ruby asked sceptically.

'I LOVE it!' roared Tom, his trained diaphragm startling the pretty waitress nodding off on a stool. 'The kids really get into it. They laugh their heads off if I trip over. And when I go to pour a bucket of water over them and it turns out to be feathers, well, you should see their faces.' He paused, as if the air had been let out of him. 'I'm not selling it to you, am I?'

It was time to tell him. 'Tom, I have a fear of clowns. They scare me. I can't help thinking they're psychopaths.' She gripped her chopsticks harder. She'd gone too far. 'Sorry. I didn't mean to insult you.'

'I'm not insulted,' said Tom. 'Well, not exactly.'

'I can't help it. Maybe I was frightened by one once,' gabbled Ruby. She noticed something. 'You've still got a smudge of white. There. On your neck.' She leaned across the table and touched Tom with her forefinger. Her finger tingled, and Ruby bit her lip.

Wiping his neck with his napkin, Tom said, 'I'm not a psycho, honest. My most antisocial character trait is that I hum loudly in queues. I'm very normal. I verge on boring.' He waved away her laughter. 'Really. You'll find out. At least, you might,' he said, keeping his eyes down.

'I suppose you can't help being a clown,' reasoned Ruby kindly.

'I'll keep it away from you.' Tom cleared his throat. 'I mean, if we . . . if you . . . if we manage to go out again, see each other. I'll never talk about it. I'll be like a spy, I'll keep you in the dark about my job.'

'There's no need for that.' Ruby recognised his discomfort talking about whether they might actually be in the foothills of a relationship. He wanted something to grow between them, she could tell. 'Let's just take things as they come. It's my problem, after all, not yours. Unless you have a pathological dread of cleaners?'

'No. Cleaners are fine. They're good, nice people.' He raised his glass of goat's wee. 'And some of them are beautiful.'

'Oooh, you big silly!' Ruby suddenly channelled her long-dead Nana: she'd be wittering 'Give over!' or 'Lawks a lawdie!' if he gave her any more compliments.

'Never mind the C word,' said Tom, through a mouthful of something with tentacles. 'What about the H word? Have you really got a husband?'

The question was so light and airy, the answer so dungeon-dark. Ruby envied Tom his innocence. ''Fraid so. I'm divorcing him,' she said, hurriedly, in case Tom might suspect her of Carl-style misbehaviour. 'He's in jail.' She said it all in one breath, watching surreptitiously for his reaction. Any hint of contempt and she'd be out of there before her chopsticks hit the plate.

'Jail?' Tom seemed surprised, but his expression didn't betray any hint of *What the hell have I got myself into?* 'What for?' he asked, very interested.

'All sorts. He's a proper old-fashioned criminal. Gambling, protection, tax evasion, fraud,' Ruby ticked off Manny's misdemeanours on her fingers as if memorising a shopping list. 'And . . .' she hesitated, ashamed. 'And violence. Plenty of violence.' She paused as Tom laid waste to a spring roll. 'Specifically to men seen out with me.'

The spring roll got a reprieve. Mid-chew, Tom regarded her questioningly, as if gauging whether or not she was joking. Nothing about Ruby's grave little face could suggest she was anything but deadly serious. 'Jealous, is he?'

'You could say that. Possessive. Manipulative. Controlling. Domineering. Spiteful.'

'I can see why you married him,' said Tom, with admirable levity for a man who'd just found out that he was in the queue for a good old-fashioned duffing up.

'*I* can't,' said Ruby, miserably. 'I don't want to be heavy about this—'

'Not doing a *great* job on that front, Ruby,' interrupted Tom.

'But,' Ruby carried on, 'I have to be straight with you. You see, he was in jail, but he's escaped.'

'This is getting better by the minute.' Tom swept the restaurant with an anxious gaze, before muttering, 'Don't know why I'm bothering to look for him, I've no idea what the bloke looks like.'

'He probably busted out because he got the divorce papers. He's contesting it.'

'I would too,' said Tom, evenly.

'Look, about flirting,' began Ruby clumsily, her mouth setting off before her mind had tidied its desk.

'Yes?' prompted Tom, that amused pout in place again when Ruby paused.

'I can't do it. And it makes me feel awkward when you do it. So . . .'

'No more flirting.' Tom sighed. 'In that case I'll just tell you quickly that you've got the nicest face I've ever seen and leave it at that.'

Ruby's nice face assimilated this last, rather high quality compliment. 'Thank you,' she said meekly.

'How did it go?' Maria looked tiny in a pair of men's pyjamas.

'It went,' said Ruby, maddeningly. She felt serene and she wanted to be alone to take out the jewels of the night she'd just passed and admire them at her leisure.

'Detail!' spat Maria. 'Gore!'

'He's very nice. Very very nice.'

'Nice?' Maria seemed disappointed. 'Is he hilarious? Sexy? Fascinating?'

'He's a nice man. We talked about things.' Not particularly private things: Ruby's secrets were still her own. They'd survived under tarpaulin for all these years, no need to reveal them all at once. Time would tell if Tom was the right person to share them with: after all, even Maria didn't know everything about Ruby. 'He's interesting, and interested.

I had a lovely evening.' Ruby felt light-footed and feathery, despite a surfeit of strange Chinese wine. 'That's all. I like him. And I'm going to see him again.'

'I knew it, I knew it.' Maria went into a cheerleader routine, high kicking and punching the air, as she chanted, 'You're gonna fall in love with Tom! He's gonna save you from Manny!'

Slightly piqued, Ruby could have contradicted Maria: saving Ruby was Ruby's job. However, it was late and she was too placid to disagree with anyone. 'There is one problem,' she said, ominously.

Maria stopped prancing.

'He's a clown.'

'Oh, all men are,' chided Maria, batting the problem away. 'So he's a bit silly sometimes. Ignore it.'

'No, he's a clown,' persisted Ruby. 'An actual clown. That's his job.' She almost laughed at Maria's blank face. 'He clowns for money.'

'Dump him,' said Maria.

26

Miss Delmar phoned Ruby on Thursday morning, coughing like a threshing machine, to cancel that afternoon's ballroom class. 'Tell Joe to practise his sugarpush,' she hacked.

'Er, right,' said Ruby.

Joe was devastated. 'But Suzie and I need to practise for the September show!' he wailed. 'And I bought her some Maltesers!'

It would take more than Maltesers to sweeten the dour Suzie, but Ruby commiserated with Joe's woes. 'Let's go somewhere fun instead,' she suggested, tucking his biro-pocked hand through her arm. 'Ever been to an adventure playground?'

As Ruby had suspected, Joe hadn't. Bishop's Park, Fulham's sprawling pleasure-seekers' paradise on the Thames, boasted an adventure playground, along with tennis courts, bowling greens, a theatre and a lot of middle-aged men showing their knees. 'Voilà!' said Ruby, aping Olivia, as they approached the adventure playground.

Looking around the wooden platforms, dangling ropes

and flimsy bridges, Joe asked 'What's so adventurous about it?'

'Erm . . .' Ruby stuck out her lower lip. 'You swing from the ropes,' she said encouragingly. 'And, er, climb the trees. And scramble along the bridges.' She read Joe's face. 'Or you go somewhere completely different instead. Ice cream?'

Looking relieved, Joe took Ruby's arm again. 'There's a tea place by that bit where the old people are throwing balls at the grass,' he said.

'The bowls pavilion.' Ruby was *au fait* with bowls: her parents had been champions. She remembered their starched uniforms hanging like tense ghosts in the wardrobe. Settling down on a slatted wooden bench a few feet away from the action, Ruby handed Joe a 99 with extra nuts.

'What have you got?' asked Joe, examining Ruby's ice cream with all the envious greed of his age and gender.

'Vanilla. No nuts.'

'Bo-ring.'

Ruby wondered which ice cream flavour Tom preferred: she had him down as a pistachio man. Then, as she wondered why she was wondering, Joe broke into her frozen dairy products related reverie with a giggly, rather loud, 'Look at her bum!'

It was entirely possible that the elderly, well-cushioned lady bending over to roll her heavy wooden ball had heard.

'Joe!' Ruby hissed. 'Shush!'

'But it's funny,' insisted Joe.

'It is not.' That wasn't entirely true, but Ruby had her responsibilities to consider. 'You shouldn't make personal remarks.' Nimbly she forgot the happy ten minutes she and Maria had spent earlier discussing the bottom, face and hairdo of the cashier at the supermarket. Ruby had likened the woman's figure to a sack of badgers, but was nonetheless scampering about on the high moral ground above Joe. 'If you can't say something nice, don't say anything at all.' After three minutes of silence, Ruby pulled Joe's ear. 'All right. You've made your point. Talk to me.'

Joe's circumflex eyebrows seemed to sharpen up when he was being wicked. 'I've never been to a pub.'

'I should think not, you're ten years old, man,' spluttered Ruby. 'It'll be a long time before you set foot in a pub.' She wondered if Joe's dad had ever crossed the threshold of a King's Arms or a Frog and Firkin. Hugo wasn't pubby in the least; she could imagine him backing away from pork scratchings. 'Forget it,' Ruby laughed, resolutely turning away from the expert look of pleading that Joe had assumed. 'I am immune.'

Some weapons are impossible to defend yourself from, nuclear warheads and Joe's eyes among them. With grumbles of, 'We'll have to sit outside' and, 'You're only having a Coke', Ruby allowed herself to be dragged to the Golden Lion. She hated pubs, and had been encouraged in her snobbery by Manny, who had been fond of describing his wife as 'too good' for a plain old boozer.

Parking Joe outside in the 'beer garden' (presumably where they grew all the beer), Ruby entered the gloom of the bar. Once her eyes adapted after the sunshine, she took in the usual afternoon pub mixture of carefree drinkers enjoying a summer shandy, and hardened old lags who had no idea what season it was. It was a relief to escape back out into the light with two soft drinks and two bags of crisps.

Joe was waving to her from the furthest wooden table, over by a scraggy rockery. 'It's great here!' he shouted enthusiastically.

Wondering what special area of hell was reserved for people who took other people's children to pubs, Ruby weaved through the maze of benches and tables. 'No salt and vinegar. I got chicken,' she said.

By way of reply, Joe asked her, 'What are you looking out for all the time?'

'How d'you mean?' Ruby swung a leg over the bench.

'You're doing this.' Joe imitated her, his eyes flitting shiftily left to right. 'Are you being followed?'

'Am I really doing that?' Ruby was stricken. She thought she had her Manny paranoia under control.

'Yeah. Are you on the run?' asked Joe hopefully, opening his crisp bag with his small white teeth.

'Don't be silly.' Ruby could sense Joe's expectancy. He was canny enough to smell a story. Long ago Ruby had decided to be frank with the boy, to answer any proper questions he put to her. 'Well, Joe, there is a bad man in my life, I'm afraid. He should be in jail but he's broken out.' That detail made Joe chomp his crisps a hundred times faster, like a gerbil on speed. 'I worry that he might try to hurt me.' This was, perhaps, a little too raw for a kid. 'I'm just being silly, though. I'm being a girl.' She pulled a self-deprecating face.

'Girls aren't silly,' said Joe, gravely. 'Girls are just as good as boys. Only stupid boys tease girls.' An amateur feminist, Joe had been well schooled by Olivia.

'You're right.' Ruby felt abashed, as if she'd let her whole gender down. She swerved on to the new subject, strategically leaving the other, more thorny one behind. 'You'll always get along with girls if you hang on to that attitude. Girls get sick of boys putting them down.'

'I like girls. They smell better than boys,' claimed Joe. He wasn't as easily deflected as Ruby thought: after a long slug from his Coke, he said casually, 'You don't have to worry about that bad man. You've got me now. I'll protect you.'

Manny vs. Joe? No contest. Ruby gave him a conspiratorial smile. 'Thank you, Joe.'

'S'all right.' He sniffed. 'Are you finishing those crisps?'

The next morning was Friday. Tom day. Ruby hadn't heard from him since their dinner together on Wednesday evening, but they had made a firm date to meet again at the weekend. She was relieved that he wasn't bombarding her with calls or texts; she'd needed space to assimilate the time they'd spent together. Ruby didn't travel at Maria's speed: she went the scenic route with lots of breaks for sweets.

'Hi, Milly,' said Ruby, as she walked down the familiar hall. Trying, and failing, not to be too eager, Ruby glanced about her for the note.

WBC,
How weird is this? One minute we're having dinner, the next you're cleaning my house. What a crazy couple we make.
Tom
p.s. Last door of the fitted wardrobes in the spare room.

A couple. Ruby gulped. She wasn't sure if they were a couple, crazy or not. She was a person and Tom was a person and together they made two people. No more than that. Not yet.

The PS goosed her curiosity. Without touching the streaky splashback or the jam-smeared table top, Ruby dashed up to the spare room and tugged open the last door of the run of wardrobes.

Gasping, she took an involuntary step backwards. An army of multicoloured suits crowded the cupboard, their padded fronts obscenely bobbing. There were hats of all shapes and sizes, neon waistcoats, giant squirty flowers and, most horrible of all, gigantic shoes lined up neatly along the floor.

Ruby slammed the door shut and leaned against it, panting, as if the costumes might escape and chase her round the house. The dating Gods were laughing their heads off over their ambrosia, or their Bacardi Breezers, or whatever the hell they drank up there on Mount Olympus.

When Ruby appeared at the Velvet Glove in the middle of the afternoon the place was deserted and brightly lit. The black floor tiles and the red faux leather booths displayed the scuffs and scars left by hordes of mating males. Later, like Teddy's spare chins, the darkness would once again kindly disguise them.

Teddy was rehearsing a Chicago-inspired routine up on the stage. He paced leadenly through his paces, sighing 'one two three, one two three and *kick*': tonight he'd be springing about with his usual energy, a result, he claimed, of his special cocktail of one part Jack Daniel's to eight parts fear.

'Kendall!' Ruby spotted him wiping glasses, his T-shirt its customary heavenly white. She plopped a carrier bag on the bar. 'Your cashmere sweaters. I hand-washed them.'

Kendall half laughed, half gasped. 'You go beyond the call of duty, you do.' He took the bag. 'Thank you very much. I'll see you right.'

'Don't you dare,' smiled Ruby. 'But you could give me a lemonade. And a few minutes of your time.'

Kendall threw her a guarded look. 'Oh yeah? What's this about?'

'Oh. Nothing.'

'You're a marvellous cleaner but a crap actress. Let's nab a booth.'

In the evenings Ruby never ventured near the booths. They

were the venue for much snogging and groping and God knows what else. In the cleansing afternoon sunshine that managed to penetrate the back of the bar, they looked innocent enough.

Perhaps as a way of heading her off at the pass, Kendall began, 'Our mutual friend of Italian origin tells me the date went well.'

'It did. It was . . . fine.'

'Rather more than fine, according to my informant. Maria's encouraging Teddy to buy a new hat.'

'No hats,' said Ruby firmly. 'I'm still a married woman, remember.'

'Ah, yes,' said Kendall, pulling a sympathetic face. 'Any news from our friendly neighbourhood psychopath?'

'No. He won't turn up. That would be crazy.'

'But he is crazy, my dear.' Kendall was never one to whitewash a subject.

'Listen.' It was time to broach the biggie. 'I saw you on Wednesday night. In town.'

'Really?' Kendall's look of surprise was so rare that it transformed his face. For a millisecond he looked gormless. 'So you saw us together.' His customary expression of sophisticated weariness returned.

'Yup.'

Kendall turned a beer mat over and over. 'Surprised?' he said, eventually.

'Just a bit.'

'Her name's Cath.' For a while it seemed as if Kendall might stop there, but he carried on. 'She works at John Lewis. Haberdashery department.' He looked up from the beer mat's acrobatics and said archly, 'What she doesn't know about gingham ribbon isn't worth knowing.'

Ruby didn't laugh. She sensed there was a lot more to he

'She's my age. She's divorced. She's got a nice little ground floor flat in Putney, all done out in beiges and creams. Bit of a thing for cushions. They're bloody everywhere. Cooks well. She has a cat. Unfortunately. She likes *Coronation Street* but she thinks *EastEnders* is a bit common. She has her grown-up kids and their families for a roast the first Sunday of every month.' Kendall pursed his lips and thought for a moment. 'Ruby, she's normal.'

'Is that the attraction?'

'Yes. After all these years of running a gay bar and living with the male equivalent of Dame Shirley Bassey, suddenly I'm a sucker for normal.'

There was a silence as they both listened to Teddy massacre a high note in 'All That Jazz', and then complain in a booming voice that he'd knackered his fishnets again.

27

It was that difficult second date. Except it wasn't difficult at all. Ruby had been surprised when Tom suggested meeting up on Saturday lunchtime; romance was a creature of the night in her imagination. She was even more surprised when he took her to Portobello market in Notting Hill. 'Let's have a good root around, see if we can find some bargains,' he said, his eyes gleaming with the thrill of the chase.

'O-kay.' Ruby wasn't a market girl. She'd been accustomed to sitting on gilt chairs in chichi boutiques while women whose foreheads and necks were from different decades brought darling little thises and thats for her to try on. Now that her disposable income was invisible to the naked eye, she tended to avoid shops until she indisputably needed something.

Portobello Road snaked up the hill. Dozens of stalls, side by side, cluttered both pavements. They sold just about everything – antique hairbrushes, wind-up dolls, vintage dresses, top hats, embroidered banners, stuffed birds, old coins, silver-framed mirrors. There were ivory knitting needles, moustache mugs, platform boots, blackboards, art deco lamps, digital cameras, and signed photographs of the Spice Girls.

Tom ploughed straight in, cramming a World War I flying helmet over his head. 'But is it *me*?' he frowned through the cracked goggles. He held a Victorian corset up to Ruby. 'Look at the lacing,' he marvelled. 'No wonder those poor women fainted all over the place.'

Tentatively, Ruby wandered to the next stall and put her hand on a tiny enamelled clock.

'Lovely quality, that,' rasped a toad-like man at her elbow, swaddled in scarves despite the sun.

'Hmm.' Ruby put the clock down again, and moved away.

Tom was already ahead of her, leafing through a box of vinyl LPs. Ruby feigned interest in some CDs, most of which seemed to be Wham! She took one out and studied the then-closeted George Michael, admiring the luxuriant hair that betrayed a certain skill with a curling tong. 'I used to be mad about him,' she confessed to Tom, who was engrossed in the back of a David Bowie album.

'Too many teeth,' said Tom dismissively.

'Philistine.' Ruby walked on to peer at the old books on the next stall. She squinted at the tiny opening lines of a fragile *Wuthering Heights*.

A woman speaking rapidly in a language Ruby didn't recognise barged into her, said an obsequious, 'Sorree!' and plodded on. Ruby imagined Manny in this bohemian setting: he'd be glaring at the tourists, denouncing the warm old books as 'tat'. Her mother, too, would have been edgy, hanging on to her handbag and warning Ruby against athlete's foot from second-hand shoes, fleas from second-hand clothes and beri-beri from anybody who looked as if they came from further away than Rotherham.

As if to spite these absent spirits who would clip her

bric-à-brac wings, Ruby recklessly tried on a gold lamé stiletto. She stared down at her pale, transformed foot. It looked racy and kind of avant-garde.

'Try the other one.' Tom handed her the shoe's partner. He stood back to get a good look. 'They're great,' he approved, folding his arms. 'Very you.'

'Very me?' exclaimed Ruby.

'Glamorous. Frivolous.' Tom hesitated, then said in a quieter voice, 'Sexy.'

'Oh for God's sake.' Ruby took off the shoes hurriedly. 'I'm a cleaner, Tom.' Stuffing the shoes any old how back into the pile on the stall, Ruby felt perturbed. She spent her days up to her elbows in other people's dirt: how could he call her glamorous?

Tom looked affronted. He regarded her contemplatively, as if trying to crack a sudoku. 'Time for lunch,' he said, changing the mood by holding out his hand. 'Sushi? Tex-Mex? Crepes?'

'Yes.' Ruby took his hand, noting the squeeze of his fingers. Soon, perhaps, she'd be able to go places like this with her new friends without referring to her old life. Manny's opinion didn't matter any more, and her mother's thoughts had been buried with her.

'It's too early to leave each other.' Tom checked Ruby's reaction. 'Don't you think?' They were loitering outside Hannah House, reluctant to part, talking about this, that and the other.

'You could come up and watch a DVD.' *Or kiss me a lot*, added Ruby's inner, naughtier voice.

'Sounds good.'

Ruby, shocked by her own subconscious, stood stock still. Coming to, she coughed and pressed her entry number into the electronic pad, carefully covering it with her free hand.

'Scared I'll break in one night?' grinned Tom.

'Not you,' said Ruby, minus the grin.

'Oh. *Him*.' Tom looked chastened. He darted a glance behind him as the heavy glass door swung shut again. 'The paranoia's catching,' he muttered.

'It's not paranoia if somebody really is after you,' Ruby corrected him, summoning the lift.

'No, you're right. Sorry.' Tom looked confused, and contrite. 'I didn't mean to make out you were being silly or anything, I just—'

The lift arrived and Ruby silenced him by saying, 'Tom, I know you didn't. My cow of a husband is coming between us even when he's not here.'

'Cow?' queried Tom as the lift doors shut.

Ruby's mind wasn't on the pile of dishes in Mrs Vine's sink. It was on Tom. Specifically, it was on kissing Tom. What a revelation yesterday had been. It had been easy. There was no arcane technique to master, just two mouths getting to know one another. She'd never kissed for so long before. They'd had a break for a glass of wine, but they'd soon banged the glasses down and got back to work.

Tom's face close up was a beautiful blur of hazy eyes and soft skin. If Ruby concentrated, she could still feel the breeze of his breath. She quivered, grinning inanely: Tom had turned her into a moony, daydreaming twit just by kissing her. Imagine, she thought to herself, what she'd be like if they ever—

Ruby switched that thought off. She coughed loudly – actually pronouncing the word 'AHEM!' – and piled greasy plates on top of one another with unnecessary vigour.

Looking wounded, Maria was slurping cornflakes from a bowl as she paced the floor. 'Where have you been? You went out without saying. You never go out on a Sunday morning.'

'So sorry, mistress.' Ruby bowed low. 'Had to nip out to do an extra hour for Mrs Vine. I didn't realise you kept me on such a tight leash.' She headed for the kitchen to get the wrong side of a doughnut. Or the right side, depending on your point of view.

'It's just that with you-know-who on the loose, I like to know where you are.' Maria upended the bowl and noisily drank the milk.

Wincing at the sound effects, Ruby murmured, 'You should ask for your money back from that finishing school.' Her lodger's anxiety had surprised her. And touched her.

'Right.' Maria wiped milk from her chin. 'Yesterday. Second date. How'd it go?'

'Fine.'

'I hate that word,' snarled Maria. 'You only use it to annoy me. OK. I'll try another approach. When I got back from my shift last night were you on your own in your room?'

'What do you think I am?'

'Human.'

'Well, apparently I'm not, because yes I was on my own. Tom left about eleven.'

'There's going to be another date?'

'Yeah.'

'Is it arranged?'

'No.'

'You just know you'll see each other again?'

'Yeah.'

Maria clapped her hands. 'Goody! You're at that stage already! The relaxed, we-obviously-like-each-other-loads stage!' Maria poured another bowl of cornflakes with a flourish. 'This is going well. Very well indeed.'

'Glad you think so,' smiled Ruby. It was just as well that Ruby found Maria's penchant for nose-pokery sweet, because there was no way of stopping her.

'Can I use your ensuite for doing my streaks? It's got more elbow room.' This translated as, 'I'm going to use your ensuite for doing my streaks,' and it earned a nod from Ruby.

Tailing Maria, Ruby lay on her own bed and raised her voice so that she could be heard in the bathroom. Over a few 'Ow's and 'Ouch's as Maria yanked hanks of hair through a smelly rubber cap with holes in it, Ruby broached a subject she needed to share. 'Listen. You're not going to believe this, but I saw Kendall with his bit on the side.'

The cries of pain ceased and Maria's head poked around the bedroom door, a stained and defeated old towel around her shoulders. '*No!* You're kidding!' she hissed delightedly, the yellowing cap squatting on her head. 'What's he like? Fit? Young? Boy band-y?'

'Middle aged. Plump.' Even Ruby's sympathy for Kendall's predicament couldn't dent her enjoyment of Maria's gaping mouth and ascending brows. 'Oh yeah, and he's a she.'

'NO!' This was a roar. Maria even stamped a slippered foot. 'Kendall's gay! He's gay as gay can be! He's gay with knobs on!' She paused. 'That should be *in*, I guess.'

Pulling a vinegary face at Maria's smut, Ruby said placidly, 'Obviously he's not completely gay. Some part of him hankers for a lady.'

'Is she gorgeous?'

'Not at all. She's . . .' Ruby used Kendall's word. It fitted the bill. 'She's normal.'

'Teddy must have hit the roof.' Maria shook her rubber-covered head. 'How can he compete with that?'

'He doesn't know.' Ruby felt a twinge of alarm. 'And he mustn't. It's up to Kendall to tell him.'

'S'pose.' Maria was quiet suddenly, as if somebody had just doused her with cold water. 'Who'd have thought it?' she mused, slipping back into the bathroom.

'Love is what it is,' said Ruby, lying back on her bed and hoping she didn't sound too country music. 'I bet you've got some odd passions in your past.'

Maria didn't answer: perhaps she hadn't heard.

Rolling off the bed, Ruby decided it was slipper time. Her trainers felt hot and sticky, and her toes craved some towelling action. On her knees, she eased a lacquered wardrobe door open. A gleam in the darkness puzzled her; slippers don't gleam. Leaning forwards, she gave a little gasp of surprise.

Cradling them carefully, like two newborn pups, Ruby picked up the gold shoes. 'He bought them,' she said to herself, a delighted smile twisting her mouth into various shapes.

From the bathroom, Maria prattled on about something or other, but Ruby wasn't listening. She jumped up and worked her feet into their new armour.

The gold shoes made her tired old jeans look funky. And her long legs even longer. They were, as Tom had said, glamorous, and frivolous. And damn sexy. Ruby's russet ringlets hung down over her face as she bent over her feet, admiring them as they flexed and pointed. *Even cleaners have their moments*, she thought.

28

It was starting to sound as if Simon was reading from a script. Each time he called, he had exactly the same lines to say. The police were watching Manny's known haunts, talking to his associates, there was nothing to report.

Surely, thought Ruby with frustration, Manny's *known* haunts and his *associates* were exactly what he would stay away from. Until, she thought bitterly, he approached his wife and strangled her neatly with whatever came to hand. 'Thanks for keeping me in the loop, Simon,' she said politely.

'Not at all.' Simon's erstwhile flirtatiousness was just a memory. 'I know how dangerous he is. I wish I had better news for you.'

Ruby thought of Simon's tooth. She guessed that he was almost as scared as she was. 'He can't run for ever,' she philosophised.

She wasn't sure she believed that. Manny could do anything. In her imagination he had grown taller and stronger and even more invincible. He was the sum of all fears, her very own Prince of Darkness. And still she fretted that he was eating properly.

Her back aching from a session at Drama Queen's (she'd been clearing out the kitchen cupboards while listening sympathetically to her client's tearful rants about how much she missed her bastard boyfriend), Ruby couldn't get comfortable in the orange plastic chair at the church hall. A few feet away Joe was tiptoeing backwards, propelled by a determined Suzie. Ruby was certain that men should lead in ballroom, but she didn't blame Joe for taking the easy way out. *Like his dad*, she thought.

Even allowing for Ruby's bias, it was obvious that Joe had improved. He was lighter on his feet, didn't look at the ground any more, and his growing confidence was written all over his face. Miss Delmar bestowed one or two wonky-dentured smiles on him each lesson, and had placed Joe and Suzie in the front row for the September show routines.

Groping for a bar of something bad for her in her handbag, Ruby cheered silently as Joe asserted himself and spun Suzie round on her patent shoes. *Go Joe!* she thought proudly. There was no need for Ruby to turn to hard drugs or killing for kicks as long as she could spend an hour each week in a church hall watching Joe turn and tap and step.

The pleasure was heightened by the knowledge that a certain Tom would be ringing her doorbell later that evening, bearing a bottle of pop, a takeaway and his very best kissing lips.

A small man was dispatched, with a quick cuddle and a packet of Quavers. A taller one was welcomed, with a longer cuddle and a frankly rude kiss. Ruby drowned in Tom's closeness and swayed on her gold heels.

'Whoah!' Tom steadied her.

'Sorry, I . . .' Ruby didn't want to tell Tom how profoundly he affected her equilibrium. 'It's these shoes. They're so high.'

'You don't have to wear them *every* time I see you,' said Tom gently. 'Although I'm glad you do.'

Copying a move she'd seen in countless movies, Ruby coquettishly kicked off the shoes, one at a time. Damn. She hadn't expected the first shoe to skid across the coffee table and knock a glass of Vimto on to the rug. In films, discarded footwear simply flew out of shot, allowing the heroine to get on with some serious smouldering, but Ruby's second shoe ricocheted off the TV, climbing malevolently through the air to deliver a smart thwack to the back of Tom's head.

'How'd you manage that?' he asked, impressed and scared, rubbing his scalp.

'Sorry.' Ruby gathered up the shoes. 'Does it hurt?'

'Of course it hurts.' He reached out and pulled her to his chest. He was getting braver about manhandling her, and Ruby was secretly glad that he punched through her aloof manner. 'But who gives a damn?' He kissed her, hard and meaningfully with those curved lips of his. He tipped his head back to look into her eyes, and his sigh was eloquent with desire.

'Is that a curry I can smell?' asked Ruby in a small voice.

Relinquishing her and pushing a hand through his mussy dark curls, Tom said ruefully, 'You know how to kill a moment, don't you?' He leaned down and thrust the carrier bag at her. 'Yes, Mrs Romance. It's a curry.'

'Good. I'm starving.' Ruby's bare feet slapped on the cool floor as she fled to the kitchen. Some moments had to be killed. She didn't trust herself around Tom. They seemed such a perfect fit, but it was too soon, surely, to be feeling like this about a man she'd met a few weeks ago. It was too random, that she should polish some bloke's sideboard and suddenly find herself in bed with him. Manny had always warned her that she was rash, that her instincts weren't to be trusted. *Do what I tell you and you'll be all right*, he'd insisted.

Ladling curry with unnecessary vigour, Ruby wrestled with the spectre of her ex. There he was again, towering over her poppadoms with unasked-for wit and wisdom. *What would you do with a bank account, you dozy mare?* had been one of his sayings, along with the classic *If God had meant women to have jobs he'd have given them brains.*

Ruby jumped at the pop of the champagne cork in the adjacent room. It sounded like a gunshot, and for one wild moment . . . She counselled herself to get a grip. Manny wasn't in the apartment, and he didn't have to be in her head. She could evict him, she reminded herself. She halted the ladle and turned, sensing that Tom was approaching.

Champagne bottle hanging nonchalantly from one hand, Tom slowly moved towards her. Head down, eyes locked on hers, the twilight moodiness of the apartment showed him off to perfection. Those eyes were really very blue, and they glinted naughtily at her.

Turning properly, Ruby held out one arm, gracefully beckoning Tom into her personal space. Manny had been wrong about so many things – Ruby's dependence, Tania's prowess with birth control, Sam Fox's sexuality – that it stood to reason he should be wrong about his wife's instincts.

'Come here,' she told Tom, hoping he couldn't hear the terror in her voice, just the lust.

Tom reached her arms just as the buzzer sounded. 'Leave it,' he whispered.

'But, oh, flip. I can't. I'm not made that way.' Ruby stamped across the apartment. 'Darn. Poos and wees.'

'Wash that mouth out,' ordered Tom, pouring the champagne into two flutes.

'Yes?' barked Ruby down the entry phone.

'HELLOOOOO!' shouted the most unwelcome visitors ever.

'Oh Gawd,' groaned Ruby, pressing the button to let them in, into her lift, into her perfect evening. 'I know what this is. They've come to get a look at you.'

'Who has?' Tom looked nervous, and slightly hunched, as befits a man who's just had his erotic hopes dashed.

'Teddy and Kendall.' She spoke rapidly, as the lift swooshed upwards. 'They're a couple, both men, kind of like surrogate parents.' The lift doors opened. 'Hide the champagne,' she hissed.

'I heard that!' whooped Teddy, bounding out first, comparatively restrained in very tight jeans. 'We brought our own, you greedy girl.'

'But who's looking after the Glove?' Ruby frowned when Maria followed him in.

'Power cut,' said Kendall succinctly. 'Everything's in darkness.'

'The job lot scampi is defrosting as I speak.' Teddy had stationed himself next to Tom and was appraising him frankly. 'So this is it?' he asked.

'This is Tom,' said Ruby, embarrassed.

Tom wasn't. 'Will it do?' he asked.

Smiling at his cheek, Teddy murmured, 'In an emergency.' Turning to Ruby he mouthed, '*Gorgeous!*' and pulled a face as if his piles had suddenly kicked in.

'Nice to meet you.' Kendall shook hands with his usual firm grip. 'We've heard a lot about you from Maria.'

Ruby shot Maria a look which Maria managed to ignore by giving Tom the kind of uninhibited hug that Ruby needed three years of friendship and written permission to administer. 'I'm disappointed. Thought you might be in your work clothes.'

Ruefully shaking his head down at her, Tom smiled, 'Sorry about that.'

'I have, in my time, been a clown,' admitted Teddy, scurrying to the kitchen and making a tremendous clatter finding glasses for the bottle of Moët in his grasp. 'A sophisticated one, obviously. For an older audience.'

'His outfit had no back to it,' said Kendall, with a wince.

'I'm more traditional,' said Tom, looking perturbed.

'Like our Rubes,' said Kendall, approvingly. 'She's an old-fashioned girl.'

'Married to an old-fashioned gangster,' chirruped Teddy, sloshing out champagne. 'You keep your eyes peeled, Tim.'

'Tom,' said Tom. 'And I shall.'

Teddy poked the silent Ruby in the side. 'Take that look off your face, cupcake. We're not staying long.' He took a long draught of his drink. 'You'll hardly know we're here,' he said, interrupting this promise with a prolonged burp. 'Pardonnez me,' he giggled.

Ruby looked covertly at her wristwatch. It was midnight, and she definitely knew that Teddy was there. It's hard to ignore a man impersonating Britney Spears on a coffee table.

Nestled beside Tom on the long red sofa, Ruby had journeyed through bemusement, reached irritation, and worked her way on to resignation. Teddy was an act of God, like whirlwinds or plagues or Natasha Kaplinsky's hair: there was no point resisting.

Kendall sat in the swivel chair, immersed in the *Guardian*, while Maria snored prettily on the rug. Ruby guessed that her new swain had passed muster with her dysfunctional family, and was quietly proud of the way Tom had handled the dozens of questions they had hurled at him. Kendall's had been polite enquiries about where he lived, but Maria had wanted to know how many girlfriends he'd had. Teddy had been merciless, the gay arm of the Spanish Inquisition, interrogating him with no regard for etiquette, boundaries or simple human decency.

Patiently Tom answered that no, he had never had a boyfriend, he'd never made love out of doors, he'd never visited a 'special clinic'. He declined to answer the one about having sex in his work clothes, earning him a worried glance from his date. When Teddy moved on to personal dimensions – 'It's important, believe me!' he yelped as the others shouted him down – Tom had drawn the line.

As ever, when there was a lull in the conversation, Teddy had gone into a song. Ruby surveyed the small pyramid of empty bottles on the floor. She felt pleasantly squiffy and the intense desire for everybody except Tom to explode had faded. Relaxed, right with the world, she felt at home among these people, even if one of them was high kicking in tight trousers and interjecting, 'Ooh me unmentionables!' between Britney's lyrics. As far as such a scene could be described by such a word, it was cosy. She peeked at Tom. Comfortably crumpled, he too seemed reconciled with the turn his evening had taken.

Peeking over the top of his paper, Kendall said to Tom in an undertone, 'Don't worry, son. It's not always like this.'

As he spoke, Teddy Hit himself One More Time and fell off the coffee table.

Kendall seemed to reconsider. 'Actually, Tom,' he said, 'it is.'

29

The gathering on Saturday night (Ruby liked the word 'gathering', it sounded so much better than 'drunken free-for-all') didn't seem to have scared Tom off. Judging by the text she received on the way home from cleaning Teddy and Kendall's flat he was keener than ever.

```
Have booked a minibreak for this
sat & sun. No excuses. Hope you like
Brighton.
```

Ruby did like Brighton. She loved it, adored it, wanted to be buried there. She'd never actually *been* there, but all of a sudden it was the nicest place in the known universe.

A warm feeling, similar to but nicer than the first bite of somebody else's dessert, washed through Ruby at the notion of Tom going to such trouble for her. Not many men would persevere through an accusation of orgy-mongering by his prospective girlfriend, a murderous ex on the loose, and a public probing about his past. He was a mountain goat of romance, gobbling up every tin can she strewed in his path, plodding onwards and upwards towards a distant peak.

The arthritic wheezing of the buses circling the green hissed *minibreak*. Yehudi's bow scratched out the word on his violin, and the birds twittered *minibreak minibreak* as they squabbled over worms in the grass.

Or so it seemed to Ruby as she made her way to Drama Queen's. She got in to find her client staring out of her bedroom window, wearing pyjamas so grubby they could have stood up on their own. Drama Queen gave a simian grunt in response to Ruby's bouncy greeting.

There were some lovely guacamole stains on the kitchen ceiling that absorbed Ruby for quite some time. Filling two bin bags with discarded food packaging – without Drama Queen the bottom would fall out of the Müller Fruit Corners market – Ruby realised she hadn't heard a peep from the lady of the house.

'Soup?' Ruby asked the effigy at the window. 'Sarnie? Welsh rarebit?' The view of the concrete yard couldn't be *that* fascinating.

'No thank you,' said Drama Queen politely.

She had to ask. 'So he still hasn't come back?'

Drama Queen shook her head, painfully, as if her neck hurt.

That should have been the cue for a Niagara of complaint, but none came. Drama Queen was in a bad way if even the promise of Welsh rarebit couldn't break the spell.

Hesitating for a moment, Ruby took a deep breath and sprang into action. 'First things first,' she said briskly. 'Let's get you out of those clothes.' She was rewriting her job description. She knew it wasn't a cleaner's place to chivvy her client into a clean dressing gown, or persuade a comb through the mangled bathmat on her client's head, but, Ruby reasoned, there was nobody else around willing to do it.

Clean again, Drama Queen allowed Ruby to position her like a mannequin on the sofa. Accepting something eggy on a tray, she said sadly, 'Do you think I'll ever find someone?'

The self-obsession was impressive – she was the sort who'd check her lippy while clambering into a lifeboat – but Ruby felt too sorry for Drama Queen to judge her. 'Don't be silly, of course you will,' she said. 'In the meantime, you've *got* somebody – you.'

That kind of self-help philosophy fell on deaf ears. Ruby would have liked to prescribe some time alone for Drama Queen to work out what she really wanted from a relationship: the reality would probably entail Drama Queen embarking on a carbon copy of her last fling, but Ruby nurtured a tiny hope.

'So don't forget,' said Ruby as she collected her tools to leave. 'Wash. Eat. Get some sun.'

'Why?' asked Drama Queen.

'Minibreak?' Maria snorted. '*Sex* break, he means.'

'Could you lift your mind from your gusset for a minute or two,' reprimanded Ruby from the other side of the dining table. She had forced Maria to sit and share a stir fry with her before the evening shift at the bar. It was time, she had said sternly, that they started making an attempt to live healthily. 'And how's your bean sprouts?'

'Very very beansprouty.' Maria lifted her chopsticks to her lips. 'If there's tofu in here I'll sue. I bet you wouldn't give your new boyfriend this sort of healthy muck.'

'There's no tofu,' said Ruby. Tofu scared her. She didn't understand how it was made – from toffee, perhaps? – so could never work up the nerve to buy it.

'Interesting.' Maria pursued a broad bean around her plate.

'What is?' Ruby knew she couldn't be referring to the stir fry.

'I called Tom your boyfriend and you didn't froth at the mouth.'

'Well. Hmm. Yes. No.' Ruby hassled her bean sprouts with a nervy chopstick. 'I suppose he is my . . .'

'Say it,' said Maria, the threat of something unnamed in her voice. 'Say the word, Ruby.'

'He's my boyfriend.' Ruby threw back her head and cackled. 'Ooh, that felt good!' she laughed.

'At last!' crowed Maria. 'You're moving on, girl.'

'Sideways, maybe.' Ruby corrected her. 'Moving on is impossible while Manny's out there.'

Rolling her eyes, Maria groaned, 'With any luck we'll read in the papers that they've fished a six foot two bullet-headed moron out of the canal.'

'Maria!' Ruby shivered. 'Don't.'

'Sorry,' said Maria unconvincingly. 'I just—'

'Well, don't.' Ruby put her chopsticks down, and not just because her stir fry tasted like damp string. 'I can't make a gag out of it. Not yet.'

'No.' Maria sounded small. 'And I'm a bitch to think you can. Sorry, Ruby.'

Old feelings of guilt and sorrow were rekindled when Maria made her crass jokes about the past. And fear raised its unwelcome, badly coiffed head. Ruby shoved something slimy into her mouth, hoping that her cooking would take her mind off Manny.

'Let's talk about nicer things,' declared Maria. 'Like your nookie fest in the Grand Hotel.'

'Minibreak,' corrected Ruby. 'And it's at somewhere called the Lansdowne.'

'Wherever,' said Maria airily. 'You won't see much of the sights, I bet.'

'Life is just one long *Carry On* film to you, isn't it?'

'Pretty much. And don't pretend you're any different, m'lady. I know you've been fantasising wildly about Tom in his birthday suit ever since you got that text.'

'Sorry to disappoint you, but no.' If Ruby had been Pinocchio her nose would have taken Maria's eye out. 'I love the sea. I'm looking forward to some long walks, looking around the old part of town, watching the sun set.'

'And shagging like bunnies,' added Maria sagely. 'Shame it's only Brighton.' She stretched out her olive arms, tanned to a warm brown by the recent sunshine. 'Maybe he'll take you somewhere more exotic next time.'

'Brighton's exotic enough for me, ta.' Ruby remembered the lavish, business class trips Manny had arranged. More than once, their holidays had been cancelled at the last minute because of 'work problems' (money insufficiently laundered and still showing the stains, possibly) but even when they'd got as far as a Seychelles beach or a Florida poolside, Manny had spent much of his time on the phone, barking at the guys back home. 'I've had the whole limo to the airport, hoovered sand style holidays. I'm not bothered if I never get on a plane again.'

'Mad.' Maria shook her head sorrowfully. 'I'd go to the Maldives with anybody. Literally anybody,' she stressed. 'Even our tramp.'

'Looking back,' said Ruby, slowly, unfurling a chain of thought, 'I can see that Manny took holidays without me sometimes.' She laughed softly, amused at her own naïvety. 'I didn't dare question him about the sand in his shoes after his week on business in Manchester.' She tutted. 'I suppose he'd strolled along those Manchester beaches we hear so much about.'

Across the table Maria didn't seem to be listening. Or maybe she didn't get the joke. Or maybe the interesting mix of flavours and textures in her stir fry had finally defeated her.

The good weather persisted. Perhaps nobody had told the sun about England, and its infamously shoddy summers. Yehudi had shed his overcoat and now practised 'Yesterday' in shirt sleeves that had once been white but which were now a MacTramp tartan of differing shades of dirt. The Bachelor showcased a new pair of far too short shorts every time Ruby 'did' him, and even Mrs Vine was flashing an upper-class bingo wing in strappy frocks.

Assuming Olivia Friend to be insulated against anything so frivolous as summer by her walls of books and her high-mindedness, Ruby was shocked to see her spreadeagled in a bikini on the ratty square of neglected lawn behind number fourteen Clancy Street.

The scene had none of the sensuousness associated with sun worship. Olivia looked as if somebody had kidnapped her from a shop window specialising in ill-fitting nylon swimwear and tipped her out of a third storey window.

'Can I fetch you a towel to lie on?' shouted Ruby, poking her head out of Joe's bedroom window. The ground beneath Olivia looked uneven and hard.

'No thank you.' Olivia spoke with the stiff upper lip of a woman who has been given a tough assignment that she must see through to the bitter end. 'I'm absolutely fine.'

Even from this distance Ruby could see the streaks of sloppily applied sun cream. Withdrawing her head, she left Olivia to it.

The banisters that snaked the height of the house responded gratefully to Ruby's care. Using buttery polish from a tin,

Ruby worked her way methodically along the mahogany rail. The duster buffed in tight circles, eradicating fingerprints and history as it went.

Down in the basement, Ruby burnished the snail shell curl that brought the banister to an elegant full stop, and stood back, satisfied. The back door opened and closed with a slam, and Olivia padded, barefoot, along the dark basement hall.

'How do people do it?' she barked, her hair wobbling wildly with each step, rather like Tom's work wig. Plodding into the kitchen, she pulled a dressing gown on over the multicoloured bikini that didn't improve on closer viewing. 'Sunbathing!' she proclaimed. 'It's so *boring*!'

'You should have taken a book,' suggested Ruby.

'I tried, but I couldn't get comfortable. There was no way of holding it open.' Olivia sounded exasperated. 'How do women do it?' She bit her lip. 'Why can't I do it?'

'It's not a skill,' laughed Ruby. 'You either like sunbathing or you don't.'

'Women like to sunbathe,' whinged Olivia. 'They like makeup. They like dancing. They like trivial things.'

Startled, Ruby murmured, 'You sound like my ex.'

Twitching round sharply to face her, Olivia pinned Ruby with a piercing look. 'Don't get me wrong. I'm not saying *all* women like those things, as if women are just an amorphous lump with no free will.' As Ruby pondered what 'amorphous' might mean, Olivia rambled on. 'I'm envious, actually. Some women get great pleasure from these things but I just can't see it. I'm not very womanly, I suppose.'

Olivia sounded small, quite unlike her usual formidable self. Ruby could discern the shape of the inner, weedier woman within Olivia's intimidating outline.

'I mean, I'm not even sure of my bra size, Ruby,' Olivia

admitted suddenly. 'I just snatch one that looks as if it might fit and if it doesn't I wear it anyway.' She looked down at her chest under the seen-better-days towelling dressing gown. 'Joe said something about one of his pals' mums the other day.'

Aha, thought Ruby. This was the heart of the matter.

'Said she was *fun*.' Olivia shrugged at the word. 'I met her when I picked him up from her house. She was . . .' Olivia widened her eyes at another unfamiliar word. 'She was *trendy*. Tiny little thing. Looked like her son's girlfriend. All brown and pretty, about . . .' Olivia sized up Ruby. 'About your age.' Her chin sank to her chest. 'Made me feel a hundred and two.'

'So you decided you'd learn to love sunbathing?'

'Silly, I know.' Olivia sighed. 'We waited such a long time for Joe. I don't want him to feel that I'm over the hill. I mean I'll never be a yummy mummy.' She huffed at the phrase. 'But at least I might try and be less of a dusty old hag.'

'Olivia!' Ruby couldn't bear to hear her talk like that. She admired Olivia's majestic bearing, and her tousled hair that swam about her strongly sculpted face like topiary. 'Not everybody has to be size ten and tanned. You know that,' she ended meekly, wary of teaching her grandmother to suck feminist eggs.

For an answer, Olivia asked, sharp again and showing none of her previous uncertainty, 'Do you want children, Ruby?'

Rattled by the *only yours* that sprang into her mind, Ruby said evasively, 'One day.'

'You'll make a lovely mum.' Olivia sounded warm, and slightly sad. 'One day.'

30

'You swear you didn't know?' Ruby was stern.

'I swear.' Tom was contrite. And trying not to giggle. 'You've got to admit it's funny, though.'

'It's my worst nightmare, and I'm using that phrase literally.' Ruby looked out of the taxi window and into the next vehicle, which was driven by a clown. On the back seat was a tall clown beside a smaller clown. The train they'd arrived on had been packed with clowns. Everywhere she looked, Ruby saw a clown, so she focused on her boyfriend instead. He looked very handsome (Tom was benefiting from the mysterious voodoo that renders a bloke better looking the more you like him) but he was, she knew in her heart of hearts, a clown under that wholesome exterior. 'The Brighton International Clown Convention,' she sighed. 'Anything else would have been fine. An international pimp convention. An international body odour convention. But clowns . . .'

'You could hurt a boy's feelings with talk like that.' Tom's customary pout was exaggerated.

'One clown I can cope with, but the streets are full of them.'

'Not quite,' said Tom calmly.

As they pulled away from the station, the clowns ebbed. But Ruby wasn't done harrumphing. 'You're sure you didn't know?'

Tom didn't answer. He kissed her instead. Good and proper, the kind of kissing that should be available on the NHS. She came up for air as the taxi slowed.

'The Lansdowne,' said the driver, bored.

Breaking away from Ruby, Tom paid the fare and lugged their bags out on to the pavement. With a stricken look on his face, he turned to Ruby as she stepped down from the cab. 'Honestly, they didn't tell me,' he blurted. 'I had no idea. Cross my heart and hope to—'

Whatever it was that Tom hoped to do was drowned out by Ruby's wail. She read the banner strung across the stately façade of the Victorian building that took up an entire block. 'The Lansdowne Hotel Welcomes the Fifth International Clown Convention.'

A honk from behind made Ruby jump. She spun round to be splashed by a plastic daisy on the lapel of a small man in a bald wig and a fluorescent top hat. 'Prittee laydee!' he yipped in an unplaceable accent.

Another clown, rather more esoteric than his short, amorous friend, bowed low in his pierrot suit. 'Mademoiselle, forgeev 'im,' he implored, his sorrowful delivery matching the painted tears on his lugubrious white face.

Mademoiselle took off, up the red-carpeted steps and through the revolving door, cutting a swathe through the throng of clowns in the lobby. Ploughing past padded bellies, treading on elongated shoes, Ruby elbowed her way through the sea of hilarity to say, distinctly and very loudly, to the girl behind the desk, 'I'm sorry, I'm usually a very polite and patient person but unless you hand me the key to the room booked by Tom Goodman I will have a panic attack that may end with my death and the death of many clowns.'

The girl behind the desk seemed to understand, and soon Ruby was in the lift, breathing into a paper bag as Tom rubbed her back.

'You really don't like clowns, do you?' he said.

About some things, Maria was always right. And she'd been right about the minibreak. It *was* a sex break by another name.

The door had barely shut behind them, closing out the clown-cluttered corridor, when Tom had taken Ruby into his arms.

Different, purposeful, he took the lead and, like a traditional ballroom dancer, Ruby let him.

She let him unbutton her top and she let him trail his fingertips across the flesh that billowed above the lace cups of her bra. His fingers seemed to have been electrified: their touch blazed through her.

'Do you . . . is this all right?' whispered Tom, his breath warm and starting to catch.

Nodding, Ruby pulled his lips towards hers by placing her hand on the back of his head. His hair felt healthy and springy, like a puppy's fur. There was nothing puppyish about his mouth, which was greedy for her own.

The love that Ruby and Tom made was clean and sweet, like happy teenagers discovering it for the first time. The tides that lapped up through her as she stared into Tom's honest blue eyes were overwhelming.

'Why did you cry?' asked Tom, his arms around her afterwards in the tumult of their bedclothes.

Not accustomed to talking about such things, Ruby mumbled some nonsenses.

'Was it because you know I love you?'

And then she really cried.

All the self-help books would agree. It was far, far, *far* too soon to be talking about love. It was needy, it was manipulative, it was foolhardy, it was wrong.

But Tom meant it. Ruby could tell. And he didn't seem to expect anything back. He had simply snuggled closer, held her until the frankly unattractive blubbering had subsided and then he'd fallen asleep.

She looked at him, still peaceful, from a vantage point by the tall window. She wondered if she loved him too. It felt like love. It smelled like love. But Ruby's tight leash on her own emotions wasn't to be relinquished so readily. She leaned over and shook Tom gently by the shoulder. 'Shall we look at the sights?' she asked gently.

'I am,' he smiled groggily, taking in her nakedness.

'You meant "sight" in a good way, right?' whispered Ruby, as they made their way across the lobby. They were walking close together, as if handcuffed, and she felt certain that other people could smell their desire.

'Shut up,' laughed Tom, pulling her fingers up to nibble them.

So busy was Ruby looking out for rogue clowns that she didn't spot the heavily built bald man until he was upon them. Snatching her hand away from Tom's lips she took two startled steps back, almost falling over. 'Man—' she began.

The stranger passed her, without a glance.

Tom got it. 'You thought that was him?'

'Yes,' choked Ruby, picking up speed and heading for the revolving door.

Outside on the pavement, they both turned naturally towards the sea lying like a silver rug at the end of the street. 'How could he know you're here?' Tom demanded. 'That was the idea of coming to Brighton, to help you relax. He's not a magician. He's not watching you in a crystal ball.'

By the tone of Tom's voice, this was shaping up to be their very first row. Ruby answered him petulantly, 'You don't know what it's like.'

'No,' said Tom, with a calm that seemed to come only with some effort. 'But I'm trying to understand. I'm in this too. I'll be top of the list for a broken nose when he finds out about me.'

'I'm sure he knows all about you already,' said Ruby. She noticed that Tom hadn't offered his hand again.

'Thanks for the reassurance.'

'How can I reassure you when I feel scared all the time?' Ruby went from petulant to screeching in a millisecond, and Tom looked shocked at her sudden change in volume.

'OK, OK,' he said, hands up as if dealing with a skittish pony. 'Can't we just put him behind us for two days? I'm here now, Ruby.' He closed the distance between them, but carefully. 'I'll protect you if he turns up.'

Ruby almost laughed. The thought of Tom, nice polite middle-class Tom who called a serviette a napkin, protecting her against the street-honed skills of a career criminal like Manny was pure fairy tale. The sort of fairy tale she thought she'd left behind in Esher. 'Come on, that's the sea, for God's sake!' Ruby grabbed his arm and started to run. If Manny *was* watching her, she might as well give him something to see.

*

That Saturday stretched on for ever. By the time Ruby and Tom sat on the sand watching a reluctant sun sink on the horizon, they'd explored the bijou shops in the Lanes, eaten lunch at a seafood shack, returned to their room for a reprise of the morning's delicious togetherness, strolled around the Royal Pavilion and had a reviving hot chocolate in the hotel bar.

A few yards further along the beach two clowns sat hand in hand, the sunset burning their red noses orange. 'Ignore them,' whispered Tom.

'I intend to.' Ruby nestled closer to her companion. She was wearing his floppy cotton jumper, revelling in the fact that it was too big for her. The differences between them were sensual, marking her out as the woman and Tom as the man. They'd crossed a line today, and become a couple. Their differences were their strengths. These unusually philo-sophical new thoughts surprised Ruby: perhaps all those books at the Friends' were having an effect on her.

'I suppose it's dinner time, but I don't want to move,' said Tom lazily, leaning on her.

'Me neither.'

'I fancy a steak tonight.'

'I fancy you.'

Tom shifted to look down at Ruby. He looked amused, and delighted. She looked red. 'You're coming out of your shell, young lady.'

'I want to,' she said quietly. 'It can be lonely in there.'

'Oh come here,' breathed Tom, gathering her up in a hug. He kissed the top of her head, the only part of her visible in his embrace. 'You old silly.'

It would be years, possibly decades, thought Ruby, before anything could begin to touch the perfection of that day in Brighton.

*

The Sunday afternoon train back to London was clown-free. Hands entwined, leaning on each other, the newly glued happy couple stared out of the window. All talked out, Ruby was grateful for some silence. She and Tom had discovered a lot about each other, not just where to bite to earn a shriek of pleasure. Ruby knew Tom's favourite colour (green), his favourite food (his mum's mash), his favourite TV programme (*Blackadder*) and how many children he wanted (fourteen).

A mystery had been cleared up, too. 'Just who is the Honourable Millicent Flatbush?' she asked.

'You mean you don't know?' Tom seemed surprised, and not in a good way.

'No,' confessed Ruby, shrugging unhappily at yet another hole in her general knowledge.

'You owe her a lot,' said Tom.

'I do?' Ruby wondered how. 'Did she invent kissing?' she whispered.

'She was,' laughed Tom, fending off his amorous companion, 'a suffragette. Quite a famous one. She campaigned for your right to vote, to have your own money, to be treated equally.'

'Really?' Ruby was delighted. She'd been fond of the Honourable Milly before but now she admired her.

'She'd be cheering you on, if she was around,' Tom said, with certainty. 'You're independent and responsible, just like she wanted women to be.'

Tom's remark negated all the indifferent school reports, all the disappointed sighs from her father. Ruby leaned against his shoulder and stared out at the edges of London as the train raced on.

They'd talked so much, and revealed so much, but Ruby held one nugget back. Manny had known all about it and he'd held it over her. Subtly, and, she now realised, cruelly. Tom was a different kettle of DNA, but she didn't dare risk it. It would devastate her to see Tom's expression alter when he looked at her.

Ruby stirred, suddenly uncomfortable against Tom's side. She scooched over to the window. Only a few weeks into a new relationship and already so dependent on his good opinion. She would hold back. It was the best way. To hold back just a little.

31

Miss Delmar took Ruby to one side. 'He's very . . . *enthusiastic*,' she said in an undertone, inclining her bouffant head towards the oblivious Joe on the other side of the room. 'But we're not talking championship material.' She tutted as Joe waltzed Suzie backwards into another couple.

'He loves ballroom,' said Ruby firmly, stung by the lack of praise. 'He thinks about it all week.'

'But he's not a natural,' warned Miss Delmar, fiddling with the glasses that hung from a chain around her neck. 'I've seen your face, dear, when you watch him. I just wanted to make sure you weren't nursing high hopes for your little carthorse.'

Her parade neatly rained on, Ruby managed a curt thanks for Miss Delmar. She sat down again and, chin on hand, watched Joe progress around the floor. He was brilliant, she smiled to herself, just brilliant. Miss Delmar didn't know what she was talking about.

'No, Joe. This isn't on. Your mum would go mad.'

'My mum won't know,' said Joe calmly, and with all the

self-possession of a seasoned fraudster. 'It's just an amusement arcade.'

'But you could get addicted.' Ruby held on tight to Joe's hand as he dragged her towards the winking lights and jangly music. 'You'll steal to get money for the machines, and before we know where we are you'll be clumping old ladies over the head for their pension books.'

Joe stopped dragging and frowned at her. 'I want a go on the machines,' he said. 'What you banging on about old ladies for?'

'Oh, go on then.' Ruby wasn't immune to the lure of flashing lights either. Once over the threshold, she shrieked at the sight of the Penny Falls. Joe was drawn to a simulation game that involved killing zombies. Sitting in the little cabin with his headset on, he was lost to Ruby, and once she'd squandered all the money earmarked for that night's supper she leaned on the cabin and gazed at him.

Olivia would have forty fits if she could see her son. Mouth set, body jerking with his efforts to machine-gun the undead, Joe was in another universe, one only available to ten-year-old boys. Ruby struggled to silence the bleatings of her conscience. The other youngsters in the arcade were either of Joe's design, tender, pink and overexcited, or quite another genus. Cigarettes in their back pockets, a pallor on their cheeks, they were old before their years.

'Come on, Joe.' Ruby tugged at his school shirt sleeve. 'Time to go.'

'But—' Joe seemed to clock something in her eyes and pulled off the headset with a frustrated growl. 'You should have seen my score!' he gabbled as they came out into the sun, its shining face insufficient after the artificial glare of the arcade. 'I was bloody top!' He punched the air.

Ruby stopped short, wheeling him around by the shoulder. 'You were what?'

'Top,' repeated Joe meekly, with an unmistakable air of doom.

'I do *not* want to hear that, that word again.' Ruby was aflame. This had to be her fault. 'What if your mum heard you say that?'

'She'd be too busy with her head in her books to hear.'

Wise to Joe's schemes by now, Ruby shook her head. 'Oh no you don't. Don't play me and your mum against each other. She'd be horrified. And her head isn't always in her books.' Ruby gave him a shove, more loving than vindictive. 'You're the most important thing in the world to her and you know it.'

'Don't tell her,' whined Joe.

'Don't worry, Al Capone, your secrets are safe with me.'

'Who's Al Capone?'

It evidently hadn't occurred to Joe that Ruby couldn't tell on him without telling on herself.

'An extra hour, that's all I need,' Mrs Vine had asked. 'Just to freshen up the house.' She'd paused for effect. 'While my niece and her children are staying.'

Overall on, Ruby set about the kitchen, her Marigolds a blur. Conversation wafted in from the drawing room next door and Ruby tuned in as if it was a radio play. She'd shaken hands with the niece, managing a curt, 'Hi', biting back a speech about the wickedness of neglecting a lonely old lady.

'So, Aunty, have you been keeping well?' asked the niece, a tall healthy blonde in jeans.

Huh, sniffed Ruby to herself as she rinsed a vase. *A lot you care.*

'Very well, as usual.' Mrs Vine's voice floated in. 'Apart

from my knees. And my back. And my eye. And my feet. And of course, dear, you know I'm a martyr to my heads.'

The niece murmured something but was cut short by her aunt's, '*Must* you wear jeans, dear? It rather reeks of the underclass.'

With a glance down at her own underclass legs, Ruby heard the niece say, 'It's the fashion, Aunty.'

'To look like a plumber? Really?'

'The garden looks gorgeous.' Ruby could hear the tension in the niece's voice.

'It looked better the day you were meant to come, but never mind.' Just how much Mrs Vine minded was perfectly clear. '*Boys!*' she snapped, presumably at the blond cherubs Ruby had seen plonked on uncomfortable gilt chairs. 'Do stay still. What little fidgets you are.'

'Perhaps if you let them play in the garden . . .'

The niece's suggestion was curtailed by an outraged, 'And let them trample all over my plants? I don't think so!'

There was a pause. Ruby, too fascinated by the unfolding drama to concentrate on her chores, crept nearer to the door.

Mrs Vine spoke first. 'Have you ever considered having little Rupert looked at?'

'Looked at?' queried her niece.

'To make sure he's normal,' said her aunt. 'He looks simple to me.'

Ruby put her hand to her mouth. She admired the calm of the niece as she replied, 'My son is quite normal, Aunty.'

'Hmm,' sniffed Mrs Vine. 'Pity he's so fat. He doesn't get that from our side.'

Tiptoeing back to her nice warm sink of soapy water, Ruby realised why her client was lonely. The woman was a dreadful old bat.

32

Miss Delmar's last lesson before all her protégés were lost to the mad whirl of the summer holidays was unexpectedly poignant for Ruby. The hour in the church hall was a reliable gem in her week: she would miss it.

'Practise, ladies and gentlemen, practise,' urged Miss Delmar as her abbreviated apostles filed out. 'I hope you have the twelfth of September in big red letters in your diaries. We have to be perfect for the show. So hone those cucarachas!'

'Yes, Miss Delmar,' simpered Joe, like a boy who had never seen the inside of an arcade. His position in the front row, alongside the rancorous Suzie, was assured. Whether this was down to Joe's hard work or Ruby's judicious offering of Terry's All Gold to his teacher was unknowable.

'Where to now?' asked Joe, bouncing along on the springs all children are issued with.

Ruby, whose springs had worn out some time ago, trailed behind. 'Home,' she said, allowing her conscience to call the shots. Olivia was working from home and Ruby felt the need to deliver her son to her.

'Aw, nooo,' whined Joe.

'Home,' repeated Ruby, catching up with her charge.

'An ice cream first?' Joe chanced his arm.

'On the way home.' Aware she'd opened up a chink in her armour, Ruby braced herself for Joe's attempt to exploit it.

'OK,' he said casually. 'An ice cream.' Almost imperceptibly he added, 'On the green.'

Giving in felt sweet. With a forced tut and a most unconvincing glare, Ruby made her way to her favourite bench on the parched late July grass. 'Here.' She handed Joe a five pound note. 'A 99 for me and whatever you want.' As he raced away, she yelled, 'AND I WANT THE CHANGE THANK YOU VERY MUCH!' She'd been stung by his scams before.

The green was popular, a beacon for grass-starved Londoners from the surrounding streets. Ruby took off her sunglasses and tilted her head back. A male voice, rather too close, sliced through the hubbub of traffic and ball games.

'What an unexpected pleasure.'

Ruby's eyes sprang open. 'Oh my God,' she gasped as her lungs recovered. 'It's you.'

To a paranoiac, the tramp's voice sounded uncannily like Manny's, despite the fact that Yehudi was ten years older and had started life several rungs farther up the social ladder.

'I'm disturbing you.' The tramp, his suntanned arms an intriguing shade midway between Filth and Sludge, took a step back.

'No, of course you're not.' Ruby pulled herself together. 'Really.'

Brandishing his instrument, the tramp said, 'This has hugely improved my income. People appreciate a touch of culture.' He smiled, showcasing all four of his remaining teeth, and raised the violin to his chin. He lifted his bow and lurched forward, landing spreadeagled face down on the grass with a thump.

'Yehudi!' Ruby shot up on to her feet. Then, 'JOE!' she yelled, yanking the boy off the man's back.

'Leave her alone!' Joe was mewling in a terrified vibrato as he pummelled the prone man like a punchbag.

'*Joe! No!*'

Playing possum, the tramp laced his hands behind his head and lay still, face down, not reacting to the boyish blows. His posture suggested that it wasn't the first time he'd found himself in this position.

With a mighty effort, Ruby managed to drag Joe off Yehudi's back. She dropped him on the grass and the boy lolled there, his face screwed up and rosy, a 99 blotted down the front of his shirt. 'Have you gone completely mad?' wheezed Ruby, trying to ignore the fascinated gaze of a small crowd that had gathered.

'But he's the bad man.' Even as he said it, all conviction drained from Joe's voice: he'd realised his mistake. 'Isn't he? The bad man who wants to hurt you? I've saved you.' His mouth twitched with doubt. 'Haven't I?'

Helping the tramp stagger to his feet, Ruby did her best to tune out the smell. Using a tone of voice she'd never needed before for Joe, she said vehemently, 'This is not the bad man. What made you think that? This is my friend.'

Ruby's friend tried to slink away, but Ruby had other ideas. 'Apologise!' she commanded Joe sharply, reminding herself of beleaguered mothers she'd overheard (and pitied) in supermarkets.

Sullenly righting himself, Joe mouthed something that might have begun with an S.

'Properly,' said Ruby, menacingly, again taking her cue from supermarket mums dealing with sugar-crazed shortarses.

'No need, no need,' muttered the tramp, his eyes resolutely down. Clutching his violin to his chest, he attempted a scuttled, sideways escape.

'Hang on, please.' Ruby turned to Joe, gesturing at the painfully self-conscious tramp. 'This gentleman's day is enough of a challenge without a pipsqueak like you coming along and making things worse for him. Apologise, Joe, and mean it this time.'

'I'm sorry.' Joe forced the words out on a sigh. 'I thought you were somebody else.'

His eyes still on the bubblegum wrappers at their feet, the tramp said, 'Quite all right. Could happen to anybody. No harm done.'

'Are you going to be OK? Would you like to sit down?' Ruby asked, tenderly. She was convulsed with indecision about offering him some change. Best not, she concluded, in case she added insult to (literal) injury.

Walking hastily backwards, the tramp assured her that he'd be 'fine, fine, marvellous, wonderful', and was soon swallowed up by the brouhaha of the main road, leaving Ruby and Joe facing each other. The crowd had melted.

'So, Action Man, what have you got to say for yourself?' asked Ruby.

'Are you my real mum?' asked Joe, his head cocked.

'Yes,' said Ruby, winded.

'Thought so,' said Joe. 'You're the reason I'm crap at maths.'

Hunched on the red sofa, knees tucked under her chin, there was no clue in Ruby's blank expression to the fireworks in her head.

Her plan – if a cack-handed stumble headfirst into the arms of coincidence can be called a plan – had gone wrong.

Joe was supposed never to know. That was the most important part of the plan. He was to be protected at all costs. He was the most important person in the whole set-up.

And now he knew. He didn't know much, because Ruby had been too dazed to answer his questions on the way home. She'd promised him to be as honest as she could, but later.

That promise was responsible for the pyrotechnics in her head. The truth about Joe's birth wasn't just her business: he had two perfectly good adoptive parents who loved him.

And trusted Ruby.

If she had any tears left she would have sobbed again, but she'd done so much of that on her return to Hannah House that there was a drought behind her eyes. She was, she bitterly recited, a liar, a fraud, a bitch, a home wrecker, a shopping trolley with a wheel missing that had careered through the Friends' happy, stable, normal home.

At least they wouldn't find out yet just how untrustworthy she was: Ruby had wrested a promise from Tom not to tell Olivia and Hugo about his detective work. This second promise, vital though it was, catapulted Ruby even further down into hell.

33

'I'd offer a penny for your thoughts but I don't think I'd get value for money,' teased Kendall, placing a brimming glass of something alcoholic on the bar.

'Hmm,' said Ruby, which was more than she'd said all night. The Saturday mêlée at the Velvet Glove wasn't conducive to conversation, but even so her introspection was obvious.

Lifting her chin with one finger, Kendall asked, 'Are you OK? Not sickening for something?'

Ruby rolled her eyes. 'People only say that in period dramas.' She was grateful he couldn't read her sin on her face. 'I'm fine.' Evil. Two faced. But fine.

A tutu rubbed against her jeans and Teddy pulled himself laboriously on to the next stool. 'I have made a decision,' he said sombrely, as Kendall diplomatically relocated himself to the other end of the curved bar.

'And it is?' asked Ruby with a smile, taking in his pink tights and his leotard. One of the reasons she loved Teddy despite the tantrums, the vanity and the tendency to quote

Kylie Minogue lyrics at times of stress was the shot of absurdity he brought to her life.

'I'm going to fight for him.'

'Who?'

'Who d'you think?' snapped Teddy. 'Terry Wogan? Bloody Kendall, of course.'

'Oh. Right. Good.' Ruby raised her glass to him.

'This limbo can't go on indefinitely. I'm going to win back his heart.'

'Aw,' said Ruby, with a suitably gooey look.

'If only I knew what interests him so much about this mystery man.' Kendall lifted his chin at the subtle but undeniable change that rippled over Ruby's features. ''Ere!' he squawked. 'You know something!'

'No, no, honest to God, I don't,' babbled Ruby, feeling the dangerous tug of underwater currents. This would end badly, she could already tell.

'Spill.' Teddy held a cocktail umbrella to her throat. 'Tell me what you know.' He flung the cocktail umbrella into an abandoned advocaat and leapt off his stool. 'Please, Ruby,' he whined. 'Just one word. To help me fight fire with fire. One teeny adjective to describe what this bloke's got that I haven't.'

Rejecting *ovaries* as too crude, Ruby pussyfooted. 'Apparently this other person is normal.'

'Nor – mal?' Like a visitor from another galaxy, Teddy strung out the two syllables wonderingly. 'Really? He's *normal*? That's it?'

'Yeah,' said Ruby apologetically, doing her damnedest to ignore the unsuitable pronoun.

'What's so fucking special about that?' demanded Teddy, hands on hips. '*I'm* normal too, you know!' he shouted, stamping one satin ballet pump. 'I'll show you, Kendall

Brontë. If normal's what you want, normal's what you'll bloody well get, mate.' And with that, Teddy turned to pirouette his way through the crowd, as the opening bars of *Swan Lake* came over the loudspeakers.

Facing Joe across her rarely used dining table, Ruby couldn't shake the feeling that she was being interviewed. By the look on Joe's face there was no guarantee she'd get the job.

'First question,' he began, glancing down at the crumpled sheet torn from an exercise book. 'Who's my dad?' His blitheness had melted: he'd evidently been thinking through the repercussions of his detective work.

So had Ruby. Thinking through the repercussions had robbed her of sleep the entire weekend. 'First,' she said, locking eyes with her interrogator, 'Hugo is your dad.'

'Yeah, yeah, yeah, I know.' Joe batted that caveat away. 'My *real* dad.'

Persisting with her theme, the Friends' spectres at her shoulder, Ruby said, 'Joe, Hugo is your real dad. He brought you up. He loves you.'

With a frustrated sigh, Joe clarified. 'Whose sperm made me?' he asked.

'Blimey.' Taken aback by such primary school frankness, Ruby spluttered a name she hadn't said out loud in years. 'Duncan Sweet.'

'You're joking,' laughed Joe.

'He was head boy,' continued Ruby, wondering why she suddenly felt responsible for the calibre of her first boyfriend's name. 'All the girls were after him. You have his nose.'

There was a lot of the Ruby/Duncan epic that she would leave out. Partly in deference to the magic circle she'd drawn around Olivia and Hugo, partly in deference to Joe's sensibilities: his 'real' parents' tale wasn't much of a love story. 'Duncan was eighteen. I was seventeen.'

'Pretty old, then,' mused Joe, from his vantage point at the other end of his teens.

'Hardly!' laughed Ruby. Her younger self was a baby. Mollycoddled and protected, it was obvious now that she should have stuck to swooning over pop stars for a few more years. Ruby hadn't been ready for the cat's cradle of sex. 'I don't know what he saw in me, but he chased me for a whole term.' That was disingenuous. Ruby knew exactly what Duncan saw in her. He saw her white skin and her russet hair and her leaf-like body: one of her main disappointments in him was the fact he didn't see past them. 'Nicking my schoolbag. Teasing me about my haircut. Offering me his last Rolo.'

Joe's face illustrated high-minded disgust at such schmaltz. 'Was he, like, the best looking boy in the school?' he asked hopefully.

'Absolutely.' It was easy to be honest about that. Duncan had had the face of a sixth form angel. Less important for Joe to hear about was Ruby's lack of desire for her glamorous boyfriend. He'd been too preoccupied with gelling his hair, too concerned about being top of his class. Duncan was unfinished, a hasty sketch of the man he would become, and Ruby found him rather dull. She was just too polite to say 'no'.

'Was he any good at dancing?' The question was so very casual that the answer had to be important.

Recalling Duncan getting down with his bad self to Ricky Martin at school discos, Ruby could give Joe a heartfelt 'yes'. No need to tell him that Duncan would rather be crucified at assembly than strap on a cummerbund and attempt a waltz.

275

'Your mum and dad,' began Joe carefully, tiptoeing around a new thought, 'were my real grandparents.'

'Mmm,' agreed Ruby dubiously, her fingers lacing tighter on the table in front of her.

'Were they pleased about me?'

Oh. My. God.

'Yeah!' lied Ruby. It was the biggest lie she'd ever told, a full-fat, turbocharged humdinger of a fib with knobs on. Marjorie and Stan were not pleased, even though the ignorance they'd carefully cultivated in their daughter had contributed to her predicament. She had been excruciatingly naïve, unmoved by the marathon snogs Duncan insisted on. When he'd wanted to go further she'd been baffled by his excitement, and too shy to say no.

The old wives' tale she'd relied on turned out to be untrue: you *can* get pregnant if you only 'do it' once. Even if it's in the gym cupboard with a dusty mat scraping your backside.

'Your grandparents were very pleased but they knew it would be too hard for me to bring you up on my own.' She didn't add, and never would even if Joe applied thumbscrews, how often the word 'disgrace' had been bandied in their small, stifling house.

'What about Duncan?' Ruby was grateful that Joe didn't call him Dad. 'He could have helped.'

'Well . . .' Both sets of parents had declared apartheid the moment the news broke. 'The adults kind of took over.'

The months before Ruby found the nerve to tell her mother about all five of her missed periods had been a walking coma. As Ruby's body threw out unmissable clues, she'd wandered dazed through her days, looking longingly at the big, kind wheels of double deckers, picturing herself happily crushed beneath them. Joe's grandmother's reaction to the news had been worthy of the Victorian stage; she had wailed, staggered, sunk, declared the end of the world. The expression on her father's face would stay with Ruby for the rest of her life. The orphaned, adult Ruby rationalised that her parents must shoulder some responsibility for her predicament, but it didn't help with the pain of those memories.

'I bet Duncan *wanted* to help.' Joe seemed confident of his biological father's decency.

'He had no choice.' In fact Duncan, tired of his shell-shocked sweetheart, had already begun shopping around for a new trophy girlfriend. There were whispers of giggly misbehaviour with the blonde captain of the netball team in the back row of chemistry. *Your father wasn't bothered* is not a phrase anybody should hear, so Ruby papered over Duncan's indifference. 'His mum and dad were as worried as mine. They had their minds made up. We couldn't fight them.' Duncan, after all, was just a kid back then, even though his head boy status made him the school's JFK.

His defection hadn't affected Ruby, who'd had enough to worry about. Was it freakish, wondered Ruby, to wade through all that drama and misery without her heart being touched?

'It was the best thing for everybody . . .' Ruby halted, the rock in her throat getting in the way. 'It was the best thing, especially for you, to give you up.'

There. She'd squeezed it out without breaking down. The shameful phrase that summed up her behaviour. Ruby had given Joe up.

'But you never met Mum or Dad, did you?' puzzled Joe.

'No. It was all done through an agency. They took you away from me while I was still in hospital. They told you you were going to a family who were desperate for a little baby of their own to love and take care of. I knew you'd be safe. And happy.'

'Did you ever think about me?'

Yes. Yes. YES. Blood. Guts. Furious activity – Joe's arrival was the realest thing that had ever happened to Ruby. How best to describe the way she'd thought about him in the intervening years? Constantly? That wasn't quite true, and honesty, always important to Ruby, was vital here. Joe had been a low-level hum, like a car alarm in an adjacent street. *How old would he be now? How tall is he?* Such thoughts would assail her in the supermarket or at the gym or halfway through a bap. *I wonder if he's allergic to cucumber, like me.* 'It was . . .' Ruby almost said 'hard' but didn't feel she had the right. 'It was *strange* knowing that you were growing up somewhere. I missed you,' she told Joe, almost apologetically.

Accepting this with his usual gravity, Joe threw Ruby a curve ball. 'Did you love me?'

'Yes.' Shapeless. Unformed. Chemical. At a distance. But love all the same.

'Wild,' he said, baffling Ruby with his trendy use of the word.

There was no need to describe the aftermath of Joe's birth. The secrecy, the ludicrous cover story (*Ruby's been very ill, staying in the country with an unspecified aunt we've never mentioned before*), the depression. Her parents treated her like an exotic pet which might race up the curtains at any moment.

Enter Manny stage right. The problem daughter was offloaded, her past rewritten. The hero-husband played his role well, managing to reassure Ruby that her fall from grace didn't matter, while sending out subliminal signals that it really really did.

Slumped on the other side of the table, Joe had read out all his questions, and seemed to have shrunk.

'You all right?' asked Ruby with a tenderness she'd been too inhibited to exhibit before.

'Yeah. 'Course.' Like any prepubescent boy worth his salt, Joe wouldn't readily admit to not being all right.

It was time for Ruby to ask a few questions of her own. 'When did you realise you were adopted?'

'Dunno. I always knew. I'm special, Mum and Dad chose me,' said Joe, with a soupçon of smugness.

'They were lucky to get a little bargain like you.'

'Yeah.' Joe accepted the compliment with equanimity. Sitting there like a bag of washing, his fringe going eight different ways, sherbet on the end of his nose, Joe still looked like a bargain to Ruby. 'Sometimes people say I look like Mum. We have a laugh over it. Dad always winks at me when somebody says that.'

Ruby smiled dotingly, but inside a small revolution was happening. Opening the can of worms labelled 'Giving Away Joe' had forced her to confront deeply buried emotions, ones that threatened her carefully cultivated attitude towards the Friends. An ugly, dirt-coloured stratum of jealousy ran through her now. 'Am I like you imagined?' Ruby asked a question she'd promised herself not to.

'Kind of. Don't know, really.' And that was that. Joe stood up. 'I'd better get home. I've got a holiday tutor today.' He pulled a face. 'Maths. I mean, what's the point? Mum is so mental.'

'Joe, if you want to tell your mum and dad, you can,' Ruby blurted, as she called the lift for her diminutive visitor.

Joe looked shocked. 'No way! She won't let us—' Joe stopped dead. 'Nah. It's a secret.'

The word was a paper cut. Standing on the terrace, watching the top of Joe's chrysanthemum-like head as he traipsed across the green, trainer laces undone, Ruby was weighed down by new-minted fears. When she'd first knocked on the door of number fourteen she'd sworn to herself that she wouldn't disrupt the family she found beyond it.

Joe disappeared, swallowed by the dapply blur of the trees. From this distance Ruby fancied she could hear him ticking. How long, she fretted, before he detonated?

34

Switching the downlighters on full, Maria flung herself across the end of Ruby's bed. 'Got anything to eat?' she queried.

'What? How would I . . .' Ruby couldn't be bothered to give the stupid question a proper answer, as she burrowed out from under her duvet, blinking and sniffling.

'Your hair looks nice,' sniggered Maria, tossing off her flip-flops.

'It's gone 2 a.m. Amazingly, I don't have any food in my bed, and my hair looks like it should look after I've been asleep for three hours, thank you very much. Don't you have a bed to go to?'

'Not tired.' Maria settled down.

'Well, I am.'

'Are you?' said Maria airily. 'God, Teddy's acting weird.'

'How is that news?' yawned Ruby.

'Well, when I say weird, I mean normal.' Maria didn't seem to notice Ruby's interest quicken. 'But in a weird way.'

'Like?'

'Like wearing . . .' Maria blew out her cheeks and pondered for a while. 'There really is no other word for it. The man is wearing *slacks*.'

'Oh dear.' Ruby's heart sank. It sounded as if Teddy's plan to fight fire with fire had started. The poor man had no idea what he was up against.

'And a nice Pringle sweater with diamonds across the front.' Maria shuddered at the memory. 'And slip-on brogues. The bouncer wouldn't let him in until he produced some ID.' She reached out to a foot shaped bump in the duvet and squeezed the big toe unmercifully.

'Ow!' complained Ruby.

'Here's another one!' cackled Maria, pouncing on Ruby's other foot.

'No! Honestly don't!' begged Ruby. 'Maria!'

'And another – hang on.' Maria recoiled. 'How many bloody feet have you got?'

'I did try to tell you,' said Ruby pointedly, jerking her head down at the duvet.

'Oh. Right.' Maria stood up and tiptoed backwards from the bed. 'Goodnight Ruby. Goodnight T—'

'GET OUT!' yelled a muffled male voice.

Since the abysmal boyfriend had moved on to torment another victim, going to Drama Queen's flat had become like going to church. Ruby would creep in, head bowed, before tiptoeing reverently around the statuette her client had turned into.

Persuading Drama Queen into clean clothes and feeding her something more nutritious than the snacks she favoured took extra time that Ruby didn't charge for. She was happy to be part of Drama Queen's rehabilitation.

The church analogy crumbled on Ruby's next visit, unless the house of God had changed since Ruby's lapse. Hopping around to the Black Eyed Peas in her bra and pants, Drama Queen was managing not to spill a drop of her champagne as she bounced down the hall to yell, 'Ruby! Ruby! Ruby Wuby!' in greeting.

'Hi,' muttered Ruby, as she was dragged, like prey, into the sitting room. For somebody who survived on processed foods, Drama Queen had quite a grip.

'Meet my Rafe!' yipped Drama Queen, gesturing to a long-limbed blond boy laid out on the many kilims and rugs and throws that adorned the sofa.

'Hi, Rafe.' Ruby wondered if Rafe was dead. Perfectly still, head flung back and mouth slightly open, the boy didn't move. 'Is he all right?' she whispered to Drama Queen, who, by contrast, couldn't stay still.

Dancing gimpily to the ear-splitting music, Drama Queen was unworried. 'He's fine. Rafe's very soulful.'

And very, very stoned. Ruby tried not to stare.

Chattering excitedly as Ruby ploughed through a week's worth of mess, Drama Queen filled her in on how 'lovely', how 'artistic', how 'kind', how 'sweet' and how 'am-a-zing' Rafe was.

Over on the sofa, Rafe didn't exhibit any of these qualities. He looked even deader than when Ruby had arrived.

'His parents own, like, Hampshire or something,' gabbled Drama Queen. 'Rafe's an artist. He lives for his art.' She giggled. 'And for me of course.'

'Of course.' Ruby wondered if Rafe had woken up at any point during his fledgling relationship with Drama Queen. 'You'll be careful, won't you?' she asked anxiously as she left.

Drama Queen did a double take. 'Careful of Rafe? Whatever for?'

*

Crammed around the tiny table in the flat above the Velvet Glove, Ruby, Tom, Maria and Kendall all sniffed the air.

'Something smells good,' called out Tom to Teddy, who was toiling over a large lump of roast animal. 'I love beef.'

'It's lamb,' said Kendall under his breath.

A huffy voice corrected them both. 'It. Is. Pork.'

'Whatever it is, get it over here, I'm *starving*!' Maria brandished her cutlery.

Teddy stared in haughty reproof through the shelves of the room divider. Eyes bare of mascara, he said in a saintly tone, 'Could we please all try to be a little more Waltons today? I have put much effort into my pork.' He resumed carving the joint, which, by the sound of things, was fighting back.

'Correct me if I'm wrong,' said Maria, tapping a pretty tune on the Formica with her knife, 'but wasn't there a *Mrs* Walton?'

'Well, in this version,' snapped Teddy, 'there are two Mr Waltons and one of them is armed, so watch it, miss.'

Ruby's knee kissed Tom's under the table. She enjoyed both his stoic refusal to acknowledge it with a change of facial expression, and the manly squeeze he gave her thigh. Tom's shoulders had drooped when she'd announced they were invited – or press-ganged – to Sunday lunch as part of Teddy's ongoing festival of normality, and she shared his ennui. There was more fun to be had at home than around this table, but Ruby knew where her duty lay and, apparently, Tom appreciated this. She wondered if it would be possible to tap out, YOU ARE WONDERFUL in Morse code on his leg. But, she reasoned, she'd have to know Morse code to do that.

'Come *on*!' What little manners Maria had evaporated if forced to wait for food.

Ruby and Tom, conscientious guests, admired the floral centrepiece. They admired the glass of champagne they'd been handed on arrival. They would have admired Kendall if he hadn't been sitting like a monument to Miserable Sods Everywhere.

'Oi,' hissed Ruby, leaning over the contraband centrepiece. 'He's making a big effort. You could smile.'

Kendall bared his teeth sardonically and Ruby tutted. 'Get with the programme,' she begged.

'Which programme?' he asked in an irritated whisper. 'Oh, you mean the programme where we all pretend nothing is wrong and my partner of twenty years hasn't lost the few marbles he had?'

'Read-eee!' trilled Teddy, stomping triumphantly over to the table with a platter of sliced meat and Yorkshire puddings and roast potatoes.

The appreciative noises Tom was emitting might taper off, Ruby thought, if she told him that Teddy had last cooked in 1991 – a boiled egg which had taken a cat's eye out.

'One doesn't,' drawled Kendall, 'have Yorkshires with pork.'

'One does now,' said Teddy, his nose high as he doled out rosy slices of meat to everybody.

'It's a bit . . .' Ruby reconsidered under Teddy's basilisk glare and said 'gorgeous' instead of 'underdone'.

'It's underdone,' said Kendall, peering at his slice.

'That's the way the French eat it,' said Teddy, evidently keen to brazen it out.

'The ones in hospital do,' said Kendall. 'We can't eat it, Teddy, seriously.'

'He's right,' said Tom, in a macho way that made Ruby's underwear shudder. 'Better stick it under the grill. We can wait.'

'Speak for yourself.' Maria speared a Yorkshire pudding which would have been impressive testimony to Teddy's skills if there wasn't an Aunt Bessie's carton sticking out of the bin.

'Oh, *all right*.' Teddy flounced back to the kitchen and began to swear at the cooker. Tom stood up, feeling his bruised knee (Ruby was getting rather ardent) and squatted in front of the oven. Under his composed tutelage, Teddy calmed down and the grill was switched on.

Meanwhile, Kendall was the one hissing over the gerberas. 'This is all *your* fault!' He poked an accusing finger at Ruby. 'You had to use the N word, didn't you?'

'I had to say something,' hissed back Ruby. 'Under the circumstances, "normal" was the best I could do.' She glanced over at Teddy, who was hugging Tom like a returning war hero for his ability to turn a knob. 'Although I don't know where Teddy gets his definition of normal from. He's dressing like a dad from a 1970s sitcom.'

Ruby, Maria and Kendall drank in Teddy's unflattering combo of Terylene slacks the colour of old tea and a suede gilet.

'I prefer him with mascara,' whispered Ruby. 'He looks naked without it.'

'I half expect the silly bugger to produce a pipe,' sighed Kendall as they all leaned back to welcome Teddy and Tom back to the table.

'Isn't this nice?' said Teddy unconvincingly. 'A nice, normal Sunday lunch. How nice. How . . .'

'Normal?' volunteered Kendall.

The thump thump thump of disco music erupted suddenly under their feet.

'Those bitches!' fizzed Teddy, shedding his urbane demeanour. 'That'll be Ava and Tiger Lily. They promised not to start rehearsals until later.'

'Never mind, Ted,' soothed Ruby. 'We'll ignore it.' She

was rather afraid of Ava and Tiger Lily, and not merely because they measured over six foot six in their platforms. The drag queens' glamour fascinated her, but they were both as touchy as premenstrual hornets and she gave them a wide berth.

Once Teddy had carefully burned the pork, the stop/start conversation gave way to slicing and chomping. The meat was tough, and the damp vegetables were cold, but Ruby persevered. At her side, Tom was valiant, even forking seconds on to his plate. She kept a vigilant eye on Kendall, but couldn't fault his behaviour. He didn't comment on his food, or even raise his eloquent eyebrows. Their little circle was protecting Teddy, and judging by the tortured expression on his face he knew it.

'Sorry about the lunch,' he murmured, as he cleared away.

'Don't be silly', 'It was lovely', 'Give over,' the guests demurred.

The loud clank of dishes on sink gave a clue to Teddy's state of mind. 'Anybody want to risk afters?' he asked, a touch too brightly.

'Ooh, yes!' came obedient cries from the table.

Over coffee, as the group tried to put the rice pudding behind them, Teddy pulled out a pipe. Kendall and Ruby shared a look. 'The perfect Sunday afternoon,' he said gently, puffing on the empty pipe.

From below them came the unmistakable sound of one strapping man in a bra bitch-slapping another strapping man in a bra.

'Oops,' giggled Maria. 'Ava and Tiger Lily are off. Last week,' she began with a grin, 'Ava nailed Tiger Lily's . . .' She tailed off when she realised her host with a pretend pipe was eyeballing her viciously. 'Yes,' she simpered instead. 'The perfect Sunday afternoon.'

Below the table, Tom was drawing abstract shapes on Ruby's

leg. Ruby's leg was enjoying the attention. 'Yeah,' she agreed, 'perfect.'

And that was where the conversation ran out.

Possibly the stress of being normal was too much for the little band of misfits, possibly their thoughts were elsewhere. During the gentle music of cleared throats and mindless Hmms, Kendall peeked down at his watch.

'Keeping you from something, are we?' snapped Teddy. 'Or someone?'

'I just looked at my watch, Ted,' said Kendall, low key, like a vet approaching a manic depressive chihuahua with a rectal thermometer.

'Can't wait to get away?'

From beneath them, they all heard a bass roar of, 'THEM'S *MY* NIPPLE TASSLES, YOU SLAG!'

'We agreed,' said Kendall, through gritted teeth. 'I'm not going anywhere today. This is your day and I'm sticking to that.'

'Huh. That's big of you.' Teddy wouldn't drop it: the chihuahua had hold of his favourite bone. 'Admit it, you'd rather be with him!'

'No, Teddy,' said Kendall coolly. 'There is nothing to admit. Stop embarrassing everybody, please. I'm happy here with you and our friends. I don't want to be with her, honestly.'

The ruckus downstairs stopped abruptly, as if Ava and Tiger Lily had heard the *faux pas*.

'Her?' laughed Teddy, tickled. '*Him*, sweetheart, unless you've changed even more than I thought.'

It took a second or two for Teddy to cotton on that he was the only one laughing. '*Him*, you mean, don't you?' he addressed Kendall's bowed, unhappy head, his tone still light. 'You can't be serious, Kendall.' The tone lost its lightness.

'Come on. Don't joke about stuff like that.' He sounded panicked. 'This paragon is a fella, right?'

With palpable relief, Kendall said, 'It's a lady, Teddy. I'm sorry.'

Cringing low in their seats, Ruby and Maria awaited the thunderclap. Tom, unaccustomed to how these scenes panned out, bit his lip and looked compassionately at Teddy. 'Would you like us to go?' he asked, gently.

Perhaps such *politesse* triggered a scrap of self-control in Teddy. 'Not at all,' he said, Duchess-like. 'Let's all finish our coffees.' He took a dainty sip and gagged slightly.

'Look, we really should—' Ruby's bottom left her chair.

'SIDDOWN!' barked the Duchess.

Ruby's bottom obeyed.

'Ted,' Kendall began. 'We should discuss this in private.'

'Oh, should we?' Teddy's calm was novel. And chilling. 'It didn't seem to come as much of a surprise to these ladies.' A glare that could curdle custard was bestowed on each lady in turn. 'Who is this trollop of yours then?'

'Nobody you know.' Kendall had the look of a man with a thousand angry ants in his pants.

Beside Ruby Tom shifted, chewing his lip. Ruby felt his discomfort, and wanted out every bit as much as he seemed to.

'I do hope you won't think me inquisitive,' said Teddy, with shaky sarcasm, 'but why the sudden change of heart, Kendall, my love? I mean, you've enjoyed decades of playing with the boys, and now all of a sudden you're a ladies' man. You understand,' he said, through teeth beginning to clench, 'my bafflement.'

'I didn't mean for it to happen.' Kendall looked on the brink of tears, his long sharp nose the same shade of scarlet that Teddy favoured for his lip gloss. 'It just did.'

'Ah,' said Teddy, encouragingly. 'You just woke up one morning and thought *Oooh, where can I find me some lady-bumps?*'

'Don't be so vulgar,' snapped Kendall.

'But I am vulgar, hadn't you noticed?' Teddy said bitterly. 'With me boas and me high heels and me triple *entendres*. My vulgarity has kept this place afloat for the last ten years. Nobody comes through the doors to watch you change the sodding beer barrel.' He stopped abruptly. 'Do you love me?'

Ruby flinched, and felt Tom do the same on his uncomfortable Formica chair. They shared a pained look before Kendall answered.

'Don't be so bloody stupid, man.'

Not the ideal answer to such a question. Ruby went hot, imagining how Teddy must feel.

Kendall wasn't finished. 'Do you want drama, Ted, or do you want to really talk? I warn you, I've had enough histrionics to last me a lifetime.'

'*You* warn *me*?' Teddy was incredulous.

'If you're ready to listen I might make you understand. You might learn something.'

'Do you take lessons in condescending?' demanded Teddy, his mouth wobbling. ''Cos you're bloody good at it.'

'Guys.' Tom laid his hands palms down on the table, making everybody jump. 'This is none of our business. You two have a lot to talk about. We're going.' He stood up.

Ruby dithered, half up, half down. She noticed that Maria was resolutely stuck to her chair. She admired her boyfriend's candour, but couldn't bear to leave while Teddy still needed her. She avoided Tom's searching look.

Teddy folded his arms. 'If anybody should go,' he said ominously, 'it ain't you two.' He threw Kendall a challenging look.

'Are you telling me to go, Ted?' Kendall asked evenly.

'Yes.'

If anybody had thought to drop a pin, it would have sounded like church bells. Ruby, somehow managing to maintain a squat above her chair that would have been quite beyond her at the gym, willed Kendall to stay put.

Kendall wasn't tuned in to her wavelength, because he turned and left the room without another word.

Whispering huskily, Maria said confidently, 'He's going nowhere. He's having a huff.'

'*That*,' said Tom, pointing to the ceiling, 'sounds awfully like a man packing a suitcase to me.'

Teddy was silent, and still, lips pursed and back straight, as they listened to Kendall's feet on the stairs. When the front door banged shut he blinked and said hoarsely, 'I didn't think the bugger would actually go.'

'You all right?' asked Maria dubiously, leaning over to peer at him.

'Well of course I'm not fucking all right,' snapped Teddy.

'No, s'pose not,' said Maria sheepishly.

Ruby, ignoring Tom who was discreetly executing an expert mime entitled 'I Have Had As Much As I Can Take And It Is Your Duty As My Girlfriend To Get Me The Hell Out Of This Madhouse', said, 'Shall I go after him?'

With a loud scoff, Teddy turned down her kind offer. 'What for?' He looked down at his slacks. 'At least I can get out of this gear and back into my chiffon.'

'Don't you want to . . .' Ruby faltered. She didn't like this new model Teddy, who took things like a man.

'Cry? What's the point?' Teddy shrugged and left the table. 'I've got a bar to run.'

When the door closed behind him, Ruby and Maria went into a huddle. 'Oh my God,' said Ruby.

'Oh my God,' echoed Maria.

'Why isn't he sobbing? Stabbing himself with his false nails? Chasing after Kendall with the curling tongs?' Ruby was at sea.

'He's in shock,' said Maria, with all the confidence of a woman who watched both *Casualty* and *Holby City*.

Butting in, Tom suggested, 'He needs some space.'

Ignoring him, Ruby said, 'Should we, you know, do something?'

'I'll stay with him until the bar opens,' said Maria. 'You two get off.' Maybe she'd noticed Tom's discomfort.

Ruby frowned. 'I can't take this in. I mean, Kendall can't leave.'

'He just did,' sighed Maria. 'I had a feeling the end was coming, but I thought it would be dramatic. Not . . .' Maria gestured helplessly with her hands. 'Not like *this*.'

'I feel bad leaving Maria to look after Teddy,' fretted Ruby as she sprinted along the street, forcing Tom to keep up.

'Maria will be fine. Teddy'll be fine,' said Tom briskly. Putting out an arm to enfold Ruby he said, more gently, 'Hey Rubes, slow down. I've been dying to get you on your own. I thought we'd never get out of there.'

'I can't hang about, Tom.' Ruby dodged his arm and looked at her watch. 'Bums. I'm already late for the Friends.'

'You mean . . .' Abruptly, Tom stopped walking and threw out his hands. 'It's a Sunday. We spend Sundays together.' He pouted. It was sexy and irritating at the same time. 'At least I thought we did.'

'Tom, don't start.' Ruby regretted it as soon as she said it. It was a phrase for naughty children, not lovely new boyfriends who dared to show their exasperation after being force-fed bad food and worse behaviour. 'Oh no! Not that face, please!'

she cried as the shutters came down over Tom's wholesomely happy features and turned them sullen. 'Come round tomorrow night.' She took a step towards him and reached out a forefinger to trace a line down his chest. 'I'll make it up to you.'

'I just thought that, after spending all my afternoon with your crazy friends, you might . . .' Tom tailed off.

Ruby didn't remove her finger but the tracing stopped. 'Do you really think they're crazy?' They were straying into marshy territory. Perhaps, she reasoned, Tom couldn't appreciate how vital her friends were to her in her new life. After all, he'd never had to build a new life: his old one was perfectly fine.

'A bit.' Tom was mellowing. He pushed at his shiny curls with an impatient hand. 'Ignore me. I can't complain when I think about what poor old Teddy must be going through. I'm just disappointed. You could have told me you were working today, Ruby. I'm your bloke. You should tell me stuff.'

Stuff like stalking her long-lost son? Ruby withdrew her finger. If Tom could get so aerated about a trivial detail, what would he do when he discovered the bigger stuff she'd neglected to mention, the soap opera, jaw-dropping stuff? 'We need to talk. Come round tomorrow. About eight.'

Tom's face fell. 'I've blown it,' he said, his voice suddenly deep.

'What? NO! Hell, no,' laughed Ruby.

'*We need to talk* is code for *You are a shite boyfriend and I'm going to dump you from a great height.*'

'It's code for we need to talk, silly.' Ruby took a step backwards, her green eyes holding his blue ones. 'There are things I need to share with you.'

'That doesn't really make me feel any better.'

Another glimpse of her watch got her moving. 'Tomorrow!' she called over her shoulder.

'Tomorrow,' echoed Tom, broodingly.

35

'I do feel awful dragging you over here at the weekend.'

'S'fine,' panted Ruby, wishing Olivia would put her energy into holding up the other end of the massive bookcase they were manhandling down the stairs, instead of the careful display of her liberal bleeding heart. 'Oh oh!' she panicked, as she felt the veneer slip out of her grasp.

'Got it. You're fine,' called the invisible Olivia from a few steps down.

Clearing out the loft so that Joe could have a bigger bedroom was a project close to Ruby's heart, but she hadn't realised what hoarders her employers were. She noticed that Hugo had vaporised, although Joe did his ostentatious bit by sauntering down the stairs now and then holding a small lamp or a large book.

Joe had let her in, and Ruby had found herself saying, 'Hello you,' in an altered voice. His 'Hi' had been as nonchalant as ever.

'Everything OK?' she'd asked meaningfully, as the thumps of Olivia's Birkenstocks got nearer.

'Yeah,' Joe had said with a half laugh, seeming surprised by the question and its intensity. 'Do you like my new T-shirt?'

'It's absolutely stunning,' said Ruby. High praise indeed for a limp white garment with Snoopy on the front.

And then Olivia had joined them, resplendent in a boiler suit, warning, 'It's dusty up there!' and the not awfully significant Mother and Son moment was over.

Once the loft was cleared and Ruby's hair resembled her chum the tramp's, Olivia insisted they sit down and recover. 'Joe darling! Joe! Join us,' she hollered up the stairs.

Twitchy, Ruby refused a biscuit and watched Joe covertly over the rim of her mug. He was unchanged, as cute, as bored looking, as fundamentally Joe-esque as he had been before the revelations. Relieved that he was leaving no clues for Olivia to spot, Ruby nonetheless felt an itch of disgruntlement. Had Joe simply slammed shut the door they'd eased open? Was that it? Had she lost him a second time? Surprised by her reaction – not at all the rational, generous, selfless attitude she prided herself on – Ruby pushed it to the back of her mind.

The back of Ruby's mind was a messy place. A little like the Friends' loft.

It was a very Mondayish Monday. People stepped in front of Ruby in queues, her last pound coin rolled down a drain and she was struggling with the tiredness that follows a sleepless night.

Not just any old sleepless night. Ruby had been dragged out of her bed to take over from Maria on Teddy Watch, so it had been a sleepless night punctuated by alternating screams of 'I WILL STAB HIS COCK OFF!' and 'I LOVE HIM SOOOO MUCH!' Babysitting a hysterical cross-dresser had proved to be a draining business, and Ruby pushed her hoover around Mrs Vine's elegant rooms like a curiously domestic out-take from *Dawn of the Dead*.

When last seen Teddy had been sleeping like a baby, albeit a large and drunken one. Ruby had left him a key to the penthouse and two paracetamol as a parting present.

There had been no call from Tom. Which was, Ruby felt, fine. Absolutely fine. After all, they were due to see each other later on. So it was fine that he hadn't called. Ab. So. Lutely. Fine.

Juggling the phone along with a J-Cloth, Ruby said expectantly, 'Tom?'

'I CAN'T GO ON!'

Ah. 'Teddy,' sighed Ruby.

'Am I old, Rubes?' asked Teddy desperately.

'Err, no.' Ruby frowned. 'Of course you're not old.' Not compared to Bruce Forsyth. Or the white cliffs of Dover. 'You're young at heart,' she assured him.

'I don't want to be bloody young at bloody heart!' wailed Teddy. 'I want to be young all over. I bet this Cath creature is young. Young and big boobed with ovaries the size of a London bus. He's gone mad, I tell you, Looney Tunes. A skirt-lifter, after all those years of preferring gentlemen. Is it me, Ruby? Honestly, is it my jowls that have driven him to this?'

Sick of discussing Teddy's jowls, Ruby had an answer that was both diplomatic and, she suspected, true. 'This is all about Kendall, Ted. It's something he's got to do. He'll come back when he's sorted his head out.'

'Huh. I won't want him,' fibbed Teddy with gusto. 'I'll have moved on. Traded up. He wasn't so great, anyway. His feet smelled, you know, and every one of his front teeth was a crown.'

There was a pause, and Ruby strained her ears to hear an odd thumping sound. 'Teddy?' she asked, like a loving but stressed mother to a Ritalin-riddled child. 'Are you hitting yourself on the head with your handbag again?'

Bones aching, head throbbing, Ruby was spent. Flaked out on the sofa, she wondered if it would be feasible to remain there for the rest of her life. She closed her eyes. Still no word from Tom, but soon he would be there. He would feel, smell, taste good and she – there was a pause for a tiny gulp here – *needed* him.

That realisation made her whistle and scratch her nose very aggressively. Her mobile interrupted her confusion.

'I'm bringing fish and also chips!' said Tom. 'And I'm sorry for being an arse yesterday.'

'Listen, don't come over tonight.' Ruby plunged straight in.

'But you want to talk.' Tom's tone had changed completely, as if he'd flicked a switch marked 'wary'.

'Yeah I know, but . . .' Ruby sighed. 'Oh, Tom, I was up all night with Teddy, and it's been a terrible day and . . .'

'Fine. Great.'

Tom wasn't to know that 'need' had become something of a swear word in Ruby's dictionary of love. 'I'm sorry.'

'Me too.'

There was a pause, tense enough to taste. 'Will you come round tomorrow?' asked Ruby tentatively.

'Unless there's another drama in your unpredictable life.'

'Everything will have calmed down by then.' Ruby crossed her fingers.

'Look. Why don't I just come over anyway?' Tom asked reasonably. 'I might make you feel better.'

He didn't understand. An oddly distant Joe, a hysterical

Teddy – Ruby couldn't handle a resentful Tom as well. 'Don't,' she said, a tad too hastily for politeness.

Coldly Tom asked, 'Where do I come in your pecking order, Ruby? Bottom? Nowhere?'

Ruby stared at her mobile, amazed. Her cool, calm, rational boyfriend had hung up on her.

Showered, blow-dried and the other side of a glass of terrible wine, Ruby looked at her watch. It was past eight. By rights Tom should be here now, and they should be feeding each other fish and chips.

How Ruby envied Tom the clean page of his mind. He was free to focus on their relationship. Burdened and muddled, Ruby couldn't do that. She was clear on one point however: she should have let him come over.

The buzzer interrupted her thoughts, lifting her chin and her mood with it. Dashing across to the intercom, she attempted sexy sternness. 'You were told not to come!' she scolded, pressing the button to send the lift down before flying to her bedroom. With only a minute or so there wasn't much she could do to render herself smooch-ready. A ruffle of the hair, a slick of gloss to the lips and a spin to check her rear view was all she managed before she heard the lift doors sneak apart. 'Help yourself to a drink, you naughty little gatecrasher,' she called out, hurriedly anointing her eyes with mascara.

Taking a deep breath, she strolled, super casual, out to the reception room.

Manny held up a glass in salute. 'Cheers,' he smiled.

It was all wrong, as if a tiger had turned up to a picnic.

Ruby's smile went rigid, pasted to her face. As her husband took a languid step in her direction, she took a hasty one back.

'No hug? No kiss?' His voice was all good humour. His teeth glowed white and sharp in his smile. 'You've redecorated. Shame.' He shook his head indulgently. 'You never did have no taste, babes.'

'No,' said Ruby lamely. Behind her frozen expression, she was frantically devising a way of handling Manny, how to be with him. A little voice in her head whispered that it didn't matter what she did: the tiger was in charge.

'Can you guess why I called round?' he asked chattily. For a fugitive, Manny was looking sharp. He was in one of his handmade suits, with a pristine white shirt. A sizeable diamond glittered on his pinkie.

'Erm . . .' was Ruby's reply; she hated the tremor in her voice. The harder she tried to think, the more she shut down. The promise of harm was much more menacing than she'd imagined in her daydreams, where she'd outwit Manny with some cunning plan. The reality was a seizure that changed her body language utterly. She was aware that her smile had melted, to be replaced by a look of wary misery. The outcome seemed inevitable: his hands would leave their mark on her. Ruby had never been hit or slapped or touched with anything except tenderness in her life. Yet another lesson she could do without was coming up.

'Cat got your tongue?' Manny cooed. 'Not scared of me, are you, babes?'

'Course not,' quaked Ruby. At least she was managing to retain eye contact with this sleek predator who had dynamited her placid living room into a terrifying mess of bright colours and hard edges. All her hard-won treasures seemed dangerous now: Ruby visualised being slammed against the second-hand furniture she loved.

'Then answer me, Ruby.' Manny took another step forward.

Ruby mirrored it with another step backwards.

'Why, darling, do you think I'm here?' asked Manny smoothly.

His gaze was intense, yet cold. Ignorant about drugs, Ruby wondered if cocaine was one of the ones that made you violent, or one of the ones that calmed you down.

She had her answer soon enough. Manny raised his arm and his glass tumbler flew across the room, whistling past her head before smashing against her bedroom door. 'I asked you a question,' he said, wiping his mouth. 'It's not a bloody multiple choice. Answer me.'

'Your insurance,' squeaked Ruby hastily. 'You came for your insurance.'

'At last,' beamed Manny. 'Now, Ruby, my darling dutiful wife, would you be so kind as to tell hubby where you've put his stash?'

If only she had an answer. Tears threatening, Ruby pleaded, 'Honest to God, Manny, I've no idea what this stash is.'

'I am getting bored,' warned Manny.

'You'll get into trouble for this,' blurted Ruby.

'Trouble?' The tiger's laugh was a rasping growl. 'Oo-er. You don't say.' Manny lowered his head and fixed her with his brilliant gaze. 'Babe, my life is trouble. Settling a score with my missus can't make it any worse.' Another step forward.

Another step back. The crunch of glass under her slippers. Sooner or later she'd hit a wall. 'If you go now I promise I won't tell.' Every second that ticked past without those paws round her neck was a bonus. Ruby was starting to warm up. Keeping him talking was, she felt, one way to keep him at bay.

'I've only just got here. There's an awful lot more fun to be had before I leave.' Manny gave Ruby a frank and filthy look up and down the length of her body.

A snapshot presented itself, in vivid colour, of what Manny could do to her. It galvanised Ruby. 'You won't be having any fun here, Manny Gallagher,' she said, as firmly as she was able. 'Remember, you don't tell me what to do any more.'

Manny leaned over and swept a vase off the dining table. It crashed to the ground. Ruby expected him to roar and spring at her, but instead he seemed to pull himself together. 'Do not annoy me,' he panted. 'Co-operate and perhaps I won't introduce your nose to the back of your head.'

The sideboard caught his eye. He bent to fling open and slam shut each of its six doors in turn, only taking his eyes off Ruby for the second it took to scan each section's interior.

Swearing under his breath, Manny banged the final door with especial force. 'This way.' He motioned Ruby to follow him to the kitchen.

Ruby carefully kept the distance between them constant.

'Stand by the window,' said Manny brusquely, as if training a dog.

Phone, thought Ruby, amazed that it had taken so long for her brain to thaw to the point where it came up with this magical word. Covertly she looked about for her mobile as Manny ransacked the kitchen cabinets.

There it was, snug in his chest pocket. Damn Manny for being so quick witted, and damn her for being too tight fisted to install a landline. Ruby eyed the carving knife on the draining board. Just a few hours earlier, she had been using it to unscrew the fuse in the toaster plug: now it throbbed with gory potential.

Images flickered through Ruby's head. She could grab the knife. Brandish it. Stick it in his bespoke tailoring. Ruby wilted. She couldn't do it. She wasn't made that way. She lacked the streak of self-preservation it would take. Instead she was hampered by empathy: she couldn't hurt her Manny like that.

That 'her' was sharper than the knife. Even now Manny had the power to provoke something next door to love in Ruby.

'Oops.' He must have followed her line of sight. He picked up the knife delicately and threw it into a drawer. 'Little girls might prick themselves if they play with big sharp horrid knives.' He leaned over and pushed Ruby back out into the main room, the first time he'd touched her since he'd arrived.

Ruby tensed, and hastily took herself out of his reach.

'I don't have time for all this fannying around.' It may have been accidental but Manny stopped directly in front of the intercom, the other object of Ruby's desire. 'Tell me where it is, and I'll leave. Just like that.'

'I don't even know *what* it is.' Ruby only knew she was crying by the tang of salt on her lips. 'Why don't you give yourself up, Manny?'

Afterwards, Ruby wondered what she'd expected from this approach: Manny simpering *Excellent idea, I never thought of that*, perhaps. Instead, he sighed, 'You are officially ten times thicker than I remember. I'm in a hurry, darling. Do I really have to smash up every corner of this dump?' Manny reached over to a shelf and pushed a pile of magazines to the floor.

'Can't we talk?' Vague memories of Hollywood movies about negotiators talking down madmen with guns stirred in Ruby's beleaguered mind.

'What the fuck do you want to talk about?' Manny sounded exasperated. His exhaustion was apparent now: his face was grey. 'Why do birds always want to talk? Yada yada yada. Feelings. Emotions. I bet you don't want to talk about how you done me over, nicked me penthouse, cashed in me insurance, broke my . . .' He faltered, and ran a stubby hand over his face.

'Your what, Manny?' demanded Ruby quietly.

'THAT'S ENOUGH!' roared Manny, lurching towards her, arms outstretched. 'IT STOPS HERE!'

Ruby spun round and ran, her slippers skidding on the cold floor. She didn't even have time to scream.

Her nightmares were coming true: it's terrible to discover that they can. The tiger was off its leash and she could feel his breath hot on her neck. The Manny she'd loved was dead and she was fleeing the Manny the rest of the world knew. Even as she ran, Ruby felt hopeless. It could only end one way.

An unexpected noise stilled Manny and Ruby as efficiently as if some unseen hand had hit their pause buttons.

'Ruby darrrrrling!' sang a husky baritone from the direction of Maria's bedroom. 'Come and join me on the bed!'

Ruby reeled around to face Manny. She was crouching, ready for him.

He, meanwhile, had straightened up, his face in shock. 'You've got a man here!' he snorted, incredulous. He turned as the bedroom door opened, the red mist over his eyes almost visible.

'It's not—' Ruby never got out the 'what you think' because Teddy materialised.

The leopardskin négligé fluttered. The wig had been tamed to hang in a sleek wave over Teddy's kohl-rimmed left eye. He stopped short when he spotted Manny, letting out a girlish 'Oh!' as his hand flew to his breast.

'What the . . .' gaped Manny, taking in his wife's (very) fancy man.

A glance over at Ruby told Teddy everything. 'This 'im?' he demanded in a much deeper register than that initial 'Oh'.

On a nod from Ruby, Teddy roared, 'RIGHT!', tugged out his earplugs and pushed his lace-trimmed sleeves up to the elbow before launching himself at Manny.

Too surprised to react, Manny was bowled over. He rolled back on the rug, amazement written large on his broad face. In Manny's narrow-minded neighbourhood, blokes in negligees didn't throw mean right hooks.

'Run, pet!' Teddy didn't have much breath to spare. As Manny hit the floor, his street fighter's reflexes kicked in. The two men were soon entwined, rolling about on the rug as if – Ruby couldn't resist the analogy – they were making passionate love.

Grunts, groans, gasps. They made all sorts of strenuous sounds as the strange amoeba they'd spawned tumbled about the floor. Ruby darted past, heading for the intercom.

The dash was badly timed. Manny reared up, with Teddy clinging to his back, and whirled around, knocking Ruby flying against the coffee table.

Winded, she cried out at the pain in her ribs. She raised her head to see Teddy's fingers gouging Manny's cheeks. Manny backed against the lift, bashing Teddy's spine on the unyielding metal.

Groaning, Teddy slithered down Manny's back to hit the floor with a dull whump.

Rallied by the sight of Manny's elegant Chelsea boot raised above Teddy's face, Ruby launched herself at her husband, grimacing at the pain from her torso. 'Don't you dare!' she yelled, before finding herself flying backwards through the air as if she had wings. She met the coffee table again, hard.

Ruby's little foray had won her fresh bruises, but it had also won Teddy enough time to stagger back up on to his platforms. With a grunt, he folded Manny in his arms and aimed punches upwards at his belly as they waltzed drunkenly around the room. Manny's yelps of pain were smothered, his face pressed into Teddy's shoulder.

Panting, Ruby skirted them as they shuffled crazily to and fro. Finally she got her hands on the intercom just as it buzzed loudly. 'WHO IS THIS?' she yelled into the grille, over the noise of a burly homosexual pasting a burly heterosexual against a wall.

'I know you told me to stay away but—'

'TOM! GET UP HERE!' shrieked Ruby, adding a hasty, 'OH, AND POLICE MURDER HELP!' because the situation seemed to merit it. She nipped neatly out of the way as a slap from Teddy sent a groggy Manny pirouetting across the floor.

'Think you're 'ard?' bellowed Teddy, his negligee torn and tattered. He grabbed Manny by the lapels, mid-spin, bringing their faces nose to nose. 'You're not so handy with somebody your own size, are you?'

'Poof,' slurred Manny unwisely, sagging in Teddy's grasp.

'Too right, mate,' laughed Teddy. 'All poof, all man.' He let go of his opponent, watching as he swayed dopily on unsteady feet. 'Be sure to tell your prison chums that you got sent back by a bloke in stockings, won't you?' He lifted his hand lazily for the final smackeroo.

'Hang on.' Ruby stepped between them. 'May I?'

'My pleasure, pet.'

Ruby took a deep breath. 'Ta-ra, Manny,' she whispered, and gave him the lightest of taps on his cheek.

Manny folded to the floor just as the lift doors delivered Tom. Flushed with panic, he stared down at the crumpled gangster and then up at his girlfriend's raised right hand. 'Remind me never to get on the wrong side of *you*,' he gasped.

*

The chalky circle of lamplight kept midnight at bay. Cosied up to Tom, Ruby finally unclenched. Not many fairy tale heroines get to wake up twice, but tonight Ruby had finally broken the curse: Manny was out of her life for good. She was no longer afraid. She couldn't be frightened of the drooling, open-mouthed lump the police had hauled away. Ruby had faced up to him and survived. Such a momentous night called for fireworks, but Tom's kisses were enough.

'You know, don't you, that it was all Teddy's doing?' she double-checked, tucking her head into a spot on Tom's shoulder that could have been made for it. 'Wouldn't like you to think you're dating a female version of the Hulk.'

'I just wish I'd got here earlier.' Tom sounded sulky. 'I could have protected you.'

That spot was suddenly uncomfortable. 'I don't need you to protect me,' said Ruby carefully. 'I mean, thank God Teddy had let himself in while I was at work and fallen asleep. I'll always be grateful to him, but even if I'd taken a beating, tonight had to happen. I had to exorcise Manny by facing him.'

'I know,' said Tom. 'But . . .'

'But what?'

'It would be nice to be needed occasionally.'

'Tom, I'm a big girl.' Ruby fought to stay serene. She'd left behind one role, she didn't want to step into another for Tom's benefit.

'I care about you. It's natural that I want to protect you. Some girls would like that.' Tom reached down to nuzzle her ear, only to discover it had been sharply pulled out of nuzzling distance.

'That's the kind of thing Manny used to say,' Ruby said curtly.

'Do *not* lay that on me.' Tom echoed her spikiness. 'I'm no Manny. Christ, why can't it ever be you and me? We're never alone. Any more skeletons in your closet you'd like to introduce me to? Anybody else I have to share you with?'

Ruby bit her lip. It wasn't Tom's fault that hearing Joe described as a skeleton made her want to hit him. 'No,' she fibbed. 'Could you stop . . .' There was no better word than the one dangling on the tip of her tongue, '. . . *nagging*. I've had a hell of a night.'

'Nagging?' Tom sounded insulted. 'I only –' He halted, and Ruby felt his body, so close against her own, droop. 'We're going wrong, Ruby.'

'I know.' Ruby steeled herself for what might come next.

'Does it scare you as much as it scares me?' asked Tom, plaintively.

'Yes!' Ruby was glad that they were in accord about something. 'Give me time, Tom. For some reason this whole relationship doodah isn't easy for me. I must have been off sick from school the day they covered it.'

'Take all the time you need.' Tom squeezed her. 'I just need to know what it is you want from me. If anything.'

'This.' Ruby put a hand either side of his lovely, thoughtful face and told him with breathless urgency, 'Tonight, Tom, this is all I need.' She kissed him, hard and desperately at first, before allowing herself to sink into the warmth of him.

36

Picnics are good things. They raise the spirits with their cheerful rugs, their Scotch eggs, and their general air of playing hooky.

Unless you're Teddy. He was looking down at a mini quiche as if it had insulted his mother. 'I'm not in the mood,' he said, dropping it back on to his Flintstones paper plate and readjusting his broad straw sunhat. His look today was lacklustre – jeans, floral shirt and sandals. He hadn't pulled on a sequined boob tube since Kendall's departure a week earlier.

Tom snaffled the abandoned quiche. 'Are you on stage tonight?' he asked.

With a dismissive shake of his head, Teddy pulled on enormous sunglasses, retreating still further from the hot, happy people lolling around on Parsons Green.

'You have to get back in the saddle some time,' Ruby scolded him as she tried to balance a can of something fizzy on one of the tiny hillocks in the rug. 'Your audience need you.' She winked down at Maria, sunbathing alongside her. They had prophesied that this would be the clinching argument.

'Fuck my audience,' said Teddy.

Perhaps not.

Some progress had been made. Two nights ago the girls had finally shoehorned him off their sofa and cajoled him back to the Glove.

There had been total silence from Kendall. Ruby had left him a message, begging him to give Teddy a call, but none came. It surprised Ruby how much she missed him. It was as if the stabilisers had been swiped from her trike. She couldn't begin to imagine how Teddy must feel.

Maria, prone on the lumpy grass, shielded her eyes with one hand to ask, 'Scale of one to ten, Teddy?'

This had been a daily question for the past week. One was desolate, ten was ecstatic.

'Three,' decided Teddy after careful contemplation.

'That's an improvement,' said Tom, the curl of his lip betraying something Ruby preferred not to dwell on.

'We'll winch you up to eight in no time,' said Maria, pulling down the straps of her cami.

'Don't think so, love,' sighed Teddy. 'Not unless you've persuaded Johnny Depp to take me line dancing.'

Despite herself, Ruby had grown quite fond of Rafe. There was no way of knowing if this fondness would endure if he ever woke up.

A fog of marijuana smoke hung over Ruby's head as she scoured Drama Queen's sink. 'Everything OK?' she asked.

'What?' Drama Queen seemed thrown by the question. 'Oh. Yes.'

'Happy?' Ruby nonchalantly inflicted violent death on millions with one squirt of her germicidal spray.

'Er, yeah.' Drama Queen backed away, her pretty face puzzled. 'Look, I'll be in there. Shout when you've finished.'

Instead of shouting, Ruby lingered to put together a ham sandwich (with mayonnaise, just the way Drama Queen liked it) and a side of crisps. 'There you go!' She placed the tray on her client's lap.

Drama Queen was wearing that puzzled look again. She glanced across at Rafe, but he was busy being dead and didn't help. 'Er, did I ask for this?' she said eventually.

'No, but I just thought . . .' Ruby took in the look on Drama Queen's face: she had thought wrong. 'I'll put it in the fridge,' she said meekly, taking the tray back.

'Your money's on the hall table,' shouted Drama Queen after her, flicking on the TV.

Ruby let herself out. So, she thought, she'd misjudged her relationship with Drama Queen. A cleaner – even the world's best – is, when all's said and done, just a cleaner.

37

Joe practised his fallaway rock and swivel down in the basement kitchen as Ruby scoured the greeny-grey goo that was always stuck to the hob. 'Head up,' she counselled, her frame quivering as she wrestled the grime. 'Bottom in!'

'Maybe I should get together with Suzie for some practice.' Joe glided, like a moose in labour, across the sun-chequered floor. 'We need to be sharp for the show in September.'

'Good idea.' Ruby kept her amusement to herself.

'Has that bad man been bothering you?' Joe tripped over his own feet and slammed into the dresser. Straightening himself hurriedly, he resumed sashaying.

'He's gone away. For a long time,' said Ruby with satisfaction. She moved on to the grill. An old foe, Ruby squared up to it. Soon it would be gleaming and ready for its close-up, Mr De Mille. Out of the corner of her eye she watched Joe stumble about the kitchen.

A special warmth stole over her, a central heating that only Joe could inspire. She would never tire of watching him, he could never bore her, however many times he insisted on telling her the plot of his favourite Artemis Fowl.

Feet sounded on the stairs. Fast feet. Ruby looked across at the door, opening her mouth to smile, but the black look on Olivia's face stopped her.

'Oh God,' groaned Joe, as the look fell upon him.

'Darling . . .' began Olivia, crossing to the table with Hugo, pensive and concerned, at her shoulder.

'You're obviously going to tell me off but can it be quick?' interrupted Joe. 'I mean, do we have to talk about it and go on about the underlying meaning and stuff?'

'Shall I . . . ?' Ruby motioned to the door.

Hugo smiled his puppyish grin. 'Lord no,' he said kindly. 'We don't have any secrets from you, Ruby.'

Hoping she'd imagined it, Ruby ignored the flicker of a look that Joe seemed to throw her way.

'We'd like an explanation, Joe. For *these*.' Olivia slapped Joe's collection of ballroom dance magazines on the table. 'And these.' They were joined by a pair of polished dance shoes. 'And *this*.' Olivia placed his membership card for Miss Delmar's Academy neatly on top of the pile.

Joe gulped. He wrinkled his nose. He put his hands in the pockets of his hideous shorts. He didn't seem about to say anything.

'Mummy's been on the phone to this Miss Delmar,' said Hugo, with a sternness that didn't suit him, as if he'd forced his plump body into a sharp suit. 'Apparently, you've been going to a ballroom dancing class when we've believed you to be at extra sitar.'

'If you know,' said Joe sullenly, 'why are you asking?'

It was a good question, but Ruby was the only adult in the room who thought so. Shoulders taut with tension, she wiped the teapot with the hem of her overall. Her skin prickled all over, as if tiny mice were nibbling at her beneath her clothes. She kept her back firmly turned on the unfolding courtroom drama.

'*Ballroom*, darling!' Olivia held the word out with tweezers, as if it might bite. 'Of all the silly, mindless, time-wasting activities . . .'

'I'm good at it!' declared Joe loudly.

'So what if you are?' scoffed Olivia, whose usual self-control was eluding her. 'Where will such a talent get you? And don't use that tone of voice with me, young man. You're in big trouble.'

'For liking something *you* don't like?' Joe's hands burrowed deeper into his pockets and his brow dropped low over his eyes.

Hugo upped his volume too. 'For telling barefaced lies, buster!'

Scrubbing at a patch of worktop she'd already cleaned, Ruby struggled to control her breathing. This conversation was hurtling downhill. Straight towards her.

Hugo carried on, talking to the dishevelled top of his son's head. 'We're very, very disappointed in you, Joe.' From such a mild man this amounted to foaming at the mouth. 'For one thing, that academy is a tube ride away and you know you're not allowed on public transport alone.' Hugo frowned, as if something else, even more dastardly than illicit tube-boarding, had occurred to him. 'And where did you get the money for these jaunts?'

Joe didn't answer.

Ruby turned her head to take in Olivia and Hugo's tableau of Parental Dismay.

'Well?' prodded Olivia, arms folded. 'We're waiting.'

Joe opened his mouth, but it was Ruby's voice they heard. 'I paid for the lessons. I took him to Miss Delmar's every week.' She put a hand on his head. 'It's my fault, not Joe's.'

'You?' Hugo seemed thrown. 'So you knew.' He frowned at Joe. 'You went to Ruby and you—'

'It was my idea,' interjected Ruby, making sure that she was hung for the sheep, and not a paltry lamb. 'I've been very irresponsible.' Maybe it looked heroic, stepping in to own up and save a child, but Ruby knew that her employers only had half the story: she'd been far, far more irresponsible than she was choosing to admit. She'd lose her job, that much was certain, but at least her big secret would stay hidden.

'It wasn't all her,' insisted Joe gallantly, in a small, obstinate voice. 'It was me too.'

The kitchen was turning into the set of *Spartacus*. Hugo seemed confused. As usual. 'Ruby, why on earth didn't you come to us and—'

The no doubt rambling question was interrupted by a succinct one from his wife. 'Ruby, what's your maiden name?'

An icicle slithered down Ruby's spine. With a dry mouth she answered, 'Lawless.'

With the clarity of a chisel hitting stone, Olivia said, 'I knew it.'

'You knew what?' Hugo's gaze flipped from one woman to another, his podgy features churning. 'What does it mean? Who's Lawless?'

'*Think*, Hugo,' ordered Olivia calmly. She was composed but brittle. 'Ruby Lawless. Eleven years ago?' She made encouraging faces at her husband.

Hugo's eyes widened as the semaphored message sank in. 'Oh good God,' he breathed, turning to Ruby. 'You're—'

'Yes, Hugo, Ruby knows who she is,' said Olivia hastily, motioning to Joe with a jerk of her head.

Joe spoke. 'So do I. I know who she is. It's cool.'

315

If a trapdoor could have opened under Ruby's feet she would have willingly plummeted all the way to hell rather than look at Olivia and Hugo's faces.

Olivia said nothing, but her eyes clouded ominously.

Hugo said plenty. The couple's usual roles were reversed as he found his tongue. 'How bloody dare you?' he roared. 'You come into our house, like a sneak thief, and do something like this!' He was unrecognisable, his familiar chubby face puce. 'What were you thinking? What are you after?'

'I didn't really think,' admitted Ruby miserably, her hands knotted in front of her.

'Dad, don't,' muttered Joe, who, like everybody else, seemed glued to the spot.

'I'll deal with you later, Joseph Friend!' yelled Hugo before aiming his scattergun back at Ruby. 'I've never heard anything like it. You worm your way in, gain our trust and then you approach our son and tell him . . . tell him . . .' Hugo juddered to a stop.

'It wasn't like that. Honestly. I just . . .' But Ruby couldn't explain herself. Now that the whole affair had exploded, the light from the resulting mushroom cloud exposed her behaviour as the muddled procession of blunders it really was.

With sudden force Hugo blurted, 'You can't have him!'

Bile rose in Ruby's throat. 'That's not what this is about, Hugo, I swear.'

His wife's hand on his sleeve prevented Hugo from going any further. 'I'm sure it's not,' said Olivia calmly. She didn't seem able to lift her eyes to Ruby's as she said, 'The best thing is for you to go, please, and leave our family alone.'

'But I want her,' exclaimed Joe, taking a step forward, arms folded around himself and a panic-stricken scowl etched on his funny face. 'Don't make her go, Mum.'

'Joe, my love, we'll talk this through and we'll—'

'I DON'T WANT TO BLOODY TALK!' bawled Joe, spectacularly shedding his nonchalance. 'I want Ruby to come here, just like always. Why doesn't what I want matter?'

'Darling, of course it matters.' Olivia sounded forlorn and helpless as her son pushed brusquely past her and charged out of the kitchen.

'Happy now, Ruby?' Hugo was grimly triumphant. 'And to think how I raved about you. Going on about the happiness you brought to the house. I looked on you as one of the family and all the time you were busy turning our little chap against us.' Hugo took a pace towards Ruby and said forcefully, 'Because he is ours, you know.'

'Hugo,' said Olivia, quietly.

'Not yours.' Hugo wasn't finished. 'Got that? You gave him away, remember?'

Olivia's voice sharpened. 'Hugo!' she snapped. 'There's no need for any of this. Ruby's going, aren't you?'

'Yes,' muttered Ruby, crossing rapidly to where she always left her bag, on a battered rocking chair by the door. She felt like a tent peg that had been hammered neatly into the ground.

'And you're not coming back. Ever.' Olivia was calling up the stairs as Ruby barged, blind with tears, towards the front door. 'You know that, don't you?'

'Yes,' whispered Ruby shakily, closing the door behind her. She swayed a little before tottering down the familiar stone steps flecked with moss that she'd swept a hundred times.

The front door opened again before she reached the bottom. 'Ruby, wait.' Hugo's cheeks were still red, lending him the look of an overheated choirboy.

Turning, Ruby held up a wet face. 'Yes?'

'Keys.' Hugo held out his hand.

It took for ever to find the house keys in the anarchy of her overstuffed bag.

Hugo slammed the door.

There was only one person Ruby wanted to speak to.

'Darling?' Tom's tone was soft, as she knew it would be. The bliss, Ruby suddenly thought, of a sensitive man after so many years with a walrus. 'What is it? Something's happened.'

'I need to see you.' And smell you. And have your arms around me while you tell me it's going to be all right.

'Come to this address. Now.' Tom didn't hesitate, or fob her off, even though he was working. 'It's fifteen minutes away and then we'll sort it out, whatever it is, you'll see.'

That was a big claim, but Ruby in her shame and sorrow was prepared to believe it.

The address Tom had given her was a large terraced house in Chelsea. Inside, past the sturdy railings and the glossy front door, a children's party was in full swing. Privileged kids make much the same sort of noise as their counterparts further down the food chain, and Ruby had to raise her voice over the din when a thin woman dressed in clothes so tasteful they were almost offensive answered the door. 'Is Tom there?'

'Tom?' The woman's frown cleared. 'Oh. The clown. Hold on.'

A moment or two later, Tom came padding down the plush stair carpet in red shoes that stuck out like kippers. 'Ruby!' he said, sounding relieved to see her in one piece. 'I've got about twenty minutes. What happened?' He closed the door behind him and took her hand. 'Let's find somewhere to sit.'

'OK,' said Ruby uncertainly. This creature with a bald wig

sprouting turquoise tufts didn't feel like her Tom. She had a disloyal urge to yank her hand away from his white-gloved grasp.

The narrow street opened into a garden square. Tom, scrutinising her expression, led her to a bench. 'You've been crying,' he said.

'Mmm,' agreed Ruby, tight lipped, conscious of the stares his scarlet dungarees with massive yellow buttons were drawing from passers-by. 'You know, Tom, I can't help feeling awkward talking to you when you're dressed like that.'

'I forgot,' laughed Tom. 'I'm so used to it, but yeah, your phobia and everything.' He whipped off the wig. 'Is that better?'

So no was the only possible reply. Tom's beautifully disordered black hair only made his whitened face stranger. Ruby looked down at her own nice normal-sized trainers, airbrushing her boyfriend's ginormous feet out of her peripheral vision. It was time to push the truth out. 'The Friends just sacked me.' Best to start with a small detail, she reckoned. Gain a toehold in the rockface.

'Whaaat?' Tom was outraged on her behalf. 'Why? You're the best cleaner in the world. I've seen that in black and white.' He found even more outrage where the first batch had come from. 'And after all you did for, the kid, what's he called, Joe! Bastards.' He drew her to him. 'Forget them, Rubes. They're dickheads. They don't deserve you.' He lowered his voice. 'Are you worried about money? 'Cos if you are, I can help you out.'

That managed the impossible and got a laugh out of Ruby. *If only,* she thought, *I could worry about something as trivial as money.* 'Careful, Tom. You're straying into Manny territory. I'm OK for money.'

It sounded as if Tom was making an effort to keep his

tone light when he said, 'Don't compare me to Manny again, if you can help it, Ruby.' Leaning his head down to her bowed one, close enough for her to smell his shampoo, he said gently, 'Come on, lovely girl. Tell me what's brought this on. There's more, isn't there? We'll sort it out. Promise.'

'Promise?' Ruby heard herself ask, like a toddler who's been pledged a lolly.

'Cross my heart,' smiled Tom.

Gratitude flooded Ruby. Thank you, God, she thought, for sending me such a forthright, reliable, generous man: he hadn't flinched, just crossed his heart. 'It starts eleven years ago.'

Under the white greasepaint, Tom's brow puckered in surprise.

'Before I met . . .' She hesitated. 'Before I met you-know-who.' She hesitated again. This was hard. She'd never told anybody before. The Q and A with Joe had been the first time Ruby had said certain names out loud for a decade. She looked into Tom's earnest face and took a deep breath. He deserved this, even if it was a little late in the day. 'I had a baby,' she said. 'By accident.' She pulled a horrified face. 'Oh God, what a crap way to put it. I mean, I was so naïve and silly I didn't realise what was happening. I had sex once – once! – and the result was a baby boy.' She stalled, staring into Tom's eyes, which had become even more earnest and, to her, infinitely more beautiful. 'Oh Tom, that baby was Joe.'

'Joe Friend?' said Tom, his voice pirouetting upwards. 'That's . . .'

'Yes, it is whatever you're about to say.' Ruby managed a weak smile. 'He was adopted, by Olivia and Hugo.' She scanned Tom's face. 'I was only eighteen, Tom. I was a *young* eighteen, too. I couldn't fight them, my mum and dad. They said it was for the best. I blanked it all out. I—'

'Hey!' Tom squeezed her hand. 'Calm down, missus. You don't have to justify yourself.'

Oh but I do, whined Ruby to herself. 'I didn't know anything about the couple who wanted Joe,' she carried on. 'I even tried not to read the form when I signed it, but I saw some details and they stayed with me. Like a scar. So when I passed their house, it was like a . . .' Ruby struggled to find an adequate metaphor. 'A thunderclap,' she ventured. 'A bolt of lightning. It was *awful* and *wonderful* all at the same time.' Her face crumpled and she pressed a disintegrating tissue to her eyes. 'And then I saw him and my heart almost burst and now I can never see him again and I know I was wrong, I know just how bad I am but I couldn't, I had to, I was, I mean—'

'Shush, shush.' Tom folded her up in his arms. 'Cry it out.'

Eventually worn out by her own tears, Ruby calmed down. 'So?' she said fearfully, pulling away to look at Tom.

'I had no idea.' He spoke like a zombie.

'Well, no,' began Ruby. 'It's not the kind of stuff you tell people.' With an internal 'ouch' Ruby regretted that *people*. She was beginning to understand Tom's sensitivities, and she knew that being classified as mere 'people' would trample them.

'Would you have told me if the Friends hadn't found out?' asked Tom, chewing his lip.

'Of course,' said Ruby. It sounded insincere, even to her own ears. 'Yes, yes, I was going to,' she insisted, ramping up the certainty. She buttoned her lip, guessing that Tom needed time to digest what he'd heard.

Tom exhaled heavily, and seemed to snap out of it. 'What a mess,' he said, hugging her to him again. 'You poor love.'

'Do you think less of me?' asked Ruby fearfully, her cheek pressed against the oversized buttons on his chest.

'Don't talk rubbish.' Tom jiggled her with mock impatience. 'What you must have gone through . . .' His voice tailed off.

'It hurts,' whispered Ruby, opening the door to her heart a chink.

'I know, I mean, I don't know, but I can imagine.' Tom echoed her bleakness. 'Poor Ruby.'

They sat in silence for a while, the clown and his girl.

38

Arranging the tablecloth just so on Mrs Vine's dining table, Ruby wondered what her client would make of the cleaner's big secret. Perhaps Mrs Vine would banish her, like a Victorian housemaid who'd been ravished by a cad. More likely, the snooty old thing would consider giving babies away a perfectly appropriate hobby for the underclass.

Watching the old lady sit in her conservatory, tutting at articles in her *Daily Mail* about naughty immigrants and naughty teenagers and naughty unemployed people, Ruby wondered why she continued to do little unpaid extras for such an ungenerous old soul. The dry cleaning, the errands, the careful plumping of Mrs Vine's chair – Ruby felt it was her duty to do these things.

Without me, there'd be nobody to care about her, she thought. *It's all part of the job.*

There were other people to tell.

Maria was so shocked she had to eat a whole packet of HobNobs before she could speak. Crumb-flecked on the end of Ruby's bed, she made a few attempts before she managed an entire sentence. 'You mean you . . . But why did you . . . you should have . . .'

'I've been mad, I know.' Ruby was lying back among her pillows. 'It was never going to work. With hindsight I can see that.'

'Bloody hindsight,' grumbled Maria. 'Have you ever noticed it always comes along *just* too late. You could do with a bit of hindsight right at the beginning, before it all goes tits up. Mind you,' she mused, 'then it wouldn't be—'

'*Hindsight,*' they said together.

There was no name for the strange crime Ruby had committed. Was she a Fraudulent Cleaner? A Biological Con-Mother? If she could name her sin she could find a support group, like AA, and stand up to say, 'My name is Ruby Gallagher and I may have ruined some nice people's lives.'

As the days passed, her recklessness swam into clearer focus. Ruby could only condemn the woman who'd sauntered so carelessly up the steps to number fourteen Clancy Street back in January. Reckless was too kind a word: ruthless was a better one, a word that Ruby shied away from as if it was a hand poised to slap her.

When Ruby was lenient with herself, she acknowledged the aching emptiness that had propelled her to the Friends' front door. She had never, ever meant to tell Joe. Her folly had been to imagine that she could control the chain of events her business card set in motion.

When Ruby was hard on herself – a mere ninety per cent of the time – she couldn't forgive that callous girl, the one who behaved like the self-seeking, princessy madam that Manny described.

Manny. There he was again, popping up in her subconscious like a mole on a new lawn. The man himself was safely locked away in a high security prison from which Simon vowed he couldn't escape. His trial would be, apparently, an open and shut case after which the judge would gleefully throw away the key. The divorce was chugging along. There was no reason to think about Manny.

Yet here he was again, as regular as repeats of *Only Fools and Horses*. Only not half as funny.

Tom. *Think about Tom*, Ruby counselled herself. A far better man, and one who would arrive at Hannah House later on bearing a takeaway and an erection.

Pausing in her vigorous polishing of the Divorcee's tiled fire surround, Ruby recalled a livid phrase of Tom's. 'We're going wrong,' he'd said. She resumed polishing with even more elbow grease. He was right.

It was obvious to everybody that Ruby and Tom were well suited, that they fancied the respective pants off each other, that something precious happened between them: he had become important to her in a profound, odd, hard to describe way. But Ruby also knew that they were striking bum notes far too often, that sometimes their togetherness was strained by a fog of misunderstanding.

Tom was a straightforward man. Perhaps he resented being catapulted into her soap opera of murky secrets, bullyboy exes and long-lost babies. Did clean, transparent Tom really need a dark, demented girlfriend like Ruby? Instead of answering her own question, Ruby Mr Sheen-ed the tiles to within an inch of their lives.

Feeling traitorous, Ruby looked up and down the street before she rang the bell. Unless Teddy had access to an intricate network of surveillance cameras there was no way he could know she was at Cath's door, but Ruby's conscience spurned such namby-pamby detail.

'You came!' Kendall's face was pleated with pleasure as he opened the door.

The speech which Ruby had been polishing, packed with pithy observations about how compromised she felt meeting Cath behind Teddy's back, was doomed to be unsaid. 'Oh Kendall!' she breathed soppily and subjected him to a long hug. Holding him at arm's length like an indulgent aunty, she cooed, 'Let's look at you.' She frowned. 'Oh dear God, it's gone!'

'I know.' Kendall put a hand to the rudely nude flesh between his nose and his upper lip. 'Cath wasn't keen.'

Sans moustache, Kendall was a different creature altogether, especially when Ruby factored in the beige safari-style shirt that had replaced his trademark white T. 'Off to Kenya, are we?' she smiled.

'Are you coming in or do you have more personal remarks to make?' Kendall rolled his eyes as he led her down the hall.

'Ooh, it's been *ages* since you were all waspish with me,' giggled Ruby delightedly as she was led into a neat and orderly sitting room.

For a moment she thought the sofa was camouflaged. Her eyes adjusted and she realised that everything in the room was beige. The sofa, the walls, the carpet, the cushions, Kendall and even the Siamese cat daintily projectile-vomiting on the rug was beige. The resulting hairball, which struck Ruby on her ankle, was beige.

'Thought you didn't like cats,' said Ruby, sitting down.

'Oh, Pompom and I are great chums.' Kendall reached out a hand and the slender apostrophe of silky fur slunk from the room.

'So I see.' Ruby had many questions, but they seemed too

provocative for such a conservative room. An 'Are you happy?' might disarrange the doilies, a 'Do you want to come home?' would surely shatter the standard lamp. She contented herself with a simple, 'I miss you.'

Kendall's reply, a non-denominational 'Hmm', was drowned by a merry yodel of 'Any room for a small one?' from the doorway.

The infamous Cath, turner of homosexuals and patron saint of the Normal, was amongst them. Almost obscured by a three-tier plate of cream cakes, she was composed entirely of curves, a plushly upholstered woman whose round, dollish face was beaming.

So far, so good. Cakes and smiles were right up there on Ruby's list of Good Things, even if adultery wasn't. 'Hi!' she said toothily, keen not to let Kendall down. 'I'm Ruby.'

'Oh I know who you are,' said Cath, setting down the cakes.

Feeling Kendall's keen gaze upon her, Ruby managed an 'I've heard a lot about you'. Kendall's desperation that the two women bond was almost tangible. 'You have a lovely flat,' Ruby fibbed, adding *if you like beige* to pacify her scruples.

'Horn?' asked Cath abruptly, proffering the plate of cream cakes. 'Or are you more of a tart?'

The snigger on Ruby's lips transformed into a genteel cough. 'Oh, a horn,' she said politely, leaning over to take one. There wasn't the ghost of a titter from Kendall, who had swapped a man who lived and breathed *double entendres* for a woman who didn't recognise one when it bore down on her like a juggernaut.

'And you, dear?' Cath turned to Kendall. 'Something fruity, I dare say?'

The cake helped with Ruby's nerves; she would never

327

succumb to the lure of Class As while there were pâtisseries around. She managed to make polite chit-chat with Cath, who steered the conversation around the weather, the news and Pompom's digestive problems without ever veering near controversial territory.

'We're considering a long weekend in the Trossachs, aren't we, dear?' Cath looked at Kendall.

'Mmm-hmm,' nodded Kendall, licking apricot glaze off his fingertips.

One of the questions popped back into Ruby's head. 'Where are you working these days?' she asked Kendall.

'Oh yes.' The reply came from Cath. 'He's working for, well, *with* one of my sons. In the air conditioning business.'

'Never!' The coincidence tickled Ruby. 'My folks were in air conditioning.'

'Then you'll know,' said Kendall smoothly, 'how fascinating it is.' They enjoyed a shared twinkle.

'Kendall can turn his hand to anything,' mused Cath approvingly. 'My son wasn't sure at first, but now he wouldn't be without Kendall.' She was luminous with pride. 'I don't know what I ever did to deserve him.'

'Oh hush, Cath,' said Kendall.

Or rather, Kendall number 2. Ruby didn't recognise the safari-shirted man with the thickening torso and the burgeoning career in air con. Perhaps, she thought, all his essential Kendall-ness had been in his facial hair: Cath was his Delilah.

The question mark over his pliable sexuality was the least of the puzzles this new Kendall presented. Ruby was more intrigued by his transplant from the racy, night-time world of the Glove to this taupe Nirvana. He seemed perfectly content at the side of a woman who, although perfectly *nice*, had no spark.

As Cath proffered a choux bun, Ruby over-smiled to compensate for her hasty judging of this particular book by its (beige) cover. Cath launched into an account of her family, giving Ruby time to speculate that Kendall might well have had enough 'spark' to last him a lifetime. Perhaps he had been pining for just this brand of undemanding wholesomeness during the years spent refereeing drag queen cat fights.

'Greg, my eldest boy,' Cath was saying. 'Now, you'd like him, Ruby. Quite a looker. Good head on his shoulders. What he doesn't know about caravanning isn't worth knowing.'

'He's quite a chap,' said Kendall gnomically.

Ruby could smell a story here.

'He'll come round, dear,' said Cath comfortably. 'Eventually.'

'Greg doesn't *approve*.' Kendall drew out that last word in a way Ruby recognised as dangerous.

'My boy worries about me, Ruby. It's natural,' said Cath cosily, in a woman-to-woman tone. 'It's all this silly gay nonsense. He can't quite believe Kendall's over it.'

So caravanning Greg and Ruby had something in common. She was prepared to accept that her friend must be bisexual, but a hetero Kendall was unthinkable.

'I've made my choice,' said Kendall quietly.

'And I'm it!' squeaked Cath triumphantly. She splattered Ruby with whipped cream as she dug her newly acquired live-in love in the ribs. 'After all, there's gay,' she said confidently. 'And there's *gay.*'

'I'd rather,' said Kendall, 'we didn't get into this.'

Getting right into it, Ruby had to ask, 'And . . . which one is Kendall?'

'Oh, the latter, obviously.' Cath didn't elaborate, just carried on demolishing a bun. 'Greg'll come round. He'll have to. Kendall's given up a lot for me,' she said, nodding to under-line this fact. 'I'll stand by him. We're soulmates.'

'Yes,' said Kendall, eyeing Ruby with meaning. 'I've found my niche.'

'About time,' said Cath comfortably. 'After putting up with that ghastly Teddy all these years.'

Ruby put her cake down. This rarely happened.

'I mean, what a monster!' blustered Cath, blithely. '*Me me me.* Making Kendall's life a misery.'

It was impossible for Ruby to be rude to Cath, in her tidy sitting room in front of her ironed boyfriend. Even though she wanted to, Ruby wouldn't list the things that Cath didn't know about Teddy. His kindness, his humour, his energy, his rough wisdom. All she could do was leave.

'Thank you for the lovely tea and cake,' said Ruby all in one breath as she stood up. 'I have to be . . . at a place in, erm, ten minutes.' Her swearing was coming along nicely, but the lying sometimes let her down.

'Aw no. We wanted to show you photos of our allotment,' wailed Cath.

'Another time,' smiled Ruby, knowing there would be no such thing. 'Nice to meet you.' She stuck out a rigid hand to her hostess.

'You come back any time you like,' grinned Cath, pumping her hand. 'Do you need to use the little girls' room? Shall I put some cake in a piece of foil for you?'

Cath's kindness only added to Ruby's unease. 'No, honestly, I'm fine, no thanks, really.' She batted away various good-hearted offers as she made her way to the front door. Cath retreated to the kitchen, trailing 'Toodleoo!'s.

Pulling the door behind him on the step, Kendall said 'Hey!' in an undertone, as Ruby darted to the gate. 'You don't have to be anywhere in ten minutes, missy. Give me a moment.'

Shamefaced, Ruby turned.

'So. That's my Cath,' said Kendall searching her face.

'It's very hard . . .' began Ruby. 'I mean, I know you as one person and with her you're somebody completely different.'

'Maybe I'm happy,' suggested Kendall.

'Are you, though?' It seemed a key question.

'Yes, as you ask.'

'Then so am I,' said Ruby. 'And Cath's very nice.' Slightly homophobic. Utterly deluded. But nice with it.

'We never got a chance to talk,' said Kendall reprovingly. 'How are things with the lovely Tom?'

'Good. Then not quite so good. Up and down.' Ruby shrugged. 'Relationships. You know.'

'And Maria?'

'Still very much Maria.'

'Good. And what's-his-face, your little favourite?'

'Joe?' answered Ruby, the word rolling like a rock in her mouth. 'Fine. Great.'

'Will you come again?' asked Kendall curtly.

'I don't know.' Ruby watched Kendall try to conceal his wince. 'It's not easy listening to that gay or *gay* stuff. I mean, Kendall,' she hissed, 'you and Teddy were lovers! For years!'

'All right, all right!' Kendall flapped his hands and peered nervously behind him down the empty hall. 'I've been frank about it all. She just has a certain way of seeing things. Where's the harm if it gets her by?'

'It's a fairy tale,' insisted Ruby in an urgent whisper.

'I know a certain someone who lived in one for years.'

Startled, Ruby admitted huffily, 'Well, yes, s'pose . . .'

'So . . . maybe you and Cath have more in common than you think.'

Choosing to ignore the ever-so-Kendall razor edge, Ruby agreed. 'Maybe we do. We both love you, that's for sure. Cath worships you. I suppose that must be nice, after . . .' Ruby tailed off, uncomfortable with her treasonable thoughts.

'After being called a slap-headed ladyboy for years?'

'That's not all he called you,' Ruby reminded him gently.

'Look, Cath's good to me. And I'm good to her.'

'Sounds like a recipe for success.' Ruby's voice was clotted with emotion. She could sense a heavy curtain about to fall. 'Good luck, Kendall.'

'Good luck, Rubes.' Kendall's nose twitched like a rabbit's and he jammed his hands deep into his pockets as he turned back to the house.

On the pavement once more, Ruby turned just as the freshly painted front door began to close. 'Aren't you going to ask after Teddy?'

The door clicked shut.

Some of Ruby's routes were altered to bypass Clancy Street. She had a dread of bumping into a Friend, catching her breath at every pint-sized, Joe-style boy she passed.

Her mobile squeaked on the way home from Drama Queen's and her heart lifted a fraction, as it always did, in the ludicrous hope that it was Olivia or Hugo calling to say – what exactly? *Thank you so much for making fools of us, do come round and do it again*? Ruby hadn't got that far with her fantasy.

The number was unfamiliar. 'Hello,' said Ruby in her customary friendly way.

'Ruby, it's Tania.'

'Oh.'

'Don't put the phone down.'

'What do you want?'

'You don't mess about, do you?' laughed Tania.

'Why beat about the bush?' Tania sucked the energy out of Ruby. She could just picture her, sitting in one-size-too-tight black, chain smoking and scowling. 'This can't be a girly catch-up, so what do you want?'

'Money.'

'Really? I want world peace.' Ruby was almost impressed by the woman's nerve. 'A – I don't have any money and B – if I did, why on earth would I give it to you?'

'You're minted,' said Tania, with rude certainty. 'Stands to reason. You cashed in Manny's insurance and he told me how much it was worth.'

'Oh, change the record, will you?'

'You've got that money. You're a liar, Ruby.'

'Charming. You, erm, do rudes with my husband and bear him a child behind my back but *I'm* the liar.' How Ruby wished she could use words like 'shag' when occasion demanded: she vowed to practise.

'I never lied to no one. He did the lying.'

'I don't want to discuss the finer points of it all,' sighed Ruby. 'This conversation is going nowhere. I'm just about making ends meet. There is no magic pot of money.'

'There's that posh flat.'

'My home, you mean.'

'Sell that. It's Manny's, really.'

'It's mine,' said Ruby wearily. 'I have the documents to prove it.'

'Sell it,' repeated Tania.

'Aren't you listening? *I don't want to.*' Ruby was becoming exasperated. It was none of this angry stick insect's business, but she was attached to the penthouse. It had given her a roof over her head when she needed one. Ruby didn't see 'capital' when she looked at Hannah House, she saw 'home'. 'There's not only me to consider. Maria lives there too. I'm not going to chuck her out because your middle-aged hoodie of a boyfriend let you down.'

'Maria?' Tania snorted. 'No,' she said, with darkest sarcasm, 'we mustn't upset your bestest friend in the whole wide world, must we?'

An alarm bell jangled far off in the clutter of Ruby's mind. She paused. Her thumb hovered above the button to end the call. Her thumb stayed put and she heard herself ask, 'What exactly are you trying to say?'

'Did you know about cheese and chocolate?' Maria asked from where she lay stretched out on the red sofa. Watching Ruby come in and put her bag down, she carried on. 'For some reason they go together. It's insane. It's wrong. Like P. Diddy marrying Judy Finnigan. But, trust me, Parmesan and Galaxy is the nuts.' She gestured to the plate balanced on her bare midriff. 'Try some.'

In the weird monotone patented to scary children in horror films, Ruby said, 'You slept with Manny.'

'Shit.' Maria shot up to a sitting position, sending meteorites of cheese and chocolate hurtling to the rug.

'Not once,' said the super-calm and spooky Ruby as she lowered herself into the towelling swivel chair. 'Many times. While I was at home, waiting for him.'

'Now look,' gabbled Maria, springing to her feet. 'It wasn't like that.'

'You shagged him in the office at the club.' That tricky word slipped out easily. 'In the loos. In his car. Under the table in a restaurant. Classy, Maria. Quite the little Audrey Hepburn.'

Maria's lips were so pursed they'd disappeared. She and Ruby eyeballed each other for a long moment before she let loose an extended, weary sigh. 'I really, really, really wanted to tell you,' she said quietly, approaching Ruby and taking her hand.

Looking down at her fingers like defrosting shrimp in Maria's grasp, Ruby said, 'So why didn't you?'

'The same reasons you didn't tell the Friends, I suppose.' Maria spoke carefully. 'Because there was never a right time. Because I was ashamed. Because I worried it might ruin our friendship.'

'Might?'

'Don't, Ruby,' begged Maria, twisting her friend's hand and throwing her head back like a child pleading to stay up late. 'Don't go cold on me. Let's have a clean slate. Ask me anything you want.'

'I've heard enough about your affair, thanks,' said Ruby, dully.

'It wasn't an affair,' scoffed Maria. 'It was something or nothing. He was bloody horrible to me.' She pulled an expressive face at the memory. 'Low self-esteem. Too much Jack Daniel's. Who knows why I did it?' Maria paused. 'Actually, d'you know what? I *do* know why I did it. Because it felt like an adventure, banging the boss. God help me, I actually thought I was living the high life. What a fool. He told everybody, of course.'

'Except me,' said Ruby pointedly. 'He didn't tell me.'

'I didn't know you then, Rubes,' said Maria urgently. 'You were just an idea, a stranger. The wife. He told me . . .' she hesitated. 'He told me all sorts of garbage about your marriage.'

'He was married, Maria. There are other fish in the sea. Single fish.'

'You're right.' Maria hung her head. 'Manny can be very forceful.'

'Yeah, I'd noticed.'

'Of course. Sorry.' Maria winced. 'This is coming out all wrong. I'm trying to explain as best I can. It's important.' She thought for a moment. 'It was like a project, a mission, he was *fixed* on me. He wouldn't take no for an answer.' She swallowed hard. 'I was flattered. I was too flattered to see that it was a game, a bet with himself. I thought he was mad about me.'

Ruby pulled her fingers away. 'I thought you and I were mates.'

'We were. We *are*.' Maria sounded desperate, a sweaty counterpoint to the eerily calm Ruby. 'I'm glad, in a funny way, that you know. It means we can start again, put it behind us. I can make it up to you, instead of feeling guilty all the time.'

'Well, I wish I didn't know. You're so . . .' It was a dangerous moment to open up, but Ruby did it anyway. 'You're so important to me, Maria. You rewired me, connected me to the world. You believed in me when I felt like a freak, when everybody and everything was letting me down.'

'And all along I'd let you down too.' Maria masochistically finished the line of thought.

'Well, yes.' Ruby's unexpected and lovely friendship hung in shreds. Suddenly weary, she put her hands, scented with Fairy Liquid, up to her face. 'Look, you're going to have to go. I can't see past this. Sorry. Take a week. Longer. But you have to go.'

Managing a truncated laugh, Maria said, 'Don't apologise, you idiot. Of course I'll go. I'll get out of your face right away.' She shrugged and said in a small voice, 'I don't have much to pack.'

39

Shocked, Teddy's painted lips made a perfect 'O'. He pushed his Liza Minnelli wig up an inch in distress. But once again, he was shocked at the wrong aspect of Ruby's tale of woe.

'You mean to tell me,' he blustered, leaning right over the bar, 'you threw your best friend out on the street over some extracurricular rumpy-pumpy?' He laid a hand across Ruby's forehead. 'Have you gone bananas? You need your bumps felt, girl.'

'She had sex with my husband behind my back,' clarified Ruby loudly enough to ensure that every head in the half full bar swivelled to tune in. 'Then she came oiling around offering friendship without alluding to that rather important factette.'

Delighted wide eyes all round. This was quality eaves-dropping.

'That girl doesn't *oil*,' scoffed Teddy, adjusting his sequined boob tube. Despite his glittery get-up he spoke with the lofty certainty of a High Court judge. 'And of course she didn't *allude* to the fact that she'd been making the beast with two backs with your willy-wipe of a husband. I mean, would *you*?'

Ears waggled to hear Ruby's granite-like response. 'I wouldn't have done it in the first place.'

A whispered, 'Whoooh, get her,' was heard.

'No, of course not,' said Teddy with distinct lack of sympathy. 'Park your arse and polish your halo while I get you a nice glass of Holier Than Thou juice.'

When a long cool drink was set in front of her, Ruby mumbled, 'A little understanding wouldn't go amiss.'

'Don't get me wrong.' Teddy leaned forward on brawny folded arms encircled by diamanté bangles. 'You've been let down. It hurts. But think, Ruby. *Why* does it hurt, pet?' He didn't wait for any theories. 'Because you love *her*. Not *him*.' He waved a hand dismissively at the bulk of Manny's philandering ghost. 'Womanising halfwits are ten a penny. But a friend . . .' He straightened up and wiped the bar surface distractedly. 'They're precious. You hang on to friends. You forgive them.'

'That's asking a bit much,' said Ruby, speaking in a whisper and spoiling all the fun for the busybodies around her.

'You'd be doing yourself a favour,' said Teddy sagely. 'Grab love where you find it, darling. You never know when you might need it.'

Ruby looked up to meet Teddy's eyes, but he was looking beyond her, possibly into the recent past. She touched his hand and brought him back to the moment.

'I grabbed you,' Teddy reminded her.

At least somebody's life was looking up. The clues were all there; No. 7 cleanser in the bathroom cupboard; towelling headband by the sink; bra drying on the bedroom radiator. The Bachelor was getting some lady action.

Twirling Henry like a lover up and down the flat, Ruby surmised that the Bachelor must rather like this girl. Dirty pots and pans testified that he'd been cooking: previously she'd lugged a slag heap of ready meal containers down to the basement bins. There was no icing of discarded underpants on the bedroom floor, the porn had fled and the bed was neatly made.

'Some lucky female's getting the gold card treatment,' smiled Ruby as she shook his sheepskin rug vigorously.

A key in the lock and a familiar heavy-footed clump alerted her to the return of the man of the house.

'Oh. Hi.' The Bachelor hovered in the doorway of his room. 'I'd hoped to get back before you arrived. Clear stuff away.'

'That,' Ruby pointed out gently, 'would be silly. I'm the cleaner, not you.'

'Yeah. Sure. But.' The Bachelor hovered on. 'Are you OK with me having, erm, you know . . .'

Stoically managing not to laugh, Ruby said solemnly, 'Your romantic life is none of my business.'

'Brilliant.' The Bachelor grinned with relief. 'You're being really big about this, Ruby.'

Chasing dirt along his skirting boards, Ruby shook her head at the Bachelor's arrogance. 'Men,' she thought.

It never left her handbag. Sometimes she longed to touch it, and scrabbled about for it: at other times her fingers retreated from it as if it was contaminated.

It was only a clip-on bow tie. An innocuous, cheap little number in black polyester satin Ruby had picked up for Joe's show.

The show would rumble on without Joe or the bow tie. Only four weeks to go before September beckoned kids back to school. Suzie would have to seek out other toes to torment.

Ruby rubbed the bow tie on her cheek, ignoring the massed ranks of packaged mince vying for her attention in the supermarket freezer. The shiny fabric was soft against her skin, drenching Ruby in a tidal wave of memories. She closed her eyes and could sense Joe, his gawky shape, his yeasty boy smell and his awkward, surprising, endearing ways.

It was careless to lose such a treasure once, but twice . . . Ruby cursed her butter fingers. A supermarket trolley prodded her peevishly in the thigh, but she ignored it. Far from the half-fat, ten per cent fat, economy and prime cut mince, Ruby was tangled in both the recent past and a decade ago, dealing with fresh pain that felt remarkably like the old pain. But worse.

Concentrate on the shepherd's pie you promised Tom, Ruby counselled herself. She nudged some mince. It was hard to care about whether to buy five hundred grams or go berserk and plump for the full kilo when she longed to hear one of Joe's daft questions: 'What if the Queen was a man?'

'Potatoes,' she recited under her breath. 'Oxo cubes. Onions. *Joe.*'

'Mmm. Grffle. Bngh.' Tom couldn't stop eating long enough to form recognisable words, but his face said it all as he munched through his third helping of Ruby's pie.

'So you like it?' laughed Ruby, disproportionately proud of herself. She was such a novice at cooking that she still experienced a jolt of delight when people ate her food without keeling over. The clatter of pans and the hiss of the hob helped the apartment to feel less empty. 'It's true what they say, the way to a man's heart really is through his stomach.'

'Sometimes,' agreed Tom, when he could speak again.

He reached over to drag her from her chair, plonking her on his lap. 'And sometimes it's through his trousers.' He must have enjoyed Ruby's blush because he let out a small, '*Aww!*' before kissing her all over her face and telling her, 'But most of the time the way to a man's heart is through his heart, Ruby, and you're already there.'

'Am I?' asked Ruby, her frown not matching the moment.

'You know you are,' said Tom, his irreproachably straight if slightly over-large nose a centimetre from her own. He paused. That frown was catching. 'Don't you?'

'Yes.' Ruby couldn't quite go the whole hog and make it sound sincere. She threw her arms around his neck to grab the moment back.

Tom withheld his lips. He was studying her.

'Nooo!' she half howled. 'We always do this. We start talking when we should be kissing. No analysis tonight, Tom, please!'

Tom kissed her. It was a capable, effective, trust-me-I-know-what-I'm-doing kiss but Ruby could taste the difference between this kiss and those others that preceded pulling each other's tops off and heading for the bedroom as if there was a pack of dingoes after them.

'Go on, then,' she sighed, sliding off his lap and returning to her chair. 'Talk.' She threw her head down on the table in exaggerated despair, but eventually lifted it again when Tom stayed schtum. 'Well?' she prompted.

Pushing his plate away, Tom said, 'Don't know if I've got the energy. We always have the same conversation.'

Perturbed by the lack of a glint in his eye, Ruby sat up straight.

'You know the one I mean,' he continued. 'I ask how you are. You say you're fine with a big artificial smile. Then I try to get you to be honest with me. That can take quite a while.

Then you admit you're missing Joe. Then, after another while, you admit you're missing Maria. Sometimes we even manage to miss Kendall. But all the time you're trying to fob me off, use me as an emotional hot water bottle to dull the pain without ever really engaging with me or inviting me into your thoughts.'

'Is that how you see me?' Ruby was flitting from guilt to resentment, unsure where to land.

'Then, if we keep talking, I'll ask you that question you hate, the one you always make me feel like a self-centred heel for asking.'

'Which one's that?' murmured Ruby, sulkily pushing peas around her plate with a forefinger (she'd plumped for resentment).

'The one where I ask you where I figure in all this.' Tom stood up abruptly. The scrape of his chair on the shiny floor grated on Ruby's ears. 'Maybe I sound like some egomaniac who can't accept that you have other people and things in your life.' He gripped the back of his chair and hung over it, to say passionately at her bowed head, 'But don't you see? What I'm really asking is if you care, just a bit. If you can let me in. Because I'm here and I'm real and I'm ready to go all the way with this.'

Slowly, Ruby looked up. She took in Tom's ardent face with its cleanly drawn features and the two new points of high colour on its cheeks. 'I'm not used to this,' she whispered. 'I've never had an ordinary relationship before.'

'Ordinary?' Tom almost spat the word. He gripped the chair so tightly his knuckles were bleached. 'This isn't ordinary. This is love. So you can stop trotting out that excuse. I've never been in love like this before either, you idiot!'

Ruby swallowed. She could feel it, whatever *it* was, slipping away. Tom was saying beautiful things with a snarl. She had zero confidence in her own ability to steer them back on course because, as she told Tom, 'Being with Manny for so long has left me useless at this.'

'There he is again!' Tom threw his hands in the air and stalked over to the tall windows. 'Manny. Manny. My mate Manny. It always comes back to him. I know Manny Gallagher so well I could take a degree in him.'

'What do you want me to say?' pleaded Ruby, lost in the maze that always sprang up around them when Tom insisted on 'talking'. 'I can't rewrite my past. I can't pretend I'm not sad about Joe, that I don't wish Maria hadn't betrayed me. I can't go over Manny with Tipp-Ex. What,' she repeated wildly, 'do you want me to say, Tom?'

There was an immediate answer, calm and quiet. 'I want you to ask me how I am.'

'Eh? But I do.' Ruby's mouth twisted. 'Don't I?' she asked, in a low voice.

'I wouldn't mind, I really wouldn't give a damn,' said Tom, 'if I thought you saw a future for us. I'd just hang on. I'd stick around indefinitely. But I can't shake the feeling . . .' Tom hesitated.

Ruby could see a neon sign flashing over her boyfriend's head. IMPORTANT (POSSIBLY SHIT) MOMENT COMING UP! She tensed.

'. . . that you aren't really into this. Into me,' ended Tom blankly.

The gap he left for her denial widened until Ruby could have herded Teddy's entire wig collection through it.

'There's my answer, I guess,' whispered Tom hoarsely, turning his back on her.

Ruby wanted to holler *Don't give up on me!* She wanted to tell him that she cared. That his face was her favourite face. Some evil stone in her throat stoppered her up and she watched him pull on his faded, cosy sweatshirt and head for the door.

As Tom reached for his rucksack, a voice in Ruby's head told her that it was better this way, that it had to end sooner or later like everything else. In that moment, Ruby knew that Tom was right: she'd been withholding in the hope of lessening the pain when it all flew apart.

Standing waiting for the lift, Tom said, 'I know you want me to be gone, and I've said far too much, and you probably think I sound like a naff greetings card, but honestly Ruby, you need to learn how to be loved.'

'Bye then,' said Ruby to the empty room.

Dawn reeked with the smell of burning bridges. Too wimpish to drink alone, Ruby drowned her sorrows in Munchmallows and Jammie Dodgers and Fun Size Mars Bars.

Undoing the top button on her jeans, she let another wrapper flutter down to join its fallen brethren on the rug. 'I'll throw myself into my work,' she vowed, like a character in one of those thick sagas her mother used to read. 'I'll work. I'll save. I'll look after Teddy. I'll heal.'

Trying to be philosophical, Ruby was looking upon her love affair with Tom as a casualty of war. They were, she reckoned, never meant to be (that idea required a full size Mars Bar – sometimes those Fun Size buggers just don't do it). Perhaps it was bad timing. Or perhaps she was every bit the misfit that Tom had described. Ruby vowed not to pick at the corpse. From now on, it was onwards and upwards.

Or at the very least not backwards.

40

Wheee! Look! There goes Ruby Gallagher! Throwing herself into her work!

Over the next couple of weeks, Ruby cleaned as if she was trying to break through her clients' houses into another dimension.

The Bachelor's mirrors gleamed like the sun, the Divorcee's chrome coffee machine could only be viewed through smoked glass, and Mrs Vine's antimacassars were as white as a puritan's dance card.

Ruby approached five new customers and three of them took her on. She found herself hoovering an open plan loft apartment, a dinky cottage dense with bric-à-brac, and an artist's studio above a newsagent's.

It felt bracing, like a dip in the Channel. Ruby glowed with the satisfaction of being useful. She had a place in the world. She was independent. She was building up a nest egg. Ruby baked pies for Teddy, indulged the Drama Queen, hid the Divorcee's gin. She was exhausted every evening and slept deeply on her big bed.

The divorce was on course. There were no mixed feelings any more: Ruby was salivating for it. She wondered how she would celebrate, and decided on a nice supper somewhere posh with Teddy. If he was available: Teddy had started to make noises about dating again. Ruby knew these noises were really bleats to stave off the silence. She recognised them from her own vocabulary.

Intimately acquainted with the TV schedules, Ruby formed attachments to the most unlikely programmes. One evening a dull little documentary about the history of the house brick had held her hand for that awkward hour between when she began to yawn and the moment she judged herself sleepy enough to nod off.

In fact, Ruby's life was a fairy tale all over again. She was Rapunzel this time, trapped high up in Hannah House, watching life buzz past far below. Her hair wasn't long enough to reach the green.

There was no hopeful checking of her mobile. She knew Tom wouldn't call. He lived in straight lines. Tom's 'Goodbye' meant just that. It made it easier. Ruby had had her fill of jumping out of her skin when the phone rang.

As for calling him . . . those remarks still smarted. They stung all the more because they were true. Ruby wasn't like other people, and it was a relief not to pretend any more.

It was her karma, she'd realised, to miss people. She was getting good at it. Ruby could conjure up Tom in the same gleaming detail as she imagined Joe, Maria or Kendall.

'Joe,' breathed Ruby like a little prayer as she channel-hopped on the lookout for televisual opiates. 'Tom.'

Rapunzel's solitude was, she believed, less to do with choice, more to do with karma.

Teddy, who had never believed in fairy tales, or karma, or

keeping his nose out of other people's business, had a different opinion. 'Pride,' he sneered. 'I reckon you prefer it up there in your nice hygienic ivory tower.'

Visits to Drama Queen were strictly business these days. Clean. Collect money. Do not pass go.

Today, something was amiss. Ruby's nose tingled as she entered the flat. No sickly sweet smoke, she realised. The flat had reverted to its pre-Rafe scent of toast and filthy pyjamas. Inwardly, Ruby sighed. More flipping heartache.

As she warily opened the door to the sitting room, a mad-eyed creature in dishevelled nightwear sprang at her.

'He has somebody else!' shrieked Drama Queen.

'Rafe?' asked Ruby. 'Are you sure?' The boy hadn't the energy to blow his nose, let alone two-time.

'Don't use that disgusting name in this house!' Drama Queen put Marmite-stained hands over her ears. 'He's got some girl in Bournemouth, and one in Oxford. And I have reason to believe there's a bitch in East Molesey.'

It was hard not to be impressed.

'And they're all thinner than me!' howled Drama Queen.

This was tedious. It was never-ending. And all Ruby could earn by getting involved would be a knock-back when the next gentleman caller shambled along. She stood, irresolute for a moment, as Drama Queen sobbed into a tissue that had given its all some time ago. 'Soup?' she said, eventually.

'Ooh, yes.'

'And we'd better get you into some clean things.'

To deserve the title of World's Best Cleaner, Ruby reckoned she had to roll up her sleeves and get stuck into all sorts of messes.

*

'Rabbits,' yawned Ruby dutifully on the first of September. Summer was losing its grip. Café tables had been whisked back inside. Knees were no longer bare.

Absentmindedly demolishing a family bag of Hula Hoops, she grimaced at her sitting room. It felt stale. It was, naturally, spotlessly clean but was in sore need of a kick up the bum.

Tugging and panting, Ruby heaved the red sofa over to the other side of the room, and placed the low table at a different angle. That meant the TV would have to move. Pushing the swivel chair along the glass wall, a blurred figure far below on the pavement caught her eye and deceived her into thinking it was Maria.

Another glance told Ruby she was right. It was Maria. Hands in pockets as always, Maria was beetling towards the doors of Hannah House with an air of purpose.

'Oh God!' Ruby's hand went to her mouth. How should she be? Stern? Flinty? No, no, she scotched that approach as she arranged herself casually in the swivel chair. Disappointed yet philosophical? Mature and accepting?

Waiting for a shrill announcement from the buzzer, Ruby considered and then jettisoned anger, snootiness, piety and indifference. As the tension grew, she faced facts: she would leap about like a kangaroo the moment Maria walked in.

Tension can't grow indefinitely. After five minutes of posing in the chair Ruby had to admit that, unless Maria had managed to get hopelessly lost in the lobby, there would be no visitor today. Evidently, Maria hadn't been heading for the doors at all.

'Doesn't matter,' Ruby told herself, and continued shunting the furniture around. 'Doesn't matter a bit.'

*

The tramp was picking his teeth with the violin bow. 'Fancy a song?' he asked as Ruby passed, laden with carrier bags full of Teddy's favourite food.

'No, no, you have a rest,' smiled Ruby.

'You can't beat a good tune.'

'That's true.' *But you can flog it to death.* Ruby paused and dug out a pound coin.

'Thank you, young lady.'

The Velvet Glove, minutes away from closing time, was disgorging bon viveurs, some of whom could still walk, as Ruby passed its door. Vivid blue and fuchsia speckles of light daubed the pavement each time the door delivered another disoriented drunk back into the arms of the chilly real world.

Ruby let herself in and struggled up the stairs to the flat with her carrier bags. Huffing and puffing, she backed through the sitting room door.

The twilit room erupted with noise and colour. Streamers popped as disco music poured out of powerful speakers. Ruby spun round to blink in the glare of flashing fairy lights.

'Wha—?' she croaked, squinting at the scene in the centre of the room. A forest of gold balloons sprouted from the sagging sofa. Arranged among the cushions, holding aloft a champagne bottle and wearing the briefest gold briefs known to man, was Kendall.

'SURP—' was as far as Kendall got before his smile fell in on itself. 'Oh, it's you,' he said, crestfallen. Abandoning his wanton pose, he reached out and flicked off the music with one toe. 'I thought it was Teddy.'

'You're back,' said Ruby stupidly.

'It would seem so.' Kendall patted the seat beside him. 'Sit down and recover.'

Lowering herself to sit beside him, Ruby took Kendall in.

He looked his old self, even though the neat moustache was obviously stuck on. His pepper and salt crop was just so, and he smelled of Imperial Leather as ever. The absence of clothes was novel, and Ruby wished she could stop her eyes flickering down to his gold pants. Kendall was far more strapping downstairs than his conservative presentation suggested. 'What does this mean?' she asked.

Kendall plonked a cushion on his lap. 'Is that better?' Evidently he'd noticed the route her eyes kept taking.

'Thanks,' said Ruby weakly.

'This means,' said Kendall, returning to her question, 'that I have come to my senses.'

'You're back for good!' Ruby clasped his arm in delight.

'Ow. Yes.' Kendall grinned too, his moustache wobbling. 'I've missed you, Rubes.'

'Me too, me too,' squeaked Ruby giddily. 'Teddy really thought he'd lost you. No phone calls. No letters.'

'I thought it was fairer that way. Cleaner.' Kendall sighed. 'I had to give poor Cath a fair crack of the whip.'

'Is she devastated?'

'Hmm.' Kendall pondered the question. 'Not exactly.' He sagged. 'It just kind of petered out. No histrionics, no throwing things.' He sighed. 'I felt rather insulted, to tell you the truth. When I said I was leaving, she helped me pack.' He shared a comfortable laugh with Ruby. 'God, I was *bored*,' he admitted. 'Cath has such an orderly, stable life. Everything runs like clockwork. Dinner at seven. Telly at eight. Knitting disgusting garments for the gruesome grandchildren. Some nights as we sat there, watching some godawful game show or watching the cat show us its bumhole on the rug, I longed, *longed*, for a drag queen to come down the chimney, kicking and biting.' He let Ruby laugh, then continued, 'There were no surprises. Not one. And if I'm honest, I disappointed her.'

'You?' said Ruby, loyally. 'Never.'

'I couldn't work up an appetite for the finer points of air conditioning. I didn't want to wear matching windcheaters. I found it hard to pretend that the cat was a person. I just wasn't Cath's type, in the end.' He shook his head. 'Gay, straight, whatever, I think I'm Teddy's type; that's pretty specific.'

'We assumed you were blissfully happy.'

'I was wallowing in regret,' confessed Kendall. 'Too much beige can clog your arteries. God, I love this dump.' Kendall beamed around at the room. 'Even though it's blue.' He pursed his lips. 'My least favourite colour.' He raised that eyebrow that Ruby had missed so much. 'I kept remembering the thud of the music from downstairs, Teddy's hairclips scattered everywhere.' He reached out and took a crinoline lady ornament from a shelf. 'All his crummy tat. Cath never ran around in the nude singing songs from *My Fair Lady*, you know.'

'I bet,' giggled Ruby.

'She didn't annoy me or nag me or make me want to throttle her with my bare hands once.'

'What a bitch.'

'How has it been?' asked Kendall uncomfortably.

'How d'you think it's been?' asked Ruby.

'Bad.'

'That's how it was. Mood swings. Drink. Hysterics. Writhing around on the floor in a fluorescent leotard.' She could have gone on, but the guilt on Kendall's angular face stopped her. 'But he was getting better. Teddy's made of sterner stuff than I thought. He's a fighter.'

'I broke the poor sod's heart.' Kendall's head drooped. 'And it's a big heart.'

'True. Answer this, Kendall.' Ruby eyeballed him. 'Have you made your choice? Is this it?'

'I've been homesick and that man is home. I'm staying put.' Kendall raised an eyebrow. 'If he'll have me.'

Ruby harrumphed happily, then held up a finger. They both listened. 'The music's stopped. He'll be up any minute.'

Kendall sprang into position and his cushion hit the floor. Shading her eyes, Ruby coughed. 'Kendall, I had no idea . . .'

'Never mind my magnificent appendage,' said Kendall matter-of-factly. 'Shoo, sweetheart.' He flicked the fairy lights off. As Ruby fumbled for the door in the darkness, he hissed, 'Hey, what about you? Have you been OK?'

'Tomorrow,' promised Ruby. 'It can wait.' She gave him the once-over. 'Tummy in, please. Chin up.'

The sound of a key in the front door silenced them. Ruby mouthed, 'Good luck' as she slipped out of the room.

Meeting Ruby at the turn of the stair, Teddy said, 'You're going the wrong way, you silly old tart.'

'I, erm, forgot something,' fibbed Ruby.

Looking doubtful, Teddy refused to move out of her way. 'What, exactly?'

'Er, paprika.' Ruby squeezed past him. 'Liquorice.' She took the stairs two at a time. 'Tripe.'

'Are you running out on me?' shouted Teddy crossly, hands on hips.

'I've left you a tasty dish in the sitting room.'

His delighted whoops followed her all down the street.

41

Spending time with the reunited Teddy and Kendall was like being force-fed meringue. Ruby was as fond of romance as the next girl, but slumped between the loved-up pair on her big red sofa, she concocted an excuse to cut short their visit.

'Is that the time?' she exclaimed, waving her watch theatrically. 'I have to do my client in the flat downstairs! He goes ape if I'm late!' This was a lie: the Bachelor, despite his macho ways, had never complained about anything, even when Ruby had left a damp J-Cloth on his signed photo of Pammy Anderson.

'Aww,' wailed Teddy, as if he had planned to stay for ever.

'Come on, Ted.' Kendall hauled his beau up, saying with his usual perspicacity, 'I think we're a bit much at the moment.'

'Not you,' gushed Teddy, stroking Kendall's cheek. 'You're never too much. Look at that face!' he ordered Ruby. 'Did you ever see anything so adorable? I could eat a plate of him!'

Kendall looked at the ceiling. 'I'm sorry,' he said. 'Normal service will be resumed as soon as possible.'

'Yes,' chirruped Teddy, who seemed to have swapped personalities with Snow White and really could chirrup. 'We'll be spewing abuse soon, but for the moment, we're in lurve.' He stopped short and reached out to hug Ruby, crushing her against him. 'Oh sweetie pie, here I am yakking on about love and you carrying around that sore old broken heart.'

'I'm fine,' mumbled Ruby. 'Honest.'

'Best mate gone. Little Joe gone,' lamented Teddy. 'Boyfriend gone.'

'She's aware of all that,' said Kendall, trying to extricate Ruby from the sticky vines of his lover's grasp.

Relinquishing her reluctantly, Teddy held her at arm's length and regarded her with pulsating pity. 'You poor cow,' he half sobbed. 'You poor poor poor cow.'

Muttering, 'He was a great loss to the Samaritans,' Kendall bundled Teddy away.

'You'll always have us!' yelled Teddy, the sentiment only slightly marred by a boisterous fart.

A whole hour early, Ruby let herself into the Bachelor's flat, relishing the special silence of an empty house.

Peeking in at the kitchen, she saw a sink stacked with smeared dishes. *Perfect*, she thought, eager to get them sparkling again. She decided to leave the kitchen until last, the way a child saves their favourite ice cream flavour.

Backing into the bedroom, faithful Henry ambling noisily alongside, Ruby edged around the bed. This apartment was much smaller than hers, and the Bachelor's penchant for dark, oversized furniture didn't leave much floor space. She reached over to release the blinds, and they sprang up with a neurotic twang.

The duvet, bunched up on the circular bed, moaned.

Ruby jumped, and tugged Henry closer for reassurance.

'Whatsit?' grumbled the duvet.

'Sorree,' trilled Ruby, backing out. The lump in the bed was undeniably female and she foresaw losing her client over this.

'Whosthatthere?'

The lady all wrapped up in the covers was obviously only half awake. If Ruby tiptoed out, the Bachelor need never know.

A snore escaped the leather bed.

Ruby stopped tiptoeing. Reaching over, she prodded the dozing bundle with the tip of Henry's nozzle. She wasn't particularly gentle about it.

'Chopfarg!' snarled the duvet.

'Maria!' exclaimed Ruby.

'Jesus Christ on a bike!' Maria sat bolt upright, wearing a Kaiser Chiefs T-shirt that Ruby recognised from the Bachelor's drawers. 'You're not meant to be here yet!' she gargled through dry lips, bringing the alarm clock right up to her sticky eyes.

'*I'm* not meant to be here,' echoed Ruby sarcastically. 'What the hell are you doing here?' Clouds parted. 'You're the new girlfriend!' Ruby was as baffled as she generally was during *CSI Miami*.

Looking peeved, Maria rubbed her eyes. 'We've been so careful. He said you were all right with it.'

A forgotten conversation popped into Ruby's head: she and the Bachelor had been at quite impressive cross-purposes. 'Well, once again I'm the last to know who you're sleeping with.'

Shutting her eyes at her own bitchiness, Ruby heard Maria rush from the room. Robotically, she straightened the room, giving Maria plenty of time to lock herself in the bathroom. She ventured out to the hall and heard the rattle of a teaspoon in the kitchen. Shoulders squared, Ruby crossed the narrow hall.

Short brown legs sticking out of her T, Maria held out a Kelly Brook fan club mug. 'Cuppa?' she asked.

'Oh. Dunno. Ta.' It was an ambush: nobody made a cup of tea quite like Maria. The ratio of tea to milk was perfect, the sugar perfectly judged.

'Have I lost my touch?'

Ignoring the open goal, Ruby declined to comment on how quickly Maria had found her way into the Bachelor's bed. Instead she shook her head.

'How's life on the top floor?' asked Maria brightly.

'Much the same.' Ruby pondered for a moment. 'Quiet,' she said, looking down into the depths of her drink.

'Great news about the boys, innit?'

'Yeah, great.'

'Heard from Tom?' Maria recoiled from the look Ruby threw her. 'Sorry. None of my biz.'

'No, it's not.' Ruby plonked her mug on a nearby radiator cover. 'Look, I have to get on.' She turned and headed for the Bachelor's sitting room.

A moment passed before small feet padded after her on the shagpile. 'This is fate,' said Maria, as Ruby bent to polish a nest of chrome and glass tables. 'It's our chance to talk.'

'We've talked,' said Ruby brusquely, wondering who was in charge of her brain today; somebody hard as nails and really rather rude.

'Not properly,' persisted Maria. 'There were things I didn't know back then, like . . .' She faltered, wringing the hem of the T-shirt in her hands. 'Like how much I'd miss us.'

'Tough.' The rhythm of Ruby's duster sped up.

Making a disappointed noise in her throat, Maria backed away.

Suddenly Ruby recognised the voice she was using. *Mum*, she thought. She remembered how it felt to be on the receiving end of Marjorie's judgemental iciness. She straightened up, breathing quickly.

With a bound she was out in the hall. 'Me too!' she blurted to Maria's back. 'I missed you. Loads.'

'You did?' Maria whirled round.

'So much.'

They faced each other, pulsing with excitement. And uncertainty.

'I wanted to . . .' began Maria.

'I couldn't . . .' shrugged Ruby.

'I was frightened you'd . . .'

'I felt all . . .'

They ground to a halt.

After a short silence, Maria managed some coherent sentences. 'Listen. I need to say sorry. I should have told you about Manny early on. That way you could have decided whether or not you wanted to know me. I kind of tricked you into being mates.'

'Rubbish,' said Ruby vehemently. 'You're my mate. I spoke when I should have listened.' Her new-found certainty spurred her on to say, 'Manny's a sleazeball, anyway. He's an expert at getting girls into bed. Falling for his crap doesn't make you a bad person.'

They seemed to have swapped viewpoints. 'But I should have taken a minute to think about his wife,' Maria pointed out. 'I should have had a conscience.'

'You did,' said Ruby fervently. 'Your conscience led you to my house the day Manny dumped me.'

'I suppose,' Maria agreed.

'And I'm glad it did.' Ruby ploughed on with this new line of thought. It was tough but it made her feel better, like a long run or a cold shower. 'I never needed a friend so badly in my life and suddenly there you were.'

Maria smiled idiotically.

'Come to think of it,' laughed Ruby, 'I'm *glad* you shagged my husband!' She held her arms out and her little friend ran into them.

Maria squeezed Ruby tight. 'You said *shagged*,' she laughed. 'Just like that. I'm so proud of you.'

Collapsing on to the Bachelor's black leather sofa, Maria asked, 'Can I come home?'

Dropping down beside her, Ruby said, 'You'd better. I'm starting to talk to myself.'

'Yay!' Maria punched the air. 'I don't like living with a boy. There's too much togetherness and not enough crisps.'

'When did you and the Bachelor kick off?' Ruby was keen to piece the jigsaw together.

'We've always flirted like flip. I mean, he's gorgeous, isn't he?'

Ruby just stared.

'OK, obviously not,' giggled Maria. 'But *I've* always fancied him. That posh, city boy look does it for me. All groomed and smart, but underneath his suit . . .' she growled expressively.

Ruby, who could only see a nerdy bloke in pinstripes, shrugged.

'You know me,' said Maria. 'I like men. All sorts. All shapes. So, anyway, I met him mid-flee in the foyer, crying and everything, and he was dead nice. Said I could stay at his. He'd take the spare room.'

'Oh. So you aren't . . .' probed Ruby.

'Of course we bleedin' are!' guffawed Maria. 'The spare room thing didn't last.' She cuffed Ruby on the arm. 'Don't look so shocked, princess. You know what a slapper I am.'

'Won't he be hurt if you just move out?'

'Oh, Ruby, you're priceless,' smiled Maria. 'He'll probably be relieved. It's run its course. We've had fun, and the best game of strip Scrabble ever. And now it's over. No bones broken. We're not Romeo and Juliet.' She shot her friend a look. 'Or Tom and Ruby.'

'Hah,' snorted Ruby, taken by surprise. 'We were nothing special.'

'I know special when I see it.' Maria was serious now. 'Call him. Be brave. It worked for me.' She gave Ruby a wheedling look, then yelled, 'Come on! Help me pack! I'm going to nick all his best T-shirts!'

Damp footprints across the marble floor. Used teabags slumped like drunks on the draining board. The last slice of angel cake mysteriously AWOL. Maria was back.

'I'll clear up that pile of Edam rind in a mo,' said Maria, peering up at the kitchen calendar as she spooned frozen yoghurt into her mouth.

'Don't worry about it,' said Ruby indulgently.

'The twelfth . . .' said Maria to herself. She screwed up her eyes and counted under her breath.

'The twelfth?' asked Ruby sharply. She'd been hoping that date might slip by unmarked.

'Twenty-four, twenty-five,' mouthed Maria, unfurling her fingers as she went. 'Phew,' she concluded. 'Thought I was late, but I'm not.' She put her hands together and gazed heavenwards. 'Thank you, O patron saint of sluts. There'll be no baby bachelors running about.' She poked Ruby in the chest, smearing her embroidered motto with yoghurt. 'What are you all dewy eyed about, missus?'

'It's Miss Delmar's show tonight,' blurted Ruby. 'He was looking forward to it so much.'

'And so were you,' said Maria with such perfect empathy that Ruby had to leave the room.

42

They were like flashbacks from 'Nam. One second Ruby was diligently running a cloth along Mrs Vine's skirting boards, the next she was plunged back into a small brightly lit room, heels hoicked up in straps and a soundtrack of her own feral grunts.

Joe had taken his time being born. Ruby reached the limits of her endurance only to discover that stern old Mother Nature expected more. So another mountain was scaled.

The universe had shrunk to that boxy room. Ruby couldn't remember anything before the exhaustion. Surely, she'd always been there in an itchy gown, her private parts spotlit for the benefit of a gaggle of masked strangers.

And then suddenly: Joe. Dangling in the air, his palms waggling like a tiny Al Jolson. A new line had been drawn: Ruby couldn't remember anything before *him*.

A dead wasp by the skirting board called her back to the present.

*

All morning Ruby was ambushed by memories. She remembered the rolling waves of agony, the blood in Joe's thick nest of hair, the indignity and the pride. That sense of standing close to the centre of things, of *almost* understanding the meaning of it all.

These memories had been locked up long ago. Assailed by them, Ruby didn't have a clue what to do. If she wallowed in them, they would break her. Losing Joe a second time gave them a new poignancy that was unbearable.

But then . . . Ruby had thought the pain of his birth was too much to bear and she'd been wrong. 'I'll get through this,' she told herself, outraging Mrs Vine by going home early for the first time ever.

It would help to sit with Maria. Just sit, chat, and take the mickey out of daytime TV.

'Hell-ooo!' called Ruby hopefully when she got home. No reply. Daytime telly isn't half as funny when you're on your own. Just kind of sad.

The day ignored her, the hours passing without any help from the inert girl on the sofa. Red eyed, Ruby feigned interest in the magazine lying open on her lap but the past still had its claws in her.

Dusk dimmed the scarlet sofa to a sulky grey. The buzzer startled Ruby and she sprang up, fuzzy-headed.

'Who is it?' she asked the intercom warily. Ruby couldn't face Kendall and Teddy's sledgehammer sympathy.

'Oh dear,' a rabbity voice answered. 'Ah. Well. Now then.'

'Hugo?' Ruby goggled at the intercom. 'Come up.' Rubbing her groggy eyes, she dashed about switching on lamps, plumping cushions and having kittens. Fizzing like a shaken can of Lilt, she waited for the lift to ascend. As the doors slid open, the bubbles waned: maybe they'd come to lynch her.

'This is incredible,' she gasped at the sight of the Friends in technicolour 3D. They appeared to be unarmed. 'Comeincomeincomein.'

Olivia strode boldly into Ruby's living room, to stand with her feet planted apart like a heroic statue. 'Are we welcome?' she asked over-loudly, one of her huge shapeless bags raised in front of her like a shield.

'Very.' Ruby noted the utter lack of Joe and bit back her disappointment. She had to keep calm, to divine where this was going.

'One never knows,' said Hugo, all tweedy uncertainty at his wife's shoulder. The passage of time had intensified the couple's characters; Olivia was now a warrior queen incarnate, whereas Hugo seemed to have sprouted tiny pink mouse ears and a tail.

'Drink?' Ruby was uncertain of the etiquette when entertaining people who had adopted your child, a child you had subsequently taught to rumba in secret.

Holding up one hand as if controlling traffic, Olivia said 'No', very firmly and rather too loud. She dropped the bag and stuck her chin even higher in the air. A new headband curbed her excitable curls and Ruby detected a smudge of gold eyeshadow above each anxious brown eye. Along with the worn velvet cape thing over her shoulders, these were evidence of Making An Effort. Ruby briefly wondered why, a thought she managed to have in tandem with where on earth one bought velvet cape things, before tuning in to what Olivia was saying.

'There are some facts we cannot ignore.' Olivia's aristocratic brow was clear, but those gilded eyes betrayed all sorts of emotions trampolining behind them. 'You are Joe's birth mother,' she said, as if starting a speech.

'Yes,' Ruby agreed, weakly.

'That is a fact,' continued Olivia.

At her shoulder, Hugo nodded vigorously.

Panic-stricken without really knowing why, Ruby nodded too. 'Erm, yes,' she confirmed, feeling that it was called for.

'Nobody can change that,' chipped in Hugo, apologetically.

'No.' Ruby was uneasy. Had they come to her home just to hurl random data at her?

'And nobody,' Olivia continued, keeping up the heroic stance, 'would want to.'

Good. That was good. Wasn't it? Fear of seeming dim in front of this Valkyrie meant Ruby was second-guessing and analysing when she knew she should simply open her ears and listen.

'Of course they wouldn't,' simpered Hugo.

Olivia held Ruby's gaze for a long moment before saying, 'If I'm honest, Ruby, part of me knew who you were the first day you came to our house.' She pursed her lips. 'God knows how.'

'Mother's intuition?' suggested Ruby, instantly regretting it. Those fierce brown eyes flickered: Olivia suspected her of sarcasm. 'I mean, you are, after all . . .' Ruby tapered off, too damned scared of Olivia to defend her *faux pas*.

'I feel responsible.' Olivia made her confession in a flat voice. 'I should have vocalised.'

'Well . . .' Ruby shrugged, glad that they seemed to have skated over one little bump. 'Vocalise schmocalise.' More instantaneous regret. Would she, Ruby wondered, ever say anything sensible again?

'The truth is that you made me feel inferior.' Olivia's long-fingered hands seemed to be trying to strangle one another.

'Me?' snorted Ruby with a cartoonish look of amazement. '*I* did?'

'I felt naked, undone.' Now Olivia was looking at the floor. 'Ruby, you're such a natural. Joe and I are always at loggerheads. I'm always trying to teach the poor child something, instead of just rubbing along with him. You guided him without confronting him. I felt as if I had ten thumbs when you were around, making Joe laugh, sharing secrets.'

Miserably, Ruby muttered, 'How you must have hated me.'

'I did try.' Olivia lifted her eyes. She squared those broad shoulders. 'The reason we're here today is to . . .' She halted and Ruby eschewed the whole breathing thing for a while. 'We're here to tell you that we can't condone your underhand, sneaky, disingenuous,' Olivia was building up a head of steam, '*wicked*—'

A touch on her arm from Hugo halted the barrage. Olivia collected herself and began again. 'We can't condone the manner in which you chose to re-enter our lives, but we do . . .' she stumbled and Hugo stepped forward to take up the baton.

Speaking gently, he said, 'We realise you acted on deeply held emotions. You suffered anguish that Olivia and I can only imagine. As she said, we can't condone what you did but—'

Olivia butted in. 'We understand.'

Her lungs rebooted and Ruby put a hand to her mouth, incredulous. 'You do?' The two people in front of her were transformed from bookish scruffbags into angels. It had never occurred to Ruby to hope for such generosity.

'I scrutinised my anger.' Olivia veered off into the kind of Friend-speak that made Ruby go cross-eyed. 'I realised that it emanated from a selfish part of the ego. Your very existence threatened my status as a mother, a position I found challenging at the best of times.'

'True, true.' Hugo took his wife's hand.

A tear, fat and salty, skidded down Ruby's cheek. 'I swear I never meant to,' she whispered.

Olivia had a lot more to say. 'Your decision to put Joe up for adoption was made under great duress. You were immature. You possibly received partisan advice that did not take your needs into account.'

Ruby couldn't have put it better herself. And God knows she'd tried. 'It was a long time ago,' she said, even though she'd been reliving it all day.

Eyes glistening, Olivia said fervently, 'As soon as I put myself in your shoes, my animosity evaporated. I had an epiphany. I experienced a profound affinity with your core sentiments.'

That sounded like it hurt.

'She could see how you felt,' translated Hugo thoughtfully.

'That's . . . nice.' It was a lukewarm word, but Ruby still had no clue about the bottom line.

'I went through years of yearning to have a child.' Olivia was very still. 'Now that I have one, I have to do what's best for Joe.'

'That's what mothers do,' interjected Hugo.

'That's what you did.' Olivia pointed at Ruby. 'When you gave him up.'

Oh, that tiny word was beautiful; Olivia had said 'given him *up*' and not 'away'. Two letters long, the word beckoned out more of Ruby's tears.

'So,' Olivia sounded choked. 'We bow to the inevitable.' She took a breath. 'You need to know Joe and he needs to know you.'

The blood pounded in Ruby's ears. She wasn't up to breaking the silence.

Hugo was. 'The lad's missed you,' he said. 'And so have we.'

'Sorry, but I really can't take this in,' said Ruby eventually. 'You mean I lie to you, encourage your little boy to lie to you, and now you're rewarding me?'

'It's not that simple,' said Olivia, with what sounded like impatience. 'Nothing is.'

Pulling up a chair from the dining table, Hugo sat down heavily. 'It's a simple human tragedy, one that's happened over and over again, throughout history. Pain, shame, loss, lies. Every soap opera is full of tales like this because it's so human, so *ordinary*. Heartbreaking, but ordinary.' He looked up at his wife, still planted stolidly on the white floor. 'We're all just people trying to get by. We're all flawed and complicated and accident prone. And we all want some happiness out of life. So, we said to each other, it is what it is. Why not accept the situation and make the best of it?'

Her heart hammering, Ruby wanted to blurt that this was fate, that somehow she'd been *meant* to give her baby to the Friends, but she guessed that they were too intellectual to allow fate much houseroom.

Hugo shrugged and crossed his legs. 'Who knows, Ruby? Perhaps this was all meant to be.'

'Oh Hugo,' whimpered Ruby, grateful for this apparent mind-reading.

'After all,' said Olivia, with some effort, 'why can't Joe have two mother figures?'

'He's only got one mum,' said Ruby firmly. Having dodged the title for so long there was no way she could casually deprive Olivia of it now.

'I'm not greedy,' smiled Olivia, a storm playing out in her eyes. 'There's enough love to go round.'

That did it. Ruby gave in to her instincts and rushed Olivia like a prop forward. The two women teetered in an awkward, heartfelt embrace and Ruby heard a small, most un-Olivia-like voice whisper,.'Thank you. Thank you for my Joe,' before Hugo's cough parted them.

'We should be getting on.' Hugo pointed to his watch.

'Lord, yes. We're late.' Olivia wiped her cheeks hastily with the backs of her hands as she strode to the window. 'Let's hope we didn't get a parking ticket.' She peered down at the street. 'Nope. Seems to be fine.'

Glancing down, Ruby yelped. Eight storeys below Joe leaned, arms folded, against the SmartCar. A street lamp's glow brought his cummerbund to blinging life.

'Joe's doing the show?' yipped Ruby.

Frizzy ringlets nodding, Olivia said, 'Of course.'

'But you both loathe ballroom,' laughed Ruby.

.'And we loathe McDonald's and skateboards and wearing the same underpants for a week, but we're not ten-year-old boys,' Olivia pointed out. She seemed to have recovered her habitual demeanour. 'Come on, Ruby. Chop chop.'

'Me?' Ruby double-checked. 'Me also too?'

Olivia nodded. 'But only if you hurry up.'

The lift couldn't travel fast enough for Ruby. Now Olivia's stab at grooming made sense; she was making an effort for Joe. Ruby tapped her foot impatiently, noting the indulgent, amused glances passing between the Friends. She wondered if they would ever know how much the last few minutes had meant to her. It's a powerful thing to offer an orphan girl a family.

Clattering through the lobby ahead of Hugo and Olivia, Ruby rummaged in her bag.

'Hi, Rubes.' Joe's inner lights were on, despite the carefully cultivated air of boredom.

Ruby handed him the satin bow tie. 'Put this on, ball-room boy.'

*

'So, tell me. Was Joe the best dancer in the show?' asked Maria, legs tucked beneath her on the end of Ruby's bed.

'Not even his two mothers could claim that,' chuckled Ruby. 'He was hopeless. He did his best, bless him, grinning from ear to ear the whole time.'

'Like you.' Maria pointed with the damp cotton wool she was using to remove her makeup. 'That smile is stapled to your face.'

'Who gets a second chance like this?' burbled Ruby. 'It's amazing. I know I don't deserve it but I'm grabbing it with both hands.'

'Can it, you know, actually work, though?' asked Maria dubiously as she swiped cleansing milk across her forehead.

'We think so.' Ruby couldn't sound anything but smug at that 'we'. Sitting in the Friends' kitchen long after Joe had gone to bed, the three adults had hammered out a manifesto for a new kind of family life. 'We're not constrained by convention and we won't conform to the narrow contours of society.' Ruby parroted Olivia, carefully ignoring the wry curl of Maria's lip.

'And in English?'

'That means, thicko, we're not going to think in stereotypes. Just because Olivia has adopted Joe it doesn't mean she can't accept me as another female figure in his life.'

'So he'll have two mummies?'

'Not exactly.' In the lamplit basement it had seemed brave, bohemian and entirely possible: now it felt a bit silly. Ruby groped for the right words to anchor the idea, stop it slipping away. 'Olivia is his mum. Hugo is his dad. I'm his biological mum and part of the extended family. I'll be around to help. I'll be involved.' Ruby suddenly found a way to express herself exactly: 'Joe and I will be allowed to love each other,' she sighed. 'And along the way I'll build a special relationship with Hugo and Olivia.'

'Sounds nice,' said Maria approvingly. 'Miles better than my dysfunctional mob.' She flicked her bottle of cleanser shut. 'You don't look like somebody who can sleep. Fancy a cheese on toast party?'

Ruby did. But then, Ruby always did.

43

There had been an invasion. An army of boys had annexed fourteen Clancy Street. Joe's birthday party was the result of cunning strategy. Ruby had rehearsed her plea after surfing the books on Olivia's shelves – 'Joe needs diversity of socialisation to ensure healthy shaping of the self,' she'd recited, almost breaking her teeth.

Joe had threatened to stop eating.

Olivia had given in.

The cosy, book-filled house was transformed. Uncle Teddy and Uncle Kendall were in charge of catering. Under their supervision the basement kitchen was churning out hot dogs and burgers and fries.

'No salad?' mewed Olivia, who had put on her best, most shapeless dress. 'Not even a carrot stick?'

'The customer is always right,' declared Teddy, 'and today's customer laughs in the face of salad.' He tweaked his apron: his Alice in Wonderland outfit was a touch tight. 'Boys want fried rubbish and that's what we'll give them.' He passed another platter of hot dogs to a waiter and sent him up the stairs with a proprietorial slap on the rump.

Bemused, Olivia looked over her glasses and asked, 'Why are the waiters in those tight little shorts?' She looked concerned as one oiled member of staff returned with an empty tray. 'It's October. The poor things will catch their deaths. Can't you at least let them pop their tops on?'

'EU rules,' said Teddy sadly. 'My hands are tied.'

One guest was of a very different vintage to the others. Mrs Vine had been deposited in the drawing room with a glass of sherry and Hugo. The Friends had been open to the idea of welcoming a 'mature feminine influence' into the family when Ruby had suggested it. If they regretted that decision, they kept it to themselves, even when Mrs Vine wondered aloud if Hugo was a eunuch.

A regular at the Sunday lunch table, Mrs Vine had settled in comfortably to her role, even if she interpreted it as, in Maria's phrase, 'mature feminine witch-bitch'. Evidently there was room in the new, non-traditional family for all sorts.

More mini-men than Ruby had ever seen in one place were swarming through the house. Handing out plastic cups of fizzy stuff, she noticed how swiftly boys bonded.

Boy A – 'I do kung fu.'

Boy B – 'I do karate.'

Boy A – 'My brother does karate.'

Boy B – 'Let's go and draw on Toby.'

There was a handful of girls, including Suzie, who had made quite an effort.

'I love your leggings,' Ruby told her admiringly as she handed her a cup.

'Yeah,' said Suzie, bored.

'I like your leggings too,' said Joe, joining them.

'God! Can people stop going on about my leggings for, like, *one minute*?' drawled Suzie.

Joe flashed Ruby an 'Isn't she wonderful?' grin, and Ruby flashed him a 'You poor deluded bugger' one.

Silver streamers criss-crossed the ceilings of every room, and balloons lay in squeaky drifts. Hugo seemed fascinated by the glitterball in the sitting room and might have sat there all day gazing at the patterns it made on the walls if Ruby hadn't nudged him.

'How's it feel to have your house turned into Lilliput?' she whispered, careful not to wake Mrs Vine, who was upright and fast asleep in the best chair.

'Rather nice,' he said, surprised. 'We should do this every week.'

Thundering past them, Olivia snatched a felt tip from a small hand just before it could draw a bra on the oil painting of a nude above the fireplace.

'Hmm,' mused Ruby, catching Hugo's eye. 'Perhaps not *every* week.'

'Sometimes things need shaking up,' said Hugo, watching his wife.

Noise levels were rising. If Ruby shut her eyes it was easy to imagine she was in the midst of a herd of wildebeest, some of whom were carrying trumpets. 'Oi, birthday boy.' She collared Joe on the stairs, hoofs flying as he migrated north with his herd.

'Whaaat?' he whined.

The long-suffering offhandedness gave Ruby perverse pleasure. 'Manners, mate,' she chided. 'Don't you owe me a thank you? For your birthday present?'

Crinkling his brow, Joe remembered. 'Oh yeah. *Strictly Ballroom* DVD. Brill.'

'I thought we could watch it on one of our Wednesdays.' Designated babysitting nights, they punctuated Ruby's week with pleasure. 'Well?' she prodded. When Joe had that unattentive look on his face, he reminded her sharply of her mother, and the way she'd half listened to Ruby or her father at times. *What would my parents say to all this?* was a masochistic game Ruby occasionally played. She guessed that they would be appalled, but it was hard to make decisions on behalf of the dead; perhaps they would be delighted. Being allowed to love Joe had created a sweet, peaceable feeling that oozed over her complicated memories of Marjorie and Stan. She could look at Joe, catch wispy fragments of them both, and be glad.

'Sure. Whatever.' Joe's ear was cocked towards the loft, where his fellow wildebeest were jumping on his bed.

'You can escape as soon as I get a cuddle,' said Ruby.

'For God's sake,' whined Joe, instantly moving in.

His bony arms felt delicious around Ruby's torso. She hung on until his inevitable, 'Is that enough?'

'Yes. Off you pop.' Ruby ruffled his fringe as he darted away. She had convinced Olivia to spend twenty pounds on a proper haircut, but within days Joe's fringe had reasserted itself. He didn't get it from Ruby, or from Duncan Sweet. Some parts of Joe were mysterious.

The lure of adult conversation drew Ruby back to the basement.

'Doesn't he look handsome?' asked Teddy rhetorically, applying baby oil to the chest of a waiter. A waiter who looked ready to implode with embarrassment.

'The Bachelor!' quacked Ruby.

'Thought I'd help out,' said the Bachelor, valiantly acting normal despite a gravelly-voiced Alice in Wonderland massaging

373

his left pectoral. Far from his natural habitat of bars, gyms and lap dancing emporiums, the Bachelor was obviously here because of—

'Maria!'

'That's my name, don't wear it out.' Maria slapped an empty platter on the table, and snatched another one up.

'What's going on?' Ruby gestured at the Bachelor as he left the room with a tray of burgers, one hand persuading his shorts to cover his buttocks.

'It's not my fault if he can't get the message,' shrugged Maria, avoiding eye contact.

'If you didn't want him here, he wouldn't be here,' said Ruby with certainty. 'Maria. You like him.'

Twiddling with a frankfurter, Maria lifted her head haughtily. 'I know you think he's an idiot.'

'When did I say that?' exclaimed Ruby, aware that she thought it.

'Loads of times. Not in so many words. You took the mickey out of his lads' mags and his weights and his fur bedspread. You think he's naff.'

You forgot the bum ogling, thought Ruby. 'You evidently don't agree,' she smiled.

'I don't have high standards like you,' said Maria. 'He's nice to me. He's . . .' She seemed to be struggling.

'Local?' suggested Ruby.

Maria sniggered. 'You can't deny it's handy. I don't even have to leave the building.'

'Truly a match made in Heaven.'

'Nope.' Maria shook her head. 'I'm not looking for that. For the moment, he'll do. We have a laugh. We're a good fit.' Maria held up a tuna and sweetcorn sandwich, freshly made by the burly Alice. 'You know when you eat a sandwich? What do you expect from it? You expect it to be as good as a sandwich and no better. You don't,' she emphasised, learnedly, 'expect it to be two weeks in Hawaii.' She flung the sandwich back among its compatriots. 'The Bachelor is a very nice tuna and sweet-corn sandwich.'

'May I ask you one thing?'

'Sure.'

'Do you always call him the Bachelor?'

'What else would I call him?' asked Maria.

'You're weird.'

'No, you're weird.'

'No, you're weird.'

'No, you're weird.'

'No,' Ruby shook her head. 'You're—'

'Excuse me.' Teddy tapped her on the head with a baguette. 'You're supposed to be looking after the kids, not behaving like them.' He clicked his fingers at Maria. 'Be off, wench.'

Two giggling girls tore past Teddy, almost knocking him off his Mary Janes. 'I'm too old for this malarkey,' he complained, wiping his brow. 'I'd only do it for our Joe.'

Ruby felt a spurt of gratitude towards her curmudgeonly, odd, cross-dressing parent substitute who had slipped so easily into his role as Joe's curmudgeonly, odd, cross-dressing Uncle substitute. 'He loves coming to see you at the Glove, having a little dance on the stage.'

'Joe's brought me and Kendall even closer together.'

'Things are all right with you two, aren't they?' Ruby asked.

'It's such a relief to have him back.' Teddy's gooey smile morphed into pursed lips. 'Not that it's perfect. He still sashays around with a broom up his chute. But we were meant to be, me and him. We're making it up as we go along, like you and Joe and Olly and Huge. One big happy, gay-around-the-edges, could-do-better family. Hey!' Teddy peered closer at Ruby. 'Why the long face, pet? That was the kind of speech that gets you bawling at the end of a made-for-TV movie.'

'I'm just wondering if I've missed my chance of two weeks in Hawaii.'

'Eh?' Teddy was lost.

A hand tugged at his frock, and an affronted child complained, 'You said ages ago you'd play Doctor Who with us.'

'Did I?' responded Teddy vaguely.

Kendall emerged from the larder to say, 'You did.'

Taking the boy's hand, Teddy rolled his eyes. 'I can't run up and down stairs at my age,' he complained out of the corner of his mouth. The doorbell rang, and Teddy's demeanour improved. 'Ah!' he cooed. 'Right on time.'

'Who is?' As far as Ruby knew, all the guests were present and correct.

'I called in a pro. A children's entertainer.' Teddy cocked his head to one side. 'I think they used to call them clowns.' He gave her an outrageous wink.

'Teddy!' gabbled Ruby. 'You're a star!'

Parting the sea of youngsters by the simple means of shoving them out of her way, Ruby raced up the stairs. Breathless, she pounded along the pitted floorboards of the entrance hall, as cogs whirred and pennies dropped.

Through the front door's stained glass, Ruby discerned a crazy Afro. It made her heart leap, all her old prejudices about clowns suddenly shed. 'Tom!' she squeaked, throwing open the door.

Beneath the greasepaint, the red nose and the fluorescent freckles, the clown was wary. 'No,' he said slowly, 'Laugh A Minute Larry. Have I got the right house?'

'Oh my God,' came a deep, disgusted voice from behind Ruby that she recognised as Suzie's, 'it's a clown.'

'You're at the right house,' said Ruby, smiling politely and itching to scream *But you're the wrong clown!*

After an initial display of cool, the children caved in and the house rocked to Laugh A Minute's banjo. Mrs Vine muttered darkly about 'children these days' and accepted another sherry while Olivia scrabbled about for her headache tablets.

Out on the front steps it was chilly but quiet. Ruby sat at the top, knees to chin, contemplating her stupidity and making a mental note to warn Teddy to be more careful with his winks. She looked down at her gold shoes. They seemed dull in this light.

A hand reached over her shoulder and offered her some red liquid, which turned out to be the worst wine Ruby had ever tasted.

'Thought you might appreciate a more grown up beverage,' said Hugo. Motioning to the step, he said, 'May I?'

Ruby shrugged.

For a while Hugo said nothing at all. He sat down near enough to lean on, and as if drawn by some kind of corduroy magnet, Ruby did just that. 'What's got to you, Ruby?' he asked kindly. 'Is it Joe? We get things a bit wrong sometimes, I know, but it will all work itself out.'

'No, no.' Ruby smothered that suggestion. 'God, no.'

'Must be the clown ex, then.'

Seeing Ruby's surprise, Hugo said, 'Quite often I'm listening when you and Olivia think I'm away with the fairies.'

'Sounds silly,' said Ruby, hoping to turn her abrupt change of mood into a funny anecdote, 'but when that clown came to the door I thought it was him.'

It didn't sound at all funny. It sounded sad and small.

'Tim,' said Hugo.

'Tom.'

'Ah.' Hugo tutted. 'Obviously I don't listen as well as I thought. Am I right in deducing you miss this chap?'

'A little bit.'

'Just a little bit?' Hugo scratched his head. 'Yet here you are, sulking on the steps while our boy's birthday party rages inside.'

'Well . . .'

'I've got to know your face pretty well,' Hugo continued. 'It's a nice face. It's not telling me that you miss Tim, er, Tom a little bit. I would call this *pining*.'

Leaning harder against his comforting jacket, Ruby risked a terrible admission. 'My heart is breaking, Hugo.'

Leaping up, Hugo yelled, 'You should be ashamed of yourself!'

'Me?' stammered Ruby, discomfited by the sudden gear change.

'Look at you,' berated Hugo. 'Wilting, trembling, *waiting*. Did suffragettes chain themselves to railings so you could sit around moping? Did Millicent Flathurst go on hunger strike for you to be so passive?' He didn't seem to notice Ruby's surprise at hearing her old friend's name. 'You are a modern woman. You can do what you like. If you want a relationship with Tom, Tim, Tom, Tim, Tom, then call him. Now.' He thrust his mobile at her. 'Do it. You are a powerful female in charge of your own destiny.' He lowered his voice. 'You are not a princess locked up in a castle, dependent on the whims of men.'

Hugo could have no idea how strongly the fairy tale analogy resonated with Ruby. She snatched the phone and punched out Tom's number, just as Hugo's very own powerful female threw up a window and shouted, 'Hugo! Get up here! Some infant has vomited on your thesis!'

'Yes, dear.' Hugo sprinted indoors.

'Where are you?' asked Ruby when a voice answered.

'Oh. You.' There was a hesitation. 'Just off the green, as it happens.'

'I'm at Clancy Street.'

'And . . . ?'

'And, erm,' Ruby hadn't thought this far. 'I thought, maybe, you know,' she stumbled.

'No, Ruby, I don't know,' said Tom, gravely.

'That you might, oh God, that we, that we could . . . or something.' Ruby fizzled out.

'I'm just turning the corner into Lilyville Road. Passing the doctor's. Waiting for the lights to change.' An undercurrent of excitement, like sexy subtitles, coursed under Tom's bland description of his progress. 'Crossing the crossing.'

Ruby caught her breath. He was coming. She turned to look in the direction he would appear. She wanted to cry, shout, jump. She stayed perfectly still.

'Going past the dry cleaner's,' Tom announced calmly, like an air traffic controller talking down a stricken 747. 'There's the newsagent's, the post office, a skip with a bath in it, your tramp. And here's the corner of Clancy Street.'

Suddenly there he was. The same crumpled clothes, the same quick stride. Ruby swallowed.

'Passing the house with the roof extension.' Tom carried on in his monotone. 'The house with the For Sale sign. The house with the horrible replacement windows. And now,' he said into the phone as he slowed to a stop, two feet away from her, 'I'm looking at a beautiful girl in gold shoes with a strange look on her face. Either she needs to do a poo or she's going to tell me she loves me.'

'She loves you,' said Ruby into the phone.

Ruby held up a warning finger to hold Tom back as he groaned gratefully and held out his arms. Still talking into the mobile, she said, 'She also needs to say she's sorry. She got it all wrong. She confused pride with independence. She knows better now. And she's got a question for you.' Ruby didn't want to spoil things by crying, but one damn tear wouldn't co-operate and escaped down her cheek. 'How are you?'

'Me?' smiled Tom. 'Never better.'

'COME HERE!' yelled Ruby, flinging Hugo's mobile into a nearby geranium pot.

The least smooth clinch in the history of clinching ensued: a fumbly, grasping, hungry, clumsy, almost-falling-over manoeuvre that only ended when the jeers of a clutch of boys at an open window became too loud to ignore.

'She's quite pretty!' shouted one tiny critic.

Joe said proudly, 'That's my sort of Mum thing.'

Sitting up, much later, in bed, Ruby's rediscovery of just how comfy it was to snuggle against Tom was disrupted by his murmured, 'Happy?'

Ruby's eyes shot open. 'Yes,' she answered, amazed. Maybe it really was as simple as making shepherd's pie; you just assembled the ingredients – people/self-respect/a touch of luck – and put them all together and there you were: happy. (*Really* happy if you'd remembered to make a shepherd's pie at the same time.) 'You? You happy?' she asked ungrammatically.

Tom laughed, 'What do you think? I just made love with

my best girl and I feel as if tiny sex fairies are massaging every inch of me.' He kissed the top of her untidy head. 'At the risk of boring you, I love you, Ruby.'

'Ooh, bore me, bore me!' begged Ruby.

'And poor old Millicent missed you too. The house just hasn't been the same.' His warm arms sneaked around her. 'Don't change a bit, Ruby. I want you to have your own thoughts even when you're lying with me. I'm not—'

Ruby pressed a finger to Tom's lips. 'Let's not mention his name ever again, eh?'

'Fine by me.'

Monday morning marked an impressive thirty-six hours in bed. It hadn't been all slap and tickle, there had been an awful lot of chit-chat, a brief argument over who was the worst duvet hog, and a horrific half hour trying not to listen to Maria and the Bachelor lick Nutella off each other in the master bedroom.

'Don't you have work to go to?' asked Tom, his curls really outdoing themselves: he looked as if he'd spent the weekend in a wind tunnel.

'Not today. I booked today off.' Ruby's matted hair also gave some clues as to how enthusiastic the reunion had been.

'Psychic as well as the best kisser in Europe.' Tom was impressed.

'Not really. I took the day off to attend the first day of Mr Unmentionable's trial.'

'Right.' Tom sat up, all decisive and manly, unaware of the thong tangled in his hair. 'I'll come with you.'

'No, Tom.'

'I'm either your man or I'm not. We've talked about this.'

'And that's why I'm not going,' said Ruby. 'So get off your high horse before its hoofs tear the sheets.'

'Not going? Why not?' Tom stared, confounded.

'Because it's nothing to do with me.' Ruby could mean those words for the first time. 'I have better things to do.' She drew Tom back down into the warmth of the bed. '*You*, for example.'

'Eww.' Maria screwed up her nose as she entered Ruby and Tom's darkened love nest on Monday evening. 'You two might consider a shower,' she suggested, switching on the light and making the pair in the bed blink like kittens.

'I didn't hear a knock,' complained Ruby, grateful that Maria had only walked in on a debate about the best roast (Ruby was adamant it was chicken, while Tom got almost violent defending pork) and not their earlier attempt to perfect a new Kama Sutra position they'd christened the Traffic Warden.

'I'm not one of life's knockers. Look at this.' Maria tossed the evening paper across the bed. 'Page seven. Towards the bottom.' She waited for them to riffle to the right place.

Ruby pushed the paper away, but Tom read out the small headline. '*Gangland Connections In Esher Case*.' He made a noise in the back of his throat. 'Not exactly a front page splash. He'll be disappointed.'

Snatching back the newspaper, Maria told them, 'Never mind that rubbish. Get a load of *this*.' She refolded the page and read out, '*Tramp Finds Fortune – "I Had No Idea It Was A Stradivarius" Says Homeless Man*.'

Ruby's mouth dropped open. 'At least somebody benefited from Manny's insurance,' she said.

*

382

Manny went to prison for a long, long time. Whether or not he made friends with a mouse is unknown: Ruby was far too busy polishing south-west London to find out.

West End Girls

Jenny Colgan

The streets of London are paved with gold . . . allegedly.

They may be twin sisters, but Lizzie and Penny Berry
are complete opposites – Penny is blonde, thin and
outrageous; Lizzie quiet, thoughtful and, well, definitely
not thin. The one trait they do share is a desire to
DO something with their lives, and as far as they're
concerned, the place to get noticed is London.

Out of the blue they discover they have a grandmother
living in Chelsea – and when she has to go into hospital,
they find themselves flat-sitting on the King's Road.
But, as they discover, it's not as easy to become It Girls
as they'd imagined, and west end boys aren't at all
like Hugh Grant . . .

'Hugely entertaining and very funny' *Cosmopolitan*

978-0-7515-3763-5

Operation Sunshine

Jenny Colgan

Evie needs a good holiday. Not just because she's been working all hours in her job, but also because every holiday she has ever been on in her life has involved sunburn, arguments and projectile vomiting – sometimes all three at once. Why can't she have a normal holiday, like other people seem to have – some sun, sand, sea and (hopefully) sex?

So when her employers invite her to attend a conference with them in the south of France, she can't believe her luck. It's certainly going to be the holiday of a lifetime – but not quite in the way Evie imagines!

'Colgan at her warm, down-to-earth best' *Cosmopolitan*

978-0-7515-3762-8

Diamonds are a Girl's Best Friend

Jenny Colgan

What does an It Girl do if she loses all her money?

Sophie Chesterton is a girl about town – she knows all
the right people, goes to all the right parties, and wears
all the right clothes. But deep down she suspects that her
best friends are actually rather nasty, and that her lifestyle
doesn't really amount to much. Her father wants her to
make her own way in the world, to make him proud.
But after one shocking evening her life is changed for ever.

Scraping a living as an assistant to a 'glamour'
photographer; living in a hovel on the Old Kent Road
with four smelly boys; eating baked beans from the can
– this is one spectacular fall from grace. Sophie is
desperate to get her life back – but does a girl really
need diamonds to be happy?

Full of warmth and humour, *Diamonds are a Girl's
Best Friend* is the charming new comedy from the
wonderful Jenny Colgan.

978-1-84744-158-4

A Bad Bride's Tale

Polly Williams

'Fun, laughter and tears blend with love, lust and a tangle of misunderstandings in this splendid romp' *She*

Two weeks before her wedding Stevie Jonson has got the jitters. Is she finally growing up, or compromising horribly? In love or in denial? Yes, there are good reasons to get married. Babies. Sex whenever she wants it. A justification for staying in without feeling like a loser. Contentment.

And there are very good reasons *not* to get married. Not wanting to sleep with him unless nothing on telly. Never sleeping with anyone else ever again. His mother. His new bald patch. Being called 'my wife'. And the disconcerting reappearance of a former major crush, reminder of everything fiancé isn't. As the clock ticks, a shocking secret threatens to bring Stevie's future crashing down around her.

'Inspirational ****' *Cosmopolitan*

'Poignant and fun' *Heat*

978-0-7515-4055-0

Other bestselling titles available by mail:

☐	West End Girls	Jenny Colgan	£6.99
☐	Operation Sunshine	Jenny Colgan	£6.99
☐	Diamonds are a Girl's Best Friend	Jenny Colgan	£18.99
☐	A Bad Bride's Tale	Polly Williams	£6.99

The prices shown above are correct at time of going to press. However, the publishers reserve the right to increase prices on covers from those previously advertised, without further notice.

— sphere —

Please allow for postage and packing: **Free UK delivery.**
Europe; add 25% of retail price; Rest of World; 45% of retail price.

To order any of the above or any other Sphere titles, please call our credit card orderline or fill in this coupon and send/fax it to:

Sphere, P.O. Box 121, Kettering, Northants NN14 4ZQ
Fax: 01832 733076   Tel: 01832 737526
Email: aspenhouse@FSBDial.co.uk

☐ I enclose a UK bank cheque made payable to Sphere for £ . . . .
☐ Please charge £ . . . . . . to my Visa, Delta, Maestro.

☐☐☐☐☐☐☐☐☐☐☐☐☐☐☐☐☐☐

Expiry Date ☐☐☐☐   Maestro Issue No. ☐☐

NAME (BLOCK LETTERS please) . . . .

ADDRESS . . . .

. . . .

. . . .

Postcode . . . . Telephone . . . .

Signature . . . .

Please allow 28 days for delivery within the UK. Offer subject to price and availability.